THE **AFTERMATH**

also by samuel c. florman

The Introspective Engineer

The Civilized Engineer

Blaming Technology

The Existential Pleasures of Engineering

Engineering and the Liberal Arts

samuel c. florman

THE AFTERMATH

a novel of survival

thomas dunne books   st. martin's griffin   new york

THOMAS DUNNE BOOKS.
An imprint of St. Martin's Press.

www.stmartins.com

Design by Victoria Kuskowski

Library of Congress Cataloging-in-Publication Data

Florman, Samuel C.
    The aftermath : a novel of survival / Samuel C. Florman.—1st ed.
       p. cm.
    ISBN 0-312-26652-9 (hc)
    ISBN 0-312-31112-5 (pbk)
    1. Comets—Collisions with Earth—Fiction. 2. Survival after air-
plane accidents, shipwrecks, etc.—Fiction. 3. Natal (South Africa)—
Fiction. 4. Engineers—Fiction. I. Title.

PS3606.L68 A69 2001
813'.54—dc21   2001041969

First St. Martin's Griffin Edition: March 2003

10 9 8 7 6 5 4 3 2 1

for hannah, lucy, sylvie, julia, and rachel

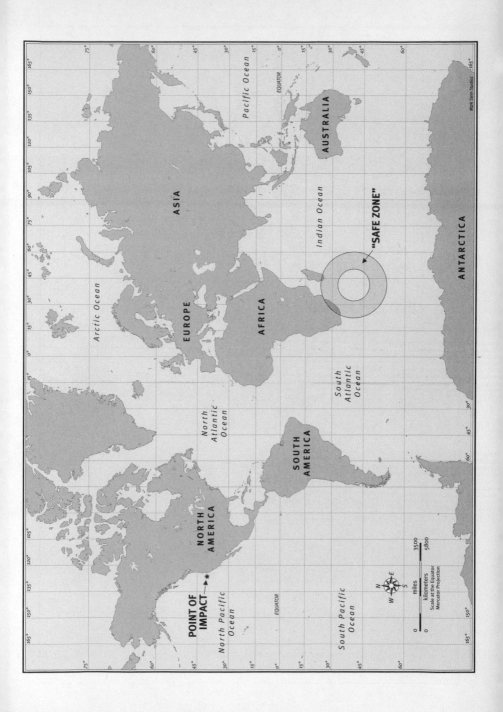

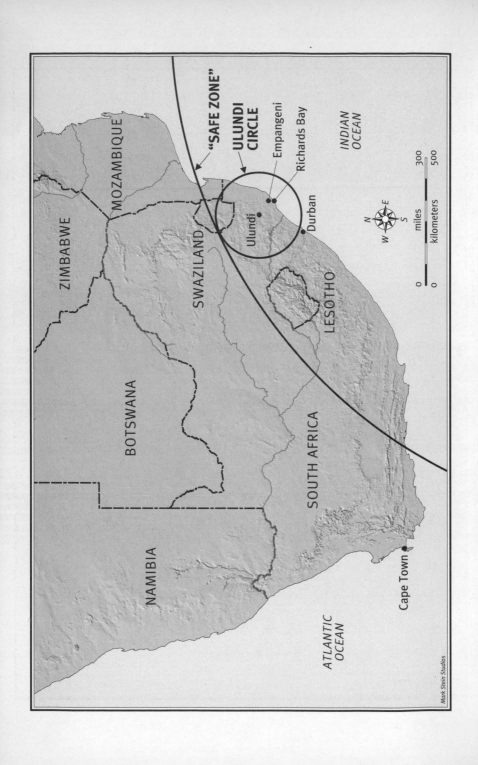

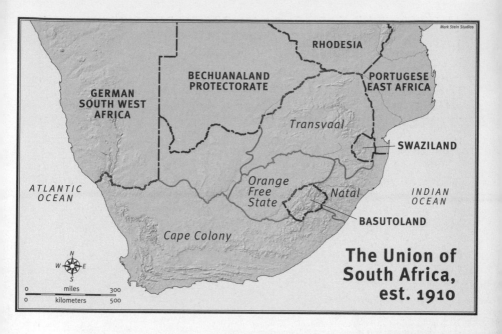

RHODESIA

BECHUANALAND
PROTECTORATE

GERMAN
SOUTH WEST
AFRICA

PORTUGESE
EAST AFRICA

Transvaal

SWAZILAND

*ATLANTIC
OCEAN*

*Orange
Free
State*

Natal

*INDIAN
OCEAN*

BASUTOLAND

Cape Colony

N
W E
S

miles   300
0
kilometers   500
0

The Union of
South Africa,
est. 1910

Mark Stein Studios

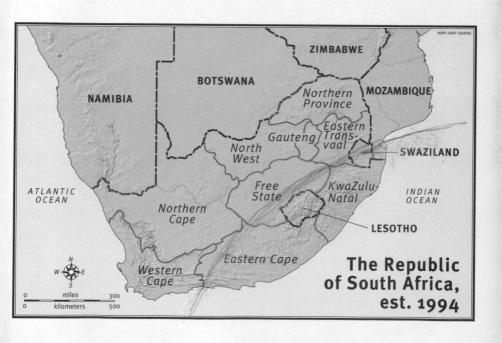

ZIMBABWE

BOTSWANA

NAMIBIA

*Northern
Province*

MOZAMBIQUE

*Eastern
Trans-
vaal*

Gauteng

SWAZILAND

*North
West*

*ATLANTIC
OCEAN*

*Free
State*

*KwaZulu-
Natal*

*INDIAN
OCEAN*

*Northern
Cape*

LESOTHO

Eastern Cape

N
W E
S

*Western
Cape*

miles   300
0
kilometers   500
0

The Republic
of South Africa,
est. 1994

Mark Stein Studios

THE AFTERMATH

FROM THE JOURNAL OF WILSON HARDY, JR.

When the comet struck, I was on a cruise with my father. It may sound ludicrous, irresponsible even, to be off on a cruise when the world blows up, but how else can I put it? That's the way it was, just a year ago tomorrow, a date for the history books yet to be written—if we ever print books again—December 25, 2009.

Can you imagine the world being destroyed on Christmas? In olden days, when children hung stockings by the fireside expecting presents from St. Nicholas, some parents would fill the stockings of naughty kids with coal to teach them a lesson. Maybe that's what has happened to the human race. Some lesson!

But then why, you might ask, wasn't I incinerated, pulverized, or drowned with the rest of the human race? I guess everyone who survived has been wondering the same thing. How many of us are there? About twenty-five hundred from the cruise ship—fifteen hundred passengers and roughly one thousand crew—plus approximately twenty-five thousand people who were already residents of the place in which we find ourselves. That is not very many out of a world population that had recently passed seven billion.

As for the Event, the odds against it ever happening in the first place are even more remarkable. The experts used to say that the chance of encountering a comet or an asteroid ten kilometers wide—like the one that hit near the Yucatan peninsula sixty-five million years ago, supposedly killing off the dinosaurs and two thirds of all other species—was once in a hundred million years.

Not only was last year's comet larger than that infamous monster, but it was the second such projectile to come hurtling toward the earth in just two years. It makes you think that someone, or something, out there was not happy about what was going on here.

When I say out there, I should really say *way* out there, because that's where comets come from—a far, far, almost unimaginably far distance. Like many people, I used to confuse comets with asteroids; but, as I now know only too well, they're very different things. An asteroid is a solid piece of rock, sort of like a small planet. It travels around the sun in nearby circles and we can keep an eye on it—on them, for there are many thousands. A comet is more mysterious, coming from the outer reaches of the solar system, beyond the planet Pluto, formed—so the astrophysicists tell us— in a remote molecular mist called the Oort cloud.

How and why these strange entities are formed, nobody really knows. But once they take shape and start to move, they are gravitationally bound to the sun. Unlike planets and asteroids, however, they travel in extremely elongated orbits, disappearing from our view for years at a time—for centuries at a time. Some of them are familiar to us—like our good friend Halley, who shows up every seventy-five to eighty years, and whose comings and goings we can calculate with great accuracy. But others can appear at any moment, coming from any direction, and usually going undetected until they are practically upon us. I remember back in 1996, when I was in elementary school, the comet Hyakutake was first sighted less than eight weeks before it passed by the earth. Less than eight weeks! And then it came within nine million miles of the earth—a tenth of the distance between the earth and the sun—practically a stone's throw in cosmic terms.

Studies have shown that the nucleus of a comet consists of sand and small bits of rock, embedded in ice, mostly frozen water, but also frozen gasses such as carbon dioxide, methane, and ammonia.

As this dirty snowball enters the central part of the solar system, the sun's heat vaporizes some of the ices, creating the spectacular coma, or "tail." A big asteroid can do just as much damage as a big comet. But the comet, vividly aglow like an avenging angel, has a more fearsome aspect.

Yet, when I think back to before the Event, fear hardly entered the picture. That may seem hard to believe. But the first comet was handled so effectively, with near-pinpoint nuclear blasts, that it looked as if the problem was nicely under control, now and forever. The technique had been worked out carefully, first in computer modeling, then in testing with nearby asteroids. The concept was simple enough—just a slight nudge to a charging assailant, sort of a technological judo maneuver. But the geometry of interception had to be exact, the timing had to be exquisitely precise, and the power of the bombs had to be increased far beyond anything previously employed.

Early in the new millennium, the U.S. Congress—at the request of a new president and with months of political debate and horse trading—had authorized the Department of Defense, NASA, and the Department of Energy to proceed on a crash program of intercept technology, using ion propulsion rockets, massive new computers, improved radar and lasers, and radically new techniques for nuclear explosion. One feature of the new methodology was to use the neutron flux from the bomb explosion to heat a portion of the surface of the intruder. The suddenly heated surface layer would blow away from its home sphere, generating a powerful recoil. This, plus the force of the nuclear blast itself, would achieve the desired change in direction. Until it all worked with a genuine threat, a certain amount of trepidation was inevitable. But, with that first comet, everything functioned perfectly. It was, as they say, a piece of cake.

When the time came, the Americans and the Russians each sent two nuclear bombs out into space and exploded them together near the monstrous mass, nudging it to one side, sending it harmlessly off on a slightly altered course. One bomb would have done the trick, but using four was part of an elaborate fail-safe program. It also provided a political and public relations bonanza for the governments of both nations, along with acclaim for the engineers, scientists, and military leaders who led the effort.

When the second comet was sighted a few months later, there was hardly any public anxiety at all, merely anticipation of another exciting media event. Our cruise was already planned, and there wasn't any discussion about canceling it. On our luxury ship we would be able to get all the news via television and the wireless Internet, and thus not miss any of the excitement.

A few people in our group, members of the American Institute of Aeronautics and Astronautics, had to drop out because of their work with NASA, both as full-time employees and as consultants. Although the methodology for diversion of comets and asteroids was now established and tested, the agency nonetheless wanted all its people on hand. Nobody else on the passenger list thought that there was even the remotest reason to change plans.

―――――――――――

I guess I haven't mentioned that our cruise was being held to commemorate the thirtieth anniversary of the American Association of Engineering Societies—AAES—which meant that many of the fifteen hundred passengers were engineers of one sort or another. To be more specific, about six hundred of the passengers were engineers, the other nine hundred spouses, significant others, and children of engineers. That's where I come in.

Call me Ishmael. No, I'm just kidding. My name is Wilson Hardy, Jr.—known to friends as Wil, with a single "L"—and I was born and raised in Atlanta. But when I think about bearing witness to an appalling disaster, I cannot help but think about Melville's great American novel, and Ishmael: the survivor as narrator. We were discussing *Moby Dick* in a graduate school seminar at Georgia Tech, just before I left for Christmas vacation last year. Actually, I left Atlanta several days early in order to go on the cruise. I was worried about falling behind in my work. That's a laugh. I guess I won't have that Ph.D. to hang on the wall. In fact, I'm lucky to have a wall . . .

My field of specialty is the history of technology. If my father had prevailed, I would have followed in his footsteps and become an engineer. Actually, that came close to happening. I kind of liked the tinkering, but calculus and physics got me down. Also, the profession seemed awfully austere, somehow too forbidding for what I like to think is my blithe spirit. Maybe I have known too many engineers throughout my life. My father is a pretty good egg, but even he will admit that he's a bit stuffy. And he is practically a laugh riot compared to some of his colleagues. Of course, engineers have changed a lot in recent years, what with computer whiz kids in blue jeans transforming attitudes in the workplace. But my father is from the old school, and I suppose I will always think of him as typical of the profession.

Not that my choice of career was determined by negative factors. I've always liked storytelling and thinking about faraway places and long-ago times. One summer during high school I read through all of those Will and Ariel Durant books about civilization, which my parents had bought ages before from a book club, probably for just a few dollars. And I have a passion for dates: 1066, 1492, 1776— that kind of stuff. So I ended up studying history. Putting that together with my liking for gadgets—and maybe the engineering genes in my family—the history of technology seemed a likely choice. If things had gone differently I would have been in Atlanta right now, writing my thesis on the development of machine tools in early nineteenth-century England. Instead, here I am on a foreign shore, wondering how I can possibly write down the story of what has happened.

When our seminar group was reading *Moby Dick*, we spent a lot of time talking about the technology of whaling. That part was pretty cool; but in a more cosmic sense the image of that ship made its way deep into my inner landscape (or seascape, I should say). The sailing vessel, *Pequod*, captained by the mad Ahab, off in search of the white whale, sinister symbol of a hostile universe, and with a crew that represents the human race—wow, what a ship, what a story! When, shortly after the Event, my father told me that the Governing Council had chosen me to be its recording secretary— and incidentally the official historian for our community—my first thoughts were of Ishmael, the sole survivor, telling the tale of that unearthly journey. Now here am I, a mundane historian—actually a student trying to become a historian—designated to record happenings even more inconceivable.

The most I have been able to do in these pages is summarize the events in bare outline. I hope some day to take my notes, along with the minutes I've kept at many meetings, add in such materials as I can glean from other survivors, and put together a more complete chronicle. But even that will be just a beginning. A host of historians and philosopher-poets will be needed to bear witness to the phenomenon through which we have lived in the past twelve months. Luckily, there were aboard our ship, the *Queen of Africa*, a few journalists, sages, and leaders—political, commercial, artistic, and religious—many of whom have been keeping their own diaries. I'm sure that the same is true among the Inlanders, the local inhabitants.

In this slight journal, I have interwoven my private experiences with the historical facts, jotting down what I see and hear, and a little bit of what I feel. My history professors would not have approved. They discouraged expressions of personal sentiment in academic papers. And if my father knew that I was commingling my personal memoirs with his officially commissioned history, he would not be at all pleased. But for now, he is much too busy to think about such a minor matter.

I should explain that my father, as president of the AAES, is sort of provisional co-ruler of our group, along with the captain of the ship. The local folk—we call them Inlanders since that's where they live in relation to us, settled as we are along the coast—they have political leaders of their own. Matters of common concern are managed by what we call the Coordinating Committee, about which more later.

I cannot say enough about how wonderfully the people have behaved. I had seen it many times on television or read about it in books—survivors of floods, fires, or earthquakes working together bravely and steadfastly. Well, now I've experienced it firsthand. There is something about common danger—and shared tragedy—that brings out wondrous human qualities. It can't last forever, of course; but for a year now the group's conduct—with few exceptions—has been exemplary. The ship's crew, established in functional units, with a formal, military-type chain of command, performed splendidly, and the rest of us pitched in as needed with a minimum of selfishness or malingering. Since the passenger list was comprised mainly of AAES people, we have a ready-made corporate structure. Nobody talks very much about exercising authority, but the organizational chart has come in handy. We used it in the earliest days for distributing information, food, and shelter, and for matching volunteers to appropriate tasks. It was convenient that AAES is a "society of societies," thus providing communities within communities.

Unlike doctors, lawyers, and other professionals, American engineers have never had a single, central organization to which individual members of the profession belong. Since the founding of

the American Society of Civil Engineers in 1852, the main organizing thrust of the profession has been along the lines of separate
technical disciplines—civil, mechanical, electrical, chemical, and so
forth. Efforts to join together continually ended in failure, often in
acrimony. Even after the creation of the AAES in 1980, there were
quarrels and disaffections, almost dissolution. The gala cruise on
which we embarked last Christmas season was to celebrate not only
the thirtieth anniversary of the founding of the AAES, but also the
commitment of more than fifty engineering societies to a new era
of cordial collaboration.

In planning this extravagant venture, however, my father was
inspired by a vision that far transcended the realm of professional
organizations. His grand conception was to bring together the most
talented, creative engineers in the world, and to have them, as a
council of experts, consider the state of technology as we moved
forward in the new millennium. His recruiting efforts were incredibly successful. We have among us an array of engineering talent
that could not be matched anywhere.

It was no great trick to enlist the ruling cliques of many of the
constituent societies, the presidents, executive directors, and trus-
tees. These people thrive on board meetings and professional get-
togethers. They were sure to greet the idea of a seminar cruise with
delight. But my father is wise enough to know that these organizational leaders, astute as they may be, are not the world's greatest
engineers. The prodigies, the geniuses, the true pacesetters were all
too busy with their technical activities, not likely to be running
volunteer associations.

Acting with a committee, but doing most of the work himself,
my father compiled a list of the engineers best qualified to make
the seminar an event of global significance. His most important
decision—especially considering how things turned out—was not
to rely upon the elders of the profession, but rather to seek out
people at the so-called cutting edge. He began by inviting the one

hundred engineers, ages thirty to forty-five, who were selected competitively by the National Academy of Engineering to attend a "Frontiers of Engineering" meeting in Irvine, California, the previous year. Hailing from industry, academe, and the government laboratories, these individuals are by definition at the forefront of technological activity. Then further nominations were solicited worldwide, from national academies, professional societies, corporations, and universities.

The selection committee sought representation from all the major engineering disciplines, and also from the various engineering career tracks, such as research, development, manufacturing, and teaching. They also looked for ethnic diversity and gender equity (although they had to deal realistically with the fact that only 10 percent of the world's engineers are women). My father was determined to have international representation, and even though the organization being celebrated is American, about 20 percent of the participants were from nations outside the United States.

Compiling the list of invitees, while of course challenging, was simplicity itself compared to the seemingly insurmountable difficulty of arranging for them to attend. How is one to persuade several hundred of the busiest, most productive people in the world to take seventeen days out of their lives to attend a seminar on a cruise ship? Here my father came up with an idea so wondrous, and carried it out with such mastery, that I have never ceased to marvel at his accomplishment.

He took as his theme the desperate need for technologists to address, in an integrated way heretofore unknown in human history, the scourges of hunger, disease, and privation. He dreamed of engineers joining together in an effort to ameliorate the age-old calamities of poverty, war, and injustice, and the relatively new menaces of environmental degradation and large-scale terrorism. Bring our best technological minds together, he argued, and let them devote their attention to the big picture, looking up for a brief period from the concerns of their workaday world.

What should we be doing about energy, food, water, health care, education, disarmament, communications, urban blight, population pressures, and fanatical terrorists . . . ? This was the time for a holistic, interdisciplinary review of our engineering abilities vis-à-vis our most vexing human problems. This was the time for such a new beginning, just as the end of World War II was the time to found the United Nations. In the first decade of the new millennium, the world was free from cold war and superpower tensions. We had grown rich—at least some of us. Computers, the Internet, and genetic engineering had put powerful new forces at our disposal. Engineers could accomplish much, not just by meeting and talking but by having the world take note of their meeting.

Dad took his vision to the Pacific coast, to Bill Gates and his zillionaire colleagues and competitors. To fund the proposed conference, my father sought an outlandish amount of money. But in the larger scheme of things, and especially in the high-flying high-tech world, the sum was relatively insignificant: a mere $30 million. He had in mind a group of fifteen hundred people at a cost of $20,000 each, which covered the cost of the trip, including $5,000 per head for spending money. Only with an extravagent gesture, he argued, can we attract the best and brightest to our enterprise. And only with the best and brightest can the enterprise succeed.

He sold this vision, incredible as it may sound. My father, an aging civil engineer, senior partner in a firm that designs dams, tunnels, and bridges—something of a hardhat, despite his doctorate degree—sold this vision to the slickest, sleekest techies in the world. He sold them on the idea that all professional engineers, from muddy boots builders to geniuses of software application, are linked in a fellowship, and that this fellowship has the genius, the opportunity—and the obligation—to ease human suffering.

And among the invitees, who could resist? A fully paid luxury cruise aboard a brand-new ship on an exotic, seldom-traveled route, partway around the coast of Africa! Bring your family, including children (up to the age of thirty, as long as they are still enrolled students), and pocket $5,000 spending money for everyone in your party. More important than the money and the travel, how about the excitement of being with talented peers who are seeking the Holy Grail of human salvation? The inevitable attention of the world's media to this remarkable enterprise was also a plus for career builders.

Most of the people who were invited accepted enthusiastically. With fifteen hundred passengers aboard, we were a veritable village. It is hard to believe that we embarked, in such high spirits and with such high hopes, just a little more than a year ago.

————————

Today, we are indeed a village, although not at all like a village that any of us has ever seen before. But we have survived, and the mood of crisis that prevailed for so many months has recently begun to lift. It seems as if we can now look ahead to more than a few days at a time.

Yes, we have survived. But our magnificent ship is sunk, and the few precious objects that we were able to salvage from it don't really amount to very much. Complex appliances—a radio, a few flashlights, a laptop computer—only mock us now. Most of our batteries were quickly used up, and we have few sources of new energy—no fuel, other than wood and a little coal, no electricity, yet. We have the use of animal power, most notably herds of powerful oxen. And we have ample running water in nearby rivers, which we have already put to use with a number of rudimentary waterwheels. Also, we have embarked on an ambitious program of technological recovery. But we have had to start from such primitive circumstances—from so far back—that one has to wonder about our long-term prospects.

I recall in one of my history courses reading about Curtis E.

LeMay, longtime commanding general of the Strategic Air Command, who eventually became chief of staff of the U.S. Air Force. A darling of right-wing extremists, and known as a zealous proponent of carpet-bombing, he retired from the military and in 1968 ran for vice president with George Wallace on the American Independent Party line. During the Vietnam War, LeMay proposed telling the North Vietnamese that unless they put an end to their aggression, we would "bomb them into the Stone Age."

Well, yes indeed, General LeMay. Not exactly the circumstances you had in mind, but it happened very much like you suggested. We're living proof. Bombed into the Stone Age!

In the course of just a few hours we were transported back to Neolithic times, before 4000 B.C.E., when the first copper was smelted in Sumeria. Like our Neolithic ancestors, we could cultivate crops and domesticate animals. Those two talents—momentous in the history of *Homo sapiens*—date to about 10,000 B.C.E.. We could make lots of clever devices out of stone, wood, and bone. We could manufacture pottery and cloth—not very well, but we knew the basic principles and could develop the skills. Indeed, some of our Inlander neighbors, who had in the past been less reliant than we upon modern machines, turn out some very good pottery, and serviceable cloth from wool, cotton, and miscellaneous plant fibers. These skills are, come to think of it, remarkable, bespeaking a natural human genius for adaptation and survival. It took hundreds of thousands of years for hominids to progress from the first stone-cutting tools to the Neolithic revolution of agriculture and animal domestication.

Then it took six thousand years of Neolithic living to bring us to where we are—or rather, where we were twelve months ago. Thinking of this passage of multiple millennia, what hope has our small group to make its way back to the modern age? Assuming— as seems so far to be the case—that a return to the modern age is the course we wish to pursue.

1

ABOARD THE *QUEEN OF AFRICA*
DECEMBER 25, 2009, 5:00 P.M. LOCAL TIME

Jane Demming Warner, a professor of planetary sciences at the University of Arizona Lunar and Planetary Laboratory, had come on the cruise along with her husband, Jacob Warner, one of the leading computer engineers in the United States. It was to be their first vacation together in several years. Jane's life had long been devoted to the study of comets, meteors, and asteroids; but she had planned to take a break from all that for three weeks, just kick back and enjoy the trip.

Sitting on the still-unmade bed in their stateroom, wearing an old tanktop and running shorts for a planned two-miler on the track, Jane gripped the telephone impatiently, waiting for the connection to be established, grimacing at the clicking and buzzing that she heard on this her third attempt to get through to her colleagues in Tucson. She had a sick sensation in her stomach about this whole thing, compounded by a guilty feeling that she had "deserted" her post at home.

The cruise had been fantastic, everything she and Jake had wanted it to be. During the days, he was cheerfully busy with his seminar activities; and their evenings were filled with splendid din-ners, dancing, and strolls on the wide decks of the luxury ship. The stars—she had never seen them so brilliant and close other than through the business end of a telescope. She gazed up at them like a cockeyed "civilian," as if she had never noticed them before. The winter constellations of the southern hemisphere, so familiar in theory, seemed startlingly fresh in their present reality—a revelation . . . Finally a voice on the other end of the line.

"Geoff, is that you? It's Jane. What's going on there?"

Despite the tenuous wireless connection, Geoffrey Baird's voice was clear and crisp, his New Zealander accent unmistakable. "Not good news, Jane luv. Not good at all."

"What the hell is it? Be specific."

"The missiles"—he pronounced the second "i" very long; she could hear his labored breathing—"They went awry—or at least one of them did. We don't know whether it was sabotage or what. Who could possibly be that suicidally crazy? What could their objective be?"

"Stop hemming and hawing, for God's sake," Jane said, wanting to reach through the phone and shake her friend and colleague.

Just a few hours earlier, she and Jake had sat in the lounge with a group of other passengers watching news of the intercept on a satellite feed from ITN in Great Britain. Jane understood exactly what was at stake and how the nuclear explosives were supposed to thwart the comet that was hurtling toward the earth. Jake had been sipping a Jack Daniel's with a blissful grin on his face. He was having one hell of a good time away from his lucrative but stressful consulting business. She had been drinking an iced tea and looking at her watch, thinking about the best time to call her friends at the university, knowing they'd be at the lab monitoring the diversion effort closely.

"Jane, we're not going to make it. Based upon our rough calculations—"

"What do you mean? Who's not going to make it?"

"All of us, the entire bloody planet. I'm saying we're doomed. About six hours from now. The impact—"

She could not hear Geoffrey's words for the roaring in her ears. What was he saying? It couldn't be . . . it just could not be what she thought he had said. The mission a failure? The end of the world? Too fantastic, too horrific to contemplate.

"Slow down, Geoff. Have you been drinking or something?"

"No, but I wish I had a good shot of vodka right about now, Jane. We're looking at the Big Barbecue. I don't mean to be flip, but I don't know what else to say or do. We're all going under one way or the other. Some of the people here have gone home to their families . . . others of us have decided to stay, ride it out the best we can. There is a chance we're wrong. But I don't bloody think so."

She felt as if she were choking. She couldn't breathe, and she struggled to speak in response to his news. "Have you told anyone? What about the press, the government?"

"Oh, yes, the big mucky-mucks called Washington. I think they got to the Secretary of Energy or some such. But it's too late, you understand. Even if we did tell everybody, there's absolutely nothing any of us can do. We're toast, as the kids say—or mine used to say, twenty years ago."

What a decent, smart, agreeable colleague Geoff Baird was. Yet at this moment nothing he said made any sense to Jane Warner, except the first statement about there being an accident or miscalculation. Even though the chances were infinitesimally small, still, there was always a possibility that the so-called fail-safe system would not work. But how could they have missed by such a margin? With all the backup systems and contingency planning? The first time they had tried it, they had done it without seeming to break a sweat. Why now? What in the world . . . ?

"Geoff, you're going to have to walk me through this. Please stay on the line." She dropped the telephone receiver on the bed, grabbed a writing pad from the desk, and picked up the phone again. "Okay, start at the beginning and tell me what *exactly* happened and what you're basing your numbers on. I'm going to write all of this down. Maybe there's something . . ." She started to say, "something you guys missed," but she caught herself and did not finish the sentence.

Geoff Baird heard her unspoken words. "Sorry to say, Jane, we didn't miss anything. We've run the calculations at least a dozen times already. But, for what it's worth—here goes."

MANILA, THE PHILIPPINES, EARLY MORNING, DECEMBER 26

A little boy with a big name, Juan-Carlos Francisco Jaime Triunfo, sat at his mother's kitchen table organizing his precious collection of Pokémon holograph cards. J. C. was almost nine, a bit small for his age, and he was the youngest of ten children. The day after Christmas was his favorite day. There was, of course, no school. After mass, the family would spend the day together just as they had the day before, and his cousins would come over and there would be kids galore in the Triunfo house—and he would show off his fine collection to all. At midday the family planned a trip to Rizal Park, the greensward in the center of the old Spanish city that looked out onto Manila Bay. There were war monuments and playing fields and picnic nooks, and usually many people throughout the park. The boy loved it, looked forward to it. It was going to be a fine day, indeed!

The old Delco radio with the clock that had stopped working long ago sat on the kitchen table where J. C.'s cards were piled. Only his mother was awake, starting her preparations for breakfast and for the family's planned picnic lunch, her back turned to the boy. He paid her scant attention; he took her for granted. After all, that's what mothers did—prepare meals. Nor did he really listen to the music on the radio, or the occasional news broadcast. All was well in the world of J. C. Triunfo.

The Triunfo family was wealthy compared to so many others they knew. The vast majority of people who lived in Manila existed in utter, paralyzing poverty. Foreign visitors who drove the few miles from Ninoy Aquino International Airport into the business center of the city passed the world-class waterfront resort hotels on their left and a high blank wall on their right, which shielded them from the depressing sight of shanty towns and slums. The wall—and the squalor it masked—was a legacy from the Marcos regime. Subsequent democratically elected governments had not improved the lot of these people very much, in part because Muslim rebels in the outer islands drained military and economic resources and political attention.

The table shook slightly, causing the Pokémon cards to move. "Mama . . ."

Senora Triunfo was paying no attention to her youngest child. She prayed silently as she worked, her lips moving to form the familiar words. It was as natural to her as breathing, as slicing the vegetables into the soup pot or wringing the neck of a chicken destined to be the main dish. The routine of life was a comfort to her, albeit hard, unending labor. Her husband went to work at his factory job at eight A.M. every day except Sunday. He worked only half days on Saturday, Jesus be praised. But he was of little or no help around the house when he was home: he drank liquor and slept, sometimes played cards with friends. He did not beat her or abuse the children in any way. He was a decent man . . .

"Mama, the table is shaking," little J. C. said.

Juanita Triunfo, who had survived hurricanes and earth tremors and revolutions, said, "Say a little prayer, niño. God will keep you safe." She held an unpeeled plantain in one hand, a small glinting kitchen knife in the other. "One of your little cards is on the floor." She pointed with the knife.

The boy bent down to retrieve his precious possession. He could smell the mingled odors of vegetables and fruits and cooking oil. He was getting hungry and heard his belly rumbling, felt it vibrate. He sat back in the chair. Then he realized that it was not his belly that he heard and felt. The table, the floor, indeed the entire house was rumbling, vibrating slightly, and it blurred his vision and scared him. Then he heard a noise, not loud, not close—he could not tell what it was or where it came from. He had never heard a train, but he knew the sound of cars and motorcycles, of jet airplanes overhead taking off and landing at the nearby airport. What was it?

"Mama!" Now he was really frightened.

The entire household was awake, and everyone, J. C.'s brothers and sisters and father, streamed into the kitchen, their eyes wide open and questioning. What could be happening?

Throughout the city of Manila and the islands of the Philippines, indeed, across the western Pacific region as far south as Australia and as far north as Vietnam and China, the atmospheric phenomenon released by the impact of the comet was spreading its swift and inexorable destruction.

As the Triunfo clan huddled together in the kitchen, they all heard the approaching roar that had first captured the youngest boy's attention. Suddenly, an emergency message came over the radio, interrupting the music that, for several minutes, had been an inane background noise to the family's increasing sense of dread. The mother and father pressed all their children, from the eldest daughter, age twenty-two, to little J. C., between them—the protective, parental instinct at work, but to what end?

Over the past few days they had heard news about the approaching comet and the mission to deflect it; but this news had barely registered with them. They were vaguely aware that this sort of thing had happened before and that there was no imminent danger. At least that was what the news broadcasts had said . . .

"Emergency, emergency, emergency," the voice on the radio repeated. "The government requires that all persons should seek shelter immediately—"

The family listened, but within seconds the radio was dead and the increasing roar was deafening, causing the young ones to cry out in pain and fear. The older children and adults looked at each other incredulously, expressions of panic now impossible to conceal.

The room—the entire house—heated up to an incredible degree: rising quickly to one hundred, then one hundred twenty degrees Fahrenheit. Within thirty seconds it was nearly two hundred degrees! A smell, an acrid, foul odor of burning plastic and rubber and other unidentifiable substances, wafted in with the hot wind. The temperature continued to rise at a rapid rate and mercifully the family lost consciousness.

Within minutes their home burst into flame, consumed by the firestorm that sucked oxygen and flesh and every material substance into its wake. The Triunfo family and all they had ever known ceased to exist.

WASHINGTON, D.C., LATE AFTERNOON, CHRISTMAS DAY

Senator Christopher P. Hartwyck of Delaware sat in his office in the Hart Building on Capitol Hill staring at the paperwork that littered his desk. He'd had very little sleep the night before and had dragged himself in to the nearly deserted building several hours ago. As a single man, never married, with no children, he was devoted to his job and wanted to keep it for as long as he could; so he spent every waking hour in his office studying briefing papers and reading correspondence from his constitutents—or out campaigning perpetually among the people of his state. The problem was, even though he had what he wanted, he was not a happy or contented man. Sometimes he got into a funk, feeling lonely and lost, despite family and friends and career . . . Is this all there is? he would ask himself.

Just a week ago, at a meeting of the Technologies Development Oversight Subcommittee of the U.S. Senate Commerce Committee, overcome by boredom, he had struggled to stay awake and focus on the subject of the hearing called by the chairman. Facing the two-week Christmas recess, the Senate tried to clear up as much business as possible—often to little effect. The upcoming intercept launch was the topic in question, and everything seemed to be running smoothly, according to the techno nerds who testified. So what was the big deal? We did it before, no problem, and we'll do it again—nuke the confounded planet or comet, or whatever it was. We need a hearing for *this*?

But now, on Christmas afternoon, as Senator Hartwyck attended desultorily to his legislative paperwork, an uneasy feeling gnawed at his gut. Something that one of the engineers had said about the chances for success. "It is a near one hundred percent certainty that the missiles, at least one of them, will find the target and deflect it from its course."

"A 'near' hundred percent?" one of Hartwyck's senate colleagues had inquired.

"Yes, we can never state any scientific fact with absolute certainty."

"And if it goes awry? What then?"

"Senator, you will not need to call another hearing, that's for certain."

The sparse audience tittered appreciatively, and there was scattered applause. The subcommittee chairman gaveled the room to order, and the young senator from Delaware slipped from the chamber unnoticed. He had walked back to his office that day with the exchange ringing in the back of his mind.

But he couldn't linger too long at his desk—he would be late for dinner at his parents' home in Wilmington. He planned to drive there. Well, no time like the present. He carried his trench coat, just in case it got cold. It was about fifty degrees, warm for early winter, but you couldn't count on weather any more, the patterns and temperature swings were so wide and frequent. Not like when I was growing up, the senator mused.

He would not call his childhood as he remembered it idyllic—the word was not in his normal vocabulary. Nor would he term it privileged. Others certainly would: prep school at Lawrenceville, Yale College and Law School, summers at Rehoboth Beach, a few years in private legal practice, election as state attorney general when he was only twenty-seven, the U.S. Senate four years later. It seemed a predestined path, a gifted existence; almost too easy, he sometimes thought. Who knows how far he would go—president of the United States?

The young senator negotiated the D.C. grid, running through a few red lights (there was sparse traffic, no cops), until he reached the famed Beltway that would carry him to Interstate 95 North and home. He fiddled with the car radio as he merged onto the five-lane asphalt road at sixty miles per hour.

Hartwyck reached for the cellular telephone in the passenger seat—an automatic gesture. Why wouldn't you be on the phone while you were driving, legal or not? He dialed his parents' number. The radio played country music, his favorite cultural vice. He reached over to the glove box and fumbled for a cigarette from the pack he kept there. Many times over the past several years he had tried to quit smoking and failed: sometimes he stayed off for a few weeks, or even a few months. But holidays, and work pressure, and driving—all of these were triggers that made him want a cigarette. He wanted one now.

The car, a two-year-old Audi compact with about nine thousand miles on it, was like a little space capsule into which Hartwyck could escape and speed along the highway of his dreams . . . sometimes driving out into the Virginia countryside for miles and miles, where he saw more horses and cattle than human beings. That is what he longed for most, escape, but he didn't know where to or why, couldn't quite put his finger on it.

A news bulletin interrupted the music: "We have been advised by the President and the Federal Emergency Management Agency that all persons must seek shelter immediately. The comet that was headed for Earth may, in fact, approach our atmosphere, causing disruptions in various parts of the world. We do not have word yet on when this might happen, but sources at NASA say it could be within the next several minutes. The likeliest point of contact is the Pacific Ocean off the California coast. We do not know what effect this may have in the Washington, Maryland, Virginia area, but we will monitor the situation closely and keep you informed the best we can. We repeat, the President of the United States and the Federal Emergency Management Agency have announced . . ."

Hartwyck hugged the far left lane of the Beltway at seventy miles per hour, listening but not comprehending what was being said. In his mind he kept hearing the words "a near one hundred percent certainty . . . a near one hundred percent certainty . . ." The radio crackled with intense static; he changed stations, but it was the same, AM and FM. Then dead silence.

As he drove, Senator Christopher P. Hartwyck saw a shadow, like an incredibly heavy black cloud, fall over the landscape. He kept driving. As he held to the curve he saw other cars veer off to the right, saw some of them waver and crash into the wall there as drivers panicked. He did not know what to do. He looked through the front windshield into the patch of sky and saw a huge object—a rock? a plane? very large; it seemed as large as the moon, perhaps larger . . . and it was on fire! It was falling toward Earth, toward him. His heart pounded. He drove on. Seconds later, he and every living thing within a twenty-mile radius was pulverized by the impact of the million-ton fragment.

ISTANBUL, MIDNIGHT, LOCAL TIME, DECEMBER 25

The ancient city, also known through its complex and colorful history as Constantinople and Byzantium, throbbed with life in the darkness that lay like a blanket over the urban landscape of spires, minarets, and tall modern buildings.

Kadijah Raouf Baker walked from the four-story modern office building where she worked as an assistant secretary in a textile-import firm toward the omnibus stop a few city blocks away. She'd had to work an unusual night shift on a special year-end project, so she would be arriving home in the early hours of the morning. Her husband, Necmettin, would have to feed and bathe their twenty-month-old son and put him to bed. He was good that way, and she thanked Allah for Necmettin—a skilled physician, a good and attentive husband, a worthy and decent man.

The street was wet from a day-long rain, and there was a distinct winter chill in the air. Kadijah pulled her *hijab*—the traditional Muslim woman's headscarf—more closely to her face. She wore a loose-fitting woolen coat and ankle-length, long-sleeved dress, but no gloves; she did not own a pair. She and Necmettin were by no means poor, but they watched their money very carefully and spent little on personal comforts. They owned a fifteen-year-old automobile, a German import with nearly two hundred thousand kilometers on it. Necmettin drove it to and from the hospital and occasionally to the seashore for a family trip . . . but fuel and taxes were extremely steep, and often city traffic was so clogged that it did not pay to drive.

Kadijah smiled at the thought of her husband and son safe and snug at home. She would be there soon enough.

She waited at the bus station for more than a quarter hour, her back turned to the biting wind. Headlights and tires played on the slick, rutted street before her in a near-hypnotic rhythm as cars jerked and honked and splashed along. She did not look up the avenue because she knew that would slow the arrival of the bus . . . and she laughed silently at her superstitious attitude.

Even with all the hard work and worry in her life, she had faith that Allah watched over her family—including her parents, siblings, and in-laws. All is well in Allah's peace for those who call upon His name. She gripped her canvas bag at her side in a new gust of wet wind. Her own times of personal discomfort or suffering were offered up to Him for the sake of her family and her country. It was expected; it was the will of Allah.

Moments later, Kadijah sat on the swaying open-air, double-level omnibus as it sped along in the sparse after-midnight traffic. Exhaustion pinned her to the bench, and she fought to keep her eyes open. She did not want to sleep past her stop, halfway across Istanbul in a quiet residential district. She looked around at the other passengers on the bus: a shrunken old woman swaddled against the wet chill and the demonic forces of the night, sitting like a brown nut with black eyes, unmoving; a young couple, per-haps in their late teens, snuggling and discreetly holding hands, the girl's face shining, her brows black and tapered, the boy's face smooth and handsome in a childish way; another man, middle-aged, weary like Kadijah herself, hands and face soiled from some kind of heavy labor, but alert and taking in the sights on the bus itself and along the streets. This man watched the young married woman watching him, a look of challenge and interest in his deep-set eyes.

She touched the scarf that covered most of her face, finding comfort in the anonymity that it provided at this moment.

The bus rocked suddenly, as if it had hit something, and Kadijah looked up and out the window. The street was covered with water, at least a meter high and rising! But there had been no rain for a few hours . . . was this seawater that somehow had risen unexpect-edly? In this part of the city? Very unlikely; she had never heard of such a thing before. The driver of the bus attempted to maneuver the vehicle forward, but the water rose rapidly to what seemed to be two meters, then three, and suddenly the bus itself was floating like a boat.

Some of the passengers screamed, but Kadijah remained calm, gripping a nearby pole and swinging around to look out at the streets and buildings. She prayed that her husband and child were safe, that she would soon be able to see them, if the flood had not yet hit her neighborhood. All about the bus, water poured into windows and doorways, sweeping pedestrians off their feet and lifting cars and trucks in its wake. The bus itself rocked and floated and picked up speed as it passed buildings at the second-story level. The young woman could look into some of those buildings and see people there running to the windows, shouting to each other.

As she looked south, in the direction of the Sea of Marma, she noticed a crimson light illuminating the night sky and obscuring the stars. Odd . . . ominous. Then, a black wall rose in her vision, blocking out everything else, looming taller than any building in the city. It seemed distant, but how could it be far away and so huge? What was it? A thick mist fell over the bus and blew in through the open sides, like rain but warm—then hot, like a shower . . .

Kadijah knew then what it was: a wall of water. A tidal wave. But how, why? The blackness built and grew closer and a roar of wind and water pierced her ears. She could not hear the others screaming, nor herself, as the weight of the monster wave crushed the fragile omnibus and all its passengers and engulfed the city that had been the capital of empires for nearly two thousand years.

ABOARD THE *QUEEN OF AFRICA*
DECEMBER 25, 2009, 9:00 P.M. LOCAL TIME

Jane Warner had not rested or eaten a bite of food throughout the remainder of the day. She skipped dinner with a mumbled excuse to Jake. Many times she had been tempted to make a phone call: to friends at the lab, to family members, to someone—anyone in the outside world. She did not say anything to her husband, nor any of her fellow passengers, for fear of creating a panic. But during the dinner hour she did approach Dr. Hardy, the leader and organizer of the cruise, and within a few minutes of her conversation with him, he suggested they contact the ship's captain. She agreed, and Johan Nordstrom, the tall Norwegian, joined them in Dr. Hardy's stateroom. The three sat around a low glass coffee table in comfortable chairs. A tray of drinks lay there, untouched.

"Captain, Dr. Hardy, I know that what I have told you sounds fantastic; but I have it on excellent authority—and I have run the numbers myself, several times now." She glanced down at the maroon carpet on the floor of the room, finding it difficult to look at them directly. "The impact will occur at about eleven our time, which is about four in the afternoon on the East Coast, one P.M. West Coast time, in the States." Each man looked at his wristwatch. "Yes, just two hours from now," she confirmed.

Hardy removed his glasses. A widower, in his early sixties, he had a kindly if somber face, and a full head of hair streaked with gray and white. "What shall we do about it? I cannot really accept this—emotionally, that is. Intellectually, I do understand what you are saying, Dr. Warner, and I believe you, but—" He shrugged and gestured helplessly with his hands, unable to finish his statement.

Nordstrom, too, was taken aback, rapidly processing Jane's information and the implications for his ship, its crew and passengers. Inevitably, he thought of his family in Oslo, which made his heart pound painfully. There was time to contact them, and he was determined to try, before he began to prepare his vessel for . . . for what?

"I ask the same question as Dr. Hardy: What must we do? How will this—this thing affect us? Can you tell us, please?" His calm, polite tone barely masked the fear and sadness he was feeling. Like the American engineer, his well-trained professional mind fought to overcome the primitive, emotional responses of the human animal.

"It is possible," Jane replied, "that we will be crushed by fragments of the comet, or engulfed by huge tsunamis, or assailed by fire from the sky, flames that consume everything including our oxygen, or annihilated in some other way I can't even think of. In short, I don't know the answer. Or perhaps we might be spared. I'm dealing with numbers and uncertain suppositions." Then, seeing the the look of horror and incomprehension on each man's face, Jane continued: "Captain, I feel that we should do nothing until we know more—except maybe you want to confine all the passengers to their cabins by eleven P.M. Some kind of curfew, with whatever excuse you need to use."

"Sounds like a wise suggestion to me," Hardy volunteered, and Nordstrom agreed.

So, about ten thirty, the passengers were notified of the eleven o'clock curfew, with a severe weather forecast attached. The evening had been in full swing, with continuing Christmas celebrations and cocktails or dinner being served in a number of dining rooms, many of the children still awake playing with the toys they had received earlier in the day.

Jane paced back and forth in her stateroom. Jake Warner had retired early, after a busy day of kibbitzing and cocktails, and a post-dinner poker game. She was jealous of his carefree state of ignorance. As the fateful curfew hour approached, she slipped outside and went to the port-side deck rail, looking into the black sky. Cloud shards swept past the spectacular showcase of stars.

A few minutes later, straight ahead, as she looked west northwest, she saw a thin horizon line—a dirty yellow glow—that had not been there before, that was not supposed to be there at this time of night. As she watched, transfixed, the line began to turn red and widened to a band that appeared to be approaching the ship.

She heard a piercing scream, a shriek really, in the distance from another deck level. Then nothing. She stood silently, gripping the handrail, feeling the sweat of her own palms. Then another sound, a man's voice shouting and others responding—doors opening and closing. Down along the deck passage where she stood, two doors opened and people came out and, like her, went to the railing and looked into the sky.

Next, she heard words from some of her fellow passengers: "I was on the telephone and it went dead." "They said there was some disaster." "What's happening out there—look!" "I'm scared to death. What is it?" Jane began to walk slowly along the deck as more people came outside giving vent to expressions of alarm. The sky glowed more brilliantly red, and the air around the ship became increasingly warm, then oppressively hot.

Within minutes the captain came on the loudspeaker system, sounding businesslike and composed. He stated that the glow around the ship was in some way related to the comet, which apparently had made contact with the earth. The possibility of danger for the ship—and for the world—was still unknown; but there was good reason to hope for the best. He urged everyone to remain as calm as they could, and to keep the children indoors. He stated that the ship appeared to be totally secure and undamaged and that all passengers and crew were accounted for and unharmed. He assured that all systems—radar, sonar, and particularly radio—would be kept on high alert, in an effort to make contact with other ships or people on shore.

Jane heard a child start to cry, and then another. Within minutes, the emotional atmosphere was charged with fear and despair. Jane could see, however, that the children served as a calming influence on the adults. She was not a parent herself, but she could imagine how powerful is the impulse to spare one's children from anguish. Like the father in *Life Is Beautiful*, which won an Oscar several years ago—the father who, for the sake of his young son, made a game out of being in a concentration camp—the parents among the passengers put on the performance of their lives.

Passengers started to gather in clusters, exchanging rumors and bits of information. Jane overheard one animated conversation among a group who had been talking on telephones or listening to short-wave radios in their cabins. She heard them repeating certain key phrases which had been gleaned from sources in various parts of the world: "red sky," "awful heat," "roaring fire," with an occasional "Oh my God!" She could not stand it any more and went back to her own cabin, where her husband had awakened and was standing half-naked outside their door.

By this time the sky was incandescent, pulsing like the light atop a police car, and the temperature was well over one hundred ten degrees Fahrenheit.

She touched Jake's arm. "I'm going to speak to the captain," she said.

"He told us to stay in our rooms. What the devil is this? It's hotter than hell out here. Is it some kind of nuclear war or something?"

As calmly as she could, she gave him the sixty-second version of the disaster. "It's the end of the world as we know it, Jake," she concluded. "You were too busy having fun today, I didn't want to spoil it for you." She left him standing there stunned, and ran up toward the bridge.

Encountering one of the ship's officers, she asked what news was coming in from the outside world. "None," was the reply. "Not a sound." Then the officer reaffirmed what the captain had said: that the ship's systems were all functioning, antennas in place, skilled operators anxiously rotating dials. But no signals had been detected—not for the last half hour. He barred her way toward the control center, saying, "The captain ordered it, ma'am—and that means everybody. That's his exact words, ma'am."

The tension throughout the ship was now palpable. The sky

continued to glow unnaturally, and the heat coming from every angle created the feeling that the vessel and everyone aboard was in a pressure cooker.

After an hour—an agonizing hour—the red glow diminished, the sky turned a murky purple-blue, and the heat started gradually to ease. The immediate crisis seemed to have passed. Jane and the others felt relieved, dazed, and most of all, bewildered.

The first shock wave arrived at a little past four in the morning with a dull thud and a shuddering of the ship. But there was no visible damage, and Captain Nordstrom again gave a brief and calming message over the loudspeaker system. Three hours later, the *Queen of Africa* felt a second impact, this time from pressure coming around the world the longer way. Close to the comet's point of impact, the blast effects had been cataclysmic. But for these survivors, so far distant, the explosive force posed no danger either to the ship or to any passengers.

Shortly after the first shock wave passed, a large ocean swell, some fifty feet high, surged under the hull. Nordstrom and his officers had been on the alert for just such a contingency, and had positioned the ship so that the wave presented no threat to the vessel. Still, the sudden rise and descent was an unwelcome surprise to nervous systems already stressed to the maximum.

The night hours eventually passed; but the sun did not appear at its usual time. There was a heavy gray cloud cover, tinted with patches of red, particularly to the northwest, where as was later discovered, fires were raging on the land. Then, in midmorning, instead of the the sky brightening, light began to wane. Abruptly, the ship was plunged into total blackness. The outside temperature, which had been alarmingly hot, and then moderated, now began to plummet. Soon the deck railings were covered with thin sheets of ice.

Inside their seagoing coccoon, most passengers felt relatively comfortable. But their mental and emotional state was anything but untroubled. In a strange way, incredulity served to avert panic. The situation was beyond anything these people could ever have imagined, or learned to fear, so that they were dazed almost more than they were frightened.

About noon, the captain spoke again, giving reassurances about the well-being of the ship. "We were refueled and provisioned at Richards Bay the day before yesterday," he said, "so we are amply supplied and capable of cruising, if need be, through several weeks of dark and cold. Besides, my meteorologist has every expectation that the skies will soon clear." It was fairly obvious to all listeners that this "expectation" was based more on hope than on science.

Several times during the afternoon, the captain repeated his reassurances, although since he had no new information, they became less and less comforting. Finally, Jane Warner contacted him to say that she had checked her figures one more time and was now ready to report on her conclusions. So, shortly before dinnertime, the captain was able to tell his anxiously attentive audience that he had something of interest to relate. With that, he informed them about Dr. Warner and the telephone discussion she had held with her fellow academics in Arizona. He concluded his remarks by announcing that Dr. Warner would deliver a lecture that evening, revealing what she had learned from her colleagues, and sharing with everyone her analysis of their situation.

2

If ever there was, in the history of the world, an ultimate bad-news-good-news message, Jane Warner's presentation was definitely it. Her scientific terminology could not soften the horrifying reality that apparently human civilization had been destroyed. On the other hand, the ship, along with portions of the land nearby, had so far been spared—and perhaps with good reason. This was, as Jane announced at the outset, the bottom line. It was critical, of course, that the darkness abate before too long, for without sunlight there can be no life. There was no way to predict reliably when this might happen; but at least the ship provided safe haven, if need be, for a period of weeks.

From the beginning of that first day—a day without a sunrise—there had been a bustle of activity. The clergy on board held religious services devoted to memorial and supplication. Wilson Hardy asked leaders of the seminar to schedule sessions dedicated to post-disaster survival techniques. The cruise staff organized various diverting activities, such as word games, bingo, and exercise sessions. The children were entertained by a continual round of treasure hunts and capture the flag contests, anything to keep them from asking to go out on deck. But for most passengers—and crew as well—the main activities were listening to the captain's periodic reports, and peeking out the windows looking for light in the sky.

At the appointed time for the lecture, nearly all of the adult passengers, and many of the crew, assembled in the largest ballroom to hear from the woman who knew the most about what had happened. For those who could not be present because of important duties, or for whom there was no room, her remarks were carried all over the ship on the loudspeaker system.

"Yes, it seemed safe to assume that the diversion technique would work again. A real no-brainer," Jane Demming Warner said. Her words descended on the hushed audience like so much fallout, irradiating their minds and searing their souls. "To guard against the possibility of rocket failure, an additional two launches were added to the four that had been used previously. This time there were three rockets from the United States and three from Russia. Then, for assurance against failure of a bomb, each of the six rockets was armed with three nuclear warheads. All you really needed was one functioning warhead on one functioning rocket, yet the redundancy was warranted since there was time for only one attempt.

"This was a high-speed chase scene," Jane continued. "The comet raced through space at a speed of forty-two kilometers per second, literally pursuing the earth—and we move pretty briskly ourselves with an orbital speed of about thirty kilometers per second. So, the overtaking velocity was twelve kilometers per second. Things would have been even dicier if the comet had been traveling toward us head-on—at a combined speed of seventy-two kilometers per second. But consider, twelve kilometers per second translates into more than one million kilometers per day. And, to picture the arena in which the event occurred, remember that the average distance between the earth and the sun is only about one hundred fifty million kilometers."

The captain sat with his arms folded, his eyes half-closed, absorbing the information. Like nearly everyone else aboard, he had only half-listened to the news reports about the planned diversion. The event had seemed as unreal as a science fiction novel, and was now as ominous as the morning headlines that would never be published. It seemed absurd when reduced to physics and numbers, inconceivable, totally beyond comprehension.

Jane shuffled through her papers and then continued. "NASA, DOD, the Russians, and other foreign experts, working in a joint committee, selected an intercept spot about as far away from Earth as the moon is—four hundred thousand kilometers, about two hundred fifty thousand miles. Fortunately, the moon was scheduled to be on the other side of the earth at the time of impact, so it would not get in the way. That was considered fortunate. Oh, yes! Some good fortune!" She looked up from her notes, hoping to catch a smile, but saw only blank, numbed faces. "Now, four hundred thousand kilometers is pretty far away when we consider the complexities of aiming a high-speed missile from Earth; but it's awfully close when we're dealing with an overtaking velocity of a million kilometers per day. If the mission somehow did not succeed, the comet would reach our planet about nine and a half hours after the planned explosion. Many experts had argued for a more distant intercept point; but a new theory, stemming from work on a missile defense system, and stressing the accuracy of powerful lasers established on Earth-circling satellites, carried the day for the closer site of engagement. Above and beyond all the studies, the tests, and the previous successful mission, everyone was confident that we had devised an overly redundant fail-safe strategy."

Jane could tell that many in her audience were not really comprehending any of these details. Yet, judged by the absence of sound and movement, they were totally mesmerized.

"About twelve hours before the scheduled rendezvous with the comet, six rockets were launched without a hitch. Simultaneously, a European consortium sent up a rocket of their own, loaded with exotic television gear. Not to be outdone, the Chinese government launched a rocket carrying scientific recording instruments. Commercial airline flights were canceled worldwide, and astronauts working on the space station returned to Earth. No other precautions were thought necessary. At the planned time of impact, millions—no, billions of people all over the world turned on their TV sets to see the big fireworks show.

"The bombs all detonated at precisely the planned moment, the light so blinding that, as most of you saw, it didn't make for very interesting television images. There wasn't much for the commentators to say except Wow, aren't we proud of our technological genius!"

The astronomer kept her voice even, her emotions steady, as best she could. She periodically fingered her silver bangs away from her eyebrow. No one among the hundreds gathered in the vast ballroom—previously the site of dining and dancing and optimistic lectures—moved or spoke.

"My colleagues"—Jane Warner caught herself—"My late colleagues in Arizona were able to explain to me what happened. As they put it, there was 'a slight complication.' One of the rockets had gone astray, following a flight path to the opposite side of the comet—exactly opposite from what was intended. As a result, although the comet was diverted, it wasn't diverted quite enough, and it remained on a collision course with Earth. Who could have predicted that a backup system would become the cause of such a colossal failure? It was nothing less than the greatest technological screw-up of all time. Some of my friends at the lab thought it might be sabotage. If so, it was surely the Mother of All Suicide Bombings.

"At first, hardly anyone was aware that there was a problem. With all the bombs having detonated on schedule, the mission was an apparent success. And even after the first few experts who were monitoring the situation discovered the mishap, their assumption was that the comet would still miss us by a comfortable distance. But minute by minute, as new readings were taken and new data analyzed, scientists from around the world began to realize that something was wrong. Then they could not reach agreement on revised projections. By the time they reached consensus, calculated the spot where the collision would occur, and reported the appalling news to government leaders, impact was only six hours away. Even then, there were no agreed-upon predictions about what the nature of the cataclysm would be."

In her mind, Warner heard the anguished voices of her friends and longtime co-workers over the fading telephone connection. They were going to die—and they knew it. For her, on the other side of the world, perhaps there was hope.

From the lecture audience a voice rose: "One lousy little comet and the whole world destroyed? You gotta be kidding." But no one acknowledged the skeptical comment. All eyes were on the rangy female astronomer.

"It may seem impossible," Jane answered softly. "I only wish that were so." She avoided the incredulous but sympathetic gaze of her husband, who sat in the front row.

"The destruction of the world was mercifully quick," she continued, "if you can say there was anything merciful about it. The comet, which we had estimated to be almost sixteen kilometers in diameter, approached the earth at an angle of about forty-five degrees, moving at a relative speed of twelve kilometers per second, as I have said. Encountering the atmosphere at eighty kilometers above the surface, the intruder, which had for days glowed in the light of the sun, now began to burn. It was about one P.M. in the target area, off the coast of California. Here aboard our ship, off the coast of South Africa—on the opposite side of the world—it was about eleven P.M. Nine and a half hours had elapsed since the failed nuclear intercept.

"A mere six seconds after entering Earth's atmosphere, its speed having increased to 16.4 kilometers per second under the influence of the planet's gravity, the comet struck the surface of the Pacific Ocean. As best I can estimate from the information my friends shared with me, the point of impact was 40 degrees North, 128 degrees West, about 350 kilometers west of Eureka, a city located on Humboldt Bay, north of San Francisco."

A collective gasp escaped from the ship's passengers. Many of them were from Northern California. Their families and friends had suffered the direct impact of the disaster.

"The collision generated forces that within seconds turned the nucleus of the comet from solid state material to vapor. Yes," Warner emphasized, "that's right. Difficult as this may be to grasp for some of you, the huge missile was transmuted almost instantaneously to a gaseous state. A large amount of material from the earth's surface—mostly basaltic ocean crust—also vaporized, and the mixed gases expanded upward in an incendiary plume. This is the sort of event that most of us find essentially inconceivable. We've all seen large, solid objects collide; there's a lot of noise, shaking, dust, and the like. But vaporization? Yet the calculations are straightforward. According to my figures, an impactor slightly less than sixteen kilometers in diameter, with density 1.2 times that of water, traveling at a speed of 16.4 kilometers per second and striking the earth at an angle of 45 degrees, will release energy of about eighty million megatons.

"That's a lot of energy. Enough to vaporize the comet and a considerable chunk of the ocean bottom along with it. A single megaton is equal to the explosive force of a million tons of TNT. A single megaton is also equal to the energy generated by a one thousand-megawatt power plant over a period of seven weeks. The entire world nuclear arsenal was estimated to contain ten thousand megatons, and here we are talking about eight thousand times as much. I cannot go into all of the underlying science at this moment, but I hope this gives you some idea of the terrible scale and power of the event.

"The two-kilometer depth of ocean water at the site of impact presented negligible resistance. Within seconds, the blast formed a 'transient' crater of, I estimate, sixty-three kilometers in diameter.

The ferociously expanding plume quickly blew aside the surrounding air and vented most of its material into the atmosphere. Eventually, after the dust settled, so to speak, the crater was destined to be one hundred and fifteen kilometers in diameter and four kilometers deep.

"Some of the vaporized material hurtled upward at speeds exceeding the earth's escape velocity and rushed harmlessly into outer space. But, unfortunately, most of the material did not escape the earth's gravity. That's the problem—the horrible, ugly root of the tragedy. The tiny bits of matter, like projectiles from millions of Lilliputian cannons, hurtled through space above the atmosphere, following ballistic trajectories, and reached every part of the globe within about forty-five minutes."

The term "ballistic trajectories" rang ominously through the room, causing backs to stiffen and faces to turn from the speaker to nearby loved ones and friends. There were a number of stifled sobs.

"We're about as far away from the impact site as you can get, and if the holocaust reached us, you can be sure that it covered the entire globe. The phenomenon was hypothesized by the astronomer Fred Whipple as far back as 1950. The speedily disbursing vapor particles quickly cooled and condensed into tiny solid globules, most of them less than a millimeter in diameter. As these globules reentered the atmosphere—all over the earth—they began to radiate heat. Some of them burned up from friction, the way large particles do when they bump into molecules of air. Remember when you were a child, seeing those lovely meteorite showers in the late summer skies?" Jane did. That was why she became an astronomer in the first place, to capture and understand such beautiful, unearthly phenomena . . .

"But most of the particles, being truly minuscule, plummeted down between the molecules of the various gases that make up the atmosphere, agitating these molecules and being agitated in turn, in a phenomenon called 'molecular drag,' creating heat through the workings of quantum molecular forces. Instead of burning up as in ordinary combustion, many of these tiny missiles maintained their identity throughout entry, and arrived whole on the earth's surface. This global layer of debris rained in for about an hour, causing temperatures to rise above one thousand degrees Celsius—practically hot enough to melt copper—for several thousand kilometers from the site of impact, and above five hundred degrees Celsius—hot enough to ignite spontaneous forest fires—over most of the earth's surface. Yes, I know it's unthinkable, but a horrific conflagration ensued. Nearly the entire earth was engulfed in flame."

"I don't remember anything like this being predicted," said one of the young chemical engineers who slouched low in his seat near the rear of the room. "And I read a hell of a lot of technical publications."

"Well," Jane said, her face reddening, "there are apparently a hell of a lot of them that you don't read. This phenomenon was predicted by many responsible authorities, and not just because of the theoretical analyses of Whipple and others. There is compelling physical evidence that lies in the very ground under our feet. I'm sure that many of you are familiar with the story. The trouble is," she said, looking directly at her last challenger, "we scientists and engineers don't know enough about each other's specialties.

"In 1980, scientists discovered a thin layer of gray clay that seemed to have been deposited all over the earth's surface some sixty-five million years ago—at the same time that the dinosaurs disappeared. This layer contains iridium and other heavy metals that are rarely found on the surface of the earth, yet are commonly found in objects that arrive on Earth from outer space. Much of the material consists of tiny particles, globular in shape, indicating that it is condensed vapor. The layer also contains large quantities of ash, clear evidence of widespread fires. Some experts have calculated that, as evidenced by this ash deposit, ninety percent of the earth's biomass was consumed in the flames. Ninety percent of every living plant, large and small, burned to a crisp. The ultimate inferno. If this material—the condensed vapor and the ash—was deposited all over the surface of the earth at one time, how else to explain it except as debris from a comet or asteroid crashing into the earth's surface? And if the dinosaurs, plus two thirds of the other living species, died off at the same time—as the paleontologists tell us they did—well . . . The combination of theory and physical evidence is, was, compelling.

"Of course, one important question remained unanswered. Where, sixty-five million years ago, did the projectile land? Could such a huge comet or asteroid crash to Earth and create such havoc without leaving its physical footprint?

"Sure enough, in 1991, a crater that would have been caused by such a giant impactor was discovered in the Yucatan peninsula. Now the picture was complete. Apparently, this event—the fall of a huge object from the sky, followed by the deposit of a layer of material not usually found on the earth's surface—marked the end of the so-called Cretaceous period and the beginning of the Tertiary. It came to be known as the K-T Event.

"So why"—Dr. Warner posed the question that hung heavy in the already charged ballroom air—"why are we now amazed that this disaster has been repeated in our time?"

She took a long drink from the glass of water that stood before her on the lectern, and flipped back the bothersome bangs. The question seemed to energize her.

"And consider," she said, "fire is only one aspect of this scenario. Since the comet landed in the ocean, conflagration was inevitably followed by flood, more specifically, tsunamis, the largest and most dreaded of so-called tidal waves. These ocean monsters probably started with heights of more than two hundred meters and moved across the Pacific at speeds of about eight hundred kilometers per hour, maintaining crests of ten meters as far away as Australia.

Then, as they approached land, they would probably run up to thirty or forty times the height they achieved over deep ocean. Imagine San Francisco and Los Angeles inundated by ocean waves that rose to a thousand, or even two thousand meters as they approached shore, dwarfing the tallest buildings. Of course, by the time the waves arrived, these cities were likely to have been charred ruins. But to have escaped the fire would only mean being engulfed by the flood.

"The tsunamis then quickly flooded shores all around the Pacific basin. Yet, clearly, the deluge was not limited to that half of the globe. We ourselves had already seen a very large wave go under our ship, and we are in the Indian Ocean, separated from the Pacific by numerous landmasses. Obviously, large chunks of the comet separated from the main projectile, and some of these fragments must have landed in all the seas, propagating waves to attack every coastal community.

"As for people on high ground, they would have had little chance to appreciate being protected from the water. Being closest to the burning skies, they would have been the first to be incinerated. And wherever there was snow and ice—think of the Himalayas and the Andes—it would have been quickly transmuted into avalanches and huge flooded rivers, wreaking more devastation.

"Then, inevitably, there was the darkness. Although most of the vaporized material had plummeted down to the earth's surface, the very tiniest particles remained suspended in the atmosphere, along with ash from the fires, cutting off the sun's rays almost completely. We pray that this condition will not last long."

From the audience a woman's voice was heard, tremulous but insistent: "Yet our ship stayed intact, and we're alive. How can this be?"

Jane Warner was prepared for this question. She located a sheet of paper from her notes. "Of course, I can't be certain about any of this," she said, "but I've run some calculations, and this is my best guess about how we have come to be spared. As I told you before, I learned from my friends in Arizona that the point of the comet's impact was going to be 40 degrees North, 128 degrees West. The antipode to this—the point exactly opposite on the earth's surface—is 40 degrees South, 52 degrees East. But during the forty-five minutes that it took the ejecta particles to encircle the earth, the earth was rotating west to east, moving the antipode eleven degrees of longitude in the opposite direction. So when the rain of fire arrived, the antipode—the point of convergence for the inferno—had moved to 40 degrees South and 41 degrees East. This spot is in open ocean, about fifteen hundred kilometers southeast of the bottom of the African continent, pretty much in the middle of nowhere.

"Now, you might think that the point most distant from the impact would receive the least amount of rain-down, but that isn't the case. It's true that the rain-down diminishes in severity as it goes farther from its source, but when it reaches the antipode, it meets the stuff coming from the other side, creating a circle of increased intensity, a double dose, as it were. If you painted a globe red, with the intensity of the color showing the intensity of the fiery rain-down, you would see the color getting paler and paler as the distance from the impact grows—but then a sudden increase, a doubling of the intensity, the overlap of material coming from two directions, makes a small red cap at the far side. There is, however, a zone—let's be optimistic and call it a safety zone—where the amount of the descending ejecta has greatly diminished, dwindling away, before it is suddenly augmented by oncoming material at the far pole. This zone can be pictured as a ring, an annulus—sort of a flattened doughnut—centered in the Indian Ocean at the repositioned antipode."

Jane sensed that many in her audience had already tuned out; but she was nearing the end of her presentation, so she pushed ahead. "Now stay with me just a moment more," she urged. "When we measure the surface of a sphere, we speak in terms of degrees of arc, halfway round the world being 180 degrees. I'm speculating—just speculating, mind you—that at about 160 degrees from the point of impact, the rain of fire dissipated below the level of total destruction and remained providentially weak until being intensified again at about 170 degrees from the point of impact. This would provide a zone of reduced intensity—the flattened doughnut—about 1,100 kilometers wide, with its center at the location I've already cited, 40 degrees South and 41 degrees East. If we plot it on a map, we see that the anullus of sanctuary—the doughnut-shaped safety zone—sweeps down into the Southern Ocean toward Antarctica, doing nobody any good except for a few penguins, perhaps. But if we follow it northward, we observe that it just manages to cover the southeast coast of the African continent, along with the southern tip of Madagascar. Our ship, off the shore of South Africa, midway between Richards Bay and Durban, is comfortably within the magic zone. For this reason, perhaps—just perhaps—we have been spared." Then she concluded, quietly, "At least for the time being."

Hours passed, then two days—three. Living in perpetual darkness, the concept of night and day became elusive. They slept, they woke, they paced up and down the corridors and into the public rooms, gathering in groups and talking, supporting each other the best they could. They returned to their cabins to nap fitfully or lie awake thinking about the unthinkable. Captain Nordstrom saw to it that meals were served on schedule, and this remnant of order helped to keep chaotic nightmares at bay.

The darkness, of course, was not just psychologically oppressive; it was literally the greatest danger that the survivors had to fear. According to the calculations of some catastrophe scientists, which

Jane Warner shared with Nordstrom and Hardy, they might be in for a long siege of "nuclear winter" that would seal their doom.

However, after three days of gloom and ever-increasing cold, it suddenly began to rain. Torrents of water poured down, gradually washing particles from the sky. This was followed on the fourth day by brightening skies and moderating temperatures. Then rainbows appeared, surely the most resplendent display of color that any of them had ever seen. Many in the group, thinking of Noah and the Great Flood, took this as a sign from the heavens, a promise of salvation.

The returning sun brought with it the hope of life, but also a new health hazard. Considering the fires that had raged in the skies, the survivors had to assume that the ozone layer was probably devastated. Since their supplies of sunscreen lotion were limited, hats and long sleeves became the standard dress code. They all agreed that this was a small enough price to pay for survival.

When the New Year arrived, a week after the Event, conditions at sea were eerily normal. Still, nobody suggested that they observe the arrival of 2010, let alone celebrate the thirtieth anniversary of the American Association of Engineering Societies. The thought of that was too bizarre even to mention. There were a few prayer meetings, but that was about the extent of any commemoration ceremony or service.

Two days later—on the ninth day since the apparent end of the world—the captain decided to head cautiously toward shore, aiming first for Durban, which was to have been the next port of call. But when, on the following morning, the tenth day, they came within viewing distance of what should have been a large city, nothing could be seen other than piles of seeming rubble, with huge clouds of black smoke shrouding the hills behind. So the *Queen of Africa* headed slightly to the north, back toward Richards Bay.

Again they waited for the morning light, but again a mass of rubble was all that could be discerned along the shore. The enormous dock facilities that the civil engineers had observed with such interest during their recent visit had been transformed into eccentrically contoured chunks of concrete. However, they could see hills rising inland, and—most welcome sight—several patches of green in the distance. There were some lingering black clouds, indicating the presence of scattered fires, but nothing as forbidding as the scene at Durban. Also, for one long stretch they could see a sand beach with fairly calm surf, a likely landing site for small boats. All in all, the prospect appeared relatively welcoming.

Yet even as they sailed slowly at what seemed to be a safe distance offshore, there was suddenly a crunching sound, and the ship abruptly halted.

After an anxious half hour, during which the officers conducted a survey of the vessel, the captain's voice was heard over the loudspeaker system. "Regrettably," he said, "our harbor charts have proved useless in this completely altered landscape, and it seems we have struck a piece of the concrete harbor works that was swept incredibly far from the shore. Everyone aboard is safe and sound. The vessel, however, has begun to take on water and is slowly sinking." He paused to allow the passengers and crew to absorb the impact of this news. "We have no choice but to abandon ship. I do not view this as a dangerous situation, because we are close to shore and the sea is calm. There is no need to panic or to rush. We have ample time. Of course, we want to move as briskly as possible, consistent with good order."

And so it came to pass that the passengers and crew of the *Queen of Africa*, having endured fire, darkness, and the threatened end of the world, were now confronted with an experience more commonplace, perhaps, but terrifying nevertheless—the sinking of a ship at sea.

3

Captain Johan Nordstrom of Oslo concentrated on the minute-by-minute details of command, moving from one deck to another, directing his crew in the evacuation and salvage operation as his magnificent ship foundered within swimming distance of the African shore. Although there was no respite from the grief for his wife and children that had obsessed him every moment since he first learned of the Event, the demands of the current crisis provided a welcome distraction.

He strode purposefully along the deck, trailed by his administrative assistant and chief security officer. The chief engineer, Nordstrom's trusted number two officer, remained at the command center on the bridge, keeping the ship's power functioning as long as possible and monitoring the videocams which showed the main points of salvage activity.

The captain removed his cap, wiped his pale brow, replaced the cap. He felt fortunate to have been sailing on a fine new ship, equal, in the moment of crisis, to the challenge of the seas. It was also fortuitous, thinking of the complicated salvage operation, that the vessel was equipped with the latest and best materials and supplies. She was the *Queen of Africa*, a beauty of seventy thousand gross tons, modeled after the *QE2*, and conceived as the flagship of a fleet built to voyage around the continent of her name.

Up to the end of the twentieth century, as far as the cruise ship industry was concerned, Africa was the forgotten continent. But with the coming of the new millennium, the last great underutilized route for oceangoing cruise ships came into its own. This evolved synergistically with the development of new port facilities in most of the major coastal cities. Another contributing factor was the commercial development and newly achieved prosperity of many African nations. Circumnavigation of the continent became a popular trip—although much too lengthy for the purposes of this group of busy engineers.

Nordstrom's ship and crew had embarked on a seventeen-day voyage, starting in Mombasa, the main seacoast city of Kenya, calling at several ports along the southeast shore of the continent, and planning to end at Cape Town for a New Year's Day birthday bash for the AAES. These Americans—and most, although not all, were Americans—went to great lengths to celebrate the most insignificant achievements, the captain thought. But it put money in the company's coffers . . . and they had been wonderful passengers, intelligent and well behaved. They seemed to appreciate the crew and treated them well.

Nordstrom himself had often thanked his lucky seafaring stars that he had been blessed not only with a fine ship but also with a superb crew. My dying vessel was well manned, he thought. Although "manned" was an inaccurate usage since about 50 percent of the ship's company was female. It amazed him to think how in just the past few years women had taken on jobs from which they had long been excluded by tradition and prejudice.

Johan Nordstrom mentally ran through the crew roster. There was the chief engineer, the crew administration assistant, the bosun and bosun's mate, the security officer and his four masters at arms (the ship's "police force"), the radio officer and his three assistants; there were the deck officers, engineering officers, deck supervisors, deckhands, and engine-room workers. On the "hotel" side of the operation—and these were predominantly female—there was the hotel manager who headed the group, along with the purser, cruise director, administration assistant, cruise sales manager, personnel manager, and public-room supervisor. These people, assisted by thirty-five hotel officers, oversaw a veritable army: baggage masters, bedroom stewards, cruise staff, laundry workers, nursery attendants, public-room stewards, receptionists, store managers, printers, and office staff. And, of course, there was the sizable restaurant operation. Responsibility for feeding this floating city was in the hands of an executive chef and five chefs de cuisine, with a staff of more than three hundred, including twenty-two wine stewards and seventeen bartenders.

Then there were those individuals who are an essential part of any modern cruise ship, but whose worth might be less clear in a community trying to survive in primitive conditions: beauticians, hairdressers, fitness instructors, masseurs, photographers, musicians, entertainers, dancers, casino staff, and a disc jockey. Happily, the captain considered, the talents of an individual are not defined by a job description. The attributes required for practically any job aboard a cruise ship include people skills, an adventurous spirit, a good attitude, and an ability to handle stress. Nordstrom was pleased during these past several days to discover the many fine qualities demonstrated by the members of this motley and high-spirited company.

Finally, in his mental list he recorded the ship's medical staff: just two physicians, supported by two nurses and a pharmacist, yet a crucial element of the ship's company. Since cruise passengers are assumed to be essentially healthy, doctors are there mainly for emergencies between ports, so a larger number would be superfluous. Fortunately, in the present circumstances, there were among the passengers a dozen or so physicians of various specialties, some of them quite prominent in their fields. Apparently, marriages between engineers and doctors were not at all uncommon. There were also numerous passengers with varying degrees of nursing skills, and a retired laboratory technologist, making it possible to assemble an eminently satisfactory medical establishment. This group had spontaneously organized when the crisis first struck, and had been working dawn to dusk ministering to the needs of passengers and crew. The effects of stress were manifest in several cases of nervous collapse, and a half dozen of outright hysteria. A variety of tranquilizers was dispensed, along with those time-honored remedies of the seafarer—rum and brandy.

———————

The surf between the foundering ship and the beach remained reasonably calm, and there were ample facilities for safe evacuation—twenty lifeboats plus fifty-six life rafts. Nevertheless, there was a good deal of confusion and unavoidable jostling as the passengers donned life jackets, gathered together as many personal belongings as could be managed, and hastened to previously assigned emergency stations. The relative composure that had prevailed on board for ten days gave way, for awhile, to barely controlled frenzy. Transfer into the lifeboats was something of a scramble, and it was particularly difficult for some of the older passengers. In the end, there were a few bumps and bruises, but no incapacitating injuries. The crew, displaying the results of effective training, moved expeditiously.

"Sir, the first lifeboats have been launched." The bosun's mate spoke matter-of-factly to Captain Nordstrom.

"Thank you, Frederick. Keep me informed by the minute, if you please. We are gaining water all too rapidly."

"Sir," the younger man acknowledged, and with a crisp salute turned on his heels to return to his station.

Throughout the afternoon and into evening, boat after boat came and went from ship to shore and back again. First the people, then medical supplies. Next foodstuffs, some of which crew mem-

bers distributed to the passengers along with water rations that
were stored in the lifeboats. Then came bedding, a welcome sight
to those who were thinking ahead to the coming nights. As blankets
were distributed, fatigue overcame anxiety, and the beach was soon
covered with huddled forms, many of them turning restlessly in
the fading light. The weather remained dry and mild, for which
Nordstrom was grateful.

The captain considered trying to salvage some of the heavy motors and other mechanical apparatus, along with a supply of fuel
oil, but decided against it on the grounds that the fuel would so
quickly be exhausted that no good would be served. Tools and utensils, however, were carefully assembled under the vigilant direction
of one of the engineering officers. The purser made sure to gather
together vital company records, and more usefully, paper, writing
utensils, and miscellaneous office supplies.

Having noticed that, where the shore party was being established, there was a river running into the sea, the captain decided
against spending valuable time and energy transporting fresh water.
He did, however, order the crew to gather together basic pots and
pans and kitchen utensils, along with containers of dishes, glasses,
and tableware.

Finally, with little time remaining, the small flotilla salvaged
personal belongings that the passengers had been unable to take
with them in the first crossing—clothing mostly, along with gadgets such as tape recorders, CD players, VCRs, and laptop computers—presently useless, yet icons of the life they were leaving
behind and mirages of a life that they hoped might be restored.

Wilson Hardy and several of his colleagues saw to it that hundreds of technical books were saved. All the engineers had come
laden with texts in their particular fields, along with journals and
notebooks filled with information on current developments. Anyone
who, in the midst of this chaos, could give thought to the eventual
revival of civilization had to recognize that this literature was a vital

supplement to the human talents among them. The written material was also a critical resource for teaching the young people how to carry on an engineering culture of high quality into future generations.

Along with the piles of engineering books, the boatmen transported several hundred volumes of all kinds from the ship's library: Shakespeare and the Bible, classics, history, biography, encyclopedias, and popular fiction, too. The survivors would not want for spiritual nourishment and intellectual challenge to go along with the handbooks, manuals, and texts. A hundred-plus collection of children's books was salvaged from the day care center. The kids on board were not to be forgotten.

Then, with an almost festive flourish, cases of wine were brought to shore. And in the very last boats to pull clear, the band's musical instruments stood out in jaunty silhouette.

Shortly after the salvage operation was halted, the ship's top decks disappeared under the water. The event was shockingly abrupt. One moment the ship's superstructure was there, then suddenly it was gone. There was no dramatic plunge into the depths as in a movie rendition of the *Titanic*'s demise. The deliberate, seemingly willful, descent of the magnificent vessel betokened, the captain thought, a formal farewell, not only the death of the ship but also the end of an epoch.

Nordstrom personally took three round trips to and from the ship during the course of the day, finally coming to shore for good with the very last load of salvaged material. That first night he supervised the crew, who worked tirelessly.

By morning, a commissary had been established. Leaders of the kitchen staff began to organize food distribution. Provisions destined to spoil without refrigeration were prepared for early consumption. Nordstrom ordered a bucket brigade to be created, and they set to work bringing water from the nearby river. A team of environmental engineers performed some elementary tests to assure the water's potability. A group of engine-room workers was delegated to gather firewood, of which fortunately there was plenty. All of it was wet and scattered, testimony to the forceful waves that had washed over the beach just a few days before, but once lit, it burned well enough.

How does one light a fire? Johan Nordstrom considered. This is often one of the key predicaments in classic stories of castaways. He remembered Jules Verne's novel, *The Mysterious Island*, which he had encountered as a boy, and recalled that the engineer hero, Cyrus Harding, solves the problem by using the crystals from two watches to concentrate the rays of the sun on kindling. He remembered his father reading that adventure tale to him . . . and the stories of Robinson Crusoe, and the Swiss Family Robinson . . . all of those memories flooded back into his mind. Well, he thought, smiling ruefully, this was one problem that he did not require the engineers to address: the crew had salvaged plenty of matches.

As the new day dawned, cooking fires started to glow and tureens of soup were set upon them to warm. Passengers gathered around to watch, and several spontaneously started to applaud captain and crew for their successful salvage operation. Suddenly it seemed the entire company was swept up in a mood of high-spirited defiance. Nordstrom felt, momentarily, like Robinson Crusoe, to whom shipwreck was a challenge through which he could demonstrate his resourcefulness, indeed, his humanity.

Once the kitchen operation was established, the captain asked the military engineers in the passenger group, led by General Allen White, director of civil works of the U.S. Army Corps of Engineers, to establish sanitary facilities. Soon work was underway on the construction of rudimentary outhouses. One of the engineers suggested designing a gravity sewer system leading to an anaerobic digester which could produce methane gas for lighting, cooking, and an eventual source of power. The idea was commended, but put in the category of "future possibilities."

The medical staff set aside a small area designated as a clinic. But there were hardly any patients. The twenty-five hundred people who had just undergone a considerable ordeal appeared to be amazingly healthy.

Food, water, and sanitation. The immediate needs of the survivors were attended to on the first day. There was no shelter, but the weather was wonderfully mild.

"Just like the Caribbean," Wilson Hardy said to Nordstrom as the two men stood together at noon, surveying the swarm of activity along the beach. "My late wife and I went several times over the years: Jamaica, the Virgin Islands, Nevis. She wouldn't have liked these clouds. But they're good fortune for us, given the ozone problem."

"It happens to be the traditional rainy season," the captain said. He was impressed with Wilson Hardy, the organizer of the AAES cruise, a natural leader among the passengers. "We cannot rely on traditional weather patterns, however," he went on. "We can only hope they prevail. But, of course, since we're a long way from establishing a farming operation, favorable weather does not solve our major problem, which is food. Even if meals are restricted to minimal levels, our supplies are adequate only for about a month."

"Is this what you want to talk to us about this evening?"

Nordstrom had called together a committee for a meeting before nightfall. Although he might have asserted his prerogative of absolute command, he felt that the existing circumstances called for a different approach. He had asked Hardy to join him as co-chairman of a leadership assembly. He invited a few of his senior officers to join and asked Hardy to call upon leaders from several of the constituent engineering societies. General White of the Army Corps of Engineers was enlisted, as was Harold Carson, director of the Federal Emergency Management Agency (FEMA), who was also part of the traveling seminar.

Carson, especially, had been distressed not to be in Washington when the comet struck. He had told Hardy that he was responsible for a staff of nearly three thousand in ten regional offices and had oversight of emergency response activities of twenty-eight federal agencies and departments, plus the Red Cross and other volunteer organizations. He and some of his key aides, who had accompanied him on the trip, had presented a session early in the voyage devoted to the mitigation of such disasters as earthquakes, floods, fires, and a variety of storms. He very much regretted not being at his post when the ultimate disaster struck. But, as it turned out, no amount of preparedness and resourcefulness would have helped.

The captain of the *Queen of Africa* said to Wilson Hardy, "We are lucky to have you and your fellow engineers in our company; but this good fortune brings with it potential problems. Engineers are not renowned for their mastery of politics. How are we going to take a collection of intelligent, strong-willed individuals and forge them into a community that works in relative harmony? I've given this some thought," he continued, "and I believe we should work toward a consensus model—not a military organization, not a true democracy. We need to remove politics and egos from the picture, as much as possible."

Hardy considered this proposal and deemed it essentially sound. He was skeptical—thinking of some of his more opinionated colleagues—but agreed to support Nordstrom's strategy.

"As long as we can channel their special talents, get them to buy into the plan . . ."

"Well, we'll know soon enough," Nordstrom said. "We can't afford a minute's delay. Let's get our people together—we might call them the Governing Council—and meet this evening."

At 1900 hours (the old "time zone" designation was being retained), the Governing Council convened for its first session. The fifteen members sat on makeshift chairs or on the sand, facing a sawhorse table that resembled something from a western movie set. For overhead protection, pieces of canvas had been spread on a framework improvised from scrap lumber and pieces of bamboo. Hardy's son, Wilson Junior, sat at one end of the table, serving as recording secretary. There was much to be done, and little time was wasted on idle conversation.

With Nordstrom the consensus chairman and Hardy his elected co-chair, the Council quickly decided to move ahead on three fronts: First, continue to improve the camp on the beach, most immediately by providing shelter from sun and rain. To help achieve this, several military engineers would be asked to design simple lean-to structures, using wooden debris scavenged from the area, along with such canvas, tablecloths, blankets, or other fabrics as could be found among the supplies. The sand dunes, some of which were tall and steep, served well as a wall against which to rest the sundry structural supports. As for assembling the rudimentary shelters, General White's officers and Harold Carson's FEMA people would direct the effort, with passengers and crew expected to pitch in as best they could. At the same time, a cadre of civil engineers was assigned the task of designing a "next-generation" structure, employing thatch or other natural materials that might make for more comfortable and durable shelters.

Second, it was vital that a survey team seek out potential sites for a more permanent settlement away from the ocean's edge. The responsibility for this work was also assigned to General White and his team.

Third, and most important for long-term survival, a scouting party would be sent inland to see who and what might have survived the holocaust, and what the prospects were for finding sources of food. The logical objective for this expeditionary force was the

city of Ulundi, fifty miles distant—seventy-five by winding road—
perched in the promisingly green hills at an altitude of about two
thousand feet. The Ulundi decision was unanimous, although more
than a few of the members of the governing group admitted that
they had never heard of the place and had only the vaguest idea of
its location.

"Just where the hell are we?" The question was raised by Donald
Ruffin, president of the Institute of Electrical and Electronics Engineers, an acknowledged whiz-bang with fiber optics, but rather
inscrutable when it came to non-technical subjects. Lumpy and be-
spectacled, he sometimes chose to act the country bumpkin, imply-
ing not that he was dim-witted, but rather that the world about
him was run by dimwits. In the current situation, however, he was
genuinely perplexed. There had been a few shipboard lectures about
African geography, history, and culture, but Ruffin—along with
many other engineer passengers—had chosen not to attend.

"We're in Africa, Donald," Wilson Hardy responded drily.

"I know," retorted Ruffin, "but exactly where in Africa, and
what can we expect to find here other than a bunch of angry elephants?"

"We are in the Republic of South Africa," said Captain Nordstrom. Then, after a slight hesitation, he elaborated: "The province
in which we find ourselves is called KwaZulu Natal."

KwaZulu Natal! Wilson Hardy, Jr., who up to that point had
been dutifully recording the minutes in his own makeshift shorthand, looked up from his notepad. The announcement evoked in
him a thrill of excitement and apprehension. The word "Zulu" is
the embodiment of heroic ferocity, the incarnation of Africa's bold
resistance to colonial adventurers. KwaZulu, he knew from a lecture
he had heard on shipboard, meant home of the Zulus, whereas Natal was the Portuguese word for Christmas, a name selected by
Vasco da Gama when he sighted this coast on Christmas Day in

1497—512 years before the fateful Christmas just past. And, from the part of the lecture that dealt with modern South Africa, Wilson had learned that this was the area where disorder and violence had reigned just half a generation earlier, during the transition to a new government after the end of apartheid.

For excitement, mystery, and symbolic implication—along with the hint of new dangers—the fates could hardly have made a more fanciful choice.

"Who do you propose for this exploration team?" asked John Hertzler, a blue-jeaned computer genius from Seattle. He had been included on the Council at Dr. Hardy's suggestion not only because of his technical brilliance, but because he had been the designated representative of Bill Gates and the other financial sponsors of the trip. Even in death, Hardy thought, they deserved to have a voice.

Nordstrom had a ready answer. There were several South African engineers on board and the captain had recruited two of them for the scouting party. They were fluent in Afrikaans, one of the official languages of the nation, and familiar with the territory to be explored. One of them was also conversant in Zulu. The expedition was to be led by the senior deck officer, Carl Gustafsson, accompanied by the security officer, two of his masters at arms, and six seamen. In addition, Hardy had asked two prominent agricultural engineers to go along, as well as a half dozen specialists in mining, construction, manufacturing, and metallurgy. "Of course, our first interest is food," he said to the assembled Council. "But assuming we find a world in which we can live, we will quickly want to make it as comfortable a world as possible."

There was general agreement with the plan, and with the composition of the scouting party. So Nordstrom turned to the next item on the hurriedly prepared agenda, a discussion of governance. Wilson Hardy, Jr., who had scribbled down the details of the expedition plan as best he could, expected a debate about political organization, chains of command, lines of authority, or possibly a constitutional convention . . . but this was not to be.

Again it was Hertzler who interjected his opinion. "Governance be damned," he said emphatically. "As we say in Seattle, let's not waste time allocating parking places in the company lot. The product comes first." He had the group's attention. "We've got to provide our people with food and shelter, a feeling of security, and expectations of improved living conditions. Later, if we draw up a political plan—a rational plan—everybody will be with us, and administration will take care of itself. On the other hand, if we begin by debating bureaucracy and fail to hold out hope for material progress, people will lose faith in the future and discontent will breed chaos. We'll be in *Lord of the Flies* territory. So let's talk facts and figures. Where exactly are we—to reiterate the previous question—and what do we have to work with? I mean physically, not philosophically. Let's be engineers today. We can be Thomas Jefferson tomorrow."

A murmur of agreement and smattering of applause came from the engineers in the council. This was an approach to the politics of survival that they could endorse: Let's get to it, not the talking, but the real work. Let's consider what materials are available to us and how we can put them to use.

The secretary, Wilson Junior, had an almost irresistible impulse to speak up. This strategy struck him as somewhat simplistic. Who says that good technology is an adequate safeguard against bad government? Well, he considered, I'm simply the scribe for this gathering of sages. He picked up his pencil, and kept his mouth shut.

His father, having anticipated that the group would be eager to assess the area's resources, was prepared to address Hertzler's challenge. With Nordstrom's consent, he had asked two of the native South African engineers to make themselves available. They were Pieter Kemm of the Richards Bay Minerals Company and Kelvin Marshall of Sasol Limited. These men had originally been invited to join the seminar not only because of their personal talents, but also because of the unique technologies in which their respective companies were engaged. The Council would learn more about those technologies presently, but for now Hardy called upon the men to provide a general overview of the survivors' new surroundings.

Both Kemm and Marshall had been traveling with their wives and children, and so, like most of the passenger group, were spared the ultimate calamity of losing those dearest to them. Still, they found it difficult to look out at their devastated homeland at the same time that they were trying to describe it. They carried on, however, and their spirits seemed to lift as the session progressed.

"Look at this nation of ours," Kemm said, pointing to a map that hung from a makeshift easel of tree branches lashed together with nautical ropes. He was a slim, youngish-looking man of average height with red hair, and he paced back and forth as he spoke. "Let me tell you about it. We cover the bottom of the African continent, reaching from our westernmost point—where the Orange River flows into the Atlantic Ocean forming our border with Namibia—to where we are now, almost fifteen hundred kilometers—more than nine hundred miles—directly to the east, on the shore of the Indian Ocean. It's about the same distance from the Cape on the south to the farthest point in the north, where we abut Botswana, Zimbabwe, and Mozambique.

"You may have heard that this land is blessed with natural resources, and it is. But believe me, these resources are not uniformly distributed. Far from it. Two thirds of the country, running from the Atlantic coast inland, is either desert or semidesert. This bleak landscape is largely caused by the cold Benguela Current that runs north along the Atlantic shore. Near Cape Town, where the Atlantic meets the Indian Ocean, there is a narrow coastal area that has what we call a Mediterranean climate, with hot and dry summers and cool and wet winters. But the truly fertile part of the country, favored by ample rain—thanks to the warm, south-flowing Agulhas Current of the Indian Ocean—is along the east coast, and that is exactly where we find ourselves today. This coastal strip, which is fairly narrow, and runs inland only twenty to fifty kilometers before the land begins to rise, has a humid, subtropical climate. The soil will support many types of vegetation, and much of the area was committed to growing citrus produce, bananas and various tropical fruits, eucalyptus, and most of all, sugar cane, of which more than two million tons per year were produced, half of it for export. We sure as hell won't have use for all that cane; but it's good to know that we can cultivate many different crops in these conditions.

"When I was a boy, living in Durban, just down the coast from where we are now, we would raise avocados, mangos, guavas, pineapples, whatever, merely by scraping the ground and then putting the seed or pineapple cutting in the hole. In no time we would have a plant. In other words, we can grow food here without fancy irrigation systems, or fertilizers, or sophisticated agricultural techniques. You have to admit that's an advantage. All great civilizations are born where crops can be grown readily. I don't say that this coastal strip is paradise. During much of the year, it is hot and uncomfortably muggy. Farther north along the coast—closer to the equator—malaria can be a problem. Although maybe the recent events have disconcerted the mosquitoes. That would be nice. Taking it all together, however, it's my opinion that if one is going to be shipwrecked, this is a pretty good shore on which to set up housekeeping."

"It sounds almost too good to be true," John Hertzler said.

"And the best is yet to come," Pieter replied. He faced the assembly, standing still for a moment as the sun set in front of him, illuminating his face and bright hair. "As we move inland, the topography rises into fertile hills through which run numerous rivers. About one hundred kilometers from the coast the elevation varies from about five hundred to one thousand meters, and the climate becomes what is called temperate, subtropical—the summers are hot, but the winters are cool and clear. The natural vegetation is grassland and thicket, wooded valleys, grassy hillsides and ever- green forests. We overcut our trees through the years, just like people in other parts of the world; but then we came to our senses and started to cultivate lots of pine, bluegum and other varieties— the largest man-planted forests in the world—some of them not far from here. We've had enough trees to support substantial manu- facturing of paper and other timber products, so there should be more than enough wood to provide for our needs.

"I guess you could say that corn is our basic crop, our staff of life. It is grown in abundance, both for cattle and as a staple for the human population. We don't harvest as much per acre as the Amer- icans do; but we still get plenty, believe me. We also grow wheat, beans, potatoes, just about anything you could want, both on large commercial farms and in small privately cultivated gardens. Fruit like peaches and pears, which tends to be infested with worms when cultivated along the coast, does just fine in the hills where the cool winter nights make short shrift of the insect pests. And let's not forget the grain sorghum, which is good for a lot of things, not the least of which is making beer."

"Beer is nice, but I'd rather have livestock." This came from Harry Wills, one of the outspoken Texans whom Hardy had in- cluded on the Council.

"Ah, someone is curious about livestock," Pieter said. "Well, there are—or at least were—more than twelve million cattle in South Africa, both beef cattle and dairy. As you probably know, among the Zulus and other indigenous tribes, cattle are well cared for and seen as a symbol of wealth and prestige. And on the large commercial ranches, cattle-tending has been raised to a fine art. Our animal husbandry has been admired throughout the world. We have managed to avoid the deadly tsetse fly, partly through dili-

gence, but mainly through a fortuitous combination of landscape and climate. As for sheep, we have more than you can count, so you needn't worry for woolen garments, or hides, or for the occasional lamb chop. There are also lots of chickens and eggs. And pigs—many thousands of pigs. And let's not forget about the wild game. Native animals were hunted to near extinction in the past; but there are now numerous game farms in KwaZulu Natal. Many species have been protected with tourism in mind, also to stock zoos in other lands, and for purposes of ecological preservation. And, let me add, for food. I'm fond of antelope myself.

"Finally, about three hundred kilometers inland lie the Drakensberg Mountains, rising to thirty-five hundred meters, part of the Great Escarpment, which runs in a north-south direction, separating the eastern coastal area from the great inland plateau. If you ever get to the point where you can rest from your work and take in some sights, this is among the most glorious scenery in the world."

At this point, Robert Barkin of Lucent Technologies raised a question that, judging from the approving nods and comments, had been on many minds: "Aren't you forgetting about the natural disaster we've just experienced? What's left of this paradise after the ravages of fire and flood?"

"Maybe I can make us all feel a little better," said Harold Carson, the director of FEMA. "First of all, we will learn more from the expeditionary group very soon. But let me assure you that the earth has wonderfully vigorous recuperative powers. You remember when Mount St. Helens erupted—back in 1980, I think it was—burying the countryside inches deep in ash? Well, within a few months there were ferns and trees sprouting on the slopes, and nearby farmers replanted their fields the very next growing season. An even better example is the eruption of the Indonesian volcano, Krakatoa—that was in 1883, a famous date in the history of natural disasters. That big bang propagated tsunami waves that swept nearby shores to a height of more than forty meters, leaving them bare and covered with a gray, muddy deposit. Within four weeks, with the coming of rain, fresh grass appeared, and splintered coconut and banana trees sprouted new shoots. Also, as you well know, most forest fires don't do lasting damage. In fact, periodic burning is in many ways beneficial to the soil. Unless nature has some more nasty tricks up her sleeve, the earth should convalesce, and much more quickly than you'd think."

Pieter Kemm took a deep breath and came to his conclusion: "It is good to hear what Mr. Carson has to say, and that bears out my own optimism. I feel in my heart that this bounteous land will recover from the onslaught of flame and salt water, and will provide for us. I apologize if I sound like a real estate promoter, but I have given you the facts as I know them."

"Terrific," John Hertzler interjected, "and as I said, almost too good to be true. I'm looking forward to seeing those nice crops being harvested—assuming we live to see that happy day. But when I ask about resources, I'm not just thinking about filling my stomach." He patted his paunch for emphasis. "What about metals and chemicals and energy and all those things we will need to climb out of the Stone Age back into the modern world?"

"Kelvin Marshall has a lot of that information," said Wilson Hardy, "and he assures me that we'll be encouraged by what he has to tell us. But . . ." and here he wiped his brow and looked at his watch.

Several torches had been lit, and in the flickering light it could be seen that the men and women of the Governing Council were exhausted past the point of constructive deliberation.

"Let's pack it in," said Captain Nordstrom, stepping forward. "Tomorrow is another day—the good Lord willing."

FROM THE JOURNAL OF WILSON HARDY, JR.

I know that, as designated historian, I'm supposed to be preparing an account of the major events that have transpired—which I have done and will continue to do. But in my "spare time" I also want to record certain personal aspects of the story that are central and important to me personally. The most momentous of these is the appearance on the scene of Sarah—my Sarah. Another is the serendipitous formation of the Focus Group.

That's what my father called us one night early in the cruise when he found the six of us in one of the ship's bars arguing about the meaning of life. Amazed to hear us carrying on in such earnest debate, my father came up with that label, the "Focus Group," and it stuck. It was all lighthearted at first, but once he took on the burden of co-leader of our survivor society, he started to use us as a resource in the Governing Council's deliberations. Not that he looked to us for ultimate wisdom. But, pending the evolution of a formalized democratic-style government, he felt the need to refer to several "sounding boards," and we were one of those.

Focus groups had become quite the thing in recent decades, particularly with market research companies. These firms would bring a small number of people together in an informal setting and have them engage in roundtable-type discussions with a facilitator, usually aimed at seeing how one product or another might fare in the marketplace. Political parties used them too, as a way of predicting how the electorate might react to campaign ads or contemplated policies. Such groups were supposed to be a microcosm of "the public." Of course, our sextet cannot claim to be representative of the world population, even as severely reduced as it is. No way. We're all young, white Americans. On the other hand, half the group is male, half female—no small distinction in the scheme of things—and philosophically, we do represent a variety of views. Most important, we share a taste for debate.

We also share a taste for line dancing—or at least that's what first brought us together. Aboard ship, a lesson in this popular pastime was one of the social events intended to help the younger, single passengers get to know each other, and soon after we left port, I was among the first to sign up. It wasn't that I knew exactly what line dancing was, or cared, but rather that I liked the look of the young woman in front of me in the sign-up line. When she chose the three o'clock class, so did I.

Her name is Sarah Darby. She grew up in Phildelphia, majored in English literature at Swarthmore, and came on the cruise with her parents. Her mother is the engineer, an eminent authority on lasers. All this I learned as we walked away from the sign-up desk. Before we reached the end of the corridor, I was in love. In the ordinary course of events, maybe it would have turned out to be merely a shipboard romance. Who knows? And at this point I really couldn't care less. Sarah has dark brown hair, hazel eyes, an aristocratic nose, flawless skin, and a body both athletic and beautiful. At college, when she wasn't deconstructing Hawthorne, she played lacrosse.

We met again at the class that afternoon, looked intently at each other, held hands as partners, and it's been that way ever since. If the world had to end for me to be with Sarah, then so be it. That's no way to think, I know, but sometimes I get carried away.

The line-dancing class was not a big draw. In fact, only five students showed up. This five, plus the teacher, gathered in the center of one of the dining salons, standing uneasily under a glittering chandelier, glancing toward the door to see if others might be coming to join us. After a while it became apparent that the group was not going to get any larger. Sarah and I talked quietly with each other, and I didn't care if we stood there waiting forever.

As the minutes passed, I became vaguely aware that there was another pair who had eyes only for each other. Tom and Mary, as I was soon to learn, are both engineers, and they seemed to be conversing in technical terminology that to my ears was close to being a foreign language. But this was just a courting ritual. You could see that their mutual attraction was more than technological. Tom is one of the stars of our traveling seminar, one of those wizards from the "Frontiers of Engineering" program I mentioned earlier. He is—was—a star professor of materials engineering at Stanford, and has a wizard's understanding of plastics, ceramics, carbon fibers, and all such stuff. His real name is Alfred Swift, but when, at an early age, his talent for tinkering became manifest, people started calling him Tom. Tom Swift. What better name can there be for an engineer?

Mary O'Connor, a russet-haired colleen who makes me think of those old Maureen O'Hara movies I've seen on videotape (my dad loves them), is also a member of the technical species. You would never guess it by her looks. She was close to receiving her civil engineering degree from Manhattan College in New York City, following the same career path as her father, who is president of the American Society of Civil Engineers. Mary is tall, about six feet, and stands and moves gracefully, like a dancer. She looked extremely comfortable next to Tom, who is about six six, lanky, and rumpled in a suitably engineering kind of way.

The fifth member of the class was Herbert Green. Like Mary, his home was New York, but, as Sarah whispered to me at one point, the two of them seemed to come from different planets. Herb is short, quick-moving, verging on nervous, and to my southerner's way of thinking, the quintessential urbanite. In his final year at NYU Law School, Herb's special interest was environmental law. As he was happy to tell us as soon as we became acquainted, he hoped some day to save the natural world from the effects of human greed and mismanagement. His outspoken hostility to technological enterprise was a constant irritant to his father, the dean of the engineering school at Columbia University. When Tom Swift first heard one of Herb's tirades, his comment was: "Green, you bet! He wants to take us back to the forests of our ancestors."

Our dance instructor was Roxanne Ford from Texas. No college credentials for Roxy. Just a quick exit from the small town where she had been born, and which she never wanted to identify, followed by a career as an itinerant dance teacher. She loves travel, she loves people, and she loves to dance. Working on a cruise ship was her idea of paradise. I am tempted to call her a blond bombshell because that's the way she first struck me, decked out for work in a tight-fitting cowgirl costume, complete with red boots and a rhinestone-studded vest. But Roxy defies simplistic typecasting. She's a hedonist of sorts, but in a philosophical rather than a frivolous way. She takes the world as she finds it, and loves not only the people in it but the animals as well. She has traveled to the Indian subcontinent, falling under the spell of Eastern religious beliefs—reverence for every living creature, curiosity about reincarnation, that sort of thing. If I had known then what I know now, I would have understood that Roxy and Herb were made for each other. But looking at them at the time, they seemed a most unlikely pair.

In fact, we all seemed a somewhat mismatched group, standing around looking at each other and glancing not so furtively at our watches. Finally, Tom said, "Well, it looks like we're going to have to abort this launch."

"Not on your life," said Roxy. "There's just more room for

those of us who are here. Let's get started," With that, she pushed a button on the boom box she had brought with her, and a lively country-pop tune by Shania Twain poured forth.

Then she gave instructions: "Everybody stand over there with your back against the wall. Put your heels against the wall and pull your shoulders back. Try to press the small of your back into that wall and lift your stomach and rib cage up and in. Lift your chin so that it's parallel to the floor. Now, move away from the wall and try to maintain your posture. Don't look down! Try walking forward and back, taking small steps. That's the spirit!"

I don't know what spirit she was referring to, since her three male students were staggering about, each more awkward than the next. Sarah Darby and Mary O'Connor, admittedly, looked great.

"Come on, guys," Roxy urged. "Put your thumbs in your pockets and stand tall. Okay, a little more walking around, listening to the music—then we'll be ready for partners."

Roxy saw that Sarah and I were standing close together, as were Tom and Mary, so she grabbed Herb.

"Here we go, mister," she said, standing beside Herb and slightly in front, placing his right hand on her right hip, his left hand holding her left hand slightly elevated, like a couple of figure skaters. I was to learn later that this was called the modified sweetheart position. In a few minutes we were stepping around the room in pairs, and magic was at work. We were becoming sweethearts, nothing modified about it. Yet, even as each of the three couples started to fall in love, so too was a very special bond established among the six of us.

That first afternoon we followed a routine that we stuck to for ten fabulous days, until it was disrupted by the end of the world. The line-dancing class began promptly at three o'clock. Roxy removed the listing of the class from the daily notice of activities so that it remained limited to just our own little group. I can't say that we became accomplished dancers, but we had a hell of a lot of fun; and we did improve (the guys a little, the girls a lot; they were naturals). First we tackled "Cowboy Hustle" and "Tennessee Stroll," then Roxy took us to a higher level with "Country Strut" and "Eight Corners." After an hour of lively stepping, we retreated to our favorite lounge, one of the dozen or so on the ship. It was at these gatherings that we quickly became a debating club. We discovered a shared passion for discussion—for argument, I should say—that developed from the group's natural chemistry.

Herb is a born debater, someone who looks for a verbal challenge wherever he goes. He is certainly the one who got us started. As for the rest of us, we each found something within the group that evoked an urge to talk, an outspokenness that was not our usual way.

Once the debate was over, usually by six P.M., the couples went their separate ways. The evenings were dedicated to friendship, and soon more—very much more. As we sailed south from the equator into the December summer of the Indian Ocean, romance flowered under tropical skies.

Roxy had her job responsibilities as teacher and entertainer, and Tom had his commitments in connection with the seminar program; but they both managed to find time to pursue what had become their primary interests, Herb and Mary, respectively. Sarah and I were more or less completely free around the clock, and that was exactly what we wanted, to be together.

"Bliss was it in that dawn to be alive/But to be young was very heaven!" Sarah quoted Wordsworth to describe our days and nights at sea. My new love, the English major, was much given to literary quotations. "I'll try to keep it under control," she said sheepishly, by way of apology. The fact was, I adored every word she spoke.

We spent some of our mornings on shore, taking preplanned tours of Africa's southeastern coast: Kenya, Tanzania, Mozambique, and finally South Africa. But the itinerary that had seemed so appealing when I read about it in a brochure paled in comparison to what Sarah and I were discovering in each other. I'm afraid that I didn't learn as much as I might have about the interesting places we visited; my heart and mind just weren't into it. Instead, I experienced ten days of pure happiness, and then . . .

After the cataclysm, as the sky first glowed red, then darkened, as the outside air grew lung-searingly hot and then bitter cold, and as we became gradually aware of what had happened in the world, our group spent hours together talking, sometimes lapsing into long silences, and privately—although we did not at first speak of it— praying. Sarah, Mary, Herb, and I, traveling with our parents— and Mary and Herb with younger sisters—had been spared the ultimate pain of losing those closest to us. Roxy, although she wept bitter tears for the human race, acted as if she never had a family of her own, and rebuffed any of us who approached her on the subject. Tom had suffered the greatest loss of all—parents, a large and close group of siblings, and lots of nieces and nephews. He reacted with a bleak stoicism that saddened us all. Mary tried to ease his sorrow with religious consolation, but he gently dismissed her efforts.

At one point, Roxy impulsively suggested that we resume our line-dancing classes. We knew that she meant well, but we didn't have the heart for it. There is a popular image of mobs, amid the ultimate calamity, engaged in orgies of drink, dance, and sex. Supposedly this happened during the plagues of the Middle Ages, and it has been envisioned in speculative stories and science fiction books. That's not the way it was with us. An extra beer, yeah, why not? But we had no spirit for wild partying. None.

Yet, while we gave up our dancing—although we vowed to return to it one day—we still needed to talk. And one of the things we talked about was the miracle of our coming together, finding

each other, and being spared together. We marveled at the phenomenon of our dancing and falling in love at the very moment that
the universe was hurling the most awful devastation at our planet.

After the ship sank, and we found ourselves castaways on a desolate
beach, physical needs took priority over philosophical debate. We
were busy all day, helping with the basic work of establishing a
camp. Yet in the evenings we six managed to find each other and
huddled together on the sand, wrapped in blankets, looking like
refugees in some disaster zone—which is what we were.

I remember in particular one discussion we had soon after coming ashore. The expeditionary force had left that morning, headed
inland, and there was widespread worry about what they were
likely to discover. Nevertheless, when the six of us got to talking,
our spirits took wing. With the natural optimism of youth (as my
father would say), we felt intuitively that we would survive. What
we viewed with fascination and alarm was the reality of being cast
back, technologically, more than six millennia.

I recalled having studied, as part of my undergraduate course
work, the crafts of the Iroquois Indians of New York State, and
being fascinated by the ways in which they coped with life in the
Stone Age. The earliest Dutch explorers found the Iroquois manufacturing nets, twine, and rope from elm, cedar, and basswood
barks; weaving baskets, mats, moccasins, belts, and burden straps
from vegetable fibers and animal hair; tanning deerskins and decorating them with hair and shells; fashioning clay vessels and clay
pipes; carving wooden ladles, spoons, dishes, and ceremonial masks.
These so-called primitive people built impressive longhouses, manufactured excellent canoes and paddles, bows and arrows, snow-
shoes, lacrosse sticks, spears, tomahawks, and war clubs. They used
antlers to make knife handles, digging blades, awls, combs, needles,
and fish hooks. They manufactured hoes by sharpening the shoul-

der blade of a deer or the shell of a tortoise and fastening it to a stick. They fashioned stone mortars for pounding corn, grinding mineral paint, and for pulverizing roots and barks for medicine.

The Iroquois, of course, were just one tribal group among the myriad whose prehistoric handicrafts have been uncovered and studied by archeologists. Even the most sophisticated engineer cannot fail to be dazzled by the evidence of technical genius exhibited in natural history museums in every corner of the world. It is bewitching to stare at the objects in display cases and to think of living like these early peoples lived, without factories and power plants, without bulldozers and jet planes—creative and ingenious, yet dwelling in harmony with nature.

"Perhaps," I mused, "just perhaps, this is the way we ought to go."

"We may have no choice," Herb said, "depending on what the expeditionary force finds—or doesn't find."

"It sounds good to me," Roxy said. "A new beginning. A new world. A chance to develop our own Garden of Eden."

"Oh, come on," Tom said. "Don't tell me you'll be happy to live your life without indoor plumbing, television, and air conditioning?"

"To say nothing of Mozart and Shakespeare," murmured Sarah.

Roxy smiled sadly, shrugged, and remained silent.

"I can tell you one thing," Tom persisted. "The six hundred engineers in our group are not going to settle for some kind of primitive paradise. What we want is technological progress, plenty of it and the sooner the better."

"Easy does it," Herb said. "Whatever we decide to do, it's going to take time. I know you feel a sense of urgency, Tom, but remember, we have no place else to go." He winked at Roxy.

"Also," I said, "you can't think just in terms of yourself and a few like-minded Western techies. There are many different people around here with ideas of their own. Engineers are not a majority, even among the passengers. And there is considerable variety even among the engineers. Our tour group contains, by design—I know because I saw how my father and his committee put it together— a large number of young people, a balance between the sexes, a certain amount of ethnic diversity, and a twenty percent representation from foreign countries, that is, from outside the United States. Asians are particularly well represented, being leaders in the engineering profession in the United States as well as in their native lands. The ship's company also comprises many under-thirty folks, and features a striking assortment of different types. Captain Nordstrom and his officers are mostly Scandinavian. The seamen are mostly Asian. The rest are from just about everywhere.

"As for the inhabitants of this area where we landed—assuming some have survived—they are certainly mixed: not only South African blacks and whites; but, from what I have learned, a surprisingly large number of Indians and Pakistanis, more than ten percent of the local inhabitants. The population of this world of the future is likely to be diverse with a capital D—and they may not all share your high-tech views, Mr. Tom Swift."

"Is that a coincidence?" Sarah asked. "A multiplicity of races and cultures. A gene pool of amazing variety. I wonder . . ."

I looked at Sarah, who smiled and shifted closer to me.

As our debate ran its course, and the evening light dimmed along the beach, I found myself surreptitiously beginning to think about my own personal future. And almost instantly I decided that I wanted to marry Sarah. In the world that had existed until just a few days earlier, I would have carefully considered how to proceed. I was very much in love, yes, but there would have been so many practical considerations—schooling to be completed, career to be considered, Sarah in Pennsylvania, me in Georgia—plus the lack of pressure to marry, indeed the very opposite force at work, the pressure to remain single until later. Now there would be no "later" in the conventional sense. Education, career, homemaking, all were compressed into something that must be embarked upon immediately. In that previous life, at twenty-five years of age, I was just a kid. Now I was a mature member of the tribe, already past the time when I should have been starting a family.

And there was another factor that I suddenly found frightening. In that other existence, if through some terrible turn of events, Sarah should have been lost to me, I would eventually have gotten over it—would I?—and found somebody else, somewhere, out of the millions of suitable young women in the world. Here there was a limited number of young women, and the potential loss seemed vastly greater. How can I say that the woman I loved seemed more precious in a world suddenly become smaller? I will not say it; but I admit that the thought occurred to me.

Also, marriage in this coming society, the shape of which I could hardly envisage, loomed larger than marriage in the world we had left. Here, a partnership in survival entailed working together as part of an extended family, finding food and shelter, averting ever-impending hazards, striving to make a new world. I understood, as I never did before, the concept of marrying for the sake of carrying on the blood line, saving the farm—or the homestead, or the kingdom. I found myself thinking of Sarah as a mother, a breeder of a new race.

Sarah. What a name for this moment! Sarah, wife of Abraham, mother of Isaac. God vowed that she would become a "mother of nations." What was I doing, thinking so much lately about the Bible? I guess it couldn't be helped, what with fire and flood and the destruction of the world. Anyhow, putting it all together, I knew that I needed Sarah by my side. As I saw her looking at me, I could tell that she felt the same way.

The idea, unspoken, was spontaneously in the air. We all became silent. Sarah and I smiled at each other, as did Tom and Mary, as did Herb and Roxy. In an enchanted moment, it became apparent that each of the three couples had made a life commitment.

"Marriages are made in heaven," I said later to Sarah, "and that's doubly true for us, brought together by a comet." I then observed that I was picking up her habit of quoting the classics. "I guess that's Shakespeare," I added, feeling smug.

"Close," Sarah answered. "It's John Lyly, a contemporary of Shakespeare's." Then, suddenly pulling me to her, she said, "And the full quote is: 'Marriages are made in heaven—and consummated on earth.'"

In the long run, of course, even the most icily analytical engineer—my father to the nth power—could not deal with this disaster in the lucid form of logic. When the Focus Group met, we might start with reasoned debate, but would eventually resort to poetry and emotion—and silent reflection. There is no way in which we can rationalize what has happened and try to compare it with anything else. The world destroyed. We didn't really absorb it that first day, or come to grips with it. How could we? How can we even now? But there it was, and here it is.

As the immediate threat lessened, and we found ourselves on this shore, warm and dry and with food to eat, tense vigilance among the survivors gave way to elemental relief, then quickly turned to something else among most people, something difficult to define—I can only call it shock. The destruction of the world is different from the loss of a loved one, unlike even widespread calamities such as earthquakes or wartime massacres. Everyone gone. Everything gone. Impossible to grasp. Carried beyond fear, grief, and anger to shock, we came inevitably to feel awe in the biblical sense, dread of the immense, powerful, and ultimately unfathomable universe.

I've said that I would leave the serious philosophizing to others, yet here I am talking again about awe and the Bible. Actually, my primary feeling—my primal feeling—was the joy of being alive, of having survived. I've read about the guilt experienced by survivors—soldiers in battle or people in concentration camps—individuals who were astonished to find that, when grief for others seemed called for, they were overwhelmed by relief at their own deliverance. I felt some such guilt, but not as much as I suppose I should have. I was pleased that my father was spared, and achingly sad that my friends back home were gone. But I could not subdue the exhilaration I felt because of the elemental fact of my own survival.

Of course, there was one major difference between the passengers and the crew, unspoken but momentous. Most of the passengers were together with their immediate families, husbands with wives and parents with children. Most of the crew came alone. Many of them are young, single, and adventurous, but not all. There was mourning aplenty, mostly private and subdued.

To give the full picture, I must also mention the suicides. At least, we all assume that's what they were. Shortly after the full scope of the Event was known, while we were still at sea, three members of the crew disappeared, presumably overboard. Each of the three had expressed to friends their agonizing grief over having lost loved ones—and they explicitly announced their intention of putting an end to their own unendurable lives. There was no official announcement of these losses, but the news did get around. When the people and supplies from the ship reached the shore, and the captain announced that all on board were accounted for, he too was making the assumption that was universally shared.

Awe, grief, shock, wonder—all such feelings inevitably gave way to the immediate pressures of simply getting through each day. Most of the survivors—young and old, passengers and crew, workers and academics, leaders and humble laborers—found an effective remedy for melancholy in hard work. They turned the precariousness of our situation to advantage as an aid to personal healing.

4

After a five-day trek up flood-scoured hills, the expeditionary force reached Ulundi, or rather the place that had been Ulundi before the coming of fire and flood.

Deck Officer Gustafsson, speaking with Captain Nordstrom in his daily radio call, reported that the first people he had encountered were a group of Zulu youngsters kicking a soccer ball around on a muddy field. This tranquil scene, come upon suddenly after their journey through appalling wasteland, brought several members of the party to the verge of tears. A rugged master at arms dropped to his knees in a prayer of thanksgiving.

The children greeted the strangers with smiles and took them to one of the few buildings that remained standing amid charred ruins. There, Gustafsson reported, he was received graciously by a group of men who were conducting a meeting. This turned out to be the Ulundi Indaba, an ad hoc administrative organization, comparable to the *Queen of Africa* survivors' newly formed Governing Council.

About half the people present were Zulus, several dressed strikingly in tribal ceremonial regalia. Some of them were officials of the now defunct provincial government. Others were tribal elders. Apparently, both the Zulu king and the paramount chief had perished in the disaster; but other leaders, acknowledged through traditional blood lines, had stepped forward. There were also several representatives of the other tribal groups who dominated the national government through the African National Congress Party. As far as Gustafsson could tell, then and later, political rivalries, as well as tribal antagonisms, were set aside by the holocaust.

In the Indaba, the white population was represented by such political leaders as had survived, along with several executives of local businesses. The Indian and Pakistani communities also had a few delegates. Rounding out the company were a number of officials from the army and police, which forces, Gustafsson noted, were racially integrated.

Simon Kambule, a forty-year-old Zulu politician, welcomed Gustafsson and his crew into an outbuilding that had survived the disaster, partly wrecked but usable. There were benches and tables enough to seat the Indaba members and visitors. It was noontime, and the roof, even with a few holes in it, provided welcome relief from the sun.

"Welcome, gentlemen," Kambule said, speaking English with a singsong British-African accent. "We are so happy that there are others who have survived this terrible event. We wish to offer you every possible means of support, and we hope and expect that you will share with us in equal measure whatever resources you may have brought with you. Let us exchange 'vital statistics,' if you will: names, numbers, facts about ourselves. If I may, I will start off the discussion and call upon my countrymen to fill in details as I go. Then we will ask you to provide us with similar information about yourselves."

As he spoke, the charismatic African gestured elegantly, looking directly in turn at each of the newcomers. Meanwhile, water and fruit appeared—bananas, mangoes, and pineapple—brought by local women. The visitors eagerly partook of the refreshing fare.

Kambule began his narrative account with a recollection of Christmas Eve. Without warning, shortly before midnight on

December 25, the inferno had descended upon Ulundi and its environs. At first the strange glow in the night was far off in the distance, but within minutes, fire swept across the landscape and entered the city. From Kambule's description, Gustafsson perceived that although Ulundi was well within the "safety zone" as defined by Jane Warner's calculations, it had nevertheless suffered terrible damage. While spared the lethal rain-down from the sky, the city had been attacked by wind-driven forest fires from outside the zone.

Suddenly, violently, the streets became rivers of flame, the buildings instant pyres. Most of the people were in their beds and never knew what happened. In many places the fire darted in jets, as if shot from flamethrowers, enveloping some individuals, leaving others untouched. Small firestorms swirled about like tornadoes, sucking up the oxygen in certain locations, leaving it unaffected in others. Never, it seemed, had death been more capricious. People staggered about, stunned and in anguish. However, unlike most of the earth's surface, where the slaughter was total, there was in and about Ulundi a remnant, a population of survivors.

Early in the morning, just as the inferno began to subside, enormous waves of ocean water rolled across the lowlands and up into the hills, swallowing everything in their path. The water lapped at the edges of the city. For people used to living at a high elevation far removed from the sea, the flood was as incredible as it was terrifying. When the waves receded, it seemed as if everything that had existed below the high water mark was suddenly gone. Then came darkness and bitter chill. Suffering and delirium, Simon Kambule said, were beyond description.

Late on the third day, however, just when it seemed that the frigid night would be everlasting, heavy rain began to fall, the same downpour that the cruise ship passengers had experienced. The next morning, the sky lightened and the cold began to abate. Then the rainbows appeared, interpreted by many in Ulundi, as aboard the *Queen of Africa*, to be a sign of salvation.

The chaos and panic subsided. In this moment of crisis, tribal traditions provided a valuable support. The Zulus had a ready-made clan structure to fall back on, and the whites and the Indians also demonstrated remarkable resilience. Surviving family members gathered together, followed by spontaneous assemblies in each community. On the seventh day, several of the founding members of the Ulundi Indaba came together and established a rudimentary government center.

"Our first concern, of course, was medical care and food," Kambule said, "although we quickly learned that there were few medical facilities remaining. Strangely, it seems there were not that many injured who required care. Some people had been carried away by the floods—they were simply gone. The fire had been so fierce and—what is the word, idiosyncratic, perhaps?—that individuals had either been suffocated, totally consumed, or completely spared. For the relatively few who had been badly burned but not killed outright, there was little that could be done. They died within forty-eight hours." For all his apparent composure, it was clear that Kambule was tormented by these horrific memories. He shook as he spoke, and his voice wavered.

"As for food, enough of the farming lands have been spared, along with cattle and sheep, that our supplies are, for the present, more than adequate. Many open fields were unaffected by the fires, and though the brief frost has done damage, much of the crop survives. This was cause for great thanksgiving among my people, since a few more days of dark and cold might have finished us. We began to ration the food in a humane manner, making sure especially that the children were adequately fed.

"Then, when we seemed to have gained some control of the situation in the immediate vicinity of Ulundi, we decided to send out scouting parties, some on foot, some on horseback. Many of these scouts returned just hours before your arrival," he told Gustaffson. "As best we can tell, there is a circle around Ulundi, with a radius of about a hundred kilometers, where life exists. Perhaps—our estimate—twenty-five thousand people survived, along with a sizable number of animals. As I have said, many of the fields have also been spared, along with their crops. To our amazement and dismay, outside that circle—what we now call the Ulundi Circle—the earth appears to be totally scorched. And, of course, between here and the coast, below the elevation of about six hundred meters, everything but a few bushes has been swept out to sea. That is why one of our scouts was so amazed to see your camp on the beach. We were about to make plans to contact you; but you have come to us!"

The following day, the Governing Council held an open session to report on the events at Ulundi, and to decide on the next steps to be taken. Nordstrom and Hardy presided, and young Wilson Hardy, Jr., scribbled away to record everything as best he could. It was comfortably dry and cool, with a breeze from the sea blowing inland. A large group of onlookers gathered around the canvas-roofed shelter, anxious to hear the news.

Nordstrom gave the most momentous information first. There was a surviving population concentrated in the area around Ulundi, and praise God, there was food. In the near future, the Inlanders—as he labeled the new neighbors—would be sending shipments of vegetables and fruit, and even meat. A great sigh of relief could be sensed among the listeners.

The captain then reported on other matters that had been discussed. Deck Officer Gustafsson and his hosts agreed that it was important to establish joint planning between the Ulundi Indaba and the beachside Governing Council. A Coordinating Committee was to be formed. But how was communication to be maintained after the radio batteries gave out? A community hardly more than a hundred miles across is not large in the scheme of things; yet carrying on a discourse across such a distance presents a trouble-some problem.

"The short-term solution," Nordstrom said, "suggested by Hugh Russell, one of our men in the expeditionary party, is a Pony Express."

There was a smattering of laughter among members of the Council and observers, but Nordstrom, in his commanding way, obtained silence and continued with his presentation.

It turned out that Russell, a mining engineer from Utah, was also an amateur historian of his home state, and had many facts and figures about the Pony Express ready at hand. When that fabled institution was founded in 1860, Utah, then a territory, contained twenty of the 190 Pony Express stations established between Mis-souri and California. The celebrated mail service featured riders who typically covered 75 to 125 miles in a single run. The key element was that way stations were established ten to fifteen miles apart, and at these stations the riders were given fresh mounts. In KwaZulu Natal, an ordinary horse could be counted on to gallop at an average speed of twelve miles per hour; so with four or five changes of mount, a message could be carried from Ulundi to the beachfront camp, in about six hours. Of course, racehorses—on a track—can run more than three times as fast; but roads in the African hills were far from racetrack quality. And, unhappily, the province's prime thoroughbreds were destroyed when the tsunami engulfed the Greyville Racecourse at Durban.

"We will also investigate the possibilities of a semaphore sys-tem," Nordstrom said, "but as a start, the Pony Express it will be." Seeing that several of the engineers were continuing to smile and shake their heads, he continued: "Scientifically ingenious solutions will be happily accepted, gentlemen. But they have to be workable—now! Right now! And while you're snickering about America's Wild West, be advised that we will also borrow from South African frontier history. We have agreed with the Inlanders that we will assist them in trying to resurrect the ox-wagon, the symbol of the Great Boer Trek, which was used during many generations of pre–machine age commerce. Fortunately, the basic roadbeds for railways and highways are in pretty fair condition, even though rails and paving have been swept away by flood or destroyed by fire. Wheeled vehicles may be salvaged; others can be assembled from odd parts. The oxen have survived upland and can be rounded up and put to work."

Suddenly the captain sighed, took a sip of water, and sat down heavily on a wooden bench. He was exhausted from the almost ceaseless activity and strain of command, and the flippant attitude of some of his high-tech passengers was obviously grating on his nerves.

The momentary silence was broken by John Hertzler, who spoke in a loud voice but clearly was sensitive to Nordstrom's annoyance.

"We want to be helpful, Captain," he said. "And we recognize that right now we have to rely on primitive ways of doing things. But at the same time, we want to move to higher technological levels as soon as possible. And in order to do this, we have to know what materials are available for us to work with. When we met the other day, one of our South African engineers was telling us about the area's natural resources; but his presentation was limited to agriculture and animals."

At this point, Hertzler turned to Dr. Wilson Hardy for help. "You know, Wilson, you promised us that this fellow Marshall was going to fill out the picture for us. How about it? What are our prospects of working our way out of the horse-and-buggy age?"

"You're right, John," said Hardy. "Pieter Kemm gave us his report, and said that Kelvin Marshall would fill us in on the mineral resources." Then, turning around to look for Marshall, he said, "I guess this is as good a time as any. Assuming Captain Nordstrom agrees."

The captain wearily waved his assent.

Kelvin Marshall was a tall, heavy, ruddy-faced man with thin, graying hair, who rose with difficulty from where he had been sitting in the sand. The manufacture of chairs was not yet a high priority among the survivors.

"If you're looking for mineral resources," he began, "you've come to the right place. We have it all, and in huge amounts: coal and iron, copper and nickel, lead and zinc, tin and platinum, silver and gold, and on and on. Also everything you need for building: lime, clay, gypsum, and different kinds of stone. You may not want rare and strategic metals right away, but for those materials we are numero uno, a veritable global headquarters. I have the figures right here." He referred to a sheet of paper on which he had scribbled some notes. "Manganese—eighty-one percent of the world reserves; chromium—sixty-eight percent; vanadium—forty-five percent; zirconium—twenty-six percent; titanium—seventeen percent; and more.

"Ready for atomic energy? Well, when you are, we have six percent of the uranium known to be in the earth. We also have proven reserves of natural gas. The only thing that we do not have—and I'll be the first to admit it—is petroleum. But that's where my company, Sasol, comes in. We are—or were—the only people in the world to have developed an economical process for converting coal into liquid fuel. Thanks to the international boycott that deprived us of petroleum imports during the apartheid days, we solved our problem through technology. At the moment, our factories are doubtless burned to cinders like practically every other structure on the face of the globe. But the knowledge is preserved in our plans and manuals, many of which I brought with me for the seminar—and up here," he said, smiling, tapping the side of his head with his index finger.

"Let me add," he continued, "that in addition to petroleum, we have ethanol. We make it from sugar cane, and for years we've been adding two to four percent ethanol to all our petrol. Until about 1970, we used ethanol—with the trade name Union—as an alternative fuel. Speaking of sugar, we also make an alcoholic drink called Cane Spirit. Sort of like vodka. If your car runs out of fuel, and you've got a bottle of that stuff with you, no problem. You pour it in your tank, and it's sure to get you home."

General White of the Army Engineers stood and asked to be recognized. "You know, Wilson," he said, addressing Dr. Hardy, "I can see that you and Hertzler and a few others are having a good time planning the world of the future, complete with skyscrapers, computers, and airports. But let me remind you that we are scrambling around on this beach trying to provide some shelter for twenty-five hundred needy people, and we're working with turned-over lifeboats, odd pieces of driftwood, some blankets, a few patches of canvas, and just about any bit of useful debris we can find. It doesn't do us a damned bit of good to know that there's a whole bunch of coal in the ground when it's not next door, and all we've got to dig with is a few sticks."

"I take your point, General," Hardy replied. Even-tempered by nature, he had promised himself not to allow difference of opinion and dissent to make him angry when he was presiding with Captain Nordstrom over these discussions. "Pieter and Kelvin, what do you think our prospects are for actually getting at all this wonderful stuff that lies underground? As the general says, we do have immediate needs to balance against hopes for the future."

"I can tell you something about the coal," said Marshall, "since that's a big part of my business. It's true that South Africa's largest deposits are far to the north; but there are several productive collieries right here in KwaZulu Natal—at Dundee, Glencoe, Vryheid, Newcastle, and Utrecht, just to name a few. These mines may be a couple of hundred kilometers inland, but they all used to be linked by train and highway to Richards Bay, which happens to be where we are right now. I dare say that with a little fixing up these road-beds will do nicely for ox-drawn wagons."

As the discussion turned to details of mining and transport, the crowd that had gathered to hear the news from Ulundi began to disperse. But Marshall continued his dissertation undeterred.

"Two hundred kilometers too far, you say? How about the Zu-luland Anthracite Mine, right near Ulundi? Or better still, look near Heatonville, just north of Empangeni, which is just a few kilometers up the hill from here. Coal was actually mined there for a short period in the 1980s. Most South African coal is fairly near the surface, which should be good news for anyone starting out with limited labor and primitive tools. Of course, if you don't want to dig at all, just go to Nongoma. It's a bit more than one hundred kilometers away, but the outcrop seams are right there at the sur-face, ready for the picking. Local folk come with their wheelbarrows and take home some very high-quality pieces.

"So, don't worry about having access to coal, now and practically forever. We have all that we need, some of it is not that hard to get to, and the geologists tell us there is lots more. They've iden-tified a seam parallel to the coast, starting not far from here and running for hundreds of kilometers up into Mozambique.

"As you know, once you have coal, you have the beginning of your industrial revolution. Not only can we burn the coal for power, but we can also use it to make oil, and all the things one can make from oil, for example, acrylic fibers, explosives, fertilizers, ammonia, phenols, waxes, paints—our company made more than one hundred twenty products." Marshall's voice was growing louder and his motions more animated.

"Thank you, Kelvin," Wilson Hardy said, breaking in as diplo-matically as possible. "But before we can rebuild your very sophis-ticated factories, we must have some very sophisticated equipment, and for that we'll need sophisticated machine tools, and in order to make those machine tools we'll need more rudimentary machine tools, and so forth back through several generations of tools, and before we can start that process we'll require something of a steel industry. So, assuming we can get the coal, where are we going to get the iron?"

"Pieter's the one to tell you about that," Marshall said, "and he'll probably tell you that all you have to do is look under your feet."

Pieter Kemm stepped forward. "What Kelvin means," he said, "is that my company, Richards Bay Minerals, mines the sand dunes right here in Richards Bay, just down the beach a bit. It's an extraordinary story: These dark sand dunes, two kilometers wide and seventeen kilometers long, have been found to contain concentrated amounts of titanium, zircon, and high-purity iron. Through the ages, these minerals, originating in our mountains, have been washed down to the sea and then redeposited by wind and waves in the form of dunes. Since the 1970s, the mining of these dunes has provided a large share of the world market in these valuable materials. I'm sure that, as the reconstruction of the world begins, our mining and factory operations will play an important role.

"In the meantime, although the largest iron deposits lie far to the north and west, six hundred kilometers away and more, I feel certain there is enough closer by to take care of our needs for a good long while. In Greytown, just one hundred kilometers distant, the very first commercial iron in South Africa was mined and smelted in 1901. The works were on a farm named Proclamation and were operated by a Mr. C. H. Green. The ore was of good quality, and although the mine was abandoned long ago, I don't see why it couldn't be reopened. At least that's what one of my geologist friends told me just last year. In the Dundee area, already mentioned in connection with coal, iron was mined back in the forties, and I'm sure there is more to be had for enterprising pioneers."

As Kemm paced back and forth under the canvas roof, which

flapped occasionally in the breeze, a feeling of growing excitement could be sensed. The morning had started with good news about a surviving population in Ulundi, and food—precious, life-sustaining food. The thrill of these tidings of salvation was still making itself felt. And now the information about natural resources was almost an unbelievably fortuitous development. "The icing on the cake," as one engineer put it, rubbing his hands together briskly.

Pieter Kemm was almost finished, but not quite, and nobody seemed about to cut him short. "Most interesting of all," he continued, "at least from an archeological point of view, is the laterite near Empangeni, which as Kelvin said, is right next door to where we are. This laterite is a weathered rock, rich in iron oxide, close to the surface, easily accessible. It is not a high-grade ore, but it was used by early native tribes in the manufacture of iron spears and other implements. Archeologists have long been interested in the entire Richards Bay area, where there are outcroppings of various porous stones rich in iron. Studies indicate that these materials were used by native ironworkers more than a thousand years ago. Incidentally, in the early days, charcoal rather than coal was used in the smelting process, and we've had a thriving charcoal-burning industry right in this very area. Black wattle wood grows all over the place—it's something of a nuisance plant really—but it's excellent for making charcoal.

"The point is, the iron is here, available in large quantities— inland in conventional mine settings, and right along the coast in the sands and stone deposits. The coal is here, and wood for charcoal. So, if our group is half as clever as it's supposed to be, we should have a thriving steel industry going in short order."

"Hey, Pieter," an unidentified voice called out. "You've got electrical people in your audience, and we're waiting to hear you say something about copper."

"Well, the copper is mostly up north, at Phalaborwa, five hundred kilometers away, and Messina, which is even farther. However, I know there's a small deposit near the surface at Nkandla, just seventy kilometers inland. It was mined briefly at the beginning of the last century, and then abandoned as economically unviable. But it should be enough to give us something of a start.

"Finally, when we talk about distances, let's not forget that when the Boers trekked inland from the Cape Colony to the northeast in the 1830s, they covered more than a thousand kilometers, taking cattle and all their possessions, fording rivers and traversing mountain passes, using ox-wagons. And then, for many decades, they carried on active trading between the coast and their inland domains, also using that same slow but steady mode of transport."

"Ladies and gentlemen," Captain Nordstrom rose, seeming refreshed after having sat with closed eyes through these last reports, "this must conclude our introduction to the resources of our new homeland. Encouraging indeed, but I want to be sure that we do not get carried away. First of all, I share General White's worry about the immediate needs of our group. I don't like to see us all excited about iron in the ground when we don't yet have a roof over our heads. But let us assume that we'll handle these mundane problems and manage to build ourselves a serviceable camp. What I am really concerned about as we look to the future is not so much KwaZulu Natal's basic resources, which I am happy to know are abundant, but rather its people, about whom I feel much less sanguine.

"Our small company of twenty-five hundred souls is not about to work farms, excavate mines, build machinery, and otherwise create Detroit or Pittsburgh—or even Oslo, which I would prefer—on this shore of the Indian Ocean. What do we do if the survivors in this very strange corner of the world do not care to join with us in our enlightened enterprise? Officer Gustafsson reports that he has had a cordial meeting. Well and good, but that is just one meeting."

Captain Nordstrom paced back and forth for a moment with his hands behind his back. Suddenly, he looked off into the distance, pointed upward into hills, and asked, "What do we do if a hostile band of Zulus suddenly comes charging down that ravine over there, brandishing spears and chanting war songs? Or, how about the Afrikaners, one of the more eccentric groups of people in all of history? What if they decide that this catastrophe is a special sign from their Calvinist God, and that our entry on the scene is not welcome? What if black and white, in a classic end-of-the-world scenario, start to fight with each other and we get caught up in the carnage? What I'm trying to say is, let's forget about the resources for a moment and think about something even more important: the people."

FROM THE JOURNAL OF WILSON HARDY, JR.

The people. What can I say about the people of KwaZulu Natal? Only this, and without exaggeration: No novelist or playwright could have dreamed up a more fantastic, exotic, implausible cast of characters than those who awaited us in this foreign land. And—more to the point, in light of our perilous circumstances—no technocrat or social planner could have conceived a group with better survival skills. At least I dare to hope that this is the case.

Before I found myself cast away on these shores, I knew hardly anything about this part of the world. I still know very little. But once I realized that this is where world civilization is fated to be reborn, I figured that I'd better try to correct that deficiency. My father, as I have related, has directed me to keep a record of our group's experiences and activities. But I can't make much sense going forward without giving some account of what has happened here in the past. I've tried to learn about the past, not so much for its own sake—although I do love the historical narrative—but more for the light it sheds on our present situation and our future prospects.

I've read any number of books and talked with many people, both ordinary folk and so-called experts. What follows is an admittedly casual recapitulation of facts, impressions, and assumptions. It would drive my history professors to distraction, I'm certain. But I'm not working on a Ph.D. thesis any more. In a sense, this sets me free.

If the human race is to endure and reconstitute itself, there is an appropriate symmetry to having this occur in Africa. Most pale-ontologists have agreed that this is the continent where our fore-bears emerged, evolving from apelike creatures into hominids over a period of some four million years. Remains of anatomically mod-ern *Homo sapiens*, dating back 130,000 years, have been found in various locations on the African continent, including caves not far from where our camp is today. The "Nahoon" footprints, found along the coast southeast of here, and which scientists have called "compellingly human," have recently been dated as approximately two hundred thousand years old.

These human ancestors of ours, established in clans of about one hundred and fifty individuals, gradually made their way to the northern part of the continent, and then ventured across the Isth-mus of Suez. This momentous migration commenced, according to current thinking, about one hundred thousand years ago, and even-tually extended to the farthest corners of the globe. Descendants of these wanderers were destined to return to the mother continent time and again through the centuries, coming with a variety of purposes, most of them not to the advantage of the people who had stayed behind.

One of the most fateful of these returns occurred in 1652, when the Dutch East India Company authorized a certain Jan van Rie-beeck, with a party of ninety, to set up a provisioning station at Table Bay on the Cape of Good Hope. The Cape had first been rounded in 1488 by Bartolomeu Dias, a Portugese navigator; and as maritime trade developed between Europe and the Indies, the need for such a station became apparent. Neither the company nor the Dutch government planned on colonization by Dutch citizens. But, once established on shore, some of the pioneers started think-ing about making this new world their permanent home. Within ten years, more than two hundred and fifty Dutch settlers were living near the Cape, farming and beginning to move inland. In 1689, they were joined by two hundred French Huguenots fleeing from government persecution. By 1707, there were almost two thousand freeholders of European descent.

This was three centuries ago, not long in the grand scheme of things, but a very long time when we think in terms of historical change. At the beginning of the eighteenth century, St. Petersburg was just being built, George Washington's father was a boy, Johann Sebastian Bach was starting to write his music, and Isaac Newton was the newly elected president of the Royal Society. In Southern Africa, Negroid tribes—the Bantu—descending from the North, had not completed the process of replacing small bands of hunter-gatherers—the so-called San Bushmen. The white settlers at the Cape—called Boers, which is the Dutch word for farmers—occupied portions of the land almost as early as some of the black tribes migrating into the area. Small wonder that these Europeans came to think of themselves as genuine natives of the continent, as Africaners. It is with good reason that they are sometimes referred to as the "white tribe." When the British came on the scene at the end of the eighteenth century, the Boers numbered more than fifteen thousand and had begun to develop their own Dutch-based language, Afrikaans.

Ah yes, the British. As a consequence of various European wars and the treaties that followed, they occupied the Cape in 1795, and a decade later, made it a Crown Colony. They promptly set about irritating the Boers in numerous ways, most notably by banning the use of slaves. The settlers had come to rely upon slave labor and felt that they could not continue farming without it. But the British—much to their credit, particularly in comparison with other nations of the world—had outlawed slavery in 1807.

In addition to feeling harassed by the British, the Boers were driven by an innate frontier-seeking hunger. For whatever complex set of reasons, in the 1830s they embarked on the Great Trek, an event of mythic import in the evolution of Afrikaner culture. Between 1835 and 1837, several thousand families—some fourteen thousand individuals—packed their wagons, hitched up their oxen, gathered their servants, their slaves, and their livestock, and headed far inland from the Cape. To the north, they founded the Orange Free State and the Transvaal, and to the east they crossed the Drakensberg Mountains and entered Natal. The territory that the whites called Natal happened to be the region that the Zulus called home.

The word "Zulu" evokes images of ferocious warriors brandishing shields and spears. Yet, for all their warlike reputation, this tribe's entrance onto the stage of history was remarkably benign. Prior to 1800, they were one of approximately twenty Nguni-speaking clans who lived in harmony with the land, and in relative peace among themselves, in the area now known as KwaZulu Natal. These clans were patrilineal chiefdoms, consisting of a number of loosely linked family groups. The people were pastoralists, and the importance of cattle in their lives was symbolized by the position of the cattlefold in the center of every homestead. According to standard historical sources, disputes over land were few, and were normally settled by the members of two competing groups lining up to throw spears at each other, while hurling abuse as well. Casualties were few, and eventually one family group would yield and move off to another piece of available land. This sounds a bit too idyllic to ring completely true; but if there was a healthy balance between population and resources, we can believe that life was reasonably tranquil.

In any event, after 1800, conditions abruptly became more grim. The area was struck by severe drought; other tribes began to crowd in from the north; white farmers, even before the Great Trek, increased their pressure from the west; and European slave traders, with the complicity of some native Africans, conducted gruesomely efficient raids from the east coast. The result was an increasingly chaotic situation in which military prowess became the key to survival of clan and tribe.

Shaka, who became chief of the Zulus in 1816, was the man for that historical moment. A fierce and astute military leader, he revolutionized tribal warfare with two innovative tactics: He replaced the traditional throwing spear with a shorter stabbing spear, and he directed his troops to surround opponents in a U-formation, close in on them, and kill them with the deadly new weapon. By 1826, Shaka dominated the entire territory, militarily and politically, absorbing numerous clans and tribes into the Zulu family, and sending others in flight for their lives. In just a few years the tradition of Zulus as fearsome warriors had become established. It was to be embellished in subsequent battles with the Boers and with the British. (One of the most notable encounters in military history saw the Zulus, armed only with spears, prevail over the British and their guns in the battle of Isandhlwana in 1879.)

While the Zulus were establishing their tribal domination east of the Drakensberg Mountains in the early 1820s, most whites remained far away, in the vicinity of the Cape. However, word about the east coast, with its good weather and rich soil, was bound to spread, and in 1824, the British established a trading post there. They called it Port Natal. This port was later to become Durban— the city that was swept into the sea the day before we were scheduled to visit it. Shaka welcomed the British, at least to the extent of signing a treaty ceding them the port and much of the territory surrounding it. Shaka's successor, Dingane, renewed the treaty in 1835, and relations remained fairly cordial, thanks to the fact that the British initially were satisfied to remain on the coast.

However, in 1837, here came the Boers, trekking over the mountains, with settlement very much on their minds. Dingane promptly massacred the Boers' leader, Piet Retief, along with more than sixty of his followers. A few months later, under the leadership of Andries Pretorius, the Boers killed more than three thousand Zulus in the fabled battle of Blood River. They then established the Republic of Natal, with its capital inland, up in the hills at Pieter-maritzburg.

This new state had a short life. In 1843, the British annexed the area and started bringing in immigrants of their own. In less than a decade, domination of the territory had shifted from blacks to Afrikaners to the British.

As the nineteenth century progressed, the Zulus were subdued by the armies of empire, and their mighty kingdom brought low. Still, overcoming many hardships and indignities, they preserved their tribal culture and pride in their noble heritage. As for the Afrikaners, once again chafing under British control, many of them left to join their fellows in the Transvaal and the Orange Free State. However, enough stubbornly stayed behind so that Natal continued to be home to three main contending groups.

Perhaps I should say four groups, because we must include the Indians—yes, the Indians, from the Asian subcontinent. Starting in 1860, the British brought them to Natal in large numbers as in-dentured laborers for the newly established sugar plantations. At first, they were subjected to abuse and humiliating discrimination; but after a number of decades, many of them became successful merchants and leaders of the South African business community. Although they comprised less than 3 percent of the national pop-ulation, in KwaZulu Natal their representation reached more than one in ten. This is a significant presence that I never could have imagined when I first thought about the rebuilding of civilization in Southern Africa. About 70 percent of this sizable minority are Hindus, 20 percent Muslim.

Incidentally, in their early struggles for respect and civil rights, these people were led by a young lawyer named Mohandas Gandhi. That saintly man's concepts of non-violent protest evolved during the more than twenty years he spent in Natal. It will be a blessing for our future society if his spirit resides here still.

The fates, having brought together these diverse communities at the southern end of the African continent, now introduced the element best calculated to create new extremes of turbulence: a find of diamonds, followed in 1886 by discovery of the world's richest gold fields. The British, who otherwise might have lost interest in this unprepossessing corner of their empire, suddenly showed passionate concern. Since the mines were located in the north-central lands to which the Boers had laid claim, one could have predicted the coming of conflicts that would culminate in war. An announced cause of the South African War (1899–1902) between the British and the Boers was the anger of recently arrived immigrants who were not granted the right to vote in government elections. But the war wasn't about votes; it was about wealth. And, in the end, the might of the British Empire prevailed.

The brutal conflict, which lasted two and a half years, pitted almost a half-million imperial troops against eighty-seven thousand farmer-soldiers. The Boers, waging guerrilla warfare, enjoyed some initial successes. But when Lord Kitchener embarked on a scorched-earth policy, and rounded up the civilian population into concentration camps, the outcome was ordained. Some twenty-five thousand Afrikaner women and children died of disease and malnutrition in the camps, another grim ordeal etched indelibly in the tribal memory.

It is notable, I think, that for all their bravery and zeal, the Afrikaners did not fight on to a suicidal end, as a few of their number urged. Neither did the Zulus when they finally discerned the almost limitless resources of their enemies. History shows us that the Afrikaners and the Zulus—along with the other tribes of South Africa—have been essentially pragmatic when confronting adversity.

The British, too, are pragmatists of the first order, famous for their Magna Carta, for their "bloodless" revolution of 1688, and numerous accommodations between the classes.

The story of South Africa in the twentieth century is, in fact, a testimony to the possibilities of compromise. While fanaticism and uncompromising hatred festered in other parts of the world, good sense and goodwill prevailed in South Africa. This sounds strange, given what we know about the evils of apartheid. And, admittedly, democracy and order did not prevail without exploitation, conflict, and many terrible deeds. But considering the difficulties to be over-come, and the potential for unspeakable slaughter and anarchy, the democratic multiracial elections of 1994 represented a triumph for the human spirit.

The policy of *apartheid* (Afrikaans for "apartness"), long-standing in practice, was formalized in laws passed during the 1950s. Predictably, a resistance movement developed, centered in the African National Congress (ANC). Many of this group's early leaders were Zulus; but eventually it came to be controlled by mem-bers of the Xhosa-speaking tribes, led by Nelson Mandela. As dem-onstrations became more widespread, and sporadically violent, the government banned the ANC and, in 1962, arrested Mandela.

Government policies of oppression were pursued at first through direct police action—including not only arrests and assaults, but also abductions, tortures, and murders. Then the policies were pur-sued even more insidiously, by pitting blacks against blacks. The Zulus in particular, led by Chief Buthelezi under the banner of his Inkatha Freedom Party, came into conflict with the ANC and fought many bloody battles with its supporters. Buthelezi received consid-erable financial support from the government and was accused by his foes of having "sold out" to the white establishment. Other tribal chiefs were also accused of betraying the cause of democratic civil rights. Adding to the chaos and distrust, a mysterious "third force" of militaristic right-wing whites was said to be fomenting hostilities among the various black factions.

Protest evoked repression, which in turn evoked more outraged protest, as violence became ever more frightful. Although the fatalities were relatively few in each confrontation, they added up, totaling more than twenty thousand. One cannot make light of these fearful events, yet they fall far short of the mass uprising and massacre that had been the nightmare of many South Africans, black as well as white.

In Rwanda, with a population one sixth that of South Africa's, five months of genocide and mass slaughter in 1994 resulted in more than a half-million deaths and two million terrorized refugees. This is just one reminder, among too many that might be cited, of what can happen when hatred and revenge take over, as civility and negotiation disappear.

In South Africa, even while violence stalked the streets, people of good faith on all sides sought some formula for accord. Bowing to the inevitable, government leaders made overtures to Nelson Mandela in his jail cell. There followed a number of secret meetings between white politicians and ANC leaders—in New York and London—calm and congenial meetings by all accounts, in which the seemingly intractable differences between the parties were addressed. Progress was slow, but the negotiations developed an irreversible momentum. When, in 1989, F. W. deKlerk was elected leader of the governing National Party, he met with Mandela directly. This led to the release of Mandela from prison and the legalization of the ANC.

In 1992, white voters, by referendum, endorsed the concept of reform. Equally important, Mandela met with Buthelezi, raising hopes for accommodation between the ANC and the Zulu Inkatha party. In 1993, agreement was reached on an interim constitution, and in April the following year, elections were held. In the new

South Africa, the tribal "homelands" were dissolved. Nine provinces were established, one of which incorporated the old Zulu homeland and the territory called Natal: hence, KwaZulu Natal.

As if this succession of events was not miraculous enough, one must add the story of Buthelezi and the deus ex machina. Up to a week before the elections, the Zulu chief had resolved not to participate, which would have been an unhappy portent for the future. As told by Buthelezi, a mediator from Kenya was coming to see him, but he, Buthelezi, was on his way elsewhere in an airplane. However, his plane developed engine trouble and had to turn back. Buthelezi met the mediator and was convinced to throw in his lot with the democratic election. Obviously, divine intervention was responsible!

Aboard our ship, the designated experts on African history and culture were Richard and Deborah Frost, a professorial couple from Stanford with impeccable academic credentials. They had been recruited to give a series of lectures, and to lead our shore excursions. Of course, the engineers in the group whose homes were in South Africa had the knowledge and awareness that goes with being a native. But the Frosts possessed the detailed information and perspective that comes with scholarly study. One evening, shortly after we arrived on the beach, but before the expeditionary force had reached Ulundi, they shared some of their ideas with our Focus Group.

Richard started off by quoting an old Afrikaans saying: "'n Boer maak 'n plan" (a farmer makes a plan). Then he explained: "A farmer must accommodate to the weather and the soil, and plan realistically for the future. The Boers extended this Stoic philosophy to all aspects of life, and so became the world's greatest realists. At the same time, there is a streak of tenacity in these folk that stems from a belief that they are a chosen people. Not so many years ago, they taught their children in school that the Afrikaners had over-come a host of mightier enemies with help from on high."

The night was warm, with a breeze from the northwest that carried odd and unidentifiable scents from distant places inland. Our "guest lecturers" sat closely together like a newly married couple, touching, as if reassuring each other that they were there, alive and together.

Herb interrupted Richard to say, "Hey, I thought the Jews were supposed to be the chosen people."

"It's sort of the same thing," Frost replied. "It's the Old Testament tradition—the Exodus, and the experience of having survived adversity through the years. When the Afrikaners won the election of 1948, they controlled the destiny of the nation for the first time. The new prime minister, Daniel Malan, declared: 'Afrikanerdom is not the work of man but the creation of God.' "

Herb pursed his lips thoughtfully, and Richard continued.

"There are interesting comparisons we can make, not only between the Afrikaners and the people of the Bible, but also between Afrikaners and the black citzenry of South Africa. Both groups share tribal traditions—loyalty to the extended family, respect for authority, respect for one's elders, respect for one's ancestors. Today, in a world laid waste, with formal government destroyed, I believe that this shared heritage should stand us in good stead."

"I don't know," Tom Swift interjected. "I've read a lot of end-of-the-world fiction, and usually there are bands of marauders roaming the countryside living by pillage and plunder. When the formal bonds of society are removed, all hell breaks loose."

"Let's hope that there's a difference between our reality here and the nightmarish fiction you're so fond of," Richard responded with a smile. "I'm optimistic. Assuming, of course, that there's food enough to go around."

"Aren't you being something of a Pollyanna?" asked Sarah. "Our shore excursion reading material warned that there was lots of crime and disorder in KwaZulu Natal, and that was before the chaos in which the survivors must now find themselves."

"Yes, there was crime," Richard said. "Left over from years of riot and protest, and made worse by unemployment. I know that many of the young people, both black and white, had become materialistic cynics with little use for the old traditions. But I think that the catastrophe—fury descending from the heavens, if you will—might well bring renewed respect for the time-honored ways. And we know that there won't be any more unemployment problems. There will be a great need for everyone to pitch in. I dare hope for a spiritual revival, for a return to the finest tribal traditions. If there is food—let me repeat—if there is food enough for all survivors, I think that the forces of decency and cooperation will prevail. This may astonish us, and should certainly amaze such heavenly powers as have seen fit to test us by fire and flood."

At this point Mary spoke up. "There is another important factor that you haven't mentioned," she said. "The disaster occurred on Christmas Day, when families must have been gathered together. Those who survived will be moved to give thanks and resolve to work together in the Christian spirit."

"That's an interesting point," Richard said. "During the apartheid years, many of the black men got used to working in the large cities and returning occasionally to their 'official' homes. They are now free to live anywhere in the country; but it is still the custom to return to tribal centers, particularly, I would think, on a holiday like Christmas—whether they are Christian or not. You know, I keep saying 'are,' but 'were' is the operative tense."

"I'm just afraid that all the pent-up hate that the blacks must feel for their white oppressors will now come pouring out," Roxy said, expressing aloud what most of us had probably been thinking.

"This is the true miracle of South Africa," said Deborah Frost, who until this point had let her husband carry the discussion. She was a petite, tanned, athletic California girl, in contrast to her husband, who was more of an Ivy League type. "I'm sure that you've heard about the Truth and Reconciliation Commission of the 1990s. Established by the Mandela government, and chaired by Archbishop Desmond Tutu, its purpose was to try to heal the wounds of the apartheid years by exposing the crimes that had been hidden by the government. It was a quasi-religious idea. Members of the security forces and others were to confess their crimes before the commission, after which they were to be granted amnesty. So, families of victims would have the satisfaction of knowing what was done to their loved ones, and by whom. But the perpetrators would not be prosecuted. As you might expect, the process didn't work smoothly. But there were some successes, and the feared cycle of violent reprisal was averted. It was such a beautiful concept."

"Well, I don't know," Herb said. "Isn't that just another example of your wonderful pragmatism, this time by Mandela and his people? The blacks knew that the police and the army would never agree to majority rule unless they were promised amnesty."

Deborah smiled indulgently, enjoying Herb's challenge. "Yes, but it's a lot more than that. The wonder of South Africa is the absence of the pathological hatred that we find in so many places around the globe. We all know about Rwanda and Zimbabwe. And how about the Balkans, where after hundreds of years, the enmity among Serbs, Croats, Bosnians, and Kosovars blazes undiminished. The Catholics and Protestants in Northern Ireland. And the fundamentalist Muslims in Iran and elsewhere. And . . . well, you can make up your own list. In this part of the world, a guiding principle of the traditional culture is *ubuntu*. A journalist once told me that Archbishop Tutu had explained the concept to her along these lines: A person is human by dint of belonging to a community, and the essence of a community is harmony. Since resentment and anger and desire for revenge undermine harmony, *ubuntu* actually demands that you forgive. When someone refuses to forgive, that person is said not to have *ubuntu*; that is to say, he is not really human. And this same reporter confirmed that she had heard similar views—generous, forgiving, non-vengeful views—expressed by scores of black South Africans over the years."

"Maybe that's why they were spared by God," Roxy said wistfully.

"I don't think that we have to bring God into it," Tom said. "First of all, we can't say that the people were spared. Clearly, most of them weren't. I only hope that enough survived to establish a meaningful workforce. If they turn out to be nice people, I'll be delighted. But, more important, are they competent people? Are they trained?"

"Sure they are," Richard said heartily, responding to Tom's abrupt shift from philosophy to practical concerns. "KwaZulu Natal has become highly industrialized in recent years, and the population contains people with every job skill you could possibly want. Plus, as Mary pointed out, because of Christmas, many Zulu men employed in other parts of the country, especially miners and factory workers, would have been here with their families. We may appreciate their muscles as well as their industrial skills. Also, we may thank our lucky stars for the many small farms and cattlepens that are tended in the traditional Zulu communities. If we're back in the Stone Age, as you engineers keep telling me, then we won't be needing computer programmers, and other such people, at least for awhile. We'll be needing many of the skills that modern society has been on the verge of losing."

"There was once a man who warned about that," I said. "Remember the book called *Small Is Beautiful*, written by a guy named Schumacher? He proposed that we maintain our local handicrafts and other low-tech proficiencies. We read some of his stuff in one of my college courses, and I thought he was a bit of a crackpot. Who could have guessed?"

"Well, I think we may be in luck," Richard said. "Some of the skills we'll need have been perpetuated in the so-called backward villages up in those hills. And one last thing. If there's any fighting to be done in this world of the future—for example, if the villainous marauders in Tom's science fiction books ever do show up—I'll be happy to have some young Zulu men on my side. They're incredibly adept fighting with sticks and shields. It's a popular sport, and also a reminder of their martial heritage."

"That's great," Herb said, picking up a pebble and throwing it out into the water. "But what do we do if someone shows up with bullets? The Zulus might have beaten the British once—spears against guns—but I wouldn't bet on it happening again."

For a few moments, nobody said anything. Through the high cloud cover a few million stars peeked down at us forlorn creatures on the beach. Finally, Roxy broke the icy silence.

"Maybe the one good thing about this terrible disaster is that most of the weapons have been destroyed. Even if there are a few rifles or pistols lying around, the ammunition for them won't last very long. Of course, the engineers will probably start building up arsenals again; but I don't want to think about that right now. So, okay, we're back to knocking each other on the head like in caveman days. We can't do too much damage that way. And, if we make friends with the local inhabitants, everything will be just great."

On that semi-optimistic note we thanked the Frosts for their conversation and ended our meeting.

"Well," I said to Sarah as we walked down the beach toward our lean-to, "maybe we'll luck out with the local gentry, just as we seem to have lucked out with the natural resources. But we won't know for sure until we hear more news from the expeditionary party."

Sarah took my arm and murmured, "Doesn't it sound wonderful? Cooperation and forgiveness instead of conflict and spite. 'O, brave new world that has such people in it!' "

"Don't set your hopes too high," I said, squeezing her shoulder.

"That's Miranda from *The Tempest*," Sarah responded, ignoring my admonition and taking my fingers into her warm hand.

5

At his first meeting with the Ulundi Indaba, Carl Gustafsson described, with a mixture of politeness and urgency, the state of the dwindling food stores of the ship's survivors. The very next morning, a supply caravan left a farm outside Ulundi, carrying a large supply of corn and various other vegetables and fruits. Carts, sleds, pack animals, and numerous human bearers made a most colorful parade that arrived at the beachfront camp a few days later. Colorful and exceedingly welcome. Another procession brought freshly slaughtered sheep and steers. A few days after that, a number of milk cows arrived, along with several Zulu youngsters to tend them.

The *Queen of Africa* kitchen staff reciprocated with a shipment of caviar, from the ship's ample stock, that went back to Ulundi with the Inlander porters.

From the start there prevailed between the parties a spirit of friendliness, trust, and mutual generosity. Perhaps there had been fears and suspicions, instinctual although undeclared. But once Deck Officer Gustafsson shook hands with the leaders of the Indaba, a bond was sealed. Underlying the relationship was not only empathy and goodwill, but also an awareness that cooperation contributed to the survival of all. In the beginning, the survivors from the *Queen of Africa* were mostly on the receiving end, since the food shipments literally kept them alive. But lives were saved in return when

Harold Carson and his staffers from FEMA were dispatched to Ulundi to supervise sanitation, water supply, and the clearing of wreckage. As time went by, it would have been impossible to say which of the two groups was more vital to the well-being of the overall community.

Once a source of food was assured, the Governing Council's next concern was to improve the shelter facilities. Hardy and Nordstrom, along with the other Council members, briefly considered moving the camp up into the hills, closer to Ulundi. But the problems inherent in transporting all of their equipment persuaded them this was not practical. When the surveying parties completed their preliminary work, they selected a new site on the shores of Lake Mzingai, about two miles inland from where they first came ashore. The lake is a large body of fresh water fed by underground springs, and their new friends in Ulundi confirmed it as a good choice.

Shortly after news of the relocation became official—subject to approval by the general population, which was forthcoming without incident—the ex–cruise director of the *Queen of Africa*, Marjorie Waters, declared that the new site, their new home, ought to have a name. Accordingly, she concocted a name-selection contest. Ever since the first days on the beach, Majorie and her staff had been arranging little entertainments—games and contests and the like— anything that might improve morale without interfering with the urgent work that needed doing. It was, in a way, absurd for a community in crisis, on the edge of oblivion, to have a group of high-spirited social directors; and more than a few of the cruise ship survivors were heard to make critical comments. But the very absurdity had an inspirational and distracting aspect, especially with the children and older people. So Marjorie soldiered on, with the backing of the Council.

The naming contest attracted a lot of attention. The final selection, proposed by an anonymous member of the ship's orchestra, and then unanimously supported by the entire crew of the *Queen of Africa* was "Engineering Village." Wilson Hardy and the rest of the engineers and their families were deeply touched. Hardy himself had proposed "Scandinavia South," in honor of Captain Nordstrom, his officers, and the crew. Other suggestions that received honorable mention: Prevail, Memorial, New Hope, Miami Beach East, Richards Bay Redux, and Little China. But Engineering Village it was. It remained to create a place to go with the name.

The only building materials available within a practical distance, aside from driftwood, were grasses, shrubs, bamboo, and short, slim trees that had survived the tsunami by bending before its power. The civil engineers and military people knew a lot about tents and framed structures. They were even ready to launch into building log cabins, if there were any logs to be found. But they had a difficult time figuring out how best to utilize the rather flimsy materials at hand. The problem was solved one morning when a group of Zulu specialists arrived on the scene. General White and his Corps of Engineers colleagues, dubious at first, soon came to the conclusion that this was a banner day in the history of construction engineering.

The traditional Zulu dwelling, the *indlu*, has an archetypal beehive shape. A number of pliable sapling trunks or branches are stuck in the ground, and then fastened together at the top to form a dome. These are covered with a woven grass mat, and then thatch is added. Grass roping is used to bind the structure together. Thus, delicate boughs and natural threads are made into solid and utilitarian structures. The concept of building an *indlu* is simple enough; but the skills exhibited by the visiting master builders impressed the Westerners as wondrous to behold.

The floor of these dwellings is traditionally made from crushed termite soil, or anthill material, mixed with clay and cow dung. The survivors made do with sand and pounded dirt, and most of them felt that this was just as well. But some of the more adventurous young people later found out that floors made of a cow dung paste dry to a hard, smooth surface, not at all malodorous or unpleasant in any way. The early Boers learned this technique from the Zulus. They also adopted the use of thatch for roofing. For walls, however, they made use of mud bricks, baked hard in the sun. The Engineering Villagers were determined, eventually, to make bricks in kilns and to build more conventional row houses with cornered rooms; but they were grateful indeed for the interim use of the beehive dwellings.

However, one feature of the new environment had a depressing effect. This was the almost total lack of greenery. First on the ocean beach, and then on the shore of Lake Mzingai, the newcomers lived in a world of sand and dried mud underfoot and blue emptiness above. The shrubs and grasses that survived the tsunami—those not uprooted for use as building materials—were terribly sparse. The citizens of Engineering Village craved the sight of lawns and trees and thirsted for natural shade. Perhaps in good time . . .

Even as immediate needs were addressed, the leaders determined to push ahead with plans for industrial development. There was hardly any talk about Utopian schemes or "new world" concepts. The members of the Ulundi Indaba were just as anxious as the Governing Council to work their way back into the twenty-first century as quickly as possible. Rebuilding and technological rehabilitation— these were the implicitly accepted goals of the survivor society.

Several elders among the Zulus urged a low-technology approach. In this they were joined by a few spiritually inclined members of the white community and a small number of Hindus and fundamentalist Muslims. Yet the overwhelming majority of the people were instinctively, vigorously, impatiently hoping to return to the physical environment they had known. And, even more urgently, to the future they had been trying to build before the Event destroyed their world. For fifteen years, since the first democratic elections of 1994, the South African politicians had been promising decent housing, clean water, and electricity for all. This dream—mundane, perhaps, but powerfully compelling—had come through fire and flood unscathed. Disappointing as it might have been to the philosophically inclined, given the opportunity to build a new world, the vast majority of the people, without hesitation, chose to resume building the world to which they had previously aspired.

To move speedily from purpose to action, leaders of the Ulundi Indaba and the Governing Council agreed to form a Coordinating Committee. Inevitably, the first action of the Coordinating Committee was to appoint a Joint Planning Subcommittee to work on specific planning and allocation of resources. Among the engineering group there was some cynical grumbling about "creeping bureaucracy," even in these dire circumstances. But it was clear to most that a modicum of bureaucratic organization was needed.

Twenty-six days after the Event, ten days after Gustafsson's arrival in Ulundi, the Joint Planning Subcommittee held its first meeting. The date, as recorded in the minutes, was January 20, 2010/Year 1.

The subcommittee, for the sake of efficiency, was limited to thirty members, fifteen from the *Queen of Africa* and fifteen from the Inlanders. As with the Governing Council, experts were to be invited to specific meetings according to the topics being considered. Suggestions from the "public" were to be handled as candidly as possible in designated open sessions. Since most of the technical authorities were members of the shoreside community, and since the Ulundi people were better equipped to travel than the engineers, the initial meetings were held in Engineering Village.

One of the first structures planned and erected in the new municipality was a large pavilion intended to accommodate group meetings. For this assembly hall the builders made use of materials cannibalized from two lifeboats that had been damaged during the salvage operation. The structural frame consisted of an odd assortment of wooden shapes—oars, spars, masts, and planks—plus a few lengths of bamboo, with a roof made mostly of thatch. Serendipitously, it looked like a work of art, or—depending on one's taste—the product of the freshman class at a second-rate school of architecture.

"Beehive huts may be good for sleeping," said Wilson Hardy, who had ordered the new facility's erection, "and that rickety canvas-covered shanty on the landing beach was okay for early days. But when this select subcommittee holds a meeting, I want it to be in classy digs."

As recording secretary of the Governing Council, Wilson Hardy, Jr., was the logical candidate for the same job with the new group, and sure enough, he was conscripted. He was flattered, but also told his cronies that the Planning Subcommittee was lucky to have him. Since he had studied the history of technology, he knew something of what had been accomplished by past societies, and so felt that he had some sense of what might be rational goals for the new one.

Following Hardy Senior's recommendation, the subcommittee elected as its chairman Alfred Richards, CEO of a giant international construction company. Alf was a casting director's idea of a hardhat—a large man, with a craggy, florid face under a thatch of white hair. His firm had designed and built manufacturing plants in practically every corner of the globe, and what Alf Richards didn't know about infrastructure, buildings, manufacturing processes, energy systems, and development in general, according to Dr. Hardy, just wasn't worth knowing. This pragmatic doer of great deeds was under no illusions about where he was starting and what he was lacking. Seeing him in action, an observer might have sworn that he took pleasure in the difficulty. In fact, this unspoken satisfaction was shared by many of his colleagues. The less they had to work with, the more notable would be their achievement.

Another key member of the subcommittee was Mildred Fox, a senior official in the Peace Corps, whose specialty was technology transfer and engineering in developing nations. Millie was smart, high-spirited, and as an African American woman, probably fit in with some political agenda of Nordstrom and Hardy's devising. In fact, with the addition of Ichiro Nagasaka of Tokyo and Gordon Chan, born in Beijing and later a superstar at the DuPont Company, this group resembled a miniature United Nations. That the majority of the foreign members of the traveling seminar hailed from Asia was no accident. That continent had been producing more than three hundred thousand new engineers per year, compared to one hundred thousand in Europe and ninety thousand in the United States. In addition, a sizable portion of the American contingent was Asian by heritage, not surprising since Asian Americans make up more than one quarter of the Ph.D. engineers in the U.S. workforce. Most important, Dr. Nagasaka knew more about iron and steel than any other ten people in the profession, while Dr. Chan was one of the world's most eminent chemical engineers.

One evening these two august gentlemen had joined the Focus Group for an informal discussion, and Wil Hardy found them to be unexpectedly witty and good-humored. When Roxy Ford expressed uneasiness about the Chinese—who had comprised one fifth of the people in the world—not being represented proportionally in the surviving population, Dr. Chan told her not to be concerned.

"We are very smart and very industrious," he said, "so that even a small number of us will make our mark in the new society. Besides," he continued with a smile, "I have a feeling that somewhere in China there is a community that lived through the catastrophe—perhaps underground or through some other good fortune—and one day these people will emerge to reveal to the world a new and glorious civilization."

"And while they are admiring themselves," Dr. Nagasaka said with a broad grin, "we Japanese, along with the rest of Asia, will honor them, emulate them, and—without further ado—pass them by!"

In their more serious moments, both Chan and Nagasaka evinced a deep serenity that found its roots in the Buddhism to which they had both been exposed in their youth. For all their modern, scientifically based sophistication, the worldwide disaster did not appear to bring out in them the anger, frustration, or despair felt by many of the survivors, even their fellow engineers.

The Ulundi Indaba's representatives on the Planning Subcommittee were led by Stephen Healey, senior surviving employee of the provincial government. "Call me Mr. Bureaucrat," he said to the others with a wry smile. Peter Mavimbela had been head of the National Union of Mine Workers; Eric Steenkamp was an experienced mining engineer from Pretoria. Then there was Harish Kahar, a respected merchant and leader of the Indian community. Other members came from local industry and government and the local farming community. Mavimbela quickly emerged as a key figure, since everyone knew that any plan for technological development would require the cooperation of the indigenous workforce. The most clever ideas of the most brilliant people would be unavailing without the endorsement of the workers among these newly encountered compatriots.

As already noted, the Africans were every bit as anxious as the Westerners to embark on a program of technological redevelopment. And it was obvious that progress would be best served if people performed the work they were most qualified to do, that is, the work they had been doing before the Event. But how could those people who would do most of the physical labor—particularly the miners and factory workers—protect themselves from being exploited? Was the history of the world to be repeated, with a working class in chains?

Mavimbela raised the question and was not impressed by the hearty assurances he received from Alf Richards. Yet, clearly, there was no practical alternative to moving ahead based on a good faith understanding. It would be foolhardy to try to negotiate employment agreements while the survival of the entire populace hung in the balance. The workers would have to perform their tasks with the understanding that they would in due course receive a fair deal, however that might later be defined. Solemnly the group agreed that the situation was to be evaluated—along with the status of all ad hoc committees and other government arrangements—after a year. One circuit of the earth around the sun. A year of good faith.

In the most general terms, the compact ensured that everybody would pitch in to the best of his or her ability. The Joint Planning Subcommittee would do the detailed planning and make specific work assignments. However, there was to be no coercion to accept these assignments, other than family or social pressure. To the extent possible, all groups would attempt to discourage malingering. It was also agreed that food, clothing, and shelter would be shared as equitably as possible. As for personal behavior—coping with the inevitable private conflicts—it was quickly decided that each of the two main communities would be responsible for its own internal order.

"Everyone seems to be avoiding the word 'communism,' " Alf Richards said, "but that's what we've got here."

"Not in the least," was Stephen Healey's response when the question came up. "This is an emergency arrangement among sensible people. We are choosing pragmatic action over suicidal polemics."

Word spread quickly throughout the Ulundi circle, and the concept of cooperative effort—according to a centrally conceived plan—won wide acceptance. There seemed to be no better alternative.

Could the survivors work without a money economy, without feudalism, without tyranny, without legal compulsion? Yes—not without confusion and complaint, and certainly not forever—but for a year, the answer was yes. One might have expected a breakdown of civility, anarchy of the mob run riot, followed perhaps by the rise of a despot. Yet such fears were not realized. Even criminal offenses decreased to the vanishing point. "A miracle," exclaimed Hans Potter, a long-time police officer from Dundee.

The political compact could remain essentially vague; but not so the strategy for technological development. In allocating resources and assigning personnel, specific decisions had to be made. And they were.

At the subcommittee's first meeting, the basic element of a master plan was established so quickly, so arbitrarily, and so unanimously that it seemed preordained. Stephen Healey proposed it, and it came to be known as "the Half and Half Doctrine": half the population were to be counted on as able-bodied workers, and half of these in turn would be committed to agriculture and animal husbandry.

"I don't know about your folks," Healey said, "but among ours I would count on only half the people for our able-bodied workforce. Set aside the very young, the old, the infirm, and the full-time housekeepers, and half is what you're left with. The individuals I call the housekeepers—mostly the mothers of our families—work extremely hard, as we very well know. But we can't send them out into the fields and the factories if we hope to maintain a functioning society. They cook, clean, sew, and launder, and many of them keep small gardens and raise chickens as well. In our present situation; they are also the ones who fetch water, or make sure that this vital activity is attended to. We need them in the home to care for their families and to help put their shattered households back in order. Hopefully, we can engage some of them in cottage industry work—weaving and the like. Eventually, if they choose, they can go out into the so-called working world as do so many—well, as so many young women did. But not right now. As for the kids, I understand that you want them to concentrate on education. And we think that's a good idea."

"Oh yes," said Gordon Chan. "If we lose our foundation in learning, we'll really be back in the Stone Age. Then our descendants will have to spend hundreds of years—maybe thousands—regaining the knowledge that we inherited from our forebears."

"The youngsters will do chores," continued Healey, "especially when crops need harvesting. But they will have to understand that their primary responsibility is to study and to learn. And, Peter," he said, looking intently at Mavimbela, "we want this to be the case with the poorest Zulu child as well as with the most advantaged among the whites."

Not hearing any questions or objections, Healey continued: "I further propose that half the able-bodied workforce—in other words, one quarter of the total population—be assigned to cultivating food and caring for livestock. I know," and here he addressed especially the Engineering Village contingent, "that in the United States, less than two percent of the people are farmers; yet they grow food for everybody else, with lots left over for export. But that means absolutely nothing when you think of our condition here today. We have—or had—large farms and cattle ranches that were run quite efficiently. But the mechanical equipment that was so vital to those operations is gone. So are the fertilizers, the stores of feed, and all the fine facilities that we used to boast about in the province's public relations brochures. Even the small, fairly primitive homesteads are obviously less productive than they were. We're reduced to poking at the earth with sticks, and harvesting such crops as there are with our bare hands. We absolutely must have half of our workers—a quarter of our people—out in the fields making sure that we have enough food to sustain ourselves."

"Without objection, then, the plan is agreed to," the chairman stated. There was no formal vote. The subcommittee began its work in consensus mode.

Millie Fox noted that the twenty-five hundred "Outlanders" did not fall into the same categories as the approximately twenty-five thousand surviving citizens of KwaZulu Natal. Specifically, in Engineering Village there were no full-time housekeepers looking after families. Members of the ship's crew prepared food and drink for the group, and as for miscellaneous domestic chores, it was every man for himself. However, in the initial planning meeting, nobody wanted to get bogged down discussing such minutiae. The population figures were just rough approximations anyhow; and it would be a long while before anybody took the time and effort to work up a detailed census. So the subcommittee applied the Half and Half Doctrine somewhat arbitrarily by establishing the available workforce at fourteen thousand—slightly more than half the estimated total population—with seven thousand assigned to farms and ranches. This left another seven thousand to work on reconstruction and industrial development.

The agricultural operation would be headed by such senior farming and animal husbandry people as had survived, and would have the services of several professors and students from the Department of Horticultural Science of the Pietermaritzburg Campus of the University of Natal. The Engineering Village group also contained a number of prominent agricultural engineers who could be helpful. There were plenty of experienced workers, both from the large plantations and ranches, as well as from small family farms. Reports from the hill country contained good news about the number of fields and orchards that had survived. Also, the calendar was the survivors' friend: it was January, the middle of the summer in South Africa. Crops were ripening, and thousands of cattle and sheep grazed nearby.

Next, the subcommittee agreed that the leaders of the agricultural enterprise should reassign some of their workers, as soon as feasible, from tilling the fields to secondary food-related operations.

The vast field of technology known as "food processing" was taken for granted by many Westerners used to living in a high-tech culture and buying food in a supermarket. But these vital activities include milling grain, salting meat, cooking and canning, brewing and refining, pressing oil from olives or peanuts or soybeans, pickling, cheesemaking, baking, pasteurizing, packaging and storing, obtaining and preparing salt and spices, and so forth.

Also, at the earliest possible time, some of the agricultural workers were to be assigned to producing and applying fertilizer. This was another job not properly understood or appreciated by city folks, even many engineers. Each new crop takes chemicals from the earth—primarily, nitrogen, phosphorus, and potassium—and these chemicals must be replaced if a healthy soil is to be maintained. Nitrogen is plentiful in the air we breathe and can be captured by combining it with hydrogen to form ammonia. But, pending the development of a primitive chemical industry, the survivors would have to obtain their nitrogen from animal manure, slaughterhouse wastes, or recycled garbage. Phosphorus can be acquired from phosphate rock or bones or as a byproduct from slag when smelting phosphatic iron ore. Potassium is most readily obtained by mining potash deposits. If such deposits are not available, it is possible to burn vegetable wastes, such as palm leaves and banana peels, then boil the ashes in a pot and evaporate the solution. Hence the word "potash." This substance is also useful in the manufacture of soap, lye, glass, and many other products.

As for livestock, the tending, slaughtering, and butchering of animals would have to be supplemented by shearing, tanning of hides, and harvesting of other useful animal products.

Some of the engineers shifted restlessly during this "meat and potatoes" discussion, as one electronic wizard referred to it. But the members of the Joint Planning Subcommittee were agreed that everything begins in the fields. A secure food supply is the sine qua non of a vigorous civilization.

One of the Ulundi delegation observed that a small fishing enterprise had been established, using the *Queen of Africa* lifeboats, which came equipped with hooks and lines. Several Inlanders had joined members of the *Queen's* crew in fabricating nets and additional gear and in trying their luck. The subcommittee estimated that about fifty people could usefully be assigned to the task, and endorsed the activity accordingly. The prospective catch, of course, would be dependent upon how much the acid rain fallout had fouled the waters.

"So much for food," Alf Richards said, rubbing his hands together with satisfaction. "What's next?"

"Not so fast, please," Harish Kahar interjected. "In the absence of a free market, who will decide which crops are selected for cultivation? There are questions of nourishment and individual taste, perhaps even some religious considerations."

"Please, Harish," Richards said, trying not to show his impatience. "If we try to micromanage every operation, we'll never get anything done. Let's leave that to the specialists, unless they have disputes that they can't settle among themselves. As for me, I'll be happy to eat whatever the hell pops out of the ground or the sea."

Kahar did not look pleased, but he acquiesced. "All right then," he said. "The logical next topic is water."

By all indications, there was throughout the Ulundi Circle an ample supply of good water—rivers, lakes, and subsurface aquifers, plus, so far, adequate rain. But distribution was something else again. Immediately after the Event, members of each community had no choice but to carry water from the nearest fresh source—lake or river or well—in primitive containers. For the ship's survivors, the dining-room workers had handled this chore with efficiency and dispatch. The next step in this process would be to repair such networks of reservoirs, aqueducts, and pipes as had existed, and to plan and build new ones. Irrigation for agriculture was also an important consideration.

Along with the water supply, there came the question of sanitation. It would be some time before outhouses could be replaced with indoor plumbing; but for some impatient people, this was a priority of no small moment. In the interim, cleanliness and hygiene had to be monitored.

So the Planning Subcommittee established a Water Department consisting of one hundred persons. This department was directed to begin with studies, surveys, inspections, and designs. Construction projects would be undertaken as they could be scheduled within an overall development plan.

It had been a long day, and a lot had been accomplished. Alf Richards looked at his watch, and was about to suggest a break for dinner. But before he had a chance to do this, Millie Fox was on her feet and vigorously asking to be recognized.

"I've heard a lot of sensible proposals," she said. "But we're forgetting one very important matter. For anything we do, from planting corn to digging a ditch, we're going to need tools. I know we'll get around to figuring out how to make these tools; but we can't wait for that. I suggest that we send out a band of, say, one hundred workers—I would call them 'the Scavengers'—to find such tools as have survived the inferno. These Scavengers should be instructed to bring back every useful implement that is not already in the hands of a hardworking farmer."

In addition, Millie suggested, the Scavengers should be told to keep an eye out for any pieces of metal—say, steel beams in partly destroyed buildings—that might later be salvaged for recycling.

"A very good point," Alf Richards said. "We can probably have blacksmiths at work within a few weeks; but they will need materials to work with. And even if we give high priority to mining and refining metals, such operations can't produce results overnight. So, scrap metal will have to be one of our first raw materials."

Looking at his watch once more, Richards ignored a few hands raised asking for recognition and spoke out loudly.

"Ladies and gentlemen," he said. "Let's take a break for dinner and then reconvene. Our work has only begun—but it's a good beginning. I wish my board of directors had worked as smoothly as we have here today!"

6

After dinner, Alf Richards reassembled the subcommittee and called the meeting to order with renewed gusto. It was high time, he said, to talk about construction. Once food and water were secured, building had to be the priority of priorities for the survivor community. Good progress had already been made building beehive *indlus* and erecting the community pavilion. But now a master plan was needed, and an organization to put it into effect. This is where the old hardhat was in his glory. He had given the matter a lot of thought, and prepared some preliminary estimates of the size and types of work gangs that would be most effective. He proposed establishing a construction company called Shaka Enterprises in honor of the fabled Zulu warrior king. Considering the immediate tasks to be accomplished, and the resources available, he recommended that two thousand individuals be assigned to the enterprise. This body of workers would consist of skilled tradesmen, laborers, and supervising engineers, three quarters of whom would work on buildings; the other quarter on roads, pipelines, and other infrastructure. This was a large commitment out of the total non-agricultural workforce of seven thousand; but the need was great. The most urgent objective was to provide housing—shelter for everyone. Yet construction for industry was also important. After all, Alf reminded the group, the agreed ultimate aim was not just to survive in safety and comfort, but to move as rapidly as possible out of the Stone Age into an industrial society.

They would need mills for grinding grain and sawing wood; furnaces for firing brick and other clay-based products, and for smelting metals; sheds for blacksmith forges and various workshops. Roads were also critical, since transport of materials would be vital to any recovery operations. The roadbeds, which had previously carried highways and railroads, had to be reshaped and maintained, first for horses and oxcarts, eventually for mechanical vehicles of a sort yet to be determined.

The Planning Subcommittee approved Alf Richards's scheme, as he had assumed they would, and they also endorsed his choice for a top management team. One of his American associates was to be in charge of factory structures, furnaces, and dams for sawmills and gristmills; a Swiss highway engineer was given oversight of work on roads, bridges, and pipelines; and an experienced contractor from Johannesburg, who had been in Ulundi at the time of the Event, took charge of regular building construction—homes, schools, clinics, and the like.

To provide direction for the constructors, the subcommittee created a professional design team of architects, civil engineers, and other specialists, assisted by surveyors and various helpers—one hundred individuals in all.

This prompted Stephen Healey to ask a question: "If we put all these architects and engineers to work, where are they going to get the paper, pens, and pencils they'll need?"

"A good question," Richards replied. "And we've looked into that. I can report that the ship's purser has saved a goodly supply of these materials. They will be allotted according to real and demonstrated need under my direct supervision."

The Ulundi Indaba had also commandeered such writing implements and paper as had escaped fire and flood in several office buildings. With rationing and conservation, there would be enough to fill the needs of the professionals for a year or more. In the meantime, Richards went on to explain, ten or so artisans would be designated to experiment with making pencils out of wood and graphite, and pens from quills, fine-haired brushes, and when available, thin metal plate. As for the ballpoint pen, that most ubiquitous implement of the immediate past, when the current supply ran out, that would be it—at least for a number of years. Not every item could be ranked high on the subcommittee's list of priorities.

"We can think about making paper," Richards said, "as soon as wood pulp becomes available." Gordon Chan suggested that the tannery workers might try their hand at making parchment. This idea was greeted with considerable skepticism. The scheme would depend on obtaining the skins of young sheep and goats—washed, stretched, scraped thin, whitened with chalk, and smoothed with pumice—bringing the survivors "up to the Middle Ages at last," one wag commented. The process was eventually tried, and it yielded some wonderful material, although never in significant quantities.

So, the construction enterprise was established; but still Alf Richards was not content.

"Plans are wonderful," he grumbled impatiently, "but if we're going to start building, what we really need is lots of wood and lots of nails. These beehive huts have come in handy, and I know that up in the hills, folks have been fixing up their houses using stone along with blocks made from dried mud. I'm sure we'll get around to making bricks and cement, too. But we can't mark time waiting for that day. Where is the wood?"

"Fortunately," said Peter Mavimbela, "there are several forested areas up in the hills that have been spared by the flames. And we have forestry experts who can tell us how this resource should be harvested, replanted, and nurtured. But right now, just like the farmers, we're hampered by lack of tools—beginning with axes, saws, ropes, and animal-drawn sleds. Further, although lumber can be roughly shaped with axes and hand saws, we really ought to get some sawmills in operation as soon as possible."

"It's that damned chicken and the egg," Alf said. "We need tools and sawmills to get building materials, and we need building materials to construct shops and mills. Well, we'll just have to do everything at once—start with our bare hands and such tools as we can find. Then make new tools as fast as we can, and get those mills built and in operation. At least we have good running water as a source of power. Some day we'll operate our mills with steam engines, internal combustion engines, or electric motors. For starters, waterwheels will have to do. But my question still is: how in the hell are we going to make waterwheels without nails?"

"I know carpenters who can do a lot with pegs and doweling," Peter said.

"Oh Christ!" Alf Richards was shouting with frustration now. "That's for people with time on their hands. Find me some nails, for God's sake. For want of a nail, the kingdom was lost!" he cried, mangling quotes from both Shakespeare and Ben Franklin.

He was somewhat mollified when the group agreed to add nails to the list of items to be sought by the Scavengers, and to make nails a priority when the first blacksmith forges were put into operation. In the meantime, calming down, he told Peter Mavimbela that he would welcome those carpenters who knew how to work with pegs and dowels.

Whatever the initial difficulties might be, the use of wood was crucial to any development plan, and the subcommittee decided to found an embryonic lumber industry with a workforce of three hundred. The first objective of this company would be, by hook or by crook, to provide structural materials for the builders. At the same time, using branches and brush not suitable for building, they were to start making charcoal for blacksmith forges, and to gather fuel for various other purposes. As a third mission, they would produce such derivatives of wood as turpentine, potash, and tannin for tanning leather. In their second year, the lumber experts would be expected to provide pulp for the manufacture of paper, as well as raw material for plastics and other chemicals.

This seemed to conclude the discussion of wood and its byproducts; and the hour having grown late, several subcommittee members stood up and stretched, anticipating adjournment. However, Gordon Chan urged the group to wait just a few more minutes in order to consider a matter that seemed to be on nobody's agenda, but that was related to timber resource: the topic of bamboo. For this purpose he introduced Tran Hung Tho, an eminent Vietnamese agricultural engineer, who had been recommended to Wilson Hardy by a number of Asian academics.

"Colleagues," began Dr. Tho, somewhat stiff and reserved, "the tropical climate along the coast in this part of Africa appears to be most promising for the cultivation of the tall, treelike tropical grass that we know as bamboo. Indeed, several varieties of the plant are local here and appear to have survived the tsunami. I have also brought with me seeds and seedlings, which I had planned to leave with African specialists for experimental work.

"Bamboo can be propagated by dividing root clumps or by planting certain segments of the shoots, as well as by sowing seeds and planting seedlings. So there are excellent prospects for an early and abundant supply of this versatile and serviceable material."

Alf Richards's eyes grew wide as he listened with fascination to the statistics.

"Some species grow quickly, as much as one foot per day, and achieve heights of up to forty meters—that is, one hundred and thirty feet. The stems, lashed together with grasses—grasses, not nails—provide a good building material. This can be especially useful for Engineering Village, far removed as it is from the forested hills. The largest stems can be cut into planks for buildings and rafts, or used to make buckets and pipes, furniture, fishing poles, and much more. Additionally, the seeds of some varieties are eaten as grain and the cooked young shoots eaten as vegetables. The raw leaves are a useful fodder for livestock. The pulped fibers of several species are used to make fine-quality paper."

After hardly any further discussion, the subcommittee authorized a workforce of fifty to assist Tran Hung Tho in his plan to grow and harvest this amazing material.

Finally, fatigued by the long day and evening sessions, but cheered by the prospect of developing a supply of bamboo—which Alf Richards labeled "our unanticipated resource"—the Joint Planning Subcommittee brought its first meeting to an end.

Just a week earlier, across the Mozambique Channel, two hundred fifty miles from the survivors of Ulundi and Engineering Village, on the shore of Madagascar, another meeting was held. Presiding was a youngish woman who spoke the Malagasy and French languages with a distinctly American accent. She removed a colorful bandanna from her head and shook her reddish-brown locks free. The all-male gathering awaited her words attentively.

She stood before them—her "government council," a score of fierce-looking men of mixed race, not a single smile on any one of the hard, dark faces that were illuminated by smoky torchlight—and spoke with the authority of a born leader. She was their captain not by formal election, but by a unanimous, unspoken agreement. Her position was like that of an ancient Roman emperor, the *imperator*, or commander in chief, who held power by virtue of his dominant personality and ability to reward the armies.

"My men, my people," she began in a low tone, "as your queen I am not afraid to lead you into danger, into the unknown sea of this dark new world. We do not know who or what is out there; but we are not afraid of them. We will make them afraid of *us!*"

The men grunted approvingly, some applauded. "Fear is our most powerful weapon, and we must move with stealth and swiftness!"

Her unkempt hair seemed afire in the flickering orange light; and she spoke just loudly enough, not shouting, to give her voice resonance and authority. "You, my friends, have only one thing in the world to fear—me. For I promise you with every fiber of my being that he who crosses me or disobeys a single command, however small it may seem, will pay with his life."

No one moved or spoke. All eyes remained fixed on the woman, whose dark eyes glowed like coals. They had no doubt that she would carry through with her threat and that every man would support her in any such action. They noted, too, the automatic pistol, fully loaded, that rested snugly in her belt, which she tapped occasionally while she spoke as if to remind herself—and her audience—of its existence.

Where had she come from? Somewhere in the United States, they assumed. When had she come to Madagascar? No one among her "pirate" crew knew for certain; most of them did not know her given name and few thought to ask. It was clear to those who spent any time thinking about it that she was educated and of superior intelligence. She spoke well, using unusual words that they sometimes did not understand; but her strategical plans seemed to make good sense. And she gave little evidence that she cared one whit what these rough men—or anyone else—thought of her. More important than where she came from, to these hungry-eyed buccaneers, was where she was going to take them.

"We don't know if anyone else has lived through this catastrophe," she said. "But if people on this island have survived, it is very likely that others have too. We don't know if they are organized or armed, strong or weak. All we do know is that *we* are stronger and *we* are destined to create a new kingdom of Madagascar and Southern Africa. The holocaust came to us from the sky, destroying the world that was, eliminating those who held power, and inviting us to take our rightful place at the head of the table. It is *our* time to rule!"

The memories of fire and flood were raw in her mind. After all, it had only been three weeks since the disaster that had wiped out the Malagasy world, that world to which she had escaped from her all-American youth in southern New Jersey. If the destruction was global—as she suspected, having heard that a comet had been on its way toward the earth—then that civilization, too, the mighty United States, no longer existed, except in those memories of times, good and bad, that filled her dreams. Of course, she had different dreams now—of conquests and of building a new world as conceived in her fantasies.

Anne Marie Appleton grew up in Cherry Hill, a South Jersey town that looked to Philadelphia for economic sustenance and to the equidistant shore towns for recreation. It was a large brood: seven kids, including Anne Marie, who was the second youngest. Dad worked in a local insurance agency; Mom was a registered nurse. They were a solidly middle-class family, and lived in a four-bedroom Victorian-style home. The children all went to Catholic schools, followed by attendance at a local community college. When her turn came, Anne Marie, who had been a straight A student and star athlete in swimming and soccer, won scholarships and loans that made it possible for her to go to Cornell.

As she looked out at the hard faces of the men who would follow her into battle if necessary, she almost laughed aloud at the contrast between the would-be adult Anne Marie of ten years ago and the woman of today. It seemed unreal to her, this journey through time and experience that had taken her halfway across the globe.

In college, Anne Marie read history voraciously and began to experiment with radical politics and mind-altering substances. Leftwing, right-wing, uppers, downers, hallucinogens, plain old alcohol, all came into play. She dated men from alternative worlds that she had never even imagined as a parochial school girl in suburban Cherry Hill. Who knew that the universe was infinitely expandable and that academic courses and boyfriends were infinitely expendable? They had never taught her that at home, where the issues were black and white, us and them, American and foreign, right and wrong.

She took a year off and traveled to Central and South America, dabbling in revolutionary politics and drug dealing. Her parents never knew how close she came to being jailed in Peru and Colombia. She was clever enough to figure out when it was time to move on, and she had friends to help her. She became ever more fluent in Spanish. Languages were easy for her. Reluctantly, she came back for her senior year, graduated, then took her own poor girl's version of the Grand Tour of Europe: including some of the old Eastern bloc countries like Bulgaria and Romania, pushing on to Turkey and Lebanon. In those years she flirted with neo-Marxist affiliations, fell in briefly with Islamic terrorists, and learned about guns and bombs. She had willing teachers, some of them lovers. But she never officially joined any of the radical organizations that sought to recruit her. Nor did she reveal any of this to her parents in New Jersey.

Next stop: Africa. Starting in Morocco, then moving across the northern tier of the continent, she eventually worked her way south through the sub-Saharan regions that were plagued with revolution and diseases. Lucky? She looked back and wondered how in hell she had never been struck with either a bullet or malaria. She came to love and respect the people she met, the undernourished and downtrodden masses with black skin and blacker futures. She witnessed tribal massacres and military coups. She learned several languages, and improved her skills with firearms. She became adept at target shooting, but never had to fire at another person until one dark and dangerous day—a day that changed her life forever.

The city of Durban in post-apartheid South Africa was a teeming

1111111111

seaport that, like any port, attracted "all kinds." Anne Marie Appleton certainly fit that category: a bedraggled, world-weary traveler who owned no more than the clothes on her back, a few bits of costume jewelry, some paperback books (including worn copies of revolutionary tracts), and the odd penny-equivalent coin as souvenir of the many countries in which she had lived. Her clothes were a man's much-patched flannel shirt a few sizes too big, a pair of denim jeans that were much too tight, rope-soled sandals that barely clung to her feet, and a floppy hat that sometimes kept the rain or sun from her matted hair. It was rare that she ever saw or touched any local paper currency. When she did, it was in payment for a sexual favor for some stranger—or a friend. She often begged for food, or a few coins to pay for it.

She had started to drink around the clock, or at least during the time she was not unconscious on her bedroll in a city mission. She stole booze and drugs when she could, bummed tobacco at waterfront taverns. After several months she had blended into the scene, and it was as if she had been there all her life. Anne Marie Appleton of Cherry Hill was thirty years old and going downhill fast.

"I am the anti–Peace Corps," she joked to her black stevedore friends in the bars. They laughed, but kept a safe distance from her. There was something in her devil-may-care attitude that made her seem dangerous.

One night, she showed up in her favorite tavern with a large quantity of cash. She did not tell her comrades where or how she had come by her treasure, but she bought several rounds for anyone who would drink with her. When the police came, looking for a woman who had robbed and murdered an English businessman, she slipped out a back door.

She ran. It was raining and the slick streets were her enemy. Her sandals betrayed her at every turn, so she shed them and ran barefoot. The police, alerted, came in pursuit, guns drawn. Her mind was a blank; all she knew was that she had to escape. If apprehended and thrown into jail, that would be the end for her.

Drunk and nearly blinded by driving rain and tears, Anne Marie ran to the waterfront, onto the dimly lit and dangerous docks. Her pursuers sent a few warning shots into the air, but then lost sight of her in the maze of shacks and gangplanks, crates and barrels. She did not know where she was running, but she ran and ran and ran. Ahead, she saw a dilapidated tugboat hugging a dark pier. Without thinking, she leaped over a pile of ropes and aboard the craft. She buried herself beneath a tarpaulin that smelled of fuel oil and rotten fish. There she passed out, oblivious to the shouts and footsteps that echoed through the night. The police did not find her.

The young woman awoke—came to—as the boat churned to life the next morning. Luckily, she still had some money in her pocket from her previous night's adventure. She paid the tug captain to take her alongside a cargo ship scheduled to leave the harbor that day. He did, and she talked her way aboard with a story about running away from a rapist in Durban. Two days later, she disembarked in Madagascar, a mysterious, even mythical place that she had never planned to visit—let alone to live in as a fugitive from the law in South Africa.

Anne Marie sought out the neo-hippie community on the southwestern beaches of Madagascar; there, within several months, she learned Malagasy and, again, blended into the scenery. She was spent, exhausted physically and mentally, tired of running, and for the first time in years she felt homesick for New Jersey and her family. She contemplated writing a letter to her parents, asking for their help. She thought about this for days, for weeks on end. Several times she started the letter, then tore it up. As time passed, she began to feel that, without help from her family or anyone else, she was "coming back," climbing out of the dark pit into which she had descended. She cut down on her drug usage, remaining dependent but feeling "under control." She congratulated herself for getting "mellow" at last.

She started living with a Malagasy sailor—a fisherman really, who rarely worked but had lived on the beaches all his adult life. He was a native, and he taught her the culture and religion of his people, and helped her hone her language skills. A year passed, then two. Whether she had regained her mental stability or slipped into a new state of derangement, quiet and aloof, it would take a host of specialists to divine. In any case, the Event changed everything . . .

It is our destiny now, she thought, to explore the seas and seek out others who may have survived the fire and flood. If most of the island nation of Madagascar has been destroyed, and the world beyond as well, then what a magnificent opportunity for these people to become a mighty power in a world remade, and for her to be their leader. How to convey such a lofty ambition to these rough and ready pirates and petty criminals whom she now commanded?

"You men," she said aloud, "have been chosen by the Creator of the universe, Zanahary. The ancestors, the Razana, are calling us to do His will and bring others into his dominion. For too long, the evil Christians and Muslims have tried to destroy our gods and our ancestors. Ever since the Portuguese first landed here five hundred years ago, our people have been oppressed by European influences. Only under the Merina dynasty and our greatest sovereigns, King Andrianamapoinimerina and Queen Ranavolana, did the Malagasy people rise to greatness. That was a long time ago. Since then, mostly it has been a struggle against the foreigners and the oligarchs for control of the means of production . . ." Anne Marie Appleton paused, having forgotten that she was no longer Anne Marie Appleton, and having forgotten for a moment who her audience was.

"We know that our traditional capital, Antananarivo, has been destroyed, as have the wealthy landowners and politicians who kept our people poor and oppressed. Many of you were fortunate to dwell far from the evil influences of the capital city, living on the sea as our ancestors once did. Now the world is reborn, and we are remade. We have created a new clan and a new nation."

Upon assuming the role of queen and commander in chief, she had renounced all sexual relations and declared herself celibate. There was no looking back, from this point, no time for regret or second thoughts.

"The world has trembled at the hand of the Almighty Zanahary, the God of our sacred ancestors. We are a people of many races who have come from far places all over the world. Just as I have come from a distant place to be here with you—and I believe it is no accident that this is the case. I was destined from the beginning of time to be here as your leader."

Her body had nearly betrayed her when she had gone through a withdrawal and detoxification process in the days immediately following the Event. But she felt reborn now, empowered, capable of great deeds—godlike. These men did not need to know anything about her other than that she was their queen, their general, and she would lead them to glory.

"Tomorrow, we will sail in search of others who have survived the catastrophe. Some will gladly look to us for leadership. Others we will destroy or force to accept our rule. We will search for food, for guns and other weapons, and for treasure. And what we seek, we shall find! We will take what is rightfully ours by virtue of our strength. We will conquer or eliminate the weak, who do not deserve to stand in our way or to consume resources that we need."

Her former common-law husband, a sun-darkened fisherman with hazel eyes, nut brown hair, and a several-days beard spoke up. "You should stay here to keep order among the people and let us do this dangerous work. If you get hurt or killed, we will be lost." He wiped his cracked lips with a callused brown hand. "You are our queen and our leader, so you cannot risk this. Think of your people."

Grunts and murmurs greeted his words. The men of her council agreed: it was just too dangerous a mission for a woman—and especially for their supreme leader.

She raised her hand. She was no longer Anne Marie Appleton. Cherry Hill was ancient history, and her family . . . gone. Everything she had known in her previous life was gone. She had nothing to lose. "I understand your concern," she said mildly. "I am thankful that you think of me in this way. But you must stop thinking of me as a woman."

Her eyes blazed now, and her tone changed dramatically. "I am the messenger of Zanahary! He and the sacred ancestors speak through me. You will listen and obey, and after this day you shall not question a single order or any statement that comes from my mouth. I speak the words of our Creator, who made heaven and earth and everything in it. It was he who destroyed the earth but left us here to inherit what is left. We are the chosen ones, and I am the undisputed leader of the people." Her hand grazed the pistol in her belt. A bolt-action rifle stood within easy reach.

"I have put aside womanly thoughts and feelings for now. Perhaps I will never take them up again. I have no fears, nothing that holds me back from doing the will of our God. I expect you to do the same, to have no reservations or doubts of any kind. Do you understand me?" The assembly nodded and muttered their assent. She looked directly at her former lover. "You have been my partner and friend. Now you are my comrade and soldier. I love you as I do these others under my command. And I expect complete obedience. My life is protected by Zanahary and the Razana, the ancestors. Your life and all of theirs," she declaimed, her hand sweeping through the air to indicate the other men present and those who waited outside the council, everyone within her sway, "are worth less than nothing except that you serve the Queen and her people in the quest to build a new empire, the greatest in the new world. I have been spared to rule. You will lay down your life for the same purpose.

"You will know me as Queen Ranavolana, the greatest ruler of the Malagasy nation. I have come back to my people. They will rejoice when they hear of this. For theirs is a special destiny. Because of me, they will have an honored place in history."

By the time the Joint Planning Subcommittee held its first meeting in Engineering Village, the queen, with a band of her pirates, was already sailing the seas in search of conquest.

1

Wil Hardy and his girlfriend, Sarah, sat apart from everyone else on the beach looking at the still unfamiliar constellations of the Southern sky. He reviewed with her the day's proceedings of the Joint Planning Subcommittee—and she listened, as attentively as she could, considering the late hour and the brilliance of the stars.

"Are you sure you're not being too ambitious?" she asked tentatively.

"Well, there are problems, plenty of them. But they seem like nothing compared to the determination of these people to overcome them. We may be biting off more than we can chew, but that's what the human spirit is all about, isn't it? We've survived the worst—the very worst that anyone could imagine—and we're pulling ourselves together. We're on our way!"

"So much optimism, so much self-confidence. It's amazing." She rested her head on his shoulder.

There was no wind. The night was totally still, eerily calm. Suddenly, Hardy heard his name. Someone was calling for him. It was Herb, breathless as he approached the isolated couple:

"Wil! Wil, where the hell are you?"

"Over here," Hardy shouted. "What's up?"

"Captain Nordstrom and your father want to see you—right away. There's been a problem with one of the fishing boats. The fishermen are in the captain's headquarters giving some kind of report. It's all hush-hush, but they want you there right away to take notes."

"We were feeling too comfortable," Wilson said to Sarah.

"The gods are displeased," she replied with a smile and gave him a light kiss on his cheek.

Wil dashed back to their hut, picked up his pencil and notebook, and hurried to see what was happening.

The survivors' fishing fleet, which had been established just a week earlier, and endorsed that very day by the Joint Planning Subcommittee, consisted of several of the *Queen of Africa*'s lifeboats, each one with a crew of seven, six at the oars. The boats also sported such jerry-built sails as the bosun and his men could improvise. The crews were comprised of seamen from the cruise ship, along with Inlanders who had knowledge of the local waters. After sailing a short distance off shore—never more than an ordained ten miles—the crews dropped nets for trawling, along with lines and hooks. They had been having moderate luck, which is much better luck than anyone had at first expected. It was such a crew of seven that was meeting with Dr. Wilson Hardy, Sr., and Captain Johan Nordstrom.

Moments after the younger Hardy arrived, Richard and Deborah Frost entered the meeting area, somewhat disheveled and winded, as if they also had been summoned hurriedly.

"Thank you, all three of you, for coming right over," the elder Hardy said. Without further introduction he addressed a question to the Frosts: "Deborah and Richard, do you know anything about Madagascar?"

"Why, yes, we've studied the island, visited it, know a fair bit about it. A forbidding and beautiful place, I can tell you that much right off the bat," Frost said.

"Good." Dr. Hardy glanced at Nordstrom, who called in the crew of the fishing boat.

The mate in charge was Harry McIntosh, a Scot who later confessed to Wil Hardy that he had been a lot happier angling for salmon in the streams of his home country than he was bobbing about in these strange waters, wrestling with nets. But at this moment he was not talking about the salmon streams of Scotland, which probably did not exist any more. He had been telling a tale that Hardy and Nordstrom obviously found unsettling—and which he was asked to repeat for the newcomers, starting from the beginning.

McIntosh was about five five and built like a barrel, with huge forearms and a brown, sea-weathered face, with a shock of white-gray hair that stood stiffly at attention.

Just a few hours earlier, in midafternoon, the fishing boat had been drifting slowly before the wind about five miles offshore. Having made a satisfactory catch, McIntosh decided it was time to head back. Just then, one of his men tapped him on the shoulder and pointed toward the east. There, clearly limned against the horizon, brilliantly illuminated by the sun now setting in the west, was a sloop, perhaps fifty feet long, speeding through the waves.

"Her sails were bright red, seemed to be on fire, if you want my view. Anyhow, we were paralyzed, at least for a moment. Up to then we had assumed there were no other survivors on the face of the earth, and surely no other ship on the surface of the sea."

McIntosh went on, "I couldn't believe my eyes. We were all convinced at first that this must be some sort of mirage." The mate stopped and shook his head as if still in a state of disbelief. "But the sloop was real enough," he continued. "Suddenly, she tacked and started flying straight toward us. There was no way to avoid her even if we had wanted to. She could literally sail rings around us."

"Excuse me, Harry," Dr. Hardy interjected. "Just what is a sloop?"

Captain Nordstrom, impatient, gave the answer. "A single-masted vessel, Wilson, with two sails, a mainsail plus a jib. The jib is the small one in front. This could have been your typical pleasure yacht. There used to be plenty of them sailing between Durban and Madagascar—it's only about two hundred fifty miles across. The waters are called the Mozambique Channel. Of course, yachts are one thing. Red sails are another. That's something I've never come across."

"I thought it was an optical illusion," McIntosh said. "You know, red sails in the sunset, that sort of thing. But they were red, all right—painted, I guess, by that crazy bitch."

"What?" Wil Hardy blurted. "Who?"

"I'll tell you, I'll tell you," the mate continued. "Within minutes, it seemed, the sloop was upon us, and without a hail or a hello, came right up alongside and grappled fast. And that's when the crazy bitch appeared. She's a youngish woman, not bad-looking, not bad-looking at all. She was wearing a red shirt and some kind of a wild bandanna around her head. At first I thought, 'Well, that's nice, here's a bit of company.' But when I noticed she was holding a gun, my mood changed mighty quick. Then I started to look at the crew. I don't think I scare easily, but I have to tell you that those nasties fairly spooked me out of my shoes. They were Malays. Malay pirates, all loaded down with knives and guns."

"How do you know they were Malays?" Captain Nordstrom asked.

"Begging your pardon, Captain," McIntosh replied, "but I've been sailing the Seven Seas for a lot of years, and I know a Malay when I see one. I could have sworn we were in Malaysia, or Borneo, or Java, except that those places are a few thousand miles away. Anyhow, just as I'm trying to figure out how these villains could have gotten to the coast of Africa, the woman speaks up and says, loud as you please, that she is Queen Ranavolana. I know I've got the name right, because I asked her twice and later wrote it down. Although I never heard such a name, and as far as I'm concerned it doesn't make any sense. So she says she's this queen, and it's then I noticed that the boat's name, painted in black, was the *King Radama*. Also, that's no king I ever heard of.

"Now here's the queerest part of all. The moment she started to talk, I knew she was an American! I also knew she wasn't a sailor. You can tell by the way a person moves and by the terms they use whether they're boat people or not, and believe me—she's a landlubber. But she talked like she owned the ocean. Like I said, she says she's Queen Ranavolana, and for good measure she is related in some way to Captain Kidd. Crazier and crazier, and I have to say that I didn't like the way she waved her gun around. After telling us we were in waters that belonged to her, and that we had no right to be there, she ordered my men to transfer our catch of fish onto her boat. I was happy to find that this is what she wanted, and told the men to do what she asked—and in a hurry.

" 'I'm letting you off easy this time,' she said, 'but you'd better tell your people that I'm out here and that this is my territory. I may drop by your home base one of these days, just to see what you're up to. And if you're collecting any goodies, you'd better be ready to turn them over to me and my crew.'

"I assured her that we were just poor folk trying to survive after the disaster, and that we didn't have anything worth her trouble. Some of my men tried to make conversation with members of her crew, but they were a pretty surly bunch, and when they did say something it was in a lingo so strange that even Victor Lupupa here"—pointing to one of his Inlander crewmen—"couldn't understand a word. And Victor is familiar with practically all the South African languages."

"So what do you make of it, Harry?" Captain Nordstrom asked calmly and directly.

"That woman is an American, I'm quite sure of it," McIntosh answered. "And she hasn't spent much time at sea. I can't begin to guess who she is or what she's doing here. She's off her rocker, that's for sure—possibly as a result of the floods and fires. She may *think* she's a pirate, but she's just play-acting. She doesn't look like the real thing from where I stand. Of course, that doesn't mean she isn't dangerous, far from it. What I really can't figure out, though, is where those damned Malays came from, or Polynesians, or Indonesians, or whatever the hell they are. They sure aren't South Africans. And they aren't Arabs or North Africans, either."

"Can you folks shed any light on this?" asked the captain, turning to the Frosts.

"I think we can," said Richard with a wry smile. "Mr. McIntosh may have been all over the world, but he obviously has never been to Madagascar. It's that big island to the east, just two hundred fifty miles away, as Captain Nordstrom said. But even though it's just a stone's throw away geographically, it's light-years away in racial, cultural, and historical terms. Most of the residents of that island are what we call Malayo-Indonesians or Austronesians, and yes indeed, they came originally from Indonesia. Actually, if you go far enough back, we believe their forebears came from the South China coast around 3500 B.C., migrated through Taiwan and the Philippines, and arrived in Indonesia and the Malaysian peninsula about two thousand years later. Presumably they traveled those vast distances in double-outrigger sailing canoes. Eventually, they continued to expand to the east, occupying much of what we call Polynesia; and then, much later, some of them turned around and traveled to the southwest, arriving in Madagascar about A.D. 500. The language spoken today on Madagascar is very similar to the language spoken on Borneo, over four thousand miles away across the open Indian Ocean."

"A scientist friend of ours," Deborah Frost interjected, "whose specialty is prehistoric migrations, has said that this circumstance strikes him as—and I think I can quote him exactly—'the most astonishing fact of human geography in the entire world.' Of course," she continued, "you do see black African features among some of the population of Madagascar. These two shores being so close to each other, it could hardly be otherwise. But I believe that most of these darker people lived in the coastal lowlands, where they would have succumbed to the tsunamis. If your pirates looked like Malaysians, you're neither dreaming nor confused. Obviously, they come from Madagascar."

"Let's not forget," Richard said, "that Jane Warner's calculated safety zone includes the southern portion of Madagascar as well as our small slice of Africa. It stands to reason that there are survivors on that island, and maybe more than a few. It's a big island, you know, almost a thousand miles long. Of course, if just the southern tip was spared, those folks could be very hard up for food, since that part of the island is famous for its so-called spiny forest, lots of fascinating cactuslike trees, but not great for agriculture. And if they're desperate, that could explain the pirate crew. Otherwise, that part of the story doesn't ring true. The inhabitants of Madagascar, I would say, are as pleasant and easygoing a people as you'll find anywhere in the world."

"What's all that stuff about King Radama and Queen What's-her-name?" asked Dr. Hardy. "Does that make any sense?"

"Oh yes, it does indeed," Deborah said. "It's all part of the island's history, which is as extraordinary as its prehistoric origins. Richard told you that the native population arrived on the island around A.D. 500. The ruins of Arab settlements have been found dating from about 1200, and the Portuguese first stopped by for a visit in 1500. During the following couple of hundred years, although there were occasional attempts to establish European settlements, they were frustrated by disease and hostile natives. So a civilization developed in relative isolation, a historical backwater, largely ignored by Westerners. A number of separate tribes evolved, but by the end of the eighteenth century, most of these were united under one ruler.

"This king—whose name I don't remember, and you don't want to know since it has about twenty letters—had a son and successor called King Radama I. There you are with the name of your pirate ship. Radama extended his rule over practically all of the island. In this effort he was helped by the British, who had become interested in this vast landmass adjoining their trade routes to India. From England the king received arms and advisers, and, as an incidental adjunct, an influx of Christian missionaries.

"When Radama died in the early 1800s, he was succeeded by his widow, Queen Ranavalona I. Known to some as 'the wicked queen,' she determined to rid the land of European and Christian influence. During her lengthy rule, she drove out the missionaries, martyring a number of them, and also brutalized her own people. She was one rough, tough lady. Make of this what you will in trying to figure out what your pirate queen is up to."

"Incidentally, Wilson," Richard Frost said, "you and your fellow engineers would be fascinated to learn about one European who, because of his technological talents, managed to get into the queen's good graces. Jean Laborde, the son of a French blacksmith, was shipwrecked off the coast of Madagascar in the 1830s. Brought before the queen, he convinced her that he could manufacture all manner of things she craved—particularly muskets and gunpowder. Whereupon she provided him with work crews to build what amounted to an industrial complex. He was as good as his word, and better. In a large factory compound he produced munitions, bricks and tiles, pottery, glass, porcelain, soap, candles, cement, dyes, sugar, rum—just about everything needed to make the island self-sufficient. He was eventually expelled for dabbling in local politics, and his workforce, who had labored without pay, wrecked the factory buildings and machines. That was the end of Madagascar's industrial revolution."

"Sounds like someone we could use today," Dr. Hardy said.

"There's a lot I can tell you," Richard continued, "but I don't know how much more you want to hear. The French entered the picture in 1883, when they invaded the island. They came again in 1895 and stayed, making the place a French colony. The monarchy was declared at an end, and Queen Ranavalona III was exiled to Algeria. During World War II, the British attacked in order to drive out the Vichy French, which they did. After the war, with French control restored, the natives rebelled, were bloodily repressed, and eventually, in 1960, achieved independence. Subsequent experiments in government were chaotic, to put it mildly. I think that's enough history for your purposes."

"Where does Captain Kidd fit into the picture?" Captain Nordstrom asked.

"Ah yes, the pirates." Deborah Frost warmed to the subject. "They're a very important part of the saga of Madagascar. From the 1680s to around 1720, the island was a major hideout for pirates in the Indian Ocean. They preyed upon the merchant ships that carried rich cargoes to and from India and the Near East. At one time the pirate population numbered nearly a thousand. And to be sure, William Kidd—Captain Kidd—was among them. As a matter of fact, it was in the Indian Ocean, at that time, that Kidd first decided to become a pirate.

"This was a mysterious turnabout, since he had been sent there by the British Crown to apprehend pirates who were molesting the ships of the East India Company. Just as, earlier, he had been commissioned by both New York and Massachusetts to protect the American coast from buccaneers. After he was hanged in London— in 1701, I think it was—doubts were expressed about the fairness of his trial. Maybe there are questions of guilt and innocence that appeal to your so-called pirate queen."

Hardy and Nordstrom had heard more than enough historical detail; but the young scribe, Wil Hardy, was lapping it up. A thousand pirates! Captain Kidd! An island where the natives speak like the people of Borneo, four thousand miles away! Evil queens martyring missionaries! What a delicious concoction of exotica for a young historian, and for a young mind that had absorbed comic books and movie special effects and computer games. All in addition to the flora and fauna of Madagascar—tens of thousands of species unique to the island, notably more than thirty different kinds of lemurs—about which his friend Roxy had been reading, and waxing rhapsodic, ever since they learned that a part of the island was in Jane Warner's safety zone.

For the moment, however, there was nothing more to be told. The other crew members added a few details, but essentially corroborated McIntosh's fantastic story. The men seemed a capable, experienced group, but it was clear that they had been shaken by their encounter with Queen Ranavolana. It wasn't the danger that seemed to bother them as much as the eeriness of it all.

Captain Nordstrom dismissed the crew. "And thank you, gentlemen, for your clear, detailed report and your behavior under such pressure. You are a credit to all of us. Please keep this information to yourselves, as much as possible. I understand that it is a wonderful sea tale that you probably want to share with others . . . but I would prefer—and I believe I speak for Dr. Hardy and the other leaders—that you characterize the incident as simply an encounter with a few hungry people in a boat."

"Understood, Captain," McIntosh volunteered, with a significant glance at the bedraggled, still-excited crew. "We'll do our best." The men shrugged and shuffled and mumbled their agreement.

Dr. Hardy spoke up: "And our thanks to the Frosts for their erudite briefing."

When the Frosts and McIntosh's group left, Nordstrom, Hardy Senior, and Hardy Junior sat quietly for several long minutes. The seasoned engineer was the first to break the silence. "We could spend many hours speculating about this bizarre situation," he said; "but I suggest we defer that to another day and direct our attention to practical planning and action."

The captain agreed. He turned to the younger man. "It is important that you keep an accurate, complete record of all of this— very important."

"I understand, sir," Wil Hardy said.

"This incident will require us to call a special meeting of the Governing Council, followed by a session with the Coordinating Committee," Dr. Hardy said. "And we will need a clear, focused agenda. Well, there's no time like the present."

With that, Hardy and Nordstrom set to work preparing such an agenda, along with specific recommendations. Abruptly, they started to dictate, taking turns, and editing each other's comments in a remarkable display of cooperative composition. The younger Hardy turned to a clean page in his notebook and began to write as rapidly as he could:

First, we recommend that there be no change in the operations of the fishing fleet. We are not prepared to embark on a naval war, nor to put what few arms we have into the hands of our fishermen. If we have to forfeit an occasional boatload of fish, so be it. At the moment, there does not seem to be any great peril to the crews. If the raids persist and become more worrisome, or if it turns out that there are more pirate ships sailing the seas, this policy should be immediately reviewed.

Wil Hardy wrote quickly, grateful that the two leaders spoke in more or less complete sentences. But there was a gnawing feeling of doubt and fear in his gut.

Second, this incident compels us to address without delay a matter we had hoped to defer: national defense—or, since we have no formal nation to speak of, let us say military security. We suggest that Deck Officer Carl Gustafsson, representing our Governing Council, and Stephen Healey, representing the Ulundi Indaba, be designated to co-chair a Defense Committee. There are military people among both the Inlanders and the Newcomers, and a small number of them should be convened to make preliminary strategic plans.

Obviously, from what we have heard, we must consider the possibility of attack from the sea. But it is only prudent also to consider potential invasion by land. We have been assuming that outside of the Ulundi Circle there is nothing but death and devastation. Yet we seem to have forgotten about Madagascar, even though we were told it was partly within the safety zone. And there may well be other pockets of survival about which we know nothing. Not that we should expect other survivors to be hostile. But it would be folly to make no preparations at all.

Sensible, Wil thought, although far from reassuring.

The Defense Committee should make plans for armed forces—probably in the form of militia, since we cannot afford to assign people full time to military service. And the Committee must make recommendations concerning armaments—the use of such guns as we have, and the manufacture of ammunition and new weapons. This manufacture will naturally have to be processed through the Joint Planning Subcommittee. Difficult trade-offs will be entailed, since we cannot let the production of armaments constrain vital industrial development. In this domain, final decisions should be authorized by the entire Coordinating Committee.

The enterprise is inherently complex and dangerous. It is crucial that any armed forces we establish must be completely under control of the communal authorities. We do not want military juntas in a position to usurp authority. Yet to do nothing is to leave ourselves helpless in the face of potential aggression.

Wil Hardy felt a cold chill grip his spine and he tried to shake off a feeling of impending doom. No . . . it couldn't be, after all that the group had so far endured . . . He and Sarah and the rest of them were destined to survive, to meet any challenge or danger. Weren't they?

Later, when Wil crawled under the blanket next to Sarah, he was relieved that she stirred but did not awaken. Time enough the next day to talk about the strange new turn of events. Happily, compared to what the survivors had lived through since Christmas, this new encounter had to be considered a relatively minor threat. In the telling, Hardy planned to emphasize the fanciful drama of the incident while downplaying the element of danger.

Yet it was a long time before he fell asleep. Once he had started to think about pirates, it was difficult to stop. It wasn't only the existence of Queen Ranavalona that disturbed him; there was the phenomenon of piracy itself. Captain Kidd is commissioned by the British government to protect merchant ships, and he decides instead to prey upon them. Greed? Simple perversity? So be it. There had been few human societies in history without buccaneers of some kind. The aggressive impulse is as old as *Homo sapiens*, and even older. We must simply cope with this phenomenon, he thought, the way we do with the many other difficulties that fate—or Providence, or God, or bad luck—puts in our path.

Having reached this rational, dispassionate conclusion, he slept.

But even as he slept, he dreamed. Deep in his subconscious, and concurrently far off in the distant reaches of the universe, a sloop with red sails sliced through foam-topped waves, a pirate queen at the wheel . . . mysterious, romantic, ominous, and ultimately beyond the reach of logic.

8

Alf Richards gaveled the meeting to order with a wooden mallet designed to crack shellfish, an item he had appropriated from the ship's galley. He glowered at latecomers and proceeded immediately to the business at hand.

The opening presentation at this, the second meeting of the Joint Planning Subcommittee, was scheduled to be given by Ichiro Nagasaka, the group's most eminent authority on iron and steel. Nagasaka was a compact man, narrow-shouldered, with a large head and a shock of black hair combed in a stiff pompadour. His dark eyebrows flicked as he spoke. Because of his specialty, everyone expected that he would be talking about metals. But he had a surprise in store.

"I wish to introduce an important topic," he said. "Kilns."

"What?" "Huh?" Several people had not understood the word.

"Kilns," Ichiro Nagasaka repeated, "furnaces, ovens, places in which to build fires."

This seemed like a strange detour on the way to restoring an industrial society, and several subcommittee members snorted as if to say as much.

Alf Richards spoke for the majority when he asked, "What happened to iron and steel?"

Dr. Nagasaka smiled. "All in good time. We will get to iron and steel. But the fact is that we cannot even begin to plan a technological future without talking about controlled heat."

Seeing the puzzlement on the faces of his audience, the speaker continued: "Just consider: If there is a single factor that enabled the human race to move out of the Stone Age and embark on its journey toward technical mastery, one must say it was the ability to create intense fires. By intense fires I do not mean simple combustion, but rather infernos hot beyond the imagining of early peoples. Ordinary flame, burning in the open air, is good mainly for keeping warm, cooking, and scaring away animals. Granted, learning how to ignite and control such flame was a vitally important step toward advanced civilization. Yet, to garner metals from their hiding places in the rocks of the earth, fiercely hot fires were required, fires contained in blazing furnaces and brought to a feverish pitch by force-feeding them with air."

Members of the group nodded but shrugged and shifted in their seats, indicating a grudging understanding mixed with impatience. Nagasaka, unperturbed, continued.

"Human beings have been hardening clay pottery in heated, enclosed spaces for more than eight thousand years. But the heat suitable for baking clay is nowhere near as intense as that needed to work metals. To melt copper, we require a temperature of 1,083 degrees Centigrade. And that is nothing compared to iron, which has a melting point of 1,535 degrees Centigrade. So, you can see that we have to give a lot of thought to heat—how to create it and how to contain it.

"Our engineers have with them many plans and specifications to follow when we are ready to build our furnaces. But we need to address the question of which locally available materials can be used to make the refractory bricks with which to line these furnaces. In addition to withstanding intense heat without cracking, these materials must also be able to resist such destructive influences as rapid changes in temperature, abrasion by dust-bearing gases, and erosion by molten metals. Of course, the bricks or tiles that we need for building kilns have themselves to be manufactured in kilns. In order to make a kiln, a kiln is required."

Several subcommittee members nodded thoughtfully. It was clear that in practically every one of their endeavors they would be running into this Catch-22 of technological progress.

"But," Ichiro said, "we escape the predicament by starting with the most primitive oven, simply a hole in the ground with walls and roof made of stones and mud—or perhaps of crude bricks made of clay dried in the sun. Then in this primitive oven we make good, solid, fired bricks, using clay mixed with straw. These bricks in turn enable us to make a more advanced oven in which we can make superior bricks, and so forth, onward and upward. All the while we seek to find ever better clay and superior admixtures—alumina, silica, magnesite, dolomite, and the like."

Dr. Nagasaka thought that he was making good progress; but he had underestimated the effect that the mention of bricks would have on the subcommittee chairman.

"Dammit, Ichiro," Alf Richards errupted, waving his coffee cup in the air, "we can't think about fancy bricks for kilns when we haven't even talked about ordinary bricks for construction! That's one of the things I was going to bring up next. We need to build walls for our houses, foundations for our factories, and piers for our bridges. We've talked about lumber and bamboo, but that won't take care of all our needs. If we can find some decent clay—and I've been told there's plenty of good stuff around—we could start making bricks pretty darn quick."

Ichiro smiled and bowed, and thereupon gave a demonstration of how the Japanese, in group enterprise, work assiduously toward consensus. Richards also showed that, when he so chose, he could be an eminently congenial negotiator. After about a half hour's further discussion, a deal was struck. The Joint Planning Subcommittee authorized the establishment of two factories to make bricks.

These were to be located near deposits of clay, and also near a supply of the wood needed for fuel. Several potential sites were suggested, and a small panel of specialists was authorized to select the two that seemed most suitable. At both plants the main product was to be a regular brick for use in construction. But at one of the installations, ten ceramics experts plus fifteen helpers would work exclusively on development of materials suitable for building furnaces. In pursuit of this goal, they would be given special facilities, along with significant operational authority.

The basic brickmaking operation is not overly complex; but it requires muscle power and efficient organization. The clay has to be dug out of the ground, then worked into a wet mash that can be mixed with straw and put into molds. In an alternative method, called the stiff-mud process, the clay is mixed with just enough water to make it plastic, and then it is forced through a rectangular die, coming out in the form of a bar which is cut into brick-size pieces. In either case, a crew then attends to the baking, or firing, in a kiln. The subcommittee, after some rough-and-ready man-hour calculations, decided to assign one hundred workers to each plant.

"One hundred musn't become a magic number," one of the committee members piped up. "Let's not use it hastily to solve every problem that comes along."

Richards responded: "Look, in the absence of a detailed estimate, this is a convenient, functional unit for our preliminary planning. We use a figure that reflects the order of magnitude that seems to make sense. Call it 'the One Hundred Strategy,' if you like. The number of personnel assigned to each activity will, in the course of events, be subject to modification. The important thing is that we get the damned work started."

The group concurred, and then commissioned a third plant— also with a complement of one hundred—to make other fired clay products such as pipes, floor tiles, roof tiles, and cooking utensils. Finally, they authorized a fourth operation, with fifty workers, to produce cement, which is a blend of clay and limestone also fired in a furnace. After cement has been manufactured, it can be mixed with sand, crushed stone, and water to make concrete. Or it can be mixed with lime, sand, and water, to provide brick mortar.

By the time these decisions were finalized, it was almost noon. Alf Richards was delighted with the morning's work. Brick, concrete, and mortar, plus a variety of tile products; just *thinking* of these materials made the crusty old hardhat feel like celebrating.

Ichiro Nagasaka also was satisfied. He had accomplished his immediate objective. The manufacture of suitable refractory materials was one of those items that needed someone to serve as champion, or else it might have been ignored. Then, at some future point, everyone would have regretted the oversight.

After lunch, Alf reconvened the meeting and asked Dr. Nagasaka whether he did not want to go on to the larger issue of metals, especially the manufacture of steel.

Ichiro said, "Oh no. Let us move on to other things." This gave the impression that he did not want to dominate the proceedings with his personal concerns. The strategically minded members of the subcommittee read it another way, and they were right in their suspicion. Knowing that there was absolutely no chance of metals being overlooked, Nagasaka contemplated an end game in which this subject would become the final agenda item, and thus the ultimate focus of attention.

If not metals, then what next? Richards posed the question, and at first there was silence.

Then Gordon Chan spoke. "How about glass?" he asked. "That is another material which our ancestors wrested from the earth with the aid of fiery furnaces, and I suggest that we will be needing some of it in the very near future."

Surprisingly, this sensible-sounding suggestion met with resistance. The group had seemingly had its fill of agreement and consensus and was ready for a fight. Put thirty strong-willed individuals together in prolonged, intense discussions and the time comes when they need to blow off some steam. Among several members of the subcommittee there was a growing undercurrent of uncertainty. Aren't we being cavalier in simply checking off these technologies one after the other? they wondered. Could we really—all at once—grow food, tend livestock, harvest fish from the ocean and timber from the forests, make bricks and other clay products and cement, and plan for the use of metals; in other words, make progress in all conceivable directions simultaneously? Didn't something have to be postponed, and wasn't glassmaking a likely place to begin?

Simon Kambule, the leader from the Zulu community who had greeted Gustafsson's expedition—and had subsequently been asked to serve on the subcommittee—contributed to the chorus of misgivings: "We can get along without glass, for the present, I believe. The immediate needs of the people must be met. And, yes, we must also plan for a return to high technology. But glass does not fit into either category. Glass windows, drinking goblets, and the like are superfluous—mere luxuries. And glassmaking is not such a sophisticated technology that it cannot be readily developed further down the road. In the meantime, since we are not able to do everything at once, why waste any of our limited resources?"

This argument was favorably received by several members of the subcommittee, including Millie Fox. "I don't recall my Peace Corps people ever mentioning glass as a basic human requirement," she said.

Alf Richards shrugged and conceded: "Maybe you're right. We can do a lot of reconstruction work without a ready supply of glass. And, as Mr. Kambule has stated, we must not go off in too many different directions at once."

There were several more speeches along the same lines, and Kambule's argument seemed about to carry the day, when Dr. Chan rose to respond.

"Please, ladies and gentlemen," he said, quietly but commanding attention, "let us not be shortsighted. Although we may not need glass windows right away, or glass insulators until we get electricity, or fiber-optic cables until we near the final stages of our technical journey, we do not want to lose our touch in dealing with these crucial materials." Then, as his usual pleasant expression turned to a troubled frown, he added, "But there is another factor that is even more important and more immediate. Have you ever seen a science laboratory without glassware? Surely, before we're done with our preliminary planning, we'll be providing for research laboratories. They are key to our recovery and future well-being. And, believe me, they will not be of much use without basic equipment, particularly apparatus made of glass."

There was a moment of stunned silence. Then Simon Kambule, with a rueful smile, withdrew his objection. The subcommittee voted to proceed with the manufacture of glass, and to allocate one hundred workers to the undertaking.

Before leaving the topic of glass, the subcommittee considered the availability of the raw materials needed to make it—silica, soda, and lime. Silica was no problem. Surely there was more sand than anyone knew what to do with. Soda, in the form of potash, they had considered the previous day in discussing the need for potassium in fertilizers. If they did not find suitable natural deposits, they could make the stuff the old-fashioned way, by burning vegetable wastes and boiling the ashes in a pot. As for lime, the third basic ingredient—needed to make glass durable—one simply burns, or calcines, limestone.

"It is worth noting," Gordon Chan added, "that lime is a basic industrial chemical with many important applications. For example,

it is used in manufacturing paper, as a flux in making steel, and—
Mr. Richards, as a builder you probably know this—it is a key
material in the manufacture of cement and mortar."

"That is very true," said Eric Steenkamp, the mining engineer
from Pretoria, "but as far as I know, limestone doesn't just emerge
from the ground in convenient containers, and we seem not to have
made any provision for acquiring it."

So, after brief discussion, the One Hundred Strategy was applied
once again. One hundred workers were allocated to quarrying this
utilitarian rock.

While speaking of quarries, Alf Richards pointed out that a supply of granite would be very useful as a building stone, as well as
for paving roads and providing aggregate material for concrete. So
yet another one hundred were assigned to this task.

"We're on a roll," Richards roared with delight, "and while we're
talking about quarrying, we might as well get into mining." With
this he turned to Peter Mavimbela, the head of the miners' union.
"What do you think, Peter?" he asked. "To get our industrial revolution underway, what we need is iron and coal, coal and iron,
preferably close together and preferably not too far out in the boon-
docks. No matter what processes we decide to use in making steel—
and, Ichiro, with your guidance we'll be talking about that in due
course—we know what the basic raw materials must be, and we
can't have them too far apart from each other. Transporting these
materials is going to be a big problem when we first get started.
It's not like the good old days when long freight trains rumbled
into Richards Bay bringing tons of coal and ore for shipment over-
seas."

"You don't need to remind me about what it pleases you to call
the good old days," Peter Mavimbela said dourly. He was a tall
man, but stooped and gaunt, with dark, dreamy eyes that belied his
practical, political approach to life and to the issue under debate. He

seemed about to launch into a discourse on mining under the apartheid government, but then thought better of it and spoke to the technical point at hand. "I think I can find you a place—or possibly two places—that will be suitable. But there are a couple of things that we ought to get straight at the outset."

Alf Richards could tell that in Mavimbela he was dealing with a rugged individual, almost belligerent, a very different sort from the diplomatic Simon Kambule. There was a sudden feeling of suspense among the group, as if a serious confrontation might be brewing.

"Okay," Alf said. "What is it that we have to get straight?"

"First," Peter replied, "understand that this is not going be an efficient operation. We—like the farmers and timber workers and everybody else—have practically no tools. And when we finally get some, I am certain that they will be of relatively poor, or primitive quality. So we cannot go digging down into the depths of the earth. We'll have to begin by getting what we can from the surface. Where this is not possible, we will cut parallel tunnels into the hills and leave large pillars of material in place as supports for the tunnel roof. That way we won't have to install timbers, which are not available in any case. So, we'll be leaving lots of material in the ground; but that will have to do for a beginning."

"What's your other concern?" Alf Richards asked.

"My men," Mavimbela said, with barely concealed emotion. "In those 'good old days,' as you call them, the miners of South Africa were obliged to travel far from their families and live in prison-like dormitories. Now, I expect that decent housing will be provided for them—and their families—within a reasonable distance from the mines."

"That's no problem, Peter," the chairman said. "Assuming that the decent housing you're referring to is the same sort of de luxe shack that we're all living in these days." Mavimbela's acknowledgment came by way of a grim smile.

Then a follow-up from Richards: "Can you round up seven hundred men, Peter?" To the rest of the group, he said, "That is a large commitment, I know. I'm suggesting the use of ten percent of our non-agricultural workforce. But in mining, we're talking about a lot of hard work, important work, vital for our future." The subcommittee, by its silence, indicated assent.

"I can manage that," Mavimbela said, after a few moments of thought. "Many of my union members were home celebrating Christmas with their families when the disaster struck. If I assure them that the new social order is to be founded on principles of social justice, I know they will give of their best."

The two men, Richards and Mavimbela, shook hands firmly to seal their understanding.

"If you want results," the union leader added, "get us a supply of half-decent tools as soon as you can, so we might start picking away at whatever we can reach. Also, get us wheels, plain wheelbarrows if that is all you have, but then rolling trams of some kind, preferably on rails, even wooden rails—for starters. And, of course, to be at all efficient, we're going to need explosives. Mining is essentially drilling holes in the rock, inserting materials that will blow up, and then letting her rip—in a controlled way, of course. We really should have steam drills, but knowing that is impossible right now, we'll go back to drilling holes the old-fashioned way, hammering steel bits with sledges. It's tough work, but we can do it. Without explosives, though, it's pick and shovel, and that is even tougher. We can do that, too, but you won't be too happy with the results."

"You know, I hadn't thought about explosives," Richards said, scratching his head.

At this point, Gordon Chan spoke up again. "It is not such a big deal, Alf. We Chinese invented black powder more than a thousand years ago. Just mix saltpeter, sulfur, and charcoal—in the right proportions, of course. I'll be happy to tell you what those proportions are, just as my ancestors told your ancestors. Then ignite the powder with a burning fuse, and poof! Better be careful, though. That powder is pretty volatile stuff. It's a lot safer to use TNT, which is a solid organic nitrogen compound, or dynamite, which is nitroglycerine mixed with ammonium nitrate. But the trouble with the safer materials is that you need safety fuses and blasting caps, and that requires another manufacturing operation. We have people with us who have the needed chemical knowledge to mix you up whatever you'd like, and others who can make you the fuses and caps. But I'm not sure that this is the first project on which you want to concentrate."

"Okay," Richards said. "You heard the man, Peter. I think we're going to have to start with picks and shovels and make do with whatever you can get us that way. In the meantime, we'll put some people—let's say thirty or so—to work on explosives. I'm sure, also, that one of these days our police and military guys will be looking for ammunition. No way we can go back to the future without some booms and bangs in our suitcases."

The sun seemed to have raced across the sky, although no more speedily than the subcommittee had been dashing across the technological spectrum. But even with a substantial amount of work accomplished, Alf Richards felt that the urgency of his mission did not allow for an evening of relaxation. So, before adjourning, he asked Ichiro Nagasaka and Eric Steenkamp to meet with him after dinner. The objective would be to select a group of metallurgists and mining engineers, both Inlanders and Outlanders, who would visit the locations that Peter Mavimbela had designated as possible centers for a mining operation.

It so happened that both of these sites were among the places that had been mentioned by Pieter Kemm and Kelvin Marshall in their original briefing of the Governing Council. One was at Dundee, seventy miles northwest of Ulundi. The other was near Empangeni, just twelve miles north of Engineering Villlage. Dundee was more distant than Alf would have liked; but the coal and iron were known to be suitable. The area had been badly burned by the fires, but this would not now impede a mining operation. The Empangeni site was centrally located, and provided ample coal. But the iron would have to be extracted from laterite, a weathered rock, rich in iron oxide, but far from what one would call a high-grade ore. It would tax the professional skills of the engineering experts. In the end, both sites were approved, and served very well, the engineers being equal to the technical challenge.

When, the next day, they gathered for their third session, the members of the Joint Planning Subcommittee were in high spirits. Several of them had brought items that began to give the meeting pavilion a lived-in quality—odd-looking chairs; maps and charts; and even a few whimsical decorations, most notably a Boston Red Sox cap atop a driftwood giraffe.

"I think we are actually making progress," said Lucas Moloko, a government official from Ulundi who, from the outset, had been openly skeptical of the group's ambitious approach. He had been rather quiet during the first meetings, but now felt a bit looser and more confident that they were moving in the right direction.

"Can do, Lucas," responded Commodore Harry Presley of the U.S. Navy Seabees, whose specialty was the planning and construction of military bases. "That's our motto."

Yet, as deliberations continued, the mood began to darken. Repeatedly, good ideas seemed to be foiled by the problems inherent in transportation. It was increasingly clear that even the best laid plans—for making bricks, quarrying stone, mining coal, or whatever activity—would be frustrated unless the new society had the capacity for moving large quantities of material from one place to another. In this crucial sphere of activity, prospects looked bleak.

The transmission of information, surprisingly, was not as serious a problem as some had feared it might be. In the first few weeks, the Pony Express between Ulundi and Engineering Village was working as well as could be expected. Messengers to other locations—some on horseback, some on foot—were dispatched on the basis of spontaneous decisions by various ad hoc groups. It wasn't exactly the Internet, but it was adequate to the needs of the moment. The subcommittee formalized this success by commissioning a Courier Corps made up of a hundred persons.

Heavy cargo, however, presented a more intractable problem. Horseback riders and youthful marathoners—no matter how willing and fleet of foot—could not ship tons of freight across many miles of rugged countryside.

Where, historically, the Industrial Revolution began and flourished—especially in Britain, France, and the United States—water transport had been an essential element of progress. Rivers, supplemented by man-made canals, were the lifeblood of industrial development. In KwaZulu Natal, although there were many wonderful resources, a network of navigable waters was not among them. So land transport it must be, entailing enormous obstacles. But recognition of this fact prompted Commodore Presley to quote the second part of the Seabee motto.

"The difficult we do immediately," he said with a hearty chuckle; "the impossible takes a little longer." This braggadocio seemed to revive flagging spirits. As several subcommittee members noted, they were, after all, in the land of the Boers, whose forebears had carried out the Great Trek in ox-drawn wagons. Americans, also, could look to a tradition of pioneers who traveled long distances in their heavily laden prairie schooners.

"We know a lot more about building good roads and maintaining them than did those folks in early days," Alf Richards reflected. "If they had had decent roads, they wouldn't have bothered building all those canals."

But roads were not the main problem. Nor were oxen, of whom an adequate number had survived. The desperate need was for vehicles—wagons, trams, carriages—anything with wheels that could carry sizable loads. Very few such conveyances had survived the Event.

On an emergency basis, critical materials were being conveyed on patched-together carts, makeshift sleds, the backs of animals, and even on the backs, shoulders, and heads of human bearers. The Planning Subcommittee decided to endorse this spontaneous arrangement, as they had with the couriers, by designating one hundred individuals as transporters of material. They were to be known officially as the Teamsters. The subcommittee anticipated that, as more wheeled vehicles became available, these workers would indeed become drivers, transporting freight to every corner of a growing realm.

"I can hardly wait for the next Jimmy Hoffa to rise up among us," Richards commented in a momentary lapse into bitter humor.

Alf then directed the discussion into a historical mode. This was strange territory for the self-confident hardhat, who for the moment sounded positively wistful. "Dammit. We need a lot of wagons, and I suggest we allocate one hundred workers—no, make that two hundred—to produce them. But where in the world are we going to find wagon builders?"

More generally, the problem was: how were the skills of yesteryear to be recaptured?

For example: candles. As the batteries expired, making lanterns and flashlights useless, the humble candle suddenly became an object of great importance. One of the first requests made by Captain Nordstrom to the Ulundi Indaba was to send a supply of tallow—rendered animal fat, a material used at least five thousand years ago in making this precious light-giving device. The three women in Engineering Village who knew exactly how to go about dipping candles, and also making them in molds, were among the earliest community heroes.

In the quest for pioneer skills, help came providentially from three unexpected sources. First, there were a number of proficient hobbyists among both Inlanders and Outlanders. They provided precious expertise in glassblowing, papermaking, blacksmithing, and candlemaking.

The second valuable resource was Millie Fox and her Peace Corps experience. Millie had intended to chair a session on "Intermediate Technology" as the most desirable way to achieve progress in underdeveloped nations. In addition to useful technical literature, she had brought along several young engineers with field experience in just such conditions as those the survivors now faced. They provided an excellent counterbalance to the high-tech professionals who were learning the hard way what it meant to cope with Stone Age realities.

The third resource was a contingent of specialists from "living museums," including those of Sturbridge, Massachusetts; Shelburne, Vermont; Old Salem, North Carolina; and Williamsburg, Virginia. In those institutions the old trades had been kept alive by actual practice. Wilson Hardy, Jr., had urged his father to incorporate the history of technology into his plans for the seminar; the elder Hardy had accomplished this by inviting museum people in addition to several academic historians. And so it happened that from the *Queen of Africa* community there were several talented blacksmiths, millers, printers, and weavers, along with excellent plans and specifications for forges, waterwheels, mills, printing presses, and various workshops of eighteenth-century America.

Equally precious was the collection of prints and photographs brought along by another museum invitee, Foster Tillinghast of the National Museum of the Smithsonian Institution. Pumps, plows, threshers, reapers, spinning wheels, forges, steam engines, sawmills, power looms, cotton gins, clockworks, lathes, rifles, sewing machines, telegraphs . . . the whole cavalcade of American technology laid out to be seen, admired—and copied if so desired. There were also some historical museums in KwaZulu Natal that contained valuable information on the early technology of the native Africans, as well as the pioneer Boers.

This treasure trove was so remarkably comprehensive that it even evoked a backlash of mild hostility.

"I hope that we're not planning merely to repeat history," said Tom Swift, one of Hardy Junior's Focus Group. He looked askance at the pictures and records that so excited the young historian.

"Do better if you can, Tom," Wil Hardy said. "More power to you. But I'm mighty happy that we have the genius of the past to fall back on." He promptly dubbed the museum professionals and the workers skilled in the pioneer crafts the "Museum Mavens."

Once the Planning Subcommittee got to talking about these technologies of earlier times, several members began to voice new misgivings.

"You know," Harish Kahar said, "we've been arbitrarily assigning hundreds of workers to one task or another, assuming that centralized factories are the way to go. But wouldn't some of this work be better performed in a cottage industry setting?"

Millie Fox also challenged the group to think seriously about technological work that could be accomplished in the home, or the tribal compound. "Remember," she said, "in Colonial America, before the rise of factories, the farmer-artisan played a prominent role. Many farm families made their own tools, furniture, clothing, and processed foods. Beyond this, some functioned as part-time craftsmen, providing trade goods or services for the market. Hats, shoes, and pottery, for example, were products of an active hearthside production. Many country gristmills were run by farmers, operated only when customers brought in grain to be ground. The same was true of sawmills. At least this is how it was before the idea of the centrally located factory took hold."

"Starting in Pawtucket, Rhode Island, in 1793." Wilson Hardy, Jr., the enthusiastic historian, could not restrain himself.

Such debates lasted well into the evenings. Decisions sometimes entailed a choice between all-out industrial development and cottage industry manufacture, and sometimes a mix of the two. The "small is beautiful" approach won out with textiles—which young Hardy found ironic, since in the Industrial Revolution that was one of the first technologies to which the factory system was applied.

Little by little, the Planning Subcommittee covered the main areas of technological activity, allocating human and physical resources to each. Several times it was suggested that the use of metals be considered; but on each occasion Ichiro Nagasaka demurred, recommending that this topic—which he considered to be the capstone of the entire enterprise—be left until last.

After the sixth day of meetings there was some talk about taking a break, a Sabbath of sorts, but Alf Richards ruled against it. "God might have rested on the seventh day," he said, "but He saw everything that He had made and beheld that it was good. The Joint Planning Subcommittee can hardly make such a claim."

For example, health care was one key field that had not yet been addressed. Medical groups had been working since the very first days of crisis, but it was important that the subcommittee formally endorse these activities and provide necessary support. The health care community consisted of doctors and other medical professionals, both Inlanders and Outlanders, numbering one hundred twenty. They had established a hospital center in Ulundi, and clinics in several other small population centers, as well as Engineering Village. The assembled pool of talent was impressive by any standard; but the shortage of equipment and drugs was worrisome.

In the first days after the Event, nobody gave much thought to the question of pharmaceuticals. There were some medical supplies that had been salvaged from the ship and from a Ulundi hospital as well. And since, in recent years, most drugs had been prepared by chemical synthesis, and since the Engineering Village community included some of the world's greatest chemical engineers, as well as several professional chemists and even a couple of pharmaceutical scientists, it seemed that the situation could be dealt with satisfactorily. But when the experts reported that it would probably take at least three years to establish pharmaceutical factories, and that the available supply of drugs would not last nearly that long, the Joint Planning Subcommittee suddenly had an emergency on its hands. As a first measure, the medical people agreed to tighten their controls even more than they already had, only dispensing medication in the most critical situations. At the same time, a program was put into effect to produce, on an urgent basis, three items that were considered essential: an antiseptic, an antibiotic, and an anesthetic.

The antiseptic problem was readily solved with ethyl alcohol—ethanol, or grain alcohol, as it is generally called. While making fuel, the chemical engineers could at the same time be making a germicide. The process is simple: boil corn in water, and after adding sprouted barley for malt, let the solution ferment. Concentration of alcohol in the liquid can be increased by distillation.

For an antibiotic, the most quickly attainable product was the first and most famous: penicillin. The chemists—like Alexander Fleming so many years ago—cultivated some awful-looking stuff that they call mold, and from this they proposed to secure the precious curative.

As for anesthetic, it turned out that there was throughout the Ulundi Circle a bumper crop of coca leaves, marijuana, and even opium poppies, to answer this need. There were ample amounts of cocaine from the coca, hashish from the marijuana, heroin and morphine from the poppies, plus every other conceivable derivative to be gleaned from these magical plants. The requirements of the doctors were met, and needless to say, many other purposes were served as well.

The topic of drug use was addressed once at a meeting of the Coordinating Committee and the decision was to do nothing—nothing, that is, other than for the medical people and social workers to provide counseling when and where it seemed warranted. The almost unanimous view was that, while the community was struggling to survive, it could not afford to expend energy on policing behavior that was not manifestly harmful to the group. In fact, some of the leaders expressed sympathy for those individuals who, totally distraught over losses suffered in the Event, found solace in the mood-altering substances. There was also a side benefit of not having to worry about a crime problem based upon a narcotics trade.

For a general anesthetic, the doctors asked their pharmaceutical colleagues if they could manage to prepare some nitrous oxide, the famous laughing gas once beloved by dentists, but also used in past years by medical surgeons. Following the technique developed by Humphry Davy in the late eighteenth century, the chemists proposed to obtain the gas by combining zinc with dilute nitric acid, which in turn could be derived from saltpeter.

The native healers were also kept busy; and a number of individuals—blacks and whites—harvested curatives, and supposed curatives, from a variety of indigenous plants.

On the seventh day, the Planning Subcommittee turned its attention to Research and Development. The future: How were survivors, having barely escaped with their lives, to think about a high-technology future? In the effort to rebuild a suitable habitat, to bring order out of chaos, and to establish a basic industrial society, long-term planning could not be the center of attention. But—another one of those ambiguities with which they had to live—neither could it be forgotten. The Planning Subcommittee had assumed from the beginning that, although technological development would occur in several sequential stages, planning for each of the various stages should commence immediately and proceed in parallel. Even as elemental everyday needs were being addressed—food, shelter, health care, transport, and basic manufactures—design for a second stage should be underway, and also a third.

Gordon Chan set forth the strategy in these terms: "Let us commit our second stage of recovery to the creation of a chemical industry. Most of the essential raw materials are available to us, particularly considering that we know how to synthesize just about any material we want from carbon-rich materials such as coal. Researchers, guided by the formulas and techniques painstakingly developed through the past century, will embark on such syntheses, beginning with those chemicals deemed most important for our evolving society. Prioritizing will be a difficult but essential part of the process. Then chemical engineers will develop pilot plants to test manufacturing methods, and this will lead eventually to full-scale production plants."

Chan held up his hands as if to forestall the wave of protest he knew was building.

"Simultaneously—let me say it quickly, before I anger my mechanical and electrical colleagues—there must be development of sources of power: steam engines, internal combustion engines, and electric generators. Also, of course, reestablishment of instant communications; perhaps we will skip the telephone and go directly to radio. After that comes what I consider the third stage, featuring the products of the electronic revolution—with television and the computer in the spotlight."

There was a sudden restlessness among the group, evidence both

of excitement over high-tech prospects and uneasiness about looking too far ahead when present needs were so great.

"There will inevitably be frustration," Chan continued, "particularly as the electronics people wait for power, materials, and manufacturing capacity. I would expect, in general, that we'll have to
repeat most of the industrial revolutions through which our forebears passed once before, only greatly accelerated because our
knowledge base is so far advanced; but slowed down in some areas
because of our limited material and human resources. This is what
I expect. But we should also expect the unexpected. We should allow
for—in fact, encourage—technological advances that will permit us
to 'jump over' the established ways of doing things. I don't know
what these advances might be. But I would be surprised if they
didn't come along sooner rather than later. After all, we are engineers."

Gordon Chan had delivered his message; but he could not resist
adding a postscript.

"A fourth stage of development, almost as enigmatic as a fourth
dimension in time and space, will be the decisions on what technologies *not* to pursue. For example, in our tiny homeland, do we
need an aviation industry? Will we want to resume the exploration
of space? No, certainly not for a very, very long time. Yet, can we
bring ourselves to abandon any scientific or technological quest that
piques our interest? As I said, we are engineers."

The Planning Subcommittee, steering away from these philosophical depths, decided merely that there should be no stinting on
research and development leading toward the future. Accordingly,
they proposed that one hundred and fifty engineers and scientists,
plus fifty assistants, be assigned to plan the second and third stages
of development.

Pieter Kemm of the Richards Bay Minerals Company and Kelvin
Marshall of Sasol Limited, both of whom had previously reported

to the Governing Council, were to round up any surviving members of their companies and establish two centers of engineering excellence based upon their past achievements. Engineers from the *Queen of Africa* seminar were to organize themselves into working research groups based upon their special disciplines. These groups were to recommend specific research projects and gain endorsement, first, from the appropriate engineering society, and second, from the Joint Planning Subcommittee. Final approval and settlement of disputes was to rest with Wilson Hardy, as president of the umbrella society. As a diplomat of ever-increasing tact, Hardy was expected to pull off this feat with a minimum of commotion.

The subcommittee further resolved that all engineers assigned to current activities—construction, mining, brickmaking, etc.—would be expected to make themselves available to the R and D community for technical consultation where needed. And all were expected to do their share of teaching as well. It would be tricky maintaining the delicate balance between present needs and future goals. But to engineers who had been involved in research and development, and who had seen one generation of technology yield to another so rapidly in recent years, this atmosphere of tension, trade-offs, and optimizing choices would be familiar.

Finally, the subcommittee adopted a resolution proclaiming that the laboratories were to receive "every consideration" in the rationing of services and supplies. Tom Swift, who was named as one of the five directors of this enterprise, explained to Wil Hardy that this meant the R and D group would have to fight like tigers to get anything at all.

"That's okay," he said softly to his friend, with a wicked grin. "That's what we're used to."

FROM THE JOURNAL OF WILSON HARDY, JR.

What a week that was! As the Joint Planning Subcommittee reached the afternoon of its seventh working day, Alf asked for a tally of the workforce allocations made to date. I ran the totals, and they showed that of the estimated 14,000 able-bodied workers, 12,900 had been assigned to specific tasks, leaving a balance of 1100.

At this point, Ichiro Nagasaka, whom I had come to like a lot, rose to address the meeting: "I've been thinking" he said, "and I conclude that we ought to have an iron and steel industry of at least a thousand individuals." He bowed politely toward Alf, but smiled broadly at the same time. "It appears from the figures just reported that this will be possible."

"Of course," he continued, "I am not just thinking about getting iron out of the earth and using it to make steel. The idea is also to make things—first the hand tools we need so badly, and then machines, probably steam engines. And before we can start to make useful machines, we will have to make machines to make machines. There is much to be done and not a minute to lose. Can we meet tomorrow to discuss my ideas, and perhaps to endorse them?"

"Well, let's wait just a minute, Ichiro," Alf said, holding one hand forward like a policeman directing traffic. "I know that it looks as if there might be a thousand people available for your grand scheme, and I'd certainly like to hear more about how you would plan to use them. But I think we've reached a point where we have to stop for a breath and see where we are. We've been hard at work for a week, more or less with the bit in our teeth, and I think that it's time for us to review our ideas with the Coordinating Committee that established us. They, in turn, will want to review them with the Governing Council and the Ulundi Indaba. I'd also like to let all of our Engineering Village people see what we've been up to. And I'm sure that our Ulundi friends will want to bring some of their folk into the loop as well."

I could see that my father's faith in Alf Richards as a leader—and as a politician—had not been misplaced.

"Let's sum up what we've done," he continued, "and for this purpose assume that you have your thousand people as requested. We'll distribute a recap of our proposed labor allocations and ask for some feedback. I suggest that we allow five days for this process. In the meantime, work should proceed as if our recommendations have been approved. We can't afford to miss a day of activity, and I'm sure that such changes as are suggested will be at the margins—a few extra workers on this project, a few less on that."

Alf pretty much quelled further talk at that point, and the sub-committee gave me the assignment of preparing a summary schedule for distribution. So I recruited my Focus Group friends to help make duplicates—by hand, of course, in this post-Xerox world. Or this pre-Xerox world, as Tom Swift preferred to say.

"This is boring as hell," Herb complained as we wrote feverishly in tight script (to save paper and to meet an impossible deadline). "Is this what old-time monks and scribes felt like?"

"Only partly," Roxy put in. "They were celibate, remember." This got us to laugh and loosen up a bit, and we bent to our task with renewed energy.

That evening, I posted copies of the annotated list on the several bulletin boards that served for the dissemination of news throughout Engineering Village. At the same time, copies were sent by Pony Express to Ulundi and beyond. The list is, of course, part of the official subcommittee minutes; but since it is such a key part of the story, I reproduce it here as part of my personal record:

January 26, 2010

Preliminary Allocation of Personnel Resources—A Report of the Joint Planning Subcommittee of the Coordinating Committee—Submitted for Review

Agriculture and animal husbandry.

Number of people assigned to this activity	7,000
Fishing	50
Preservation of fish: drying and salting	25
"The Scavengers": collecting tools and scrap metal	100
Construction: shelter, water supply and sanitation; roads, shops and factories.	2000
Architects and engineers, surveyors and helpers	100
Artisans to work on the manufacture of pencils and pens	10
Lumber and wood products: harvesting, hand-hewing, and making charcoal; set up sawmills in conjunction with construction trades; provide wood pulp for the manufacture of paper and as a raw material for future chemical industry	300
Special task force for cultivation and use of bamboo	50
Manufacture of brick	200
Manufacture of clay tile products, including pipe, roof, and floor tiles, and containers for cooking and storage	100
Special task force for development of fire brick and other refractory materials for use in furnaces	25
Manufacture of cement	50
Manufacture of glass	100
Quarrying of limestone	100
Quarrying of granite	100

Mining; first priority, coal and iron	700
Explosives	30
Metallurgists, geologists, and mining engineers directing and assisting mining operations	50
Iron and steel industry: starting with blacksmiths and primitive smelting facilities, evolving into the basic agent for industrialization, including development of machine tools and first steam engines	1,000
Courier service, including Pony Express, for transmission of information	100
Transporters of materials: the Teamsters	100
Building of wagons and other vehicles	200
Professionals and workers skilled in crafts of pioneer days, acting as consultants	50
Manufacture of yarns, textiles, and clothing, done in "cottage industry" settings	200
Mechanics to build and repair spinning wheels and looms	25
Planners for textile industry of the future	25
Other cottage industry manufactures: shoes, leather and fur garments, hats, candles, and soap	50
Food service for work sites and population centers where eating in a home setting is not feasible	200
Schoolteachers	240
Full-time government officials	200
Police	100
Medical	120
Research and Development	200
Unassigned	100
Total of Estimated Able-Bodied Working Population (Approximately Half the Total Population)	14,000

"Jeezuzz, Wilson!" John Hertzler flapped his arms in exasperation as he paced back and forth in front of my father. "This Planning Subcommittee of yours has come up with the stupidest idea since the Soviet Union's last Five-Year Plan." Remember, Dr. Hertzler is the computer genius who was invited to represent the Silicon Valley and Seattle-based sponsors of our floating seminar. He was the first speaker when the Coordinating Committee, together with the Joint Planning Subcommittee, convened to hear reaction to the proposed allocation of personnel.

"If history has taught us anything at all," the tirade continued, "it's that industrial planning cannot be centralized. A bunch of big shots sitting up on Mount Olympus selecting a hundred people for this job, two hundred for that—that's a guaranteed recipe for failure. We've got to free up creative energies, provide incentives, bring out the entrepreneurial genius of our people. Get with the program, Wilson! This is the twenty-first century!"

"Just a minute, John," my father said, speaking softly, although I could tell he was irked. He had spoken to me in just that way a million times.

"I remember the Soviet Union, probably better than you do, because my firm actually worked there. I recall those construction jobs sitting idle because some crucial valve hadn't come—the factory wasn't making valves that month—or because some bureaucratic plant manager was dumb or uncaring or too well connected politically and couldn't be held accountable. You don't have to tell me about the benefits of the free market—efficiency rewarded by profit, incompetence punished by loss, and all that stuff. But you can't just wave a magic wand and say let's apply the free enterprise system here. We're in crisis mode. We're trying to survive and rebuild in the wilderness. Also, we don't have money and we don't have markets. Our only practical choice is to organize from the top." And then, quickly, before Hertzler could respond: "Besides, there were times when the Russians used central planning to very good effect. How do you think they made their atomic bombs, except by dictating exactly who should have what priority in ordering materials and who should work where—a hundred people for this job, two hundred for that?"

Then it was General Allen White speaking, again before Hertzler could get a word in. "It's not just the Russians, Will. On behalf of the U.S. Army Corps of Engineers, let me say a word in favor of centralized planning. Some whiz kid in a garage can create a computer, but that's not how you establish a system of interstate highways. We couldn't have built all of America the way you built Silicon Valley."

Good for you guys, I thought to myself. It's ridiculous to sit here on a barren beach and pontificate about laissez-faire capitalism. The history of technology shows us how important government planning is in the scheme of things—the Egyptians with their irrigation works, the Romans with their roads and aqueducts, the French with their bridges and canals. Sure, individual initiative is important; but you can't start building a civilization—pretty much from scratch—without state bureaucrats.

It may be true that the Industrial Revolution in Britain was driven by entrepreneurs—Mr. Watt with his steam engine, for example, and a number of families that developed ever better ways of making iron. But at the same time, the crown played a vital role, especially in armories and shipyards, where government employees made important technical advances. You can't even argue that computers are a product of pure capitalism. When, during the 1960s, crucial work was done interfacing computers with humans, who do you think financed the work at the Stanford Research Institute? The Department of Defense, of course. And everyone knows that the Internet had its origins in military communication systems adapted for educational institutions. I felt like making a speech myself, but stifled the impulse.

Hertzler retreated somewhat from his extreme position, but not completely. "In my experience, administrators and bureaucrats are the problem and inevitably direct us away from the solution that will satisfy anybody but themselves. They become tyrants . . ."

My father held up his hand and continued in a conciliatory tone, partly to keep the peace and partly because he recognized the validity of Hertzler's concerns. "You certainly have a point, John," he said, "and I'll tell you what we're going to do. In every enterprise we establish, each individual will be encouraged to use his or her initiative. We can't have anarchy; but we can have a 'suggestion box' philosophy, trying to take advantage of each worker's resourcefulness and each middle manager's ingenuity. For incentive, I think that mere recognition will serve us well. We'll try praise and possibly different types of awards—'the idea of the month' sort of thing. Money, as I said, we simply don't have. We'll sit down with you and think about how to bring tangible compensation into play as soon as possible. But we can't let this divert us while we're trying to get started."

"Okay, okay," Hertzler growled. "But what are you going to do about modifying those allocations of personnel? You know, for sure, that you're going to have too many miners and too few brickmakers, or vice versa. The scheme is so damned arbitrary."

I could see that Alf Richards, who had so far controlled his irritation by pouring himself two cups of coffee, was about ready to explode. But my father held him off with a wave and a wink, and continued.

"Look, we've given that a lot of thought, John, and I've discussed the problem at length with Alf here and some of his associates on the Planning Subcommittee. I hope you'll approve of what we're thinking. We're going to look at the situation as a problem in systems engineering."

"Well, I don't know," said Hertzler, quieter now, and thoughtful. "Sometimes I think that systems stuff is a lot of gobbledygook."

"It certainly isn't my specialty," my father said, "but Harry Robbins, who is one of the top people in the field, is a member of the subcommittee, and he has assured Alf and me that the approach will be very helpful."

It's been almost a year since this conversation took place, and during that time I've had ample opportunity to see Robbins and his colleagues at work, applying the principles of systems engineering to the problems of resource allocation within the Ulundi Circle. I can't say that I understand everything they're up to, by a long shot. And sometimes I think that there isn't that much to understand; that, in spite of their abstruse lingo, they're just using old-fashioned common sense.

What we start with is a large and complex system. And within this, a change in one part, or subsystem, is likely to affect many other subsystems. The goal, to quote Dr. Robbins, is "to achieve an optimum balance of all system elements." Well, sure. It's like when you're designing an airplane and you want to make the fuselage larger to carry more payload, you have to reconsider the engines, the fuel tanks, the landing gear, and so forth. Then each of these changes affects the aerodynamic characteristics of the craft, and you have to adjust each part again and again seeking an optimum overall design. In the good old days—pre-Event, that is—you could put all of these variables into a computer program and see the effect of each contemplated change by pushing a button. In our particular and peculiar case, not only don't we have operative computers, but I dare say that our variables are more challenging than any single industrial problem, even designing a jet plane.

Since we have a limited number of able-bodied workers, adding workers to one activity means subtracting them from another. So, an essential part of the Planning Subcommittee's work is to adjust the worker allocations. In order to make such decisions, the evaluator must be given frequent reports from the leaders of each enterprise, setting forth needs, accomplishments, and projections for the future.

But allocation of personnel is only one aspect of the problem. The webs of interrelationship are endlessly complex. For example, iron tools are needed for farming, mining, lumbering, and construction; iron nails are needed for buildings and other wooden products; iron axles and wheel rims are needed for wagons. So, given limited capacity, how many of each product should the blacksmiths make? The smiths need smelted iron, tools, and fuel for fires; the smelters need ore and charcoal or coal; these materials must be transported, which requires wagons and decent roads—and so forth, in a bewildering interplay of causes and effects. It is the essence of systems engineering to bring order out of such apparent chaos.

Kind of takes my breath away . . .

A key tool in this discipline is the flow chart, a graphic depiction of the overall system, in which geometric figures—circles, squares, triangles, etc.—are drawn to represent various subsystems and arrows represent their interactions. Such charts—and I've seen more than my share during the past year—help point out the interrelationships of processes within the main system. If a sawmill is one of our subsystems, then it's important that the millpond (built by the construction organization) be ready before the completion of the waterwheel (made by carpenters) and the metal saw (coming from the blacksmith shop). All must be in place before the lumber (gathered by the logging crews) comes to be cut into boards and beams. Transport must be available when it's time to move the materials.

Naturally, there are competing objectives, and these must be compared in alternative strategies. If we need our metals most importantly for making hand tools for agriculture and mining—thus

184 samuel c. florman

improving our food yield for the immediate future and our stockpile of metal ores for future benefit—then the blades for our sawmills will have to wait, thus delaying our supply of trimmed lumber. And if we don't use our metals for axles and wheel rims, the wagons we make now won't last as long or operate as effectively as they otherwise might. Since everything depends upon nearly everything else, the arrows of influence make for a complex pattern of lines, loops, and arrows. Scenario after scenario is tried, and likely outcomes projected.

And what, exactly, are our standards for success? We want "industrialization," but to what end? Pleasant homes and furniture and clothing as soon as possible? Or sacrifice near-term comfort for an earlier development of infrastructure? How urgently, and at what cost, do we want to develop electricity, followed by radio, TV, and a return to the computer age? In these decisions, community preferences have to be considered. Since there is no traditional marketplace and no established political forum, the public will must be sensed—mostly by direct discussion and enlightened inference.

To analyze likely outcomes of alternate scenarios, the systems engineers like to apply mathematical models. System interactions can be expressed as mathematical equations. A basic optimization problem can be analyzed using differential calculus. Probability theory can be used, along with statistical analysis, decision theory, and a lot of other advanced methodologies. Plus computer simulation. But—why do I keep forgetting?—without the computers that we don't have, the analytical process is severely limited. Also, as we look at the world from the point of view of the average survivor, pure mathematics sort of loses its luster.

Some of the most intellectually brilliant of our engineers have shown reluctance, in making broad plans for the future, to rely upon theoretical analyses. There is a pragmatic, seat-of-the-pants side of engineering that endures. Our days are filled with never-ending debates about how best to proceed.

Conceptually, however, systems engineering gives us what is needed: continuous, critical evaluation of what is happening in each subsystem of our enterprise, and awareness of the effect that each decision has on the system as a whole. Applied rigorously by the Planning Subcommittee, guided by a few diligent systems specialists, we've had pretty good results over the past year. And pretty good results are all we dare hope for. As my father likes to say, "Let's not paralyze ourselves looking for perfection. We've got to get a product out the door."

───────────

The central planning issue had barely been put to rest when a new challenge was voiced, and from an unexpected source: Captain Nordstrom.

"I cannot follow more than a fraction of what you guys are up to," said the good captain, scratching his head to emphasize his perplexity, "but I don't think you realize what a small community we're talking about. There are less than twenty-eight thousand people left on the face of the earth—that we know about—and you're planning to rebuild an industrial infrastructure. Let me remind you that the *Queen of Africa*, a ship of modest size, carried a crew of one thousand. You need a hell of a lot of people to run a high-tech world."

"Give us a break, Johan," my father replied impatiently. That's the only time I ever heard Dad call the captain by his first name. He always called him by his formal title, as did everybody else. But now he was showing annoyance in spite of himself. "You don't need all those waiters and dancing girls to run a ship."

"Yes, yes," Nordstrom acknowledged. "I'm just trying to make a point, which is that twenty-eight thousand is a small number when you're talking about modern technology. You can fit that many spectators into an indoor arena to watch a basketball game. That's simply not enough people to establish an advanced civilization. I'd bet that the world you're dreaming about would need a population of at least a million."

Suddenly I heard my friend Herb, who was present in his capacity as alternate recording secretary, whispering into my ear: "He's crazy. You couldn't squeeze twenty-eight thousand people into Madison Square Garden if you tried. For a Knicks game, not even twenty thousand. The exact figure—which is engraved in my heart—is 19,763. Oh, the poor Knicks! Never to be seen again!"

Oh, the bizarre thought processes of my eccentric friend from New York City! I hushed Herb impatiently. The captain's imperfect information about basketball arenas did not alter the fact that the question he raised was important, in fact, crucial, and had not yet been adequately addressed, at least in my humble opinion.

Actually, my opinion in this case was not at all humble, since I had recently given the matter a lot of thought. The history of technology cannot be isolated from considerations of population. I had studied this subject in school, and had done some fact-finding since the Planning Subcommittee started to do its work. In the many hours I had spent in meetings of the various leadership groups, I had been suitably quiet for a young whippersnapper. But at this point there was something I was determined to say.

I raised my hand urgently, persuading my father to give me the floor. I knew that the engineers in the group liked to think in terms of numbers, so I figured that by talking about population growth, I could get their attention and keep it for at least a little while.

"Before the Event," I began, "the world population had been growing at the rate of 2.1 percent annually, which means that it was on a course of doubling every thirty-three years. In the American colonies of the eighteenth century, the population grew at the rate of approximately 2.5 percent annually, exclusive of immigration, a doubling rate of twenty-eight years. The colonial governor of Connecticut proudly attributed this increase to 'an industrious, temperate life, and early marriage,' as well as 'the Divine Benediction.' When the HMS *Bounty* mutineers, along with their Tahitian wives, colonized Pitcairn Island—a virgin land—their long-term rate of increase was 3.4 percent. Perhaps the most interesting figure, closer to our own time and place, was Kenya during the 1980s; there the natural increase in the population approximated 4.1 percent. This reflected not only a robust birth rate but also the effects of public health advances in extending life expectancy."

Out of the corner of my eye I saw my father looking at his watch, so I picked up the pace of my presentation.

"A 4.1 percent annual increase yields a doubling period of eighteen years. A similar increase was experienced in Iran during the years after the 1979 revolution, when clerics called on Iranian women to breed an Islamic generation. Also certain Mormon groups in Utah, practicing polygamy, achieved a growth rate of 10 percent, with a doubling period of seven years!

"But setting aside the extremes on either end, I think there is no reason we cannot expect to duplicate the experience of Kenya and Iran in the 1980s. After all, our population is relatively young and generally healthy. In South Africa, before the Event, almost half the population was under twenty-one years of age. After the rigors of fire and flood, I would guess that the average is even lower. The Engineering Village people are also young, on average—thanks mainly to my father's policies in arranging the seminar, along with the hiring practices of cruise ship companies. And so far, we're all amazingly healthy.

"If we lead an industrious, temperate life," I went on, trying to add a jovial touch, "and marry early, like those colonists in Connecticut—and if we enjoy the Divine Benediction—the 4.1 percent figure should be achieved." Then I sketched out the growth pattern, roughly, thus:

Projected Population

Today	27,500
In 18 years	55,000
In 36 years	110,000
In 54 years	220,000
In 72 years	440,000
In 90 years	880,000
In 108 years	1,760,000

I stopped to let them absorb these numbers, and then continued.

"If—to follow through on the captain's concern—it would take a million people to establish and maintain an industrial society, then we can expect to reach that magic number in about ninety-four years. That's a long time, to be sure; but no longer than it took our ancestors to build some of the medieval cathedrals. Even if none of us expects to live another century, we shouldn't be afraid to start on a few long-term projects of our own. Our great-grandchildren will thank us."

So far, my audience was as attentive as I could have hoped. But I hadn't yet gotten to my main point, which was that we shouldn't underestimate what can be achieved by our present population, right now and in the near-term future.

"Remember," I continued, "at the time of the American Revolution, Boston contained no more than twenty thousand people and New York City between twenty-five and thirty thousand. The states of Rhode Island and New Jersey each had populations of only sixty thousand persons, while mighty New York and industrious Connecticut were barely at the two hundred thousand level. If we then consider what was achieved in the years immediately following the Revolution—Fulton's steamboat in 1807; dozens of textile mills along New England's rivers by the 1820s; the Baltimore & Ohio

Railroad chartered in 1827—well, we should be bursting with optimism.

"Also, we tend to forget that the early American factories turned out substantial quantities of manufactured goods with surprisingly small numbers of workers. The blast furnaces of prerevolutionary days were run by about a dozen men. The average cotton factory employed thirty-five people, a paper mill fifteen, a flour mill only three. In 1807, a sizable shop in the Pennsylvania countryside manufactured steam engines and a variety of mechanical devices for many different industries, while employing on average no more than thirty-five workmen."

I was now ready for the *pièce de résistance*.

"In the mid-1800s, the Norris Locomotive Works of Philadelphia built locomotives, each of which contained some five thousand separate parts, each part designed, then cast or forged or pressed on site"—now it was Dr. Wilson Hardy, Sr., my dear old dad, who was glaring at me, so I hastily summarized—"sixty-four of these monsters were manufactured in a year with a workforce of only six hundred. Imagine: sixty-four locomotives built from scratch in a year by six hundred men!"

"Thanks, Wil," my father said firmly, but with a slight smile to indicate that he was pleased I had done my homework and learned so much interesting history. Yet I could tell that I had said more than enough to make my point.

Captain Nordstrom most kindly wrapped up my remarks with a concession: "I guess that young Wilson here—a chip off the old block—has mustered enough facts to shoot me out of the water. So, if we need not be discouraged by the size of our population, let us go on to other matters."

Later that night, I told Sarah about my brave entry into the great debate and described what I considered my creditable showing. She grew pensive.

Finally, very quietly, she said, "If your predictions about population growth are going to prove accurate, we will have to do our
share, won't we?"

My response, half in yearning and half in panic, was, "Of course,
but shouldn't we see the general situation organized a little better
before we rush ahead with our own plans?"

Sarah had the final word on the subject: "Balzac said it was easier
to be a lover than a husband, and I guess he was right."

I assumed she was smiling, but in the darkness it was impossible
to tell.

9

On the second day set aside for feedback sessions, the electrical engineers took a turn at venting their displeasure. "Uh-oh," Herb Green quipped under his breath to Wil Hardy, "it's the 'Charge of the Electric Light Brigade.' "

The leader of the onslaught was Donald Ruffin, president of the Institute of Electrical and Electronics Engineers. He was the inscrutable fiber-optics specialist who had said he didn't know what to expect in Africa other than a bunch of angry elephants. On this occasion, he skipped the sarcasm and got right to the point.

"What we want to know, Wilson," he said, poking a finger at Dr. Hardy, "is how you civil engineers have managed to take over this operation. Yesterday, my good friend John Hertzler raised some valid questions about centralized planning; but he didn't get to the problem that our group thinks is most serious. You, along with your sidekick Alf Richards, want to keep us busy with bricks and concrete and then slowly, deliberately, reenact the Industrial Revolution."

Ruffin pulled a piece of paper from his shirt pocket, referred to some scribbled notes, and continued in stentorian voice: "I haven't heard a blessed word about solar energy, wind turbines, or atomic power, not to mention nuclear fusion. You're going to busy us with digging in coal mines when we should be thinking about new solutions for a new age. Why aren't you planning to make photovoltaic cells, which could be used to recharge our batteries and get our computers up and running? And how about superconductivity? You're proposing to bring copper from hundreds of miles away without considering the marvelous work that's been done on getting more electricity to flow through special cables made of various new materials."

"Please, Donald," responded Dr. Hardy, who seemed to grow more resolutely calm with each new tempest, "to make photovoltaic cells, first we need metals and carefully prepared semiconductor materials. And, in the last superconductive line I saw, the cable had to be cooled to minus 320 degrees Fahrenheit by running liquid nitrogen alongside it. Is that what you want us to do? We're trying to crawl in order to walk, while you're asking that we start out by flying. We're saying that the people have no bread, and you're suggesting that they can eat cake."

Hardy hesitated, as if uncertain about how to phrase his next thought. Then he continued: "And, Donald, let's not begin to pit electrical engineers against civils or any other discipline. That's not what we're about here."

"I'm not just talking about electricity," Ruffin grumbled. "What are you doing about biotechnology? Not a damned thing. And robotics? And how about materials science? We can make almost any magical stuff you can imagine just by mixing some complicated molecules together—polymers, industrial ceramics, fiber composites, semiconductors, specialty metals . . . We're capable of miracles, and you're sitting down to play with iron. We're not a primitive tribe here. Damn it, Wilson, we've got some brilliant men and women aboard, and we ought to let them loose—not try to relive history. I'm surprised you haven't appointed a committee to reinvent the wheel."

At this, a tall, determined-looking woman stepped forward. Elsa Bryson was head of the Materials Science Department at Ohio State

University, and as she straightened her black-rimmed glasses, she could hardly conceal her disdain for the last speaker's presentation.

"Dr. Ruffin," she began, "nobody here could possibly be more anxious to work with new substances than those of us whose field is materials science. But let's just reason together for a moment. How are we going to mix these wondrous materials, work with them, store them, heat them, mold them, compress them, extrude them—do anything with them—unless we have basic implements and containers? And the basic implements and containers we need—we crave!—are mostly made out of steel and glass. So please; let these folks get on with the work that needs to be done. There's plenty of thinking and planning we can do as we wait for our laboratories to take shape, and I'm sure that goes for you and your electronics colleagues as well."

"Besides," and here Tom Swift spoke up, "let's not forget that two hundred people have been assigned to an R and D operation. So it's not as if the future is being ignored. I'm one of the directors of the enterprise, Donald, and I promise you that we'll be agitating on behalf of innovation. If you can figure out how to make electricity by sticking bamboo into sand and then transmitting the current through grapevines, we'll help you work out the details starting tomorrow. And by the way, if we do reinvent the wheel, it will be the best damned wheel that the world has ever seen."

Wilson Hardy, Sr., had one more volley to discharge. "When we sailed from New York," he said sternly, "we might have been in what some people liked to call the post-industrial age, the era of wireless communications and the Internet. But, damn it, Donald, we're not there anymore—if we ever were to the extent that was advertised. Anyhow, before you guys can return to making the world go round with fiber optics and computers, we're going to have to forge a lot of steel and pour a lot of concrete." In spite of his protestations about harmony between the engineering specialties, it was apparent that this rugged civil engineer enjoyed telling his high-tech colleague a thing or two about priorities.

In due course, the "Charge of the Electric Light Brigade" flickered away into mumbles and grudging concurrence.

It soon became clear that, when all was said and done, the recommendations of the Joint Planning Subcommittee were going to prevail relatively unscathed. Nevertheless, everyone agreed that the five-day hearing period should be maintained. It was important that time be allowed so that Inlanders with a distance to travel would be able to have their say. Also, there were numerous individuals who, even if they approved the plan in general, wanted to be heard, and required time to get their thoughts together.

On the morning of the third day, for example, a group of academics made a presentation on behalf of "pure science" as opposed to engineering and technological development. This was a subject that the planners had not considered in any depth. Although many of the engineers knew a lot about science, the group contained only a few honest-to-goodness scientists—physicists, chemists, biologists, astronomers, and the like. There were several such professionals among the Inlanders and a number among the spouses who had traveled on the *Queen of Africa*. In total, however, they numbered merely a handful.

Tom Swift, speaking on behalf of the R and D directors, gave assurances that the scientists would be provided with all possible resources and cooperation. "Yet, obviously, it will be a very long time before we get around to building cyclotrons and radio telescopes." What he did not say, but thought, was: who knows when, if ever, we will recover the scientific knowledge—and genius—that was eradicated in the Event?

This rather melancholy interlude was followed by the boisterous entry of the self-anointed environmentalists. Banging on tin pans and carrying hand-painted signs, the group captured the attention they desired as they walked into the open meeting. Herb Green and Roxanne Ford stood in the front ranks, waving jauntily at the other members of the Focus Group in the audience. In large letters their placards bore a single word: WARNING.

"Ladies and gentlemen!" Alf Richards shouted above the din. "We hear your message, and agree with you that it is important that environmental considerations be taken into account in all technological decisions."

"Too vague," Roxy replied, speaking for her fellow Greens. "We want the establishment of an environmental protection 'agency,' controlled by both specialists and citizens." The public response seemed evenly divided between bravos and jeers.

Richards used his kitchenware gavel to regain order. "The chair will grant your request," he announced, speaking above the uproar. This spur-of-the-moment decision came mostly because he did not have the time or the fortitude for a prolonged debate with these activists from a world now past ... and he agreed with them, at least in part. "You two will co-chair this 'agency,' and I'll appoint two more members when I have a chance to think about it for more than five seconds."

The eco-activists accepted this victory with quiet satisfaction. However, they made it known that from this time forward they would be maintaining an active watch on all planning activities.

On the fourth day of open meetings, a sizable number of Inlanders arrived, some of them having traveled from the far limits of the Ulundi Circle. They brought with them no significant objections to the proposals for technical development. But this did not mean that they gave the Planning Subcommittee a passing grade. One well-organized group—Alf Richards called them "the United Nations Gang"—expressed serious concerns about the planners' neglect of politics, law, and economics.

"It is all very well," said Sanyova Masekela, one of the Zulu elders, "to devote ourselves to material improvements and to say that, after working together in harmony for a year, we will begin to consider social organization. We understand that Peter Mavimbela, speaking on behalf of the miners, has agreed to this concept, and we do not disavow his commitment. But a year is a long time, and there are many among us who believe that discussions should begin as soon as it is practicable."

"I and my colleagues here agree," said Ann Meijers. Ann was an experienced government administrator from Pietermaritzburg. "We come to you on behalf of blacks and whites and Indians, thoughtful South Africans all—most of whom, even before the Event, experienced upheavals that they had hoped would be enough for one lifetime. We appreciate your commitment to restoring the physical necessities of life. And we thank the fates that sent people of such talent here to our shores. But engineering is not enough, not nearly enough. We need to start work on a constitution, a legal code, and most of all perhaps, an economic system. It seems to us that we absolutely cannot delay."

Dr. Wilson Hardy's shoulders sagged as he listened to these comments. Other members of the two committees, South Africans as well as Engineering Villagers, reacted with dejection as well, but tried not to show their disappointment. Having devoted heart and soul to strategies for survival, they were reaching the point of exhaustion.

The Joint Planning Subcommittee had been directed to concentrate on technical objectives, and this alone had proved to be a daunting task, almost beyond the group's capacity. Yet here were fellow survivors exhorting them to move immediately to a different level, to do nothing less than establish the social structure of a new civilization.

The younger Hardy's Focus Group, of course, had been thinking and debating along the same lines. They were more than ready, at any time, to talk about social goals. Nevertheless, Wil felt sorry for his father and the other members of the leadership team.

Paradoxically, this most difficult of problems proved not very difficult to resolve. The matter was handled in the inevitable—perhaps the only—way: by appointing new committees. Most important, a Constitutional Committee was established, with Meijers and Mavimbela agreeing to serve alongside a number of Outlanders, and with Hardy and Nordstrom as ex officio members.

No sooner had the United Nations Gang departed than another large delegation made its appearance. They had been waiting their turn quietly and in good order, but they strode into the meeting with a firm step that bespoke resolution.

These were "the Crusaders"—Tom Swift's irreverent but affectionate nickname for them, since his Mary was one of the leaders. The Crusaders were marching on behalf of religion. This at first seemed innocuous to those in attendance. Nobody could take exception to prayers offered and beliefs expressed, particularly in time of crisis. However, these true believers were not to be satisfied with soft words and new committees. They wanted action and commitment. They wanted physical places of worship, and to that end asked for an allocation of workers and materials from Shaka Enterprises. This request drove Alf Richards to the brink of apoplexy.

"Look here, friends," he said, with a tinge of acid in his booming voice, "I think that none of us wants to create any divisions among the people, or establish any hierarchy of bishops or imams or priests. This is dangerous and counter to every effort we have made to be fair and treat everyone equally. So, if we approve one church, one mosque, one synagogue, one prayer mat, how many other requests, large and small, can we then deny? We must also consider priorities. It is urgent that we build living quarters and shelter for our people before we even think about churches or theaters or stadiums."

At this point, Millie Fox raised her hand and was recognized. She spoke softly but with a solemnity that captured the attention of all present. "I grew up a Southern Baptist," she said, "and still hold that faith in my heart. I believe that religious practice need not be in conflict with the work undertaken for the physical survival and common good of all our people. In many parts of the developing world, where I have been personally with the Peace Corps, I have seen houses of worship serve also as clinics, schools, and meeting halls. There is no reason not to build multipurpose public structures that will serve the entire community and different religious groups as well."

This idea generated applause from the audience. Alf Richards, struggling to shed his curmudgeon's attitude, pledged support for the concept. No one could know for certain how Millie Fox's proposal might work in practice—a Catholic church cum Buddhist shrine cum Muslim mosque cum synagogue cum classroom? But all agreed it was worth a try. And as the fourth day of the Coordinating Committee's open meetings ended with a multifaith love-fest, there was a widely shared feeling of progress and goodwill.

Wil Hardy awoke on the fifth and final day of the open sessions and found Sarah already up and gone. She had told him that she would be making a presentation to the meeting; she wanted to do something on behalf of the arts, but said she had not yet decided how best to go about it. Wil looked forward with apprehension to the speech that he expected her to give—and the condescending response he expected she would receive.

But when the time came for the meeting to begin, before there was even a formal call to order, band music began to blare from behind the nearby dunes. It was "Colonel Bogie's March"—the theme music from *The Bridge Over the River Kwai*—rhythmic and lilting, trumpets and fifes carrying the tune, drums and cymbals marking the lively beat. The sound was totally incongruous on this barren beach, yet in its spirited defiance, somehow appropriate.

Suddenly, there they were, striding over the crest of the hill, twenty or so musicians from the ship's orchestra, looking for all the world like a well-drilled marching band and sounding pretty good to ears that had been starved for music, for any artistic expression. The surprise was complete and the effect was stunning.

The band, however, was just the beginning. Sarah Darby had brought together every artist she could find, and they marched in a procession designed to evoke the image of Greek muses on an ancient vase. There were probably very few witnesses to this pageant who knew the first thing about the muses of antiquity. But this did not faze Sarah, who presented them as if they had come to renew the spirits and save the souls of those who found themselves here by a cruel act of fate.

Several writers, carrying tablets, represented Calliope, muse of epic poetry; several others, carrying scrolls, took the part of Clio, muse of history; and Alf Richards's daughter Jeanette, bearing a lyre made from bamboo and grass, was the muse of lyric poetry, Erato. Two of the comedians who had entertained aboard ship came next wearing papier-mâché masks, one comic and one tragic, indicating the presence of Thalia and Melpomene, muses of comedy and tragedy, respectively. Euterpe, muse of music, was embodied not only in the band but also in talented virtuosos from Inland: a classical string quartet (who had survived, along with their instruments, miraculously unharmed) and an audaciously non-classical rock group. Somewhere in the parade, Polymnia, muse of sacred poetry, and Urania, muse of astronomy (which was considered by the Greeks to be an art), were lost in the shuffle.

The center of attention was Terpsichore, muse of dance, portrayed by the Focus Group's own Roxanne Ford. Roxy, who wore her cowgirl outfit, led the small corps of professional dancers from the *Queen of Africa* through some exciting steps, more or less based on line-dance movements and more or less in rhythm with the marching band.

But the highlight of the parade was still to come. Hidden out of sight until all the other marchers had completed their routines, there abruptly appeared a troupe of Zulu dancers in colorful traditional regalia, chanting in wild yet musical cadence, beating on drums and leaping, leaping, leaping—vertical bounds that took the breath away.

This remarkable procession surprised and pleased just about everyone gathered on the beach that morning, committee members, participants in the meeting, passersby, and children. Even Alf Richards, who had grown depressed verging on paranoic during the past few days of debate and criticism, was totally disarmed by the sight of his daughter carrying her make-believe lyre. Sarah Darby, it appeared, was politically savvy as well as artistically creative. To Wil Hardy, she was even more lovable for all that.

As for achieving her goal, it was not immediately clear how much had been accomplished by this display of talent. The importance of the arts was brought home to all who were present at the parade—and all who later heard about it—which meant just about everybody within the Ulundi Circle. Yet, after the excitement died down, the leaders of the Coordinating Committee made it clear to Sarah that physical survival still had an unchallenged priority in their thinking. For the first year at least, there would be no formal allocation of people or resources to the arts.

However, since all work assignments were to be "voluntary," subject only to social pressures rather than official sanction, the planners promised to look sympathetically at a moderate number of "extracurricular" artistic activities, assuming they did not unduly hinder the main work effort. The band and other musical groups, including the Zulu dancers, hoped to travel about the Ulundi Circle on "concert tours" to benefit morale. And Sarah did not plan to stop with music and dance. She hoped to organize drama clubs to put on evening performances, and had already recruited groups of readers to recite poetry and read novels. She proposed to the Co-ordinating Committee the formation of yet another committee—to safeguard the books that had been salvaged from the *Queen of Africa* and to supervise a lending library.

For both her authorized and unauthorized work, Sarah was destined to gain universal approval. She had taken the initiative with the first notes of "Colonel Bogie's March" and never looked back.

"How the hell did you have the nerve to pull this off?" Wil asked Sarah later in the day.

"I didn't have the nerve to sit by and do nothing," she answered. "I keep telling you, but you don't seem to listen. Man does not live by bread alone."

"Yes, yes, but what I'm saying—what our community planners are saying—is 'first things first.' We're engaged in a life and death struggle here. It seems to be our fate . . ."

Sarah kissed him lightly on the cheek, as if he were a child who would some day grow up and understand. "Ah yes, fate," she said in a husky voice. "That's it exactly. As André Malraux said: 'All art is a revolt against man's fate.' "

"Your quotable intellectuals seem to have an answer for everything."

"Nobody has all the answers, darling, least of all your Coordinating Committee and Joint-Planning-everybody's-life-from-now-on-Subcommittee. I'm not making fun, Wil, just pointing out the absurdity and fragility of it all. Leaven your technical fix with a touch of art and philosophy and you improve our chances for survival—for true survival, a survival in the full sense of the word."

10

On the faraway shore of Queen Ranavolana's island kingdom, the pirate sovereign gathered her government councilors and subcommanders in her newly erected "palace." A compound had been constructed to house Her Highness and Majesty, the voice and arm of Holy Zanahary, the instrument of the Creator and the Sacred Ancestors.

The seagoing pirates had returned from their confrontation with the English-speaking survivors unsure what the next step was going to be. Their booty, although not a great prize in any traditional sense, was welcome to comrades who were making do with the most meager rations. And they raised the group's spirits with highly embellished stories of conquest on the high seas. Fellow Malagasy survivors laughed and gasped upon hearing the tales of derring-do.

The young woman who had assumed the title and role of queen, although outwardly high-spirited, was actually in a pensive mood. She had begun to calculate the potential risks and rewards of an attack on the strangers she and her men had encountered. Depending upon who they were and how many, and whether or not they had established an adequate defense against invasion, they might provide an ideal target for a successful raid—a raid that could help establish her newly founded Kingdom. The surviving population on Madagascar was a pathetic remnant that presented no threat.

And on the sea, aside from this one vessel of fishermen, she had encountered nothing but drifting wrecks. But those seven sailors, obviously based on the South African continent, represented a community whose strength was difficult to assess.

Despite the underlying fears and uncertainties, she felt as high on anticipation as she ever had on any drug. Adrenaline surged through her body. She only wished there were a way to fight the battle tonight, to draw blood, to see the fear in her "enemies' " eyes as she and her pirate company unleashed their own tsunami of violence and terror upon them.

Ranavolana—she was still getting used to the name—had surprised herself by how readily she took to leadership and military strategy. All those years, through college and her wandering times, she had always read books—Marcus Aurelius and Caesar, Sun-tzu and Mao Tse-tung. At her bedside now—it was a cot, really—she kept old paperbound copies of Mahan's *Influence of Sea Power* and Machiavelli's *The Prince*; and she perused them religiously. Since she was off drugs she retained more, absorbing the wisdom and practical advice of deep thinkers.

Altogether her pirate navy had so far collected twenty vessels of various sizes and conditions, including her own flagship, the sloop with the blood red sail. Tsunamis had cast numerous yachts up on the shores of Madagascar, along the south coast where the main body of the survivors were living, and some of the vessels had survived with little serious damage. They were there for the taking, which is what the queen's people did, moving them downhill and into the water.

She divided her command among four experienced seamen, each with a lengthy résumé as a career criminal (including prison time in virtually every South Asian port between the South China Sea and the Indian Ocean). These men were both her subjects and her teachers in the ways of piracy. She respected and feared them, listened to their counsel and watched their every move.

The Indian, Raman Patel, was small in stature, and slight enough to be blown off deck in a strong wind; but his fierce black eyes revealed the hard character of a man who had sailed rough seas for forty of his forty-seven years. He was the son of an unknown sailor and a prostitute mother from Goa. His mother had tried to put a Christian imprint on her wild son; but he spent all his time at the docks watching and learning from men of the sea. When she died, he signed on as a mess boy on a British steamer. Within two years, he joined the crew of a pirate ship based in Zanzibar.

Yook Louie was a fifty-year-old Taiwan native, tall and lank as a board, with gray-yellow skin. His hair was stiff and steel gray, his brows black, and he grew a wispy goatee, rarely trimmed. He had once been married and was certain that he had fathered three or four children by his wife . . . now, in the aftermath of the Event, all certainly dead.

Jama Chaudri was a true mongrel, and he boasted of it: half Indian, part English, a little Chinese, perhaps as much as a quarter Indonesian, with an Arab or two and even an Irishman somewhere in his family tree—and he'd fight any man who mocked or criticized any of these racial or national groups. So, he was a skilled fighter, with fists or knives, and had by his own count killed at least twenty men. He was no mathematician, though, so the number— including those he had murdered in sea raids—was possibly double that. He had been a pirate for at least twenty-five years.

Then there was Errol Waddell, the big, ebullient Australian ex-con and "retired" bosun of Her Majesty's Navy. Now in his fifties, with weathered brown skin and a shock of white-blond hair, he had seen service in the Vietnam War in the early 1970s, when his countrymen fought alongside the U.S. military services. He had spent a decade as a merchant seaman in the busy trade corridor between Singapore and Hong Kong. But he had been caught smuggling drugs and weapons into Sydney and spent another decade in national prison. The Event set him free.

Together, these four men were Queen Ranavolana's senior command structure, her seagoing Praetorian Guard. They had, among them, more than a century of experience in piracy in the "dark alleys" of the seas east of Africa and south of Asia. They had little regard for human life—their victims', their men's, even their own—and in this weird new post-Event world, they were pledged to serve their pirate queen with all the skill and ferocity they could muster. They had absolutely nothing to lose, and thus were incredibly dangerous to everyone else.

The queen's dilemma, then, was what to do with the resources at her disposal.

"We will send out a reconnaissance patrol to determine the enemy's strength and ability to defend himself." She announced this to her commanders matter-of-factly, and they received the information without visible reaction.

"Yer Highness," said Waddell, the big Aussie, "I think that is exactly what we ought to do, but—er . . . well, I think we also should patrol to the east to see if there's anyone, or anything, out that way."

"Our forces are limited," Ranavolana rejoined. "There's only so much we can do. We need to keep an adequate defense on hand here."

"Lady, we can do both," Patel put in. "And we might find some more ships that have foundered or are lost at sea. We can always make use of more." He smiled, showing his small brown teeth.

Queen Ranavolana did not smile. She steeled herself not to show any softness or humor—potential signs of weakness in the company of these men of action. She sought the opinions of others of her council. Some of them were more concerned with "internal security," that is, unrest among the Malagasy survivors than defenses—against whom? they asked. There had been no other sign of human survivors since the fishing boat encounter. She listened, absorbed what the men said, then suspended the meeting so that she could consider her decision.

The queen of the pirates retreated to her private quarters, sparsely furnished with a pallet, a makeshift desk, and a chair. On a small table in one corner of the room, there was a large candle that flickered with golden light. Here she could read and meditate and relax, dream her grandiose dreams of power. Here, in her sanctum sanctorum, anything was possible, and she could be anyone she chose: she could even be Anne Marie Appleton, the lost soul who had wondered across the world to find . . . what? Herself? The meaning of life? The ultimate high? To find . . . to be the woman her now-dead family always hoped she would be?

Now there were many people—hundreds, if not thousands— who looked to her for life and death decisions on their survival and well-being. She gazed at the candle. It had been a gift from a young woman who came to her to ask for the queen's favor upon her children who needed food and shelter.

It was still afternoon in this strange new world, but the sky was gravid with clouds that obscured the giant red orb of the sun. Night and day often melded together in a dull iron sky that gave sadly inadequate light or heat. On some rare occasions, it rained; but it was not the same rain she had known before the great disaster. It was a hard, almost steely rain—cold and piercing, blessedly brief. It was enough to dampen the earth and keep the inland plants and trees in flower, enough to provide potable water for the survivor community, enough to sustain life—barely. But, to what end? she wondered. Were these people, her people, better off for having survived?

She kept herself semidetached from them—the citizens of her isolated empire. She attempted to maintain an image of godlike dispassion, the calm of a remote ruler. Her commanders and henchmen did whatever dirty police work was necessary. The people themselves kept busy with the grim business of everyday life. There was another reason for her self-imposed aloofness. She could not bear to see so much misery close up. As much as she had, during her vagabonding years, seen suffering and death, she no longer had the stomach for it.

Her thoughts were interrupted by sounds of shouting and scuffling near her private quarters. A burly guard burst into the room and informed Queen Ranavolana that she was needed urgently by the council. She rushed out to see what the commotion was all about, heading directly for the pavilion on the beach where a large crowd was gathered. She pushed her way into the middle of the meeting area.

The council rose to greet their leader. "What is happening?" the pirate queen asked.

The tall Taiwanese captain, Louie, said, "The motorboat is missing—along with some fuel. There are two men unaccounted for, as well as some weapons and ammunition."

An ominous silence fell over the assembly, and all eyes turned to Queen Ranavolana. Her eyes burned angrily as she demanded, and received, the details. The men must have slipped away the previous night, loading the fifteen-foot motorboat with as much extra fuel and other supplies as possible. They probably rowed it out to sea before starting the motor. That was many hours ago. There was no hope of catching them now.

"Who is responsible for this outrage? Who was guarding my boats?" she asked in a low voice, her head swiveling slowly as she looked into their frozen faces. No one answered her.

The Australian spoke up: "The men who were on guard at the time have been arrested. They—"

"Bring them to me."

"But, Queen—"

"Bring them to me. Now!"

It took several agonizing minutes for the word to be circulated and the men brought forward. Their hands and feet were bound, and they were dragged before the queen and her lieutenants. The two men, who seemed pitiful and small, fell to their knees. They had been beaten severely, their eyes swollen closed, their faces broken and bloody. They trembled, speechless.

To the assembled crowd, Queen Ranavolana announced: "These men are criminals of the worst order. They have endangered all of our lives." Glaring furiously at the wretches before her, she said: "I sentence you to death, at dawn."

The evening after the artists' parade, the Focus Group held a special meeting of their own to celebrate the success of Sarah's extravaganza. It was now January 30, thirty-six days after the Event. Herb suggested that the date be observed in perpetuity as Parade Day. His motion, seconded by Roxy, passed without opposition.

"Quite a parliamentary coup," Tom said drily. "Don't get me wrong, I think it's a terrific idea. I just wonder what the greater community will think of it."

As the night sky darkened, the group lit one of their precious candles and toasted the muses, drinking the sorghum beer that a Zulu dancer had given to Roxy, his fellow artist, as a gesture of friendship. The six were in high spirits, although well aware that this party atmosphere could not last.

"It's back to the grindstone tomorrow," Wil said. "For me it's back to the good old Joint Planning Subcommittee."

"What's on the agenda?" Sarah asked.

"Ichiro Nagasaka will hold forth on the topic of iron and steel. This is the moment he's been waiting for. Frankly, it's a moment I've been waiting for, too. It's exciting to be in the center of such a momentous enterprise. Rebuilding an industrial society from scratch."

"Progress," Roxy said. "Soon there will be factories, probably standing right about here, spoiling our view of the water. I can't wait!"

"Soot-filled skies and black-lunged workers," Herb put in.

"But you have to admit that it's exciting," Wil said. "Making our way out of the Stone Age into the Iron Age."

"Iron schmiron," Roxy said with a shrug. "Everyone carries on about the Iron Age, the iron horse, and all that stuff. I say it's just bad poetry for a heartless world. Really, what's the big deal about something that's just a metal?"

"It is a big deal, Roxy," Tom replied. "A very big deal. Instead of complaining, you people should be singing hymns of praise. The universe has given us ninety-two elements with which to work, and out of those ninety-two, iron has a special place, a very special place. Without this unique element—and without the people who were able to discover its secrets—human civilization as we know it would never have evolved."

"Ninety-two elements," Herb said. "Isn't that a peculiar number?"

"It's a fabulous number," Tom said excitedly. "As you learned in your high school chemistry class."

"You're assuming a lot for this crowd," Sarah put in.

"Anyway," Tom went on, controlling his exasperation, "the elements are the basic building blocks of the material world. We list them according to the number of electrons they have spinning around in orbit, which is the same as the number of protons they have in their nucleus. You've seen those pictures of electrons in orbit around the atomic nucleus. Well, a drawing can't really show what an atom is, but speaking as an engineer—not a nuclear physicist, mind you—I would say that the image serves us pretty well."

Warming to his topic, Tom continued: "Uranium, which has ninety-two electrons, is the largest atom we find in nature. Any atom with more than ninety-two electrons is too large to hang together. The nucleus is unstable and the outer electrons tend to go flying off into space. Physicists, by using fancy, high-powered equipment—cyclotrons and linear accelerators—have managed to paste together another twenty-two or so elements; but such artificially made atoms break apart very quickly. So, to repeat, there are ninety-two elements which the universe gives us to use."

"Or to leave as we find them," Roxy muttered.

"Yes, of course," Tom said. "But since we humans seem to be curious, comfort-seeking, and innately creative, the universe couldn't have expected us to keep our hands to ourselves. Just think of it. All the world is made of this wonderfully organized stuff! For us engineers, it's the most fabulous erector set one could wish for. Maybe erector set is the wrong image, since the same atoms we incorporate into manufactured objects are the basic material of burning stars and living beings. Also, they're not material or substantial in any familiar sense. They are will-o'-the-wisp electrical 'wavicles'—sort of waves, sort of particles—if I understand the physicists correctly. But for engineers, their orderly behavior is what counts.

"And, you know—this is what's so incredible as we sit here on a beach with the world in ruins—it really doesn't matter how many comets collide or how many planets are destroyed. The elements remain, and with them the capacity to reconstitute anything that has ever been, and wonders still undreamed of. Add to this the knowledge we have of what the elements are, and how they behave, and we haven't been defeated at all. We have the makings—physical and intellectual—of a new world."

"I thought we were talking about iron," Herb said, with only the slightest hint of sarcasm.

"Yes, we were," Tom said. "And we are. Among the ninety-two elements, iron with its twenty-six electrons is very, very special. When you get a reasonably pure collection of iron atoms, they arrange themselves into a nice crystalline pattern—ideal for strength—with just the right amount of internal slip—perfect for flexibility. Then, if you take iron and combine it chemically with a little bit of carbon—that is, let a few carbon atoms arrange themselves in the interstitial spaces between the iron atoms—you get the material we call steel. It's the most useful material a tool-using, machine-making, invention-loving species could possibly want. Which means that we engineers, in discovering the secrets of iron and steel, are the makers of marvels."

Tom Swift—calm, stoical Tom—was suddenly more animated than his friends had ever seen him. "If we're concerned about rebuilding the world," he said, "we should be thinking long and hard about iron. I mean, really long and really hard. What do you think that civilization is? Poems and paintings? Pretty flags and patriotic songs? No, my friends, at the heart of civilization you will find iron and steel."

"There are other metals," Herb said. "Why is iron so special?"

"All metals share some characteristics," Tom responded, "but each one is unique. Believe me when I tell you that for tools, structures, and machines, iron has proved to be uniquely serviceable. Particularly when it's mixed with a bit of carbon to make steel. And wonder of wonders, iron is plentiful. In fact, it constitutes four percent of the material in the earth's crust. Considering its attributes and its availability—well, the whole thing is nothing short of magical."

"Not magical," said Mary, who had been quiet up to this point. "It's a miracle. God's miracle."

"You've got a pretty materialistic idea about what a miracle is," Roxy said. Her tone was critical but not unfriendly.

"That's what happens when you mix an engineer with a believer," Sarah said.

"Okay," Herb pressed, allowing his curiosity to show through in spite of himself, "but how and why is this stuff so amazing?"

"First of all," Tom said, "steel is a very hard material, by which I mean it resists penetration, it resists deformation, it resists abrasion and wear. Steel is also tough, which is different from hard: a material that is tough can absorb energy during deformation, resisting the extension of cracks. For example, in a collision, it will dent instead of shattering. In addition to being hard and tough, steel is strong, which means it can sustain heavy loads, in tension and shear, as well as in compression.

"When stressed, it will deform only slightly, elastically, returning to its original shape after the stress is removed. Yet if we stress it heavily enough—and we can calculate the forces with precision—it will deform plastically, maintaining its new shape. We can cast it, mold it, stamp it, cut it, extrude it, machine it—in so many ways fashion it to serve our needs. Hard, tough, strong, ductile; we're talking about a uniquely utilitarian substance. And all because of the ways in which iron atoms arrange themselves when they're together in a group."

Flushed with excitement, raising his voice, Tom continued: "I tell you, the stuff is precious. At the same time, there's plenty of iron in many parts of the world and limitless amounts of carbon, which means that steel is comparatively inexpensive. Which makes it all the more precious, if you get my meaning. This wonderful material is responsive to our every whim. Add more carbon and the steel becomes harder. A little less, and the steel will bend more readily while retaining its toughness. If we want a tool that is very hard on the outside, to resist abrasion, yet tough on the inside—to be able to absorb shock, for example—we simply add carbon to the outer surfaces; we call it case hardening. For other special features, we can add different materials, such as chromium to make it stainless, that is, resistant to corrosion. By using changes of temperature, we can work more miracles. Heat steel and cool it slowly—the process of annealing—the material becomes softer and more malleable, just right for molding into car body panels or cooking pots. Cool it suddenly, by quenching in liquid, and it becomes harder. And if this sudden cooling creates unwanted internal stresses, they can be relieved by reheating—that's called tempering."

Wil Hardy could not resist putting on his graduate student's hat. "Of course," he ventured, "none of the chemical reasons for this behavior were known until late in human history."

"And you're about to tell us exactly when that was," Herb quipped. "Now that Tom has lectured us on chemistry, I suppose that you're going to hold forth on the history of technology."

"I can see that you're tired and impatient at the moment. But, believe me, the story is worth telling. Just think of it. We've been thrown back into the Stone Age, six thousand years in the past, yet we intend to leap across those millennia in a flash."

"Leapin' lizards, History Man! Why don't you tell the kids all about it?" Everyone laughed, but it was clear they were fascinated in spite of themselves.

"Sure. There are really two stories, one, the saga of experimentation, the centuries of trial and error during which technologists learned to smelt iron—separate it from the stone in which it is found—and combine it with carbon to make steel. The other wonderful tale is the latter-day exploits of scientists who explained the magical processes that the artisans had developed. We tend to forget that the science that we call chemistry didn't come into being until the 1770s—three thousand years after the beginning of the so-called Iron Age. Yes, the 1770s. That's when Antoine Lavoisier suggested, and went a long way toward showing, that all things are composed of a number of simple substances, namely, the elements, as Tom has pointed out.

"Then, in the first decade of the 1800s, John Dalton put forward the idea that elements consist of atoms, and that each element consists of its own distinctive variety of atom. I may be telling you more than you want to know, but just think of what a giant imaginative leap this was. A simple concept; yet how sublime. Dalton didn't know the exact ways in which the atoms differed. But he perceived that there was a regular steplike progression from one to another.

"For awhile, it looked as if this sequence was correlated with atomic weight, each atom being one unit heavier than another. This was almost right, since as each different atom has one more electron than the one preceding it on the spectrum, it also has one more proton in the nucleus, which determines the weight. It turned out to be somewhat more complicated, since there are also neutrons in the nucleus, and they also contribute to the weight—but without changing the number of electrons. And it's the electrons that mainly determine each atom's behavior. In any event, Mendeleyev's periodic table, which demonstrated the existence of 'families' of elements, appeared in 1869. The modern model of the atom, with electrons orbiting the nucleus in a series of 'shells,' was advanced by Niels Bohr in 1913. That's practically yesterday in the history of technology. So you can see that if technologists had waited upon chemical theory, the making of iron would have been a long time in coming."

"Are you saying that science doesn't matter?" Herb prodded.

"No, of course that's not what I'm saying," Wil replied. "The history of chemistry is a super story of discovery. And there are lots of things that we can now do with metals that we couldn't do before we knew their chemical composition. But there are lots of things that technologists have done—and continue to do—far in advance of scientific explanation. In fact, I believe one could say that technology has done at least as much for science as science has done for technology. Maybe more.

"I'm thinking in particular about the precise metal instruments and glass lenses that made it possible for Galileo and Newton and company to do their thing. I suppose we ought to say that the relationship between engineering and science is one of mutual benefit. But my father has a fit when he hears engineering defined simply as applied science. That isn't the way things work. And the story of iron is a case in point."

All of a sudden, Herb stood up and made a gesture of annoyance. He turned to Tom Swift and spoke in a loud voice: "I've heard more than enough about iron and steel. You're making it sound as if we're talking about the Holy Grail."

"Maybe more important than the Holy Grail," Tom replied.

"No need to be sacrilegious, sweetheart," Mary said. "We can make our point about technology without blaspheming."

"You know," Sarah said, "some scholars suggest that the legend of the Holy Grail—the cup that Christ drank from at the Last Supper—was inspired by Celtic myths about the horn of plenty, the source of never-ending abundance. So, artistically at least, the search for salvation is related to the search for material well-being."

"I like that," Tom said; "but I think that the development of iron goes beyond just 'searching' for anything. This was not a treasure hunt. The iron was always there—in the stone—and we had to devise a way to get it out."

"Oh," said Sarah. "Then let's change our fable. What we want is the sword of Arthurian legend, driven through the anvil and into the stone. That's apt. The most powerful knights in the kingdom were unable to dislodge it. But along came young Arthur, virtuous and noble, and drew it forth as nicely as you please."

"That's a really wonderful story," said Roxy. "But I could never understand why anybody would want to go to so much trouble to pull out a sword that's stuck so tight in such a place."

"Because," Sarah said, "of what was inscribed along its blade. In Thomas Malory's words, 'Whoso pulleth out this sword of this stone and anvil, is rightwise king born of all England.' I guess Tom wants us to believe that whoso wrenches iron from the stone becomes a prince and saviour of his people."

"No offense, Sarah," Herb cut in, obviously about to say something offensive, "but don't you feel a little foolish coming up with these high-falutin' quotations all the time? We're going to have to start calling you Madam Bartlett."

Sarah flushed, but then gave back as good as she got. "No. I'll tell you what makes me feel foolish, Mr. Attorney. 'Party of the first part' makes me feel foolish. 'In consideration of the mutual covenants herein contained' makes me feel foolish. All legalese, accounting jargon, and technocratic gobbledygook makes me feel diminished as a human being. Also stupid clichés: 'Have a nice day,' 'No problem,' 'Whatever.'

"But the beautiful, insightful words of our creative geniuses— they make me feel the opposite of foolish. They make me feel inspired and exhilarated. Particularly at a time when most of humanity's literature, music, and art seems to have been totally obliterated, with only a precious remnant being carefully preserved in our small library."

It had been a long day, starting with a gala parade and ending with an engineering seminar that apparently had lasted too long. For the moment, there was not anything more to be said—about iron and steel, or anything else.

Herb, as a token of an affectionate truce, asked Sarah if he could give the final quote of the day. Sarah smiled and nodded consent.

"From the diaries of Samuel Pepys," Herb said. " 'And so to bed.' "

11

When the Joint Planning Subcommittee reconvened the next day, there were many smiles and sighs of relief. After five days of doubt and second-guessing, they had come through with their plans practically unscathed. A feeling of positive energy was palpable in the air. They were ready to proceed with their industrial revolution, and it was high time to turn their attention to metals. As Ichiro Nagasaka took the floor, he wasted no time on preliminaries.

"There is a most pressing need," Ichiro began, "most pressing indeed, as we all know, for metal tools—especially tools for farming and building. Therefore, it is essential to get blacksmiths working at the earliest possible moment. It shouldn't take long to construct simple forges, little more than a barbecue pit plus a hand-operated bellows. And I don't doubt that we'll be able to gather enough fuel to get these rudimentary shops operative. We can start by burning wood. At the same time, we'll get busy making charcoal. In a month or two the miners should have some coal for us.

"We also need iron to work with; but we can't afford to wait until we start smelting our own. Fortunately, the Scavengers are already bringing in lots of scrap metal, and I'm sure they'll find enough for our immediate requirements. What we need most of all is competent blacksmiths, and here I think we're in luck."

Ichiro had inquired among the hobbyists, museum specialists, and Inlander metalworkers, and had found enough skilled or semi-skilled artisans to operate ten forges. At least that was his hope and expectation based on hasty interviews with the selected smiths. He had decided that four forges should be located at each of the two designated iron and coal mining sites, Empangeni and Dundee. He envisioned both sites eventually being developed as large, all-encompassing centers of a metals industry, incorporating mining, smelting, and manufacturing. This would minimize transportation requirements. Having accounted for eight forges, he then proposed that the final two should be located respectively in Ulundi and Engineering Village, thus providing a convenient facility for each of the two main population centers.

Each of the forges was to be staffed by fifteen men, the skilled smith plus workers to load the fuel, stoke the fires, pump the bellows, and assist in handling the iron.

"We have already begun to stockpile wood at the various sites," Nagasaka announced. "And construction of the forges is scheduled to begin immediately."

"You've been busy during our five days of public hearings," Alf Richards noted.

"Yes," Ichiro agreed amiably. "I have persuaded the lumber people to cooperate by promising them axes and adzes for shaping timber, as well as an expedited schedule for hand saws and blades for sawmills. I have promised the leaders of Shaka Enterprises nails, which they are, you might say, desperate to acquire. In addition to these agreements, I have pledged to provide metal implements to the farmers, the miners, the wagon makers, and a few others in dire need of such tools."

"Just how the hell—" Alf Richards had to pause to control his hot temper. He started again, "How, may I ask, Dr. Nagasaka, do you intend to meet each and every one of these commitments?"

"It will not be easy, Richards-san. This is why I am recommending ten separate smithing operations, and urging that they get underway as quickly as possible."

"We can't make these forges operational overnight," Alf sputtered. "I doubt that you bothered to tell the people with whom you made these deals that there will be a slight delay while the smiths make tools for themselves."

"It is true," Ichiro confessed, "that we must start by finding or manufacturing those implements you will see in any typical blacksmith shop—hammers, anvils, tongs, chisels, pincers, rounding tools (to make bars into rods), and much else. Here again is our intriguingly paradoxical problem: needing a tool in order to make the tool you need."

He smiled enigmatically, ignoring Richards's reddening face, and then continued: "How can we forge tongs in a fire without having tongs to work with? Well, somehow it will get done, making provisional tongs out of green wooden branches soaked in water, plus odd scraps of this and that."

"Aren't you being overly optimistic?" asked Millie Fox. "I've seen new blacksmith shops established, and even when adequate tools are available, they don't start humming efficiently on day one."

"Leave the efficiency to our talented artisans," Ichiro said. "Just be sure that we supply them with materials and facilities—and most of all with that critical element we must never forget, an adequate amount of food and water."

On this count, there was no need to caution the members of the subcommittee. They had been seeing to it that every day, caravans of porters, plus ox-drawn wagons and sleds, carried life-sustaining provisions to various food distribution centers. This operation was monitored closely, and the subcommittee received detailed reports of food stores as they were accumulated in designated warehouses. The bounteous land, as if trying to make amends for the cruelty that had been visited upon the survivors, was good to the crops and livestock. Or perhaps it was the skill and enterprise of the people who did the backbreaking agricultural labor. In any event, everyone—so far—was receiving adequate nourishment. On this basis, a modern industrial enterprise could be launched with an element of confidence.

And blacksmith shops were just the beginning. Nagasaka next addressed the need to start smelting their own iron.

"We must begin," he said, "in a fairly primitive way. We may know a lot, but we do not have a lot to work with. We have no electricity or pure oxygen, both essential elements of a modern steel mill. We don't even have steam engines to blow air into a furnace. So we shall have to get into our time machine and travel backwards. Not all the way to the beginning of the Iron Age, but certainly back to the early eighteenth century. Running water must be our source of power for the bellows, and we'll have to use charcoal as our fuel and reducing agent, even as we start mining coal and look forward to converting to coke."

"And just what is a reducing agent?" asked Stephen Healey. "You know that not everyone on this subcommittee is an engineer."

"So sorry, Mr. Healey," Ichiro said. "The concept is simple. Iron ore is mostly iron oxide, and our problem in smelting is to break the chemical bonds between the iron and the oxygen. If, in a fire—a very, very hot fire—we burn the ore together with charcoal, which is mostly carbon, the carbon combines with the oxygen and takes it away in the form of carbon monoxide and carbon dioxide, leaving the precious iron behind. So the charcoal serves as both fuel and extractor of the oxygen; we call it the reducing agent."

Healey nodded to show that he got the general idea and motioned for the presentation to continue.

Dr. Nagasaka's plan was to start with four smelting furnaces, two at each of the planned ironmaking centers, Empangeni and

Dundee. Calling upon a number of experts for advice—including specialists from the living museums of bygone technology—he had prepared a design based upon the old Backburrow furnace which was built near Windermere, England, in the early 1700s.

This venerable structure, which operated with charcoal fuel for more than two hundred years (until it was adapted for the use of coke in 1920), was eighteen feet high and eight feet square, built against the side of a steep hill. This was so that workers could climb up the slope with baskets full of iron ore, charcoal, and limestone—the key ingredients—and tip the contents into the top of the furnace. The bellows were made of cow hides and were powered by a waterwheel. When the water flow in the adjoining river was inadequate, the wheel was used as a treadmill operated by the foundry crew. Nagasaka proposed that this design feature be modified to make the fallback a horizontal wheel powered by oxen rather than human drudges. Fifty workers were to be assigned to each of the four furnaces, about double the number that were needed to operate the original model from three centuries ago.

The selected experts had evaluated every aspect of the plan: size, shape, and materials. The slope of the interior walls was crucial since the dropping and mixing of the raw ingredients had to be just right. It was important to avoid a descent that was too speedy, or even worse, a jamming of the materials at an intermediate level. In the end, the designers placed their faith in the craftsmen of a bygone age, a faith that proved well rewarded when the furnaces were eventually put into operation.

A vocal minority called for a taller structure, closer to the thirty-five feet in height that was typical of American charcoal furnaces in the latter half of the nineteenth century. By way of compromise, it was decided to build one of the four furnaces to the larger pattern. This also ultimately proved to be functional, although with a few more glitches than the smaller model.

It was now the last day of January, and detailed design drawings could be completed, and the sites cleared and leveled, in about a month. But actual construction of the smelting furnaces could not begin until perhaps the end of April, when suitable brick and mortar were expected to be available. However, even the towers themselves were not a key item on what the construction people called the "critical path." This honor went to building the dams for the mill-ponds, assembling the waterwheels, and fabricating the wooden-geared mechanisms for powering the bellows.

All in all, the project would probably take the better part of six months. This meant that the operation would be ready to go in early August, just about the time the blacksmiths' sources of scrap metal were expected to be running short.

Ten blacksmith forges and four smelting furnaces. That seemed like an enormously challenging enterprise. But Ichiro Nagasaka had much more to propose. He answered a few questions, waited for the group to indicate tacit assent, and then resumed.

"Yes, we need hand-forged tools. But that is only the beginning of our industrial revolution. There then remains the crucial business of making machines." He stopped talking for a moment and rocked on his heels, hands behind his back, giving his audience time to absorb his meaning.

"You may say, okay, let's start making steam engines, internal combustion engines, turbines, and the like. We have the necessary materials, and we have designs ready to go—plans of classic machines from earlier times and even a few improvements that our mechanical engineers have worked on. Good. And you tell me that there will be fuel for these wonderful contraptions—for the steam engines, wood and coal, and for internal combustion engines, methane and eventually petroleum from coal. Excellent. But still I am unable to move ahead. Why? Because you have not given me the ability to manufacture the splendid machines you have designed.

"Ah, you say, see how our blacksmiths become daily more proficient. Bless them. They can make tools which we urgently need, and which serve to augment the strength of our arms and help us harness the power of wind and water and the beasts of the field. But give me a thousand highly skilled blacksmiths and I am still unable to make these wonderful machines that you have designed. Why?" He paused again for effect, and there was total silence in the thatch-roofed meeting pavilion. Then: "I will tell you why. Because blacksmiths are human. What we need is a precision that transcends the human. *Transcends the human.* I look out on the promised land of the industrial revolution, but I do not have the means to enter. What is missing?"

He paused once more, and then, barely whispering, said: "Machine tools. Tools that achieve precision through geometric verities rather than an artisan's skill."

Wil Hardy looked up from his writing. Machine tools had been his area of special interest, the topic of his never-to-be completed Ph.D. dissertation. He had chosen the subject when he read about how radically James Watt was able to improve his steam engine once he was able to replace crudely cast cylinders and pistons with parts that were accurately machined. The new tools, little remarked in conventional history books, played a crucial role in the Industrial Revolution.

Ichiro then intoned gravely the names of what he called "the heavenly ten": lathes for precise circularity; shapers and planers, which scrape flat metal surfaces, much the way a carpenter planes a piece of wood; milling machines, which use teethed wheels to cut grooves of diverse shapes; drill presses, which cut holes, and ream, and countersink; grinding machines, with abrasive materials, which finish off metal parts with accuracy and smoothness; power presses for shearing, bending, squeezing, and hammering; punch presses to stamp out metal parts from sheet metal and form the parts to a desired shape; metal-cutting saws; and gear-cutting machines.

Next, he revealed his plan for developing a machine tool workshop, a scheme that seemed to some rather arbitrary, even capricious; though the same could be said of many of the schemes they had agreed to already.

For each of the ten basic machine tools, a leader was to head up a development team of twenty people. Several of the proposed leaders were highly respected members of the Society of Manufacturing Engineers. A few were Inlanders who made up in practical experience what they lacked in professional credentials. The "troops" to go with these generals consisted of engineering officers and engine-room workers from the *Queen of Africa*, plus experienced mechanics from among the Inlanders. There was an abundance of talent.

Suddenly Lucas Moloko, who had been pacing back and forth in the rear of the group, turned abruptly and stepped forward. "I don't understand," he said. "You haven't explained how you're going to make *these* machines without having machines to make *them*."

"A fair question," Ichiro responded. "We must design these machines with great cunning, and make them with great care. Some of the parts can be formed by our blacksmiths with hammer and tongs. Others will be cast in molds, using the molten iron that will be produced by our smelters. We will make the molds from sand, with a binder of clay and water. The patterns for the molds will be meticulously crafted from wood. The castings will be carefully filed, and critical surfaces will be carbonized for added strength. Remember, we will make these parts using geometric principles—the screw, the circle, the inclined plane, the toothed gear. Then these devices will help us make future machines with less effort and more precision."

"What will make these marvelous contraptions run?"

"We will start with water wheels turning large shafts; the shafts will drive leather belts that will power the machines."

"Just like those fantastic photos of eighteenth century factories," Wil Hardy murmured almost soundlessly.

Nagasaka bowed to his audience, indicating that his presentation

was complete. The subcommittee members appeared to be mesmerized.

But, after a few moments of silence, Gordon Chan raised his hand,
shaking his head in mock bewilderment. Chan's field was chemical
engineering, and his main concern was the work of the Research
and Development group in planning for the future of this specialty.
However, his friendly rivalry with Nagasaka, plus his wide-ranging
curiosity, inspired a keen interest in plans for the evolving iron and
steel enterprise.

"Ichiro, my esteemed colleague," Chan said, "I recall that just
before the recent five-day recess for public review comments, you
maneuvered our subcommittee into setting aside a workforce of one
thousand for your grandly conceived—and unquestionably important—venture. By my calculation, however, you have not accounted
for nearly that large a number. Ten blacksmith shops with fifteen
workers each makes one hundred and fifty. Add four smelting furnaces with fifty people, plus ten machine tool teams of twenty—I
believe your total is only five hundred and fifty."

"Thank you, good friend, for your kind and close attention,"
Nagasaka responded. "Let me tell you what I plan to do with the
other four hundred and fifty. First of all, I want to have fifty people
working on the next stage of ironmaking—better and larger furnaces—and then large-scale conversion of iron into steel, either
through a long-established process like the Bessemer or through
some other means reflecting more contemporary technologies. We
cannot be satisfied with two-hundred-year-old methods. Fifty people are certainly not too many to be working on improvements and
change.

"As for the other four hundred, I want to assign two hundred
to supplementing the work of the miners, and two hundred to helping make and distribute charcoal and coke. I don't doubt that the
miners will get us materials out of the ground. But we'll need crews

to work with the ore, to break it up, sort it, sift it, to separate out as much useless rock as possible before bringing it to our furnaces. And then we have to get all the raw materials to exactly where we want them exactly when we need them. We cannot rely upon the miners for that.

"The same applies to charcoal and coke. The lumber people have been assigned the responsibility of making charcoal, but they are not likely to be overly concerned about our schedules. As for converting coal to coke, it doesn't appear as if anybody has been assigned that responsibility. That is probably my own fault. I didn't raise the question. In a modern steel plant, the process is designed to accommodate raw coal. But for the furnaces that we'll be using, coke will be needed as soon as we run short of charcoal, which will probably be sooner than we like to think. So, believe me, good friend, all of the people assigned to the metals operation will be put to good use."

"Oh, I believe you, Ichiro-san," Gordon Chan said. "And I believe that you will build an efficient, productive empire and come back to this subcommittee sooner rather than later for greater allocations of resources, human and material. I can't say I disagree with you in the least; but I'm sure you won't be offended if I keep a close eye on you and yours."

Nagasaka bowed deeply to Chan. He did not reply directly to the barb that had been thrown his way. Instead, he addressed the committee as a whole. "One final point," he said, waiting until he knew he had everyone's full attention.

"We have the latest technical information at our fingertips. We have brilliant engineers, talented technicians, and willing workers. We even have craftspeople who have worked as blacksmiths in museums and as hobbyists—and thank goodness that we do. But what we do not have, most emphatically, is anyone who lived in the eighteenth century, making iron, charcoal, coke, or anything else.

"Young Wilson Hardy here has studied a bit about those times, and he will tell you that craftsmanship—the talent that resides in the experienced artisan's mind and hands—counted for much. The particular smell of the smoke; the look and color of the glowing metal; the feel of the furnace, that sort of thing. So, whatever took those folks one hour to do is liable to take us five—or ten—or who knows how many. It is better that we have a few extra people on hand to help cope with the unexpected. Let the supplementary personnel be an expression of our humility."

Ichiro Nagasaka's eloquence and perseverance carried the day. The Joint Planning Subcommittee concluded unanimously that he should keep his thousand-person workforce.

"Don't make us regret this," Alf Richards said, as he raised the gavel to adjourn the meeting. But Nagasaka had already spun on his heels and was out of earshot, on his way to mobilize and motivate his army of workers.

The night turned cool and a giant golden moon was visible in the clear sky, clearer than it had been for many days. Wil Hardy, Jr., tried to convey to Sarah his excitement about the day's events, especially the launching of the machine-tool enterprise.

"This is where it really began," he said, gripping her elbows for emphasis. "Don't you see? This is where human beings took the definitive leap beyond their own nature, beyond craftsmanship, into the realm of the precisely formed machine. And the thing that made it all possible was the simple screw. The screw enabled clumsy human beings to measure with an accuracy that was intuitively inconceivable. Just think of the difference between a simple ruler and a finely calibrated micrometer! Also, the screw enabled the machinist to convert rotary motion into rectilinear motion, and so to regulate moving parts with precision. The cutting tool on a lathe, for example, could be controlled by the geometrically configured parts of a machine instead of by the hand of the operator. Through the screw, the inventors of machine tools applied the perfection of ideal shapes to the forming of physical objects. I'm not saying it wasn't a big deal to tame fire, to invent the wheel, to discover the pulley—all that earlier stuff. But this was such a defining moment, a thrilling moment for those who lived it. And we are being given the opportunity to live through it again."

"Wouldn't you rather that we had been spared this particular opportunity?" Sarah asked, with only a hint of sad irony.

"Of course. But just think of those pioneering days when a handful of toolmakers were creating the machine age. A new civilization was in the making, and they were at the heart of the drama. You know, Arnold Toynbee once said that if he'd been given his choice of societies in which to live, as a citizen and family man, he would have chosen the Dutch Republic at the height of its glory in the seventeenth century. As a historian, on the other hand, he would have elected to travel with Alexander the Great."

Sarah indulged Wil in his enthusiasm. "I suppose you're going to share with me your choice?" Her eyes met his, unblinking.

"Yeah. As a historian of technology, I am living right now in the equivalent of such a momentous epoch. I know that's being terribly self-centered, but it's how I feel. It helps me forget about all those people who are not here to feel anything. That's the silver lining in this terrible, terrible cloud. We're creating a new world, my darling."

"Will it be a new world of soot and noise and disfigured landscapes?" Sarah asked wistfully. "I worry about that."

"No. That's partly my point." Wil held her arm as they stood there in the surreally bright moonlight. "We have a fresh opportunity and the benefit of so much hindsight. We can create a machine age without the ugly side effects of the Industrial Revolution. I know we can! It will be a world your poets will appreciate." He became more and more animated.

"Is there room in your world for poets, Wil?"

"There's room for you—and you're a poet."

" 'Ah, my fierce-throated beauty,' " Sarah said.

"Your what?"

" 'Fierce-throated beauty! Roll through my chant with all thy lawless music, thy swinging lamps at night, thy madly whistled laughter, echoing, rumbling like an earthquake, rousing all, law of thyself complete, thine own track firmly holding . . .' "

He looked at her, bewildered.

"That's Walt Whitman writing about a locomotive," Sarah said, smiling. "He was an optimistic yea-sayer who lived at a hopeful time in American history. He saw the possibilities of beauty in machines and the possibilities of a beautiful life in an age of machines. I guess if he were with us today, he would say, 'Give them another chance. They'll do better.' "

"I know we will, Sarah."

Wilson Hardy, Jr., lay awake that night thinking about lathes, milling machines, and drill presses. There, on the coast of what used to be called the Dark Continent, not far from the places where wild beasts still roamed, he envisioned gleaming cylinders machined to accuracies verging on perfection. Amazing. The universe confronts us with chaos and destruction, he mused, but we puny humans, using geometry and ingenuity, demonstrate our defiance.

When he finally fell asleep, however, he dreamed of a pirate queen steering a red-sailed ship across raging seas. In this wild and frightening scene, thoughts of technology provided small comfort.

FROM THE JOURNAL OF WILSON HARDY, JR.

The first day of February dawned dark and rainy. The farmers said that the moisture was welcome, but I found my mood as dreary as the gray skies. With Ichiro's presentation, the preliminary work of the Joint Planning Subcommittee was now complete. The elation that had accompanied this achievement led to the inevitable morning-after letdown. The creative strategizing was behind us. One could predict that, from this point on, the subcommittee's work would consist mainly of modifying the decisions that had been reached, constantly reallocating resources, and responding to endless complaints and second-guessing.

As if to underscore my sense of foreboding, Donald Ruffin barged into the subcommittee's afternoon session, accompanied by members of the Electric Light Brigade, and resumed his assertion of grievances. "We've been thinking things over," Ruffin said. "It just won't do to lump electricity and electronics into the category of research and development. We can't sit around designing and designing and designing." He began to sputter in anger and frustration. "We need some material to work with, dammit—and you know exactly what it is that we need. Copper. C-o-p-p-e-r!"

"We've been over this a dozen times, Donald," Alf Richards answered. "You know what the problem is. The closest sizable copper deposit is at Phalaborwa, three hundred miles to the north. Eventually we'll establish a mining operation there and cope with the transport problems, which are daunting. But it will take awhile. We just can't do everything at once."

"Let me ask a naive question," said Millie Fox. "It may even be a stupid question. But I'm not one of you brilliant engineers, so I'll risk it. Aren't there other metals you can use?"

I personally thought that was a very sensible question. In fact, Ruffin treated it with respect.

"You know, Millie," he said, "gold and silver happen to be good conductors of electricity. But they're really too soft to stand up to use in motors and transmission lines. More important, sources are extremely limited, which is one of the reason these materials have always been so expensive. The same is true of the other so-called rare metals. We need something that's sturdy and plentiful.

"Of course," he continued, encouraged by Millie's interest, "iron fits that bill, and it will, in fact, conduct electricity. Folks used to use steel wire for the telegraph system that transmitted Morse Code dits and dahs. But it isn't suitable for transmitting large quantities of electric power. For that we need copper, or as an alternative, aluminum, which has electrical conductivity about two thirds that of copper. The catch is that the best way to obtain aluminum from its ore is by electrolysis, and this requires lots of electric power, which is what we don't have in the first place. So—cutting to the chase—copper is the only practical way to go."

After a few moments of grim silence, Ruffin spoke again: "Guys, we're not here just to grouse and sulk. We have a suggestion. You may remember that when Pieter Klemm first gave us a report on the area's mineral resources, he told us about a small copper deposit at Nkanda, just forty miles inland. Well, I've taken the liberty of having a few of our mining engineers check it out, and they tell me that there is, in fact, some decent ore there. Not a large amount. Certainly not enough to provide the many miles of wire needed for an electrical distribution system. But something that we can start with. Enough to let us build some experimental equipment, not just dream about it." Ruffin made boxlike gestures with his hands as if he were assembling a piece of machinery in the air in front of him.

"Maybe we can manufacture a few small generators driven by coal-burning steam turbines and use them to recharge some of the batteries we salvaged from the ship. That would put us back in business with the radio equipment that was saved. And just think how great it would be if we could bring some of our computers back to life. Also, we could plan to install generators in key locations such as hospital emergency rooms. Even without a distribution system, a lot can be accomplished. And without taking a large number of people away from the activities of your master plan."

Alf Richards pursed his lips, dubious but thoughtful. Ruffin sensed an opportunity and pursued it.

"Just spare a few people to mine and smelt a small amount of copper," he said. "And a few more to set up a wire-drawing operation. And, finally, tell your Scavengers to bring in some scrap copper wire. You won't regret it, I guarantee."

Then, after a pause: "Come on, Alf. You can't make your way back to the modern world without putting electrical engineers in the front ranks. When you think of it, electricity is humankind's most godlike exploit. In fact, maybe it's the main reason the deities decided to send that comet our way. They looked down, saw us lighting up the night and bouncing radio signals off of artificial satellites; they must have thought to themselves, 'Hey, enough is enough. Let's cut these upstarts down to size.' "

———

For the third time in as many days I found myself drifting into that fanciful world in which tales of past engineering achievements emerged as a key element of our own odyssey. First it had been iron and steel; then machine tools; and now, most marvelous of all, electricity. Damn it, Ruffin is right, I thought. You can't help but agree with the guy, unpleasant as he may be: the mastery of electricity is indeed humankind's most godlike exploit. And it is the means by which we can most decisively leap over centuries into the modern world. While Richards grudgingly negotiated the terms of a deal with the Electric Light Brigade, I started to jot down my personal thoughts in the margins of my minutes.

Later in the day, after the meeting was over, I went off by myself, intent on recording the ideas that had suddenly flooded into my mind. I skipped dinner, telling Sarah that I had some important work to catch up on. Seated with my back against a board I had half buried in the sand, looking out over Lake Mzingai, I scribbled away, carried off into a world of my own fancy. As night descended, I lit the candle that I carried with me whenever on secretarial duty, and the flickering light was an persistent reminder of how electricity had become central to our lives.

People have been fooling around with "static electricity" for a long time, at least since the ancient Greeks rubbed amber with fur and found that it attracted light objects such as feathers and lint. In fact, the Greek word for amber is *elektron*. But static, sparks, even lightning—these phenomena were the stuff of wonder and speculation, not dreamed of as a force for human well-being. Until . . .

For me, the story begins in 1800, when Count Alessandro Volta made his electric pile, or what we today would call a battery. As the story goes, when Volta put a coin on top of his tongue, and a coin of a different metal under his tongue, his sense of taste led him to believe that something was "flowing" from one coin to the other. So he experimented with stacks of alternating discs of two different metals—zinc and copper, or silver and lead—with moist cardboard in between each slice. Then he ran a brass wire from one end of such a stack to the other and discovered that "something"—a current of electricity—ran through the wire.

Today, we know that electricity consists of the flow of electrons, and that metals, which characteristically have free-floating electrons in their outer shells, are good conductors of such flow. We also know that if we place zinc, with its thirty electrons, next to copper, with its twenty-nine electrons, then the electrons in the zinc "want" to move toward the copper, to equalize the situation, and thus they establish a flow of current. Such chemical generation of electricity is the basis of our batteries. But batteries are necessarily small. The large-scale generation of power depends upon other natural phenomena.

The next chapter in this remarkable saga features Hans Christian Oersted, a Danish physicist, who in 1820 gave a lecture that will live forever in the annals of science and technology. The topic was electricity, and for purposes of demonstration the professor had set up a circuit powered by a Voltaic battery. On his laboratory table, close to the electric wire, there happened to be a compass, an ordinary compass like those long used on ships to indicate the direction of the North-South magnetic field. Oersted noticed that each time he flipped a switch to start the flow of electric current, the compass needle quivered. Strange. Electricity in a wire was affecting magnetism in the surrounding air. Amazing. It seems that a flowing electric current creates around itself a magnetic force.

Well, then, if electricity can make magnetism, can magnetism make electricity? For awhile this question proved mystifying. People tried putting magnets over wires, under wires, surrounding wires, but nothing seemed to happen. The great Michael Faraday solved the problem in 1831. He demonstrated that by *moving* a magnet near a wire, or *moving* a wire near a magnet, an electric current can be created.

So, by spinning a wire cage (called a rotor) inside of a magnetized casing (called a stator), we manufacture electricity. All we need is the power for twirling. This can come from a hand-operated crank, or more usefully, from turbines turned by falling water or by jets of steam. The steam, of course, can be obtained by burning coal or oil, or whatever.

We can then run the manufactured electricity—the magical flow of electrons—through wires and use it for lighting, or, among other things, to run motors. A motor is practically the same thing as a generator, except instead of spinning the rotor to make electricity, electricity is used to spin the rotor. It's all so simple, in concept, anyhow.

The design of actual machines, of course, is not at all simple. Shortly after Faraday's discovery of electromagnetic induction in 1831, a number of technologists started to fabricate small hand-operated generators. But it was not until 1873 that the Belgian engineer Zénobe Théophile Gramme built the first truly commercial electric machine. The alternating current motor of Nikola Tesla, which set the standard for worldwide use of electric power, was patented in 1888. What Tesla designed—and others after him—we can duplicate here in Engineering Village. As soon, of course, as we get Ruffin and his cohorts some copper wire.

While large-scale generation of electricity was being developed, other geniuses were gaining access to an even more wondrous mystery of the universe: electromagnetic waves that travel through space. Through space!

In the early 1860s, James Clerk Maxwell, a Scottish physicist, looked at the electricity-magnetism phenomenon from a new perspective. Since these two forces seem to create and modify each other, back and forth, over and over again—electricity makes magnetism, magnetism makes electricity—in an unending mutual propagation, one could perhaps infer that a wave was involved. After all, what is a wave but something that goes up and down, back and forth, over and over again? Maxwell theorized that when electrical oscillations are created, this generates waves: waves that travel through space. Not electrons moving through wires, but electromagnetic waves moving through space! It's difficult to grasp the concept, and we really can't come up with a satisfactory physical representation of these things. But the fact is that Maxwell developed mathematical formulas predicting the behavior of such waves, and these formulas were born out by experiment.

Physical confirmation of theoretical concepts was some time in coming. Maxwell published his wave theory in 1864, and it wasn't until 1888 that Heinrich Hertz proved that electromagnetic waves actually did exist. He showed that they could be made in a laboratory, transmitted through the air, and received by an "antenna." This was truly the greatest magic act of all time.

Using high-voltage electricity—which by this time could readily be produced—he created a spark between two coils. A few feet away, he set up a receiving mechanism consisting of two rods with a spark gap between them. As Hertz had hoped, the waves created by the first spark were detected, as evidenced by a spark appearing in the second gap.

The rest, as we never tire of saying, is history. Once it was shown that electromagnetic waves could be generated by mechanical means, and transmitted through space, it was only a question of time before the few feet became a few hundred feet, a few thousand, a few hundred thousand. In 1901, Marconi sent a radio signal across the Atlantic Ocean.

While sending and receiving these waves across long distances is marvelous, the question of utility arises. If all you can send is a spark, or a blip, you're restricted to a Morse Code–type communiqúe. On the other hand, if you can imprint lots of information on your wave—it's called modulation—then you've done something very, very special.

This is what electronics engineers have been working on for the past hundred years, first with vacuum tubes, then with transistors and minuscule integrated circuits. Maxwell's electromagnetic waves, imprinted with enormous amounts of information—speech, music, pictures—are generated, transmitted, received, unscrambled, and amplified. The result has been a cornucopia of fabulous products—radio, television, cellular telephones, whatever your heart desires, and more.

Isaac Newton said that if he could see farther than others it was because he stood on the shoulders of giants. Just so should we here in Engineering Village pay homage to the giants who preceded us: Volta, Faraday, Maxwell, Hertz, Tesla, Marconi, and many others. I fancy, not that our engineers stand on their shoulders, but rather that these great men were advance members of our surviving party, scouts who landed on the beach before we arrived, planting their banners in the sand, claiming the land on behalf of a renewed high civilization.

When later that evening I shared some of these thoughts with my Focus Group friends, they were far from overwhelmed.

"It's just physics," Roxy said. "Let's not get carried away."

"Gimme a break," I protested, "I'm not talking about the ultimate meaning of life. I'm referring to a magnificent human achievement. I'm celebrating the genius and insight that enables us to do the most extraordinarily wonderful things."

"Like snoop on our neighbors," Herb said.

"And make atom bombs," Roxy said.

Tom threw up his hands. "What's with you guys all of a sudden?" he fumed. "I thought you had a sense of respect for the natural world."

"Oh, I don't know," said Roxy. "All those invisible rays. I suddenly feel like we're drowning in them."

Tom turned to me: "You may have to fine-tune your presentation, Wil. I don't think you're getting through to this audience the way you had hoped."

I grimaced and shook my head until Mary came to my defense.

"This is God's universe," she said. "Without agitated atoms emitting electromagnetic radiation, there would be no plants, no life, no anything. The fact that we've come to understand something about these phenomena—and to use them to good effect—that's cause for pride and humility and veneration."

Herb and Roxy leaned forward and seemed to be composing their retorts when Sarah held up her hand and, like a kindergarten teacher faced with an unruly class, called "time-out." Then she said, "I don't think we need to be arguing about this. There are plenty of ways in which we can relate to the universe, and let's agree that in such matters it's each to his own. As for me, I find consolation—and inspiration—in art.'

Then, turning toward me, she added, "And in love."

"And," Mary said, "in faith."

"And"—now it was Tom joining in—"I would say, creative work."

"And in fun," Roxy said, her spirits rising.

"And in debunking whatever and whomever we please," Herb said, pugnacious but smiling.

It was my turn to say something, but there seemed nothing left to say. Then, suddenly, a thought came to me, fleeting and more mysterious in origin than the electromagnetic waves we had been considering. I heard myself say: "And in marrying and having children."

That ended the evening's debate.

12

It was well past midnight when Wil Hardy was roused unceremoniously and ordered to report to a special, secret meeting called by the Coordinating Committee. Secret? This was a first. By a firm consensus, both Inlanders and Outlanders had agreed that, although not every meeting would be open to everyone, there would be no secret committees formed or secret decisions taken by anyone in a position of authority—ever. So, this development was alarming to Wilson Hardy, Jr., and he would be sure to speak to his father about it at the earliest opportunity. Meanwhile, he was gripped by nervous excitement as he threw on some clothes, assured the half-asleep Sarah that he would be back shortly, and ran off into the night.

There were about forty men and women gathered for this post-midnight meeting, and the recording secretary recognized all of them, except two who looked like natives from some foreign island—Africans perhaps, yet somehow different. He couldn't immediately put his finger on it—that is, how they were different—and he was quickly distracted by his father and Captain Nordstrom, who signaled for him to join them.

"Son, we need you to take notes, here, but you *cannot* share anything about this meeting with your friends, even with Sarah. We must have your word on this."

"Sure, Dad, but why? What the heck is going on, anyway?"

Dr. Wilson whispered hoarsely: "Just listen and take accurate notes. I don't mean to be so cryptic, son, but you'll soon see why."

Captain Nordstrom was solemn as he opened the proceedings. "I call to order this special meeting of the Expanded Defense Committee, as authorized by the Coordinating Committee. Although Dr. Hardy or I have spoken to each of you privately, I must say for the record"—he shot a stern glance at Wil—"I must say that what we discuss here shall remain completely confidential. We do this not to exclude anyone, of either community, but rather to prevent rumors and alarm from spreading among the people. Is this understood and accepted by everyone?"

Wil Hardy looked up from his notetaking. *Expanded* Defense Committee? Rumors and alarm? He thought about Sarah asleep in their little shelter. There was something ominous afoot, and he had an urge to run back and hold her in his arms. But clearly he had to stay in place to do his job. He started to scribble in his own form of shorthand, afraid to miss a single word of the discussion.

All of the attendees indicated their assent, and Nordstrom went on: "Several hours ago, two men from Madagascar landed about ten miles from here and found their way to us by following the shoreline. They were lucky they chose to walk in this direction. If they had not—that is, if they had walked north instead of south— they could have been lost for days, or forever. Our security detail encountered them and brought them to me. One of these gentlemen began to speak to me in French, which, it turns out, was the official language of Madagascar during the French colonial period. Neither of them speaks English, so French it shall be. They have been fed and given water. They are exhausted and dehydrated, but otherwise healthy.

"I have asked two of our experts to help us: Richard Frost, a recognized authority on the history and culture of Madagascar; and René Picard, a nuclear engineer graduate of the Ecole Polytechnique, who is one of the most eminent members of the French engineering establishment Dr. Picard, of course, is a native French speaker who will serve as our translator."

"*A votre service,*" Picard said with a slight salute.

Wilson Hardy, Sr., stood and spoke. "These two men escaped from an apparently terrible situation on the island of Madagascar. The young man is a fisherman and mechanic who was able to operate the motorboat that brought them here. The elderly gentleman is Pascal Ralaimongo, a schoolteacher and respected patriarch of his village. We have asked him to describe for us the conditions existing in his homeland. Mr. Ralaimongo, if you please."

Young Will Hardy, looking closely now at the "refugees," realized that the facial characteristics he could not quite identify were Malayan, and he immediately thought of the pirate crew that had been described by Harry McIntosh and his fellow fishermen. Yet these two men were obviously not pirates. In fact, both smiled in friendship, obviously grateful that they had made it to this safe haven. Ralaimongo was a small, stooped man, with narrow shoulders and wispy gray hair. He wore a multicolored polyester shirt with long sleeves and only a few surviving buttons. His canvas trousers were worn and stained, and frayed rope held the soles of his sandals to his feet. After expressing his thanks to these kind people, he told them his story, through Picard.

It seemed that the northern part of the large island of Madagascar had been consumed by flames from the sky, and then wildfires had spread through most of the south. As in South Africa, the tsunamis had devastated all coastal communities. But, in contrast to the Ulundi Circle, where farms and livestock areas in the highlands had been spared providentially, in Madagascar the inferno and the floods had destroyed crops and animals as well as people. A group of survivors—perhaps as many as three or four thousand—with Ralaimongo as their designated leader, had tried to make do by sharing the few food resources, while also hunting, foraging, and attempting to recultivate the scorched fields.

However, as if heaven-sent devastation was not enough of a trial, the struggling band of survivors had been set upon by a group of convicts who had escaped from a demolished jail. These criminals—some of whom had been serving time for committing piracy on the high seas—were banded together, ruthlessly attacking and robbing anyone unlucky enough to be in their path.

Ralaimongo and his followers were astonished to discover that the villains were led by a young woman, an American who knew their language—among others—and was called Queen Ranavolana, after dynastic rulers of old. Just how she had become a leader was unclear to the schoolteacher. He was impressed by her linguistic facility and her intelligence; but it was obvious that she had more of an affinity for the criminals and pirates than for the general population.

She played on the pirates' fears and superstitions, encouraging them to believe that she was somehow connected to the conflagration, sent by the Creator to be their saviour. Ralaimongo also questioned her sanity. Was she crazed, unhinged by the holocaust? Or was she totally in control of her faculties, making decisions that only she could explain? Why did she choose to adopt the name of the notoriously wicked queen? And what was the meaning of the red sails, which apparently were colored with paint found in a warehouse, augmented, some of the people said, with blood? What kind of blood? Or worse, *whose* blood?

The committee members were riveted by the man's tale of horror, but he was not finished. Picard struggled to keep up and to keep his own emotions out of the translation.

"I am certain that our escape, Jono's and mine"—he pointed to the young sailor who had accompanied him on the voyage—"that our action will result in recriminations. Others will pay for our freedom. I regret this very much. However, it was necessary that someone attempt to get away to tell this story, to ask for help. We were told about the Queen's encounter with your fishermen, which was described to us as if it were a grand military coup. Supposedly, she outwitted your people and took their fish without firing a shot, frightening them into submission."

At this point, Harry McIntosh, who was included in the group selected to attend the special meeting, jumped up to protest. "She surprised us, yes. But she sure as hell didn't scare us. I told you, Captain, sir—"

"Yes, Harry," Nordstrom reassured him. "We know the truth. You do not need to be defensive. Our guest is merely reporting the propaganda as it was related to him. No criticism intended." He turned to the older man. "Continue, please, sir."

"Yes, well, she filled the people's head with nonsense. We two, among many others, could see through her lies and perceive her evil intent. Yet we were frightened and did not know what to do. The Queen was not reluctant to execute any dissenters or so-called troublemakers, anyone who disagreed with her on the slightest matter. And she had the men—these criminals—to carry out her wishes." Tears welled in the old man's eyes, then fell down his leathery cheeks. "I have seen many people killed, many good people—without justification, with no trial. My family is gone, all of them annihilated in the disaster that destroyed our island home. I have nothing more to lose. But it hurts me to see innocent people treated in such a way."

"Monsieur Ralaimongo," Dr. Hardy interjected, speaking slowly so that Picard could translate, "will you please repeat what you told us earlier about this woman's plans as they affect our community? All of us here would like to help you and your people as best we can. But it is vitally important that we understand just what we are confronting."

"She—Queen Ranavolana the Terrible—plans to invade your

settlement and strip you of every bit of food and equipment that her men can carry away. And eventually she will return with an army of occupation. She believes that she is destined to rule the entire world—that is, the part of the world that has survived the catastrophe."

These words fell on incredulous ears, and several members of the Expanded Defense Committee started to speak at once. Jane Warner, who had been added to the committee because of her knowledge of the "safety zone" line as it might have affected Madagascar, asked Picard to repeat exactly what Ralaimongo had said. At the same time several of the committeemen from Ulundi, including Peter Mavimbela, started to speak animatedly among themselves in Zulu. Within moments, the entire meeting was in an uproar of shock and anger.

Pieter Kemm stood, shaking his fist. "Captain Nordstrom, we must mobilize our people immediately! Our Zulu comrades will agree, I'm sure, to an emergency conscription. The Ulundi leadership will act responsibly and quickly. Just tell us what we must do."

"First thing," Nordstrom said, raising his hands, "is to calm down. Everyone, please. Just calm down."

The two refugees were alarmed by the response of the people present, and Ralaimongo looked to Captain Nordstrom and Dr. Hardy for guidance. Did they want him to continue to speak?

Dr. Hardy said, in an even tone intended to quell the upset, "The one thing we don't want to do is panic and run around in circles. Of course, we must take measures to defend ourselves against this possible attack. I say 'possible' not because I do not believe what Mr. Ralaimongo has told us, but only because we do not know the size and strength of the forces that might be deployed against us."

"That is true," Nordstrom said. "However, our military leaders have already debriefed our new guests, and based upon their appraisal of the situation I believe that they have some preliminary ideas." With this he turned to General Allen White of the U.S. Army Corps of Engineers.

General White, along with Deck Officer Carl Gustafsson, had sat at the head table and listened to the proceedings, but to this point he had said nothing. Now he stood and walked around to the front of the table, where he could face his colleagues and fellow survivors directly.

He stood before them, erect and poised. Although his engineering specialty had led to a career that was not specifically combat-oriented, Allen White had seen active duty as a younger officer in the U.S. invasion of Grenada and in the Gulf War. His trim gray hair and mustache (which he kept meticulously neat and precise, even in these difficult living conditions) accented a firm, angular jawline. His blue eyes were capable of warmth or ice, depending on what the situation required. And his voice was crisp, just the right volume for the size of the gathering, exuding confidence.

"Thank you, Captain Nordstrom and Dr. Hardy. Ladies and gentlemen, friends, we have indeed heard some alarming news this morning. But, as Dr. Hardy has said, we don't yet know how serious the threat is. I strongly recommend, however, that we assume a worst-case scenario and plan accordingly.

"Deck Officer Gustafsson and I have had preliminary discussions about this situation and believe that a simple and direct approach is best. In our earliest meetings—after our fishing boat's encounter with the queen—a few members of our committee suggested that we take advantage of the special engineering talent in our midst and attempt to develop one or more 'magic weapons.' We decided against this course of action. I personally have seen too many high-tech weapons that didn't perform as advertised, and I could not approve putting our faith in magic devices of any sort. We do have a certain number of rifles and pistols available, and using these judiciously, our group agreed that the tried and true methods of a modern infantry would serve us best. We find ourselves living in relatively primitive conditions, and the same situation must pertain to any potential opponents. As for the present danger, from what we understand, these so-called pirates, no matter how ferocious they may be, are in no position to overcome an armed, well-disciplined group of citizen-soldiers. They will have the disadvantage of having to cross two hundred and fifty miles of open sea, and their numbers cannot be large—I would guess, from what we have heard, two or three hundred at most."

The general paced back and forth for a moment, as if on parade, and then continued, "We propose to recruit militia troops—like in the days of the American Revolution. We will seek out able-bodied volunteers, say five hundred from Engineering Village—the ship's crew alone provides many likely prospects—and an equal number from Ulundi. There is no sense in making the troops more numerous since we probably won't be able to round up more than a few hundred guns, and while some of our support forces may not need to carry weapons, in general we don't want to send unarmed soldiers into battle. Incidentally, let me say for the record that I favor enlisting men only. On the other hand, we're not going to make an issue of it if a few women insist on joining."

The overall force, as envisioned by the general, would be a regiment comprised of two battalions of roughly the same size—one from Ulundi, the other from Engineering Village. Each battalion would be comprised of two companies, each company of ten platoons, following the standard military order. Each unit, from the smallest to the largest would have one commander and one second. For example, the regiment would be commanded by White, with Gustafsson as his second. He asked Kemm to give him a list of prospective officers to be interviewed and commissioned as soon as possible. He and the deck officer had already begun to sketch out the chain of command among the Outlanders.

At this point, Captain Nordstrom broke in: "In order to minimize unnecessary alarm, I've suggested that we simply announce that the Coordinating Committee has decided to form a defense force and that we will begin organizing soon. No special sense of urgency. In actuality, we should work like the devil to get the best officers and men enlisted pronto, and the training program underway."

"Has anyone thought of negotiating with these people? Perhaps this woman wants something we can provide—a 'trade' agreement?" The questioner was Jane Warner.

"I'll answer that, if I may," Hardy spoke up. "Based on the information these two men have brought us, there is no room to negotiate anything with the so-called queen and her own government council. It would be, in my opinion, a fool's errand. And we cannot afford to send a boat, let alone a single person, into her zone of authority without some realistic hope that something might be accomplished. If there was any chance of a different outcome, I would be all for it. Anyhow, the idea is a good one, and that's what this meeting is for. Any others?"

Peter Mavimbela raised his hand and was recognized. "I'll tell you what I have in mind," he said. "Why don't we turn the table on these criminals, launch an attack against them, catch them by surprise, and put an end to the whole business? I don't like the idea of just waiting around, expecting the axe to fall at any moment, but not knowing where or when trouble will find us. That's not the Zulu way; that's not the way of the new South Africa; and I don't think it should be the way of the new civilization we're trying to build."

"A good point," said the general, "and, Peter, I like your fighting spirit. But I must tell you that we've considered that possibility, and for the time being it doesn't seem feasible. We simply don't have the resources. We would need a navy—an invasion fleet—while all we have is a few lifeboats converted to fishing vessels. The enemy, on the other hand, seems to have a number of speedy sailing yachts. And even if we could overcome that disadvantage, we would lose the tactical edge that we have now. We would be the weary invader, having crossed the water and needing to carry supplies rather than the army comfortably planted on our home soil."

"Yes, but the element of surprise, that's what the invader has."

"It's not complete surprise if we know that they're making plans. We just have to be as alert as we can be. As for the suspense, well, we'll just have to tough it out."

"Also, Peter"—now it was Wilson Hardy speaking—"think of how mounting an invasion would disrupt the important work that is going on here. Our industrial revolution would come to a screeching halt. All our dreams for the future would have to be put on hold."

Mavimbela grimaced slightly, and nodded his head to show understanding and agreement.

Since there seemed to be no other questions from the floor, Hardy turned to General White and asked conversationally, but loud enough for all to hear, "Allen, what are your thoughts about the ultimate role of this Defense Committee? And about the army and its officers. Who should have the right to give orders to whom, and under what circumstances?"

"That's an easy one, Wilson," answered the general. "Whatever worked for the United States of America—and how wonderfully well it worked for more than two centuries—is good enough for me. Civilian control of the military. It's as simple as that."

"The question of power is never simple," said Richard Frost, "if you will forgive me for saying so. History tells us that we must expect frequent conflicts and a constant clash of ambitions. So far, we haven't even had democratic elections."

"I'm sure that the general is assuming that will happen," Wilson Hardy said. "At the end of our first year, by previous agreement, we will have our constitutional convention, our elections, and all that good stuff. I take him to mean that for now the military commanders will take their orders from the Defense Committee, which in turn will answer to the Coordinating Committee, which is, in effect, the chief governing body."

"That's exactly right," said the general." I want everybody here to understand it, and we must make sure that all of our military people understand it, too."

At this point, Wilson Hardy turned toward his son and said, "Get that down in writing, young man, and protect the principle with your life, if need be."

The recording secretary wrote carefully, feeling for the moment as if he was at a meeting of the Continental Congress. Would General White be the George Washington of this new era? And would Wil's dad be the equivalent of Thomas Jefferson, or perhaps Benjamin Franklin, or some other founding father?

It was a moving moment, although not everyone present was thrilled with the idea of basing the new world order on American traditions alone. "You know," muttered Captain Nordstrom, "there are other democracies in the world—or there were—Norway, for example, just to name one."

As the meeting reached its conclusion, a consensus developed around writing down the basic principle, as it had been discussed, without reference to any particular previously existing national constitution or heritage. This was done, and a solemn confirming vote was taken.

Approval was unanimous, and the meeting was adjourned about two A.M.

Wilson Hardy, Jr., went to his father and hugged him, surprising the older man. "Thanks. What was that for?" the elder Hardy said.

"Just felt like doing it," Wil responded.

Then, as they walked out into the darkness, he sighed deeply and said, "It looks as if we may be heading toward our first war of the new era. It's sad."

"Yes it is. Inevitable, I suppose, but sad nonetheless. We could probably be of great assistance to the people of Madagascar, and they to us. God knows there are so few of us left."

"I'm very curious about this Queen Ranavolana character. It seems she's an American. I wonder if I'll ever get to meet her."

"Not if I have any say about it." Wilson Hardy looked at his son, a younger, slimmer, taller version of himself. "You're still my boy, and I'll not have you cavorting with pirate queens."

"I don't even know the meaning of 'cavorting,' Dad. . . . Anyhow, I've got to get back to Sarah. Good night."

"Good night, son. Sleep well."

FROM THE JOURNAL OF WILSON HARDY, JR.

Well, I had to keep my mouth shut about the issues before the Expanded Defense Committee, but I hadn't had the sense to do so earlier. My own words echoed and rattled around in my mind.

"And in marrying and having children."

What had gotten into me? Perhaps it was all that talk about elementary particles and electromagnetic waves. Come to think of it, this enigmatic "stuff" of the universe has somehow evolved into living creatures. And one thing we know about living creatures: they seem determined to endure and reproduce themselves. Maybe that basic impulse, lodged deep within me, simply chose this moment to express itself.

Or possibly, thinking about the complex technological society we are determined to recreate—and pondering the number of people needed to support such a society—I suddenly reckoned there was not a moment to lose in enlarging the population.

Looked at another way, my remark was simply a cry of defiance. To hell with the scientific view and to hell with the demands of technology. And to hell with the universe itself, which has done its best to annihilate us. I have survived. Sarah and I have survived—as a couple. Why have we survived if we do not carry on, if we do not reproduce and foil the fates that tried to do us in?

But why overintellectualize the whole business? I'm simply a man in love with a woman, and I want a cozy home with a cuddly family. To want babies seems the most normal, instinctual, non-philosophical impulse one can have.

But what am I saying? I don't even like babies! At least I never have in the past. Ah, but I didn't say anything about babies. I said "children." Babies are just something you have on your way to having children. And I guess I could learn to love them. Most people seem to.

Whatever the root cause of my remark—which nobody will ever know, and who cares?—the practical effect was, as Herb put it, "electrifying." Just as we three couples had decided that we would marry—spontaneously, as a unit it seemed, back on the *Queen of Africa*—so did we now decide that the time had come to set the date. And further, the time was at hand to start thinking seriously about having kids.

Almost from the first day we landed on the beach, news had circulated of twosomes among the passengers and crew who were getting married. The shock of the Event and the uncertainty of the future seemed to bring couples together, instinctively seeking an affirmative link. Most of the ceremonies were brief verging on perfunctory, performed by Captain Nordstrom. We had clergy among us, but for the urgent, precipitate unions being ratified, the ship's captain seemed the appropriate choice. Captain Nordstorm honored the yearnings of the young couples, but begrudged the demands on his time. It followed that the wedding parties were very small, and celebration, in the sense of music and dancing, was out of the question. After we made contact with the Inlanders, we learned that some of them also were rushing into marriage. Sarah speculated that the dwindling supplies of birth control materials had something to do with it.

However, until I made my remark about marrying and having children, the six of us in the Focus Group had not considered the planning of weddings. There seemed no need to rush. The "engagements" to which we were pledged provided commitment enough. And the pressures of working for group survival made the idea of ceremony seem frivolous. But by the time of my outburst—I recall that the date was February 3—forty days had passed since the Event. Survival, at least in the short run, seemed assured. The first stage of planning for the long term had been concluded. And though the real work of building a sustainable community was only beginning, it was possible—indeed, only normal—to start arranging our personal futures.

When we gathered the evening after my impetuous outburst, the topic was foremost in everyone's mind. We skirted around it with some nervous, idle chatter, until Tom suddenly spoke up.

"It's still not the time to be talking about weddings," he said. "I'm just too damned busy to think about such a happening, much less plan it. Unless," he added, "we have a quick ceremony just to make our unions honorable. But I don't think that Mary is interested in a Captain Nordstrom five-minute special."

"You know it," Mary said. "Not that I'm happy about living in sin, mind you. But as long as we've come this far, I want to do things right, with a priest, a pretty dress, and festivities with music."

"I've always thought about having a flower-child wedding," Roxy said. "A hippie ceremony at sunrise, celebrating beauty, and at the same time repudiating the values of an over-commercialized world. But with most of the world wiped out, there doesn't seem to be much sense in making a statement of protest. So I'm game for just about anything that's nice, as long as there's plenty of dancing at the party."

There appeared to be agreement that the three ceremonies would take place at the same time. Nobody said it in so many words, but as often seemed to be our way, consensus was in the air.

"I haven't discussed it with Roxy," Herb said, "but I'd like us to be married by a rabbi and stand under a huppah."

"Under a what?" Roxy asked, her voice tinged with suspicion.

"A canopy," Herb said. "It symbolizes the home to be established by the newlyweds. We'll have a flower-covered trellis, and I guarantee that you'll love it."

"Sounds nice," I said. "Can we stand under it, too?"

"Absolutely," Herb said. "We can have a huppah big enough for three couples. Why not? Unless," he added, "Mary's priest objects, or somebody's parents, or who knows what? Once you start planning weddings, complications are sure to follow."

Considering our many debates and discussions, the Focus Group had not spent much time discussing religion. Aside from Mary, a devout Roman Catholic, religious faith didn't play a central role in our lives. Roxy, a one-time Southern Baptist, dabbled with Buddhism, but not in any coherent way. Sarah had grown up as a Presbyterian, Herb as a Jew, and I as an Episcopalian, but all in such secularized families that we were destined to wander from the fold. Tom claimed to be as close to an atheist as a thoughtful person can be, and I sometimes wondered how he and Mary hit it off so well. Love seemed to conquer all, and that, as far as I could tell, was that.

"I wouldn't worry about such things," Tom said. "With the world shot to hell, people aren't going to stand on petty formalities."

"Wrong," Herb said. "How else are we going to prove that we're still human, if we don't show that we can still be petty?"

"All kidding aside," Sarah said. "Are we going to make plans or aren't we?"

"Let's do it," I said. "I might be the one who blurted out that remark about children, but obviously we're all primed to think marriage. Yet," I couldn't help but add, "Tom's right about the timing. If we want ceremony and partying, we have to wait until the situation is a bit less hectic, until living conditions are less primitive, until constructive work projects are more firmly established. We're talking about a few months at least."

"I always wanted to be a June bride," Sarah said. "That's four months away."

"You know, June isn't spring in these parts," Tom said. "It's the beginning of winter."

"Yes, but the winters are fairly mild," Herb said, "especially at these lower elevations near the sea. Assuming, of course, that nature doesn't pull any more of her nasty tricks on us."

"Let's do it," I said again. And we did. We set the date for the first Sunday in June. It seemed far in the future then, and today, a little more than six months after the day, it seems far in the past. But it was an occasion, needless to say, that will be ever fresh in my memory.

The planning did not turn out to be petty or quarrelsome as Herb had predicted, and as I had secretly feared. Tom, as one of the leaders of the R and D operation, was literally too busy to spare a moment from his work. He had a key assignment in planning for the future, and as the weeks went by and his talents were noted by his peers, the demands on his time were relentless. Although I was much lower on the scale of ability and importance, I also found myself working long hours.

As recording secretary to the various leadership groups, I was constantly on call. I thought after the first month or so of meetings (endless meetings!), with the basic plans established, the work of oversight and governance would abate. But I should have known better. Herb, as my sometime assistant, was also needed at many lengthy meetings. So, in a reversion to the conventions of previous generations, most of the wedding arrangements were handled by the women.

Not that "the little ladies," as Herb sometimes had the nerve to call them, weren't extremely busy as well. Mary, the civil engineer, was occupied with roads and pipelines. Roxy was a whirlwind in morale-building ventures—planning athletic events and other group activities, especially dancing. Sometimes she worked with the medical people. It turned out that she had done some nursing in her checkered career. Sarah, starting within a few days of her dramatic parade, became something of a commissioner of cultural affairs. She was perpetually busy with classes, concerts, theater, and other artistic pursuits. But somehow, along with Mary and Roxy, she arranged a grand wedding celebration, one that will be remembered in these parts for many a day.

Once the planning was underway, Herb started to refer to the wedding as "the catered affair." We all picked up on the term. It was a pleasant connection to the good old days. As a catered affair, the first consideration, of course, was food and drink. Here Sarah made the very wise move of bringing Captain Nordstrom into the process. It was an open secret that the *Queen of Africa* chefs still had a hidden cache of special tinned delicacies and fine wines, and some of these were peremptorily earmarked for our great day. Also the kitchen and dining-room staffs, after many weeks of having to serve Spartan rations in austere conditions, were delighted to be involved in plans for a grand shindig.

Finally, the good captain, at a meeting of the Coordinating Committee, let slip a few remarks about the nuptials being planned. Inlanders on the committee—Stephen Healey, Peter Mavimbela, Lucas Moloko, and several others—made a few notes, and shortly before the appointed day, special shipments of meat and fresh produce came rolling into Engineering Village.

Attire for the bridal party presented a more daunting challenge. For one thing, members of the traveling seminar had been instructed not to bring along anything by way of formal dress. Even more serious, after a few months of fairly rugged living, most people's clothes were beginning to show signs of wear and tear. The new clothes being made under the master technology enterprise were simple woolen homespuns, not exactly suitable for a gala occasion. Again, the ship's crew came to the rescue. Fine linen tablecloths were found amid the salvaged supplies. And several members of the laundry staff turned out to be expert seamstresses, willing to volunteer their services for the cause. In short order, Mary, Roxy, and Sarah were fitted with lovely white gowns. Women from one of the Zulu communities near Ulundi sent a gift of beadwork that provided an elegant finishing touch.

Somewhat abashed by their sudden celebrity, the three brides announced that their gowns would be made available to others in the future who chose to add a touch of formality to their wedding ceremonies. Thinking further about all the attention being focused on the forthcoming big day, we sent out a general invitation for other couples to join in.

There was at first some interest expressed, but in the end no takers. Everybody agreed that they didn't want a mass wedding like those employed in the past by certain religious sects. And there developed a friendly willingness to let the six of us have our mini-extravaganza. Sarah, in her daily work, had become widely known and much beloved. Roxy was a favorite among the ship's crew. And Mary was one of the more popular young engineers. Tom, as I have noted, had become one of the acknowledged stars among the engineering elite. Herb and I, as ubiquitous secretaries at important meetings, had gotten on familiar terms with a lot of people. So we were not begrudged our special moment in the sun. A gala triple wedding in June it would be!

For clergy, we were faced with an embarrassment of riches. The cruise ship line often recruited clerics from the major faiths, offering them free vacations plus a small stipend. Our trip, however, was something of an exception. In designing the seminar, my father and his colleagues had conceived of a session on "Engineering and the Spirit," and to lead it they invited two Catholic priests, three ministers of various Protestant denominations, and two rabbis. (Inclusion of the Eastern faiths was considered but deemed outside the competence of the planning group.) In addition, three or four spouses of the engineer participants were ordained ministers of one sort or another, and—just in case anyone was looking for a completely secular approach—several spouses were judges. Not to be forgotten, of course, Captain Nordstrom himself was always available. So the problem was less finding acceptable people than being careful not to hurt anybody's feelings.

Mary zeroed in on Father Jim O'Reilly, a jolly, florid priest right out of Central Casting, who happened to hail from a parish very close to hers in New York City. The good father might have presented a jolly front, but he soon made it clear that in matters of faith he was a stern mentor. The post-holocaust circumstances made not the slightest difference in the way he regarded the sacred obligations of matrimony. A thousand comets, he told Roxy, would not shake his faith or his view of his responsibilities—and hers. Happily, Tom, the nonchalant agnostic, was willing to promise that any children resulting from the union would be baptized and reared as Catholics.

Roxy, following up on Herb's wishes, contacted the two rabbis. The one from Philadelphia proved too sober for her taste. But she took a liking to David Silverman, a young man recently selected to head a synagogue in Denver. Silverman explained that in ordinary circumstances, an Orthodox or Conservative rabbi would not be authorized to perform an interfaith wedding, and that even he, a Reform rabbi, would like to see the prospective bride studying Judaism and considering eventual conversion. Obviously, these were not ordinary circumstances, and David Silverman struggled with the idea that the cosmic devastation might suggest radically new reforms beyond those that were in his tradition. To whom could he turn for guidance? Assuming that Jerusalem had been destroyed once again, what did this portend for the Jewish people—for the human race? The young rabbi had always prided himself on being reasonable, within limits, but in the present circumstance how was he to judge what reasonable meant? As it turned out, Roxy was enthusiastic about the idea of studying Judaism and attended a few informal study sessions. She listened carefully to everything the rabbi had to tell her, and then disarmed and bemused him with the ways in which she sought to merge Jewish traditions into her quasi-Buddhist faith.

Sarah, aboard ship, had become friendly with Ruth Peters, minister to a Presbyterian congregation in northern New Hampshire, who had herself been married—to an environmental engineer—just before coming on the trip. After meeting the other clergy, and giving the matter significant thought, Sarah decided that Ruth would be a perfect choice. My idea of a minister ran more along the lines of a fatherly gentleman with gray hair and a sonorous voice. But this was a new world. Actually, when it came to women in the clergy, it had been a new world for quite a few years, and I just had not been paying attention. Whatever—as the kids used to say (and some of them here still do)—I was to be married to a young woman by a young woman, and soon became accustomed to the idea.

The notion of legal proprieties, of course, was something of an anomaly. The typical marriage ceremony incorporated the words "by the authority vested in me by . . ." By whom? By what? In answer to popular sentiment, the Coordinating Committee, at one of its first meetings, passed a resolution stating that all individuals who before the Event had been authorized to perform weddings would be so empowered in the new society being formed. Some day there would be debates about the laws of marriage and divorce; but not yet.

As for location, the prospective brides chose a spot on the beach where we had first come ashore. Although, as I have noted, Engineering Village was established a short distance inland, adjoining Lake Mzingai, there were still some facilities at the ocean beach, including a bamboo pavilion with a canvas roof that had served as a gathering place from the earliest days. Everyone agreed that Herb should have his huppah. In fact, we all decided to marry under the huppah—a lovely trellis, also bamboo—festooned with the wild-flowers that had bloomed during the now-disappearing summer and fall.

Music was no problem, since members of the ship's orchestra took meticulous care of their instruments, and were happy to have an occasion to display their talents. For a pre-ceremony recital, Mary, Roxy, and Sarah each chose several selections, including such semiclassical chestnuts as "Oh, Promise Me." The idea was to start with traditional melodies that would evoke the past, pay homage to a world that was no more, and proclaim our intention to preserve the best qualities of that world. This concept was carried through in the selection of two wedding marches, *Lohengrin* (Here Comes the Bride) for the processional and Mendelssohn's *Midsummer Night's Dream* for after the ceremony.

Herb protested that this was too corny, but Roxy persuaded him that this was the point, and that old-fashioned sentiment was not to be scorned. She assured him that the music planned for later in the proceedings would include material unusual enough to satisfy the most exotic taste. When he pressed her for details, she put her finger to her lips and smiled. "That's our secret," she said.

After many discussions, we decided to forgo attendants, except for immediate family. At first this didn't seem fair, since Mary, Sarah, Herb, and I had at least one parent with us, while Roxy and Tom, both of whom had come to the *Queen of Africa* on their own, had lost their entire families in the Event. But Roxy said that she never had family who would have come to her wedding anyhow . . . and Tom insisted that his loss should not affect the planning in a negative way.

The brides agreed that they would serve as maids of honor for each other, and the grooms made the same arrangements concerning the best man. Mary and Sarah were to be escorted down the aisle by their fathers. Roxy asked Captain Nordstrom if he would do the same for her, and he was delighted to accept. Mary and Herb both had younger sisters—much younger—and they would add to the festivities as flower girls. Sarah and I observed, not for the first time, that we were both the products of one-child families.

"That's why you're both spoiled rotten," Herb said, also not for the first time.

We three couples wanted to be married together, but in separate ceremonies, so a certain amount of tactical planning was required. We decided that the grooms, clergy, and non-marching parents would first gather by the huppah. Then the flower girls would do their thing, followed by the three brides and escorts. The brides were to be spaced far enough apart so that each would have the equivalent of her own processional. After the three couples had assembled, the ceremonies would be performed in sequence. Clearly, no individual ceremony could be too long. On the other hand, there was to be no feeling of hurry. A starting time of three P.M. was selected, in the hope that the sun of the late autumn afternoon would bring its warmth to the proceedings.

How to select the order in which the couples were to be married? Mary came up with the creative idea that it should be done according to the ages of the three religions: Jewish, Catholic, and Protestant in that sequence. In the absence of any more inspired notions, this is what we incorporated into our plan.

―――――――

Somehow the weeks passed.

Thinking about the wedding provided me with a welcome distraction between meetings of the Expanded Defense Committee; but thoughts of invasion and battle were never far from my mind. Luckily, among the community at large, the recruitment of a militia seemed not to be a cause of special concern. The average person was too busy to be worried by a few signs of military activity.

As we approached the month of June—which would mark a half year after the Event—our industrial revolution gathered momentum in ways that the most optimistic planners could not have foreseen. With brickworks and sawmills in operation, and cement available for mortar and concrete, the building crews of Shaka Enterprises were able to show their stuff. Buildings appeared like mushrooms overnight. Residential units were designed mainly in the form of functional attached housing—brick walls and concrete floor slabs, with thatched roofs on top of wood or bamboo framing—while open-sided sheds served to protect most factory operations. For multipurpose community structures, stone and bamboo were the materials of choice. Indoor plumbing was still a future consideration, although there were heartening signs of water lines and sewers being installed.

The blacksmith forges were busy day and night; and the tools they turned out in great quantity became increasingly serviceable. The smelting furnaces were completed on schedule, and there was great excitement when they produced the first glowing ingots of iron. The machine-tool masters waited covetously for the metals that would allow them to produce the devices they had designed. As soon as these devices were operative, steam engines were scheduled to be manufactured, hopefully by year's end. Engineers argued long into the night about which machines should have priority and which sources of energy would be developed first. There were clever designs for internal combustion engines; but it was impossible, in the short term, to develop adequate supplies of fuel. The electrical engineers were doing exciting work, but still on an experimental level, inhibited by the shortage of copper. Steam was the inevitable first choice.

"The beauty of a steam engine," as Tom Swift explained it one evening to our Focus Group, "is that you simply burn wood or coal, heat water to convert it to vapor, use the vapor to push a piston, and off you go."

"That sounds so primitive," Herb said. "All these hotshot engineers, and we'll be chug-chugging along like in the nineteenth century."

"You should be sending congratulations," Tom said, "instead of complaints about what's impossible. As a matter of fact, some of the steam experts are working on improvements to the steam engine that may astound us all. They're taking it as a special challenge: How do we improve the technology of an earlier age, using the latest knowledge we have of mechanics, materials, and thermodynamics?

"And by the way," Tom continued, "if you want to see hotshot engineers in action, come visit my R and D laboratory just outside of Engineering Village. We're making great progress on developing next-generation plastics, and we're not waiting for petroleum, either. We're extracting lactic acid from corn and turning it into a plastic that we'll use for a variety of products. Right near my operation, the electrical folk are making amazing plans for the use of solar energy, nuclear power, even fusion. You can't imagine how many exciting things are being planned."

At this point, Tom spun around, leaped into the air, and literally kicked his heels together. "We'll make this place into Utopia!" he whooped.

"Be careful what you wish for," Sarah said. "In the original *Utopia*, envisioned by Thomas More in the early 1500s, premarital sex was punished by compulsory celibacy for life, adultery by slavery, and repeated adultery by death. In that ideal community you really had to shape up or ship out."

"Well," Herb said in a deep and solemn tone, "we're all about to enter the respectable state of matrimony. That must be considered a step in the right direction."

We enjoyed a good laugh, and then launched into a semiserious debate about what sort of rules a real Utopia ought to have.

As we merrily planned our ideal society of the future, it occurred to me that a hostile force—possibly setting sail at this very moment—was scheming our destruction. Instead of dreaming about our happy tomorrows, we should be planning to fight for our lives.

In fact, there was that night another secret meeting of the Expanded Defense Committee that would keep me up well past my bedtime. I was getting used to it.

13

The dark sea swelled in white-spumed waves beneath an angry sky. The wind whipped Queen Ranavolana's fleet forward, toward its destination: the coast of KwaZulu Natal and the settlement of survivors of the *Queen of Africa*. The pirate queen stood on the deck of the *King Radama*, her flagship, with its blood red sails and crew of savage sea warriors. It was the third day out from Madagascar, the day before the planned assault.

The first mate approached, shuffling warily into her regal presence, and reported the captain's estimate that they would achieve landfall in seven or eight hours.

"Good," replied the queen. "We will land several miles up the coast from our planned attack point. Rest tonight, and strike tomorrow."

She wore a bright bandanna that held her hair in place and exposed her face to the wind and salt air. She loved the feeling of being out on the open sea. Looking around at the motley fleet that accompanied the *King Radama*, she observed a dozen boats, some of which struggled to match the pace set by her vessel. She had already pushed her pirate crews to their limit—and beyond. Could she expect them to fight tomorrow, to kill or capture all who stood in their path? What kind of resistance, if any, might there be? Had the two fugitives reached the South African coast after they had escaped by boat—and if so, what had they revealed? No matter the answers to these questions, Queen Ranavolana was confident her invading force would quickly overwhelm and subdue the enemy. It was, after all, her destiny.

"Signal to the other ships," she ordered the first mate. "And tell the captain to make full sail until we sight land."

She smiled as he scampered away. The gods, or fates, or God Himself—or Herself—had been kind to Queen Ranavolana. A month earlier, some of her pirates had discovered a ghost ship in the Indian Ocean, an abandoned cargo vessel that contained stores of rice and coffee, as well as a cache of automatic rifles and ammunition. This find was fortuitous on two counts. It gave her a greater sense of security to know that the survivors on Madagascar would be adequately fed during her absence. And it was reassuring to have her men better armed for the battle ahead. There had been great rejoicing in her island kingdom when their good fortune was announced.

For several weeks, the pirates and their "recruits"—young native men pressed into the service of the queen—had drilled relentlessly as the leadership drew up plans for the raid. In total, their force numbered about four hundred able-bodied men, trained to kill first and ask questions later; much later, if at all. Each man was armed with a machete or large hunting knife. A hundred or so carried the auto-rifles that had been salvaged from the abandoned cargo ship along with a half-dozen clips of ammunition each. Some forty or fifty were armed with pistols ranging from ancient Colt revolvers to sleek semiautomatics, with anywhere from a handful to a hundred rounds to fit each gun.

Queen Ranavolana had pored over her "textbooks" and consulted with her lieutenants in the planning phase, using maps and whatever intelligence could be gleaned from anyone who had ever been to the South African shore. She herself had spent some time there during her wandering years and she conjured up dim memories of the coastal terrain. Finally, she sent out several nighttime reconnaissance expeditions to determine the location of the targeted village and its beachfront facility.

The plan of attack evolved into a simple two-pronged maneuver: a land force of about one hundred fifty men, led by Yook Louie and Errol Waddell, would approach from the north, while Queen Ranavolana's naval force with the larger number of men under Jama Chaudri and Raman Patel would attack the beach head-on.

It was early evening when the fleet put ashore in a deserted cove. They made camp and prepared a supper of fish and rice. Afterward, Queen Ranavolana called together all the men.

"My good and strong men—my pirate army and navy—I salute you and wish you good hunting tomorrow!" She stood on a make-shift platform before a roaring campfire, and her words rang out into the night. At first the men were unsure how to react to this intimidating presence; but after an instant they erupted in cheers. Their shouts echoed along the beach and reverberated off the nearby waves.

From her childhood reading the queen conjured up memories of pirate tales, of rough men adrift upon dangerous seas. Those were days of adventure! Now she had the opportunity to create such times again. She would write the script and she would star in the show. The unsuspecting quarry would be witness to her craftiness and ruthlessness. If they resisted, well, it was the way of the world that they should pay. Too bad . . . but that was reality: *her* reality.

When the cheers subsided, she continued: "The world—a new world—is yours for the taking. Your leaders will guide you, and you must follow them without question. They know of my master plan and how it must be executed. There can be no deviation from the plan if we are to succeed in our mission. Do you understand me? Do you believe me? Do you follow me?"

An even greater cheer erupted from the massed men as they

stood for their queen, waving their machetes and guns. The sub-commanders, Louie, Patel, Chaudri, and Waddell, spontaneously lifted her to their shoulders and held her aloft for all to see. When she was lowered to the ground, she smiled at her trusted lieutenants, waved to the men, and walked away from the fire to be by herself in the darkness.

Queen Ranavolana breathed heavily, her head reeling from the frenzy of adulation. She felt high, drugged, ecstatic—yet suddenly overwhelmed by a wave of apprehension. Her plans were in place, the men raring to go into action, the element of surprise—she hoped—still on her side. Why, then, this onset of nagging doubt and distressing premonition of failure? What had she done wrong? Or, what might she have overlooked?

She came to the place where the boats were moored. They rocked gently in the low tide, shadows on the water. They looked like the pleasure craft they had once been rather than the war vessels to which they had been converted. A hundred yards away she could hear the men whooping and laughing, in contrast to the deadly quiet of this sandy cove.

One of the sentries stepped forward to confront her, but when he saw who she was, he bowed his head and stepped back to allow her free passage. She saluted him and walked on through the cold wet sand.

After days of rain and clouds, the sky had miraculously cleared, and the sun shone on the southeast shore of the African continent. A beautiful day for a wedding.

A crowd gathered in and around the pavilion on the beach. The huppah had been erected close to the water's edge, making an enchanting scene. At the appointed time the music struck up, and the brides walked down the aisle, one at a time as planned, looking positively radiant. Everyone played their parts to perfection, and the three ceremonies were performed without a hitch. The formal rites were followed by brief readings that had been selected by various members of the nuptial party.

First, Captain Nordstrom read a hymn of the Great Plains Indians provided by Roxy. She had learned it years before during a visit to a western reservation and determined then to have it read on her wedding day:

> *O Morning Star! when you look down upon us, give us peace and refreshing sleep. Great Spirit! bless our children, friends and visitors through a happy life. May our trails lie straight and level before us. Let us live to be old. We are all your children and ask these things with good hearts.*

Then Herb's parents recited the Seven Blessings, a traditional part of many Jewish marriage services. It ends with "Blessed are you, Holy One of All, who created joy and gladness, bride and bridegroom, mirth and song, pleasure and delight, love, fellowship, peace and friendship."

The three couples stood, holding hands and smiling. Happiness and love were in the air.

Next, Wilson Hardy, recalling his own wedding ceremony more than thirty years previously, read from the Episcopal Book of Common Prayer:

> The union of husband and wife in heart, body and mind is intended by God for their mutual joy; for the help and comfort given one another in prosperity and adversity, and, when it is God's will, for the procreation of children and their nurture in the knowledge and love of the Lord.

Sarah had asked her parents to read from the Song of Solomon:

My beloved spake and said unto me, Rise up, my love, my fair
one, and come away. For, lo, the winter is past, the rain is over
and gone; the flowers appear on the earth; the time of the singing of birds is come, and the voice of the turtle is heard in our
land.

And Mary's parents, beaming, but with tears in their eyes, addressed their daughter and her new husband and everyone present
with the traditional Irish blessing:

> May the wind be always at your back.
> May the road rise up to meet you.
> May the sun shine warm on your face,
> The rains fall soft on your fields.
> Until we meet again, may the Lord
> Hold you in the hollow of his hand.

Each participant spoke as clearly and loudly as possible, consistent with the propriety of the occasion, but it was difficult to tell
how much the assembled guests could make out.

"We could really use a sound system," Tom Swift muttered.
"There ought to be a special prayer for the engineers who are working to restore our electrical and electronic facilities. Damnation."

Mary hushed him, but she and the others were thinking much
the same thing—not least the clergy, who probably had never been
called upon to preach without at least the option of microphone and
loudspeaker. What had it been like for all those thousands of years,
trying to communicate using only an unenhanced human voice?
How could large groups of people function? What about those famous orators: Cicero, Henry the Fifth of England, Robespierre,
Daniel Webster, William Jennings Bryan? How many individuals

really heard George Washington's Farewell or Abraham Lincoln's Gettysburg Address. The vacuum tube, which first made possible the amplification of electrified sound impulses, wasn't even invented until 1907.

"Well, these are questions for a different time," thought Wil Hardy. "For the moment, it really doesn't matter one whit whether or not our words are heard clearly by the multitudes."

Still, to those who were able to hear the exchange of vows, and the selected readings, the familiar, hallowed words were a comfort and a consolation. And to those beyond the range of the participants' voices, the ceremony and celebration that followed was a welcome community-building event.

An invitation to the wedding had been extended to all the inhabitants of Engineering Village and to many of the Inlanders as well, although the travel involved would make it impractical for more than a few of them to attend. There were about twenty-five hundred people altogether, many of whom attended out of courtesy and curiosity, watching diffidently from afar as if observing a theatrical event. Plans had been made to serve about fifteen hundred meals.

Shortly after the recessional, the ship's orchestra broke into a spirited hora, and each of the newly married couples was hoisted aloft on chairs and carried about. They were surrounded by a crowd of revelers who held hands, circling and kicking in time with the music. Soon the hora gave way to a tarantella, and then an Irish jig, which Mary's parents led with marvelous agility. The six just-marrieds considered showing off their line-dancing skills—for old times' sake (just six months ago!)—but the wedding dresses did not accommodate those western steps. They also figured that the majority of the people present would be ready for some honest-to-goodness fox-trots, jitterbugging, and disco.

Sure enough, as the musicians shifted to jazz tunes and then rock, people all over the beach broke into lively dance. The serenity of the wedding service was transformed into the merriment of a carnival. If there were indeed evil fates who had sent the comet to crush the human spirit, they must have been astonished by the scene.

After everybody had danced to the point of exhaustion, the meal was served. Buffet tables were loaded with such a variety of spectacular dishes that one could readily imagine there had never been an errant comet, that the survivors were instead off on a grand vacation or living in an idyllic land of milk and honey. The next day, everyone knew, they would return to a diet heavy with corn meal, corn mush, and corn bread. But for the moment there was a cornucopia of beef, mutton, and fowl; a dazzling variety of vegetables and fruits; a stunning display of ornately decorated pastries; and delicious bread made from fine white flour.

Within the past week, the populace had been heartened to learn that a small crop of wheat had been harvested, and that two water-powered gristmills were turning out flour of excellent quality.

The bridal party and a few special guests sat at a large table, using an assortment of chairs and stools made of every imaginable material and in every conceivable design. The rest of the assemblage sat or stood or lounged, as all had become used to doing, some within the pavilion and others spread out like picnickers in a park.

While they ate, they were serenaded by singers and musicians who had been recruited from among the Inlanders by Roxy and Sarah. White groups alternated with black; they played rock music and folk, and sometimes a marvelous combination of both. Most sang the lyrics in English, but Afrikaans and tribal languages were also heard.

Then, as the meal came to an end, Sarah rose and walked to the central area that was serving as a stage. She wanted personally to introduce the next performers, the Zulu Male Voice Choir. Eight Zulu men—none of them young—dressed simply in shirts and trousers, stepped forward and started to sing. The sound they made was familiar yet exotic, sort of gospel with an African tribal intonation. As Wil Hardy found himself tapping his feet and swaying in place, Sarah told him a little about what he was hearing.

This was music known as *mbube* ("lion") or sometimes called *cothoza mfana* ("walk steadily, boys"). The unique art form had its roots in American minstrel shows that visited South Africa in the 1890s. Mission-educated South Africans combined elements of this minstrelsy with ragtime, western hymns, and Zulu song. From the 1930s to the 1960s, when many blacks were compelled to leave their homes—the men obliged to find employment in remote mines, fields, and factories—performers of *mbube* became enormously popular in the migrant worker communities. After hearing a few selections, Wil could understand why. Fantastic, he thought. Not only the sound and style, but also the story of how it came to be. American minstrel shows traveling in South Africa in the 1890s! Another of the quirks of history that he found so enthralling.

"So you see," said Sarah, reading her husband's mind, "art has its historical tales, every bit as fascinating as technology's."

Hardly had the choir finished taking its bows, after a few encores demanded by the audience, when another performer came, leaped really, to center stage. This man was dressed in tribal regalia, and there was no tinge of Western influence in his manner or sound. He radiated Zulu exuberance and pride from head to toe. Roxy introduced him as Ezekiel Motsima, an *imbongi*, a praise poet, a chanter of *izibongo*, praises.

As Deborah Frost had explained in one of her seminars, this ancient genre had been widely used in Southern Africa by speakers of Zulu, Ndebele, and Xhosa. In its earliest form, tribal leaders were the primary focus of the praises, and the stress was on macho virility and prowess in battle. In more recent manifestations, political groups had used *izibongo* to seek partisan advantage, praising one official or another at ceremonies, or even at trade union rallies.

There is also a long-standing practice of reciting praise poems for ordinary people on special occasions, particularly weddings. Ezekiel told the wedding party that since the most renowned *imbongis* had been swept away by the Event, he, an amateur, would do his best to serve in their stead. To these observers, however, he seemed very much the professional.

First he chanted some traditional praises for national leaders of the past. After calling out the lines in Zulu, he gave the audience rough translations and encouraged them to call out *"Musho!"* (Speak him!) if they were so moved.

He is awesome . . .
One who overflows with compassion, helper of those in danger.
Broad-shouldered one . . .
Violent flooder like the Thukela River, who cannot be restrained . . .

Then, taking up shield and spear, the *imbongi* started to intone war cries, which the audience accompanied with clapping hands.

Our blood!
It quivered!
Get out of our path!
You've provoked us!
We are the courageous ones!
Our hearts are angry—as red as blood!

Finally, in the spirit of banter and jest often employed at family celebrations, he called out praises that he had prepared for the three grooms—obviously using information supplied by Roxy. He called Herb "the jokester who upsets the people with his impudence." Tom was teased as "the man who loves machines too much, who ought to love trees." And he called Wil to task for keeping his head down in books all the time.

"Stand up," he yelled, waving his spear close to Wil's face. "Stand up, show us you can put down your pencil, kiss your new wife, and do a dance."

The young recording secretary had no pencil to put down at that moment; but he did stand up, kiss Sarah, and twirl her about in an impromptu waltz.

With that, the brides called out in unison, "*Musho!* Say him!" And the call was echoed by the surrounding crowd, most of whom had not made out the *imbongi's* words, but who were swept up in the exhilaration of the moment. "*Musho! Musho! Musho!*"

By now, it was growing dark along the beach, and several large bonfires were set ablaze. The brides had planned for the day to end with a grand songfest. To lead the singing, Roxy called upon a chorus she had helped to form among the citizens of Engineering Village. It was a curious assortment of engineers, spouses, and members of the crew. If there was one main shared characteristic, Roxy said, it was that many of the participants had, at one time or another, sung in a church choir. Indeed, the program opened with two spirituals, "Shall We Gather at the River?" and "Swing Low, Sweet Chariot." Then came such time-honored favorites as "Oh Susanna," "Good Night, Ladies," and "Coming Thru' the Rye." For some reason, members of the chorus had taken a special fancy to American Civil War music: "Dixie," "Tenting Tonight," and, inevitably, "The Battle Hymn of the Republic." All joined in, singing lustily, yet with an underlying trace of sadness. The authors of those songs lived in hard, uncertain times in which optimism and melancholy were closely mixed. "Mine eyes have seen the glory of the coming of the Lord . . ."

No one could have reckoned on the solo that came next. Donald Ruffin, the often irritating leader of the electrical engineers, was one of the last people anyone present would have expected to be a singer, much less the possessor of a magnificent baritone voice. He stepped forward and with only the slightest backing from a single guitar started to sing "Shenandoah." By the time he reached the last verse, tears rolled down the cheeks of many of his listeners.

> *Oh, Shenandoah,*
> *I long to see you,*
> *Far away, you rolling*
> *river.*
> *Oh, Shenandoah,*
> *I long to see you.*
> *Away,*
> *I'm bound away,*
> *Across the wide Missouri.*

Contemplating the vast continental wilderness of early America, feelings of loneliness welled up within Wilson Hardy, Jr., feelings that even romantic love could not keep at bay—and certainly not cocky plans for technological conquest. How much more vast and lonely is the wilderness in which we find ourselves, Hardy mused, here on the coast of Africa, with the rest of the world in ashes. This day that had dawned so bright and hopeful seemed to be ending in gloom.

"You're supposed to be happy," Sarah said, sensing his mood, although in the deepening dusk he was able to brush away the tears before she could see them.

"I'm overcome with happiness," he said, kissing her on the neck. What he said was true, even as fresh tears welled up in his eyes. Just the mood of the moment, he thought, brought on by the haunting music, and possibly one glass of wine too many.

That mood changed abruptly when he heard the shots. He knew they were shots even though he had never been in the vicinity of live gunfire. There were no firecrackers to celebrate the weddings and no cars around that could be backfiring. The noise seemed to come from out on the water. Looking in that direction, Wil saw flashes of light. The streaks pointed upward. Somebody was shooting into the air. Within seconds, a sailing ship came within range of the light from the bonfires. He saw the red sails. Then the name, painted in black: KING RADAMA.

"Good grief," Herb said, as the boat rode right up to the edge of the beach, "it's the Dragon Lady herself!"

"Jeezuzz!" Wil Hardy muttered.

Mary O'Connor Swift said, "Wil Hardy, you shouldn't be taking the Lord's name in vain on your wedding day." It was clear that she had no clue as to what was happening—and what was about to happen.

Several boats sailed into view, and the wild-looking crews leaped into the surf and made anchors fast. The queen stood in the bow of her vessel, holding the rigging with one hand, a rifle aloft in the other. She looked like a painting, Wil Hardy thought—a dark perversion of *Washington Crossing the Delaware*.

14

She was dressed in light canvas trousers and a brilliant red blouse, with her hair swept up in a large multicolored bandanna, just as she had been described by Harry McIntosh and his crew of fishermen. It could be none other than the self-anointed Queen Ranavolana.

After firing another shot into the air, the queen leaped nimbly into the shallow surf, strode onto the shore, and went directly to the table at which the wedding party was seated. The three grooms had risen, and they stood near their brides to shield them from danger.

Captain Nordstrom and Wilson Hardy, Sr., also came forward to confront the queen. She looked them up and down dismissively. At the same time, she glanced about, trying not to show her astonishment at finding the beach so crowded with people. She had expected to arrive on an empty shore and sweep from there, unopposed, into the village. She was caught offguard by this—what was it? It looked like a wedding feast. At least no one appeared to be carrying weapons. The revelers were clearly unarmed, shocked by her sudden appearance. Good. Let them be shocked; she could use this to her advantage.

"Are you having a nice celebration?" the pirate queen asked in a loud voice. Covertly she tried to calculate the size of the crowd.

"Yes, thank you," Captain Nordstrom answered, as if the question had been sincere. "Would you care to join us?"

The woman laughed scornfully. "I think the question is, 'Would you care to join *me*?' After all, you are my prisoners."

"What do you mean?" Dr. Hardy said. "You can't—"

"Silence! I can—and I have. We have the weapons, as you can see. And you are my prisoners; that is the fact of the matter. I hope there is enough food left for my men. They are very hungry." She turned toward the sea and waved her left hand, her right still gripping the ominous rifle.

As the pirate force, responding to her signal, left their vessels and moved swiftly to various points along the shoreline, there were scattered screams among the wedding guests. Each of these fierce-looking men was armed with a machete or a large hunting-style knife, and many of them carried guns as well. The guests began to fall back, a few of them turning as if to run.

Chaudri and Patel appeared at Queen Ranavolana's side and reported that their men were all ashore, ready to move on the village. Their language was incomprehensible to Nordstrom and Hardy; but the two men understood the meaning all too clearly. It had happened as predicted by the escapees from Madagascar. This was a full-scale invasion.

"Everyone go back to your homes—now!" Nordstrom called to the wedding guests, many of whom seemed to be frozen in place at their tables. "You too!" he said to the brides and their grooms. "Move quickly. Go!"

The queen and her men watched the people starting to leave the beach and move back toward the village. She was pleased that her men exercised discipline and did not pursue, awaiting orders. She addressed her two subcommanders: "Prepare to move in when I give the word. First, I will speak to these two. I assume they are the leaders of this settlement." To Nordstrom and Hardy, she said,

"Now, gentlemen, do you wish to hear my terms?" They did not reply immediately, but returned her steady, unflinching gaze.

"Well, you'll hear what I have to say whether you like it or not. These men"—she swung her arm around to indicate the menacing figures that had advanced up the beach—"they follow me, do as I tell them. And I will order them to slaughter every man, woman, and child in the village if you do not cooperate with me."

"What do you want from us?" Hardy asked.

"Food, supplies, armaments. You will surrender any weapons that you have, or else my men will take them by force. Anyone who resists will be executed on the spot. I hope I have made myself clear."

"Why do you come here as pirates and thieves instead of as friends? We are willing to share what we have, and to work with you. There is no need for this . . . this show."

"Do not think it is just a show. Understand that it is a show of force. We mean to take what we need. Why should I believe your offer to share? The world is in ruins. My people are close to starvation. They are depending on me to feed them. They are desperate—as am I. Therefore, I will take—not ask, but take—and I will send my men back for more whenever there is a need. Eventually this region will become an outpost of my empire."

"You should believe us because we tell the truth. We have no quarrel with you, no wish to withhold aid." Hardy spoke slowly, deliberately, trying to find some ground on which he could negotiate. But the young woman, very clearly an American from her speech and demeanor, would give no quarter.

"You do not understand. I am not asking for anything but demanding. And if you defy me, you will pay with your life." She lifted the rifle barrel so that it pointed at Dr. Hardy's chin. "Perhaps I have made myself clearer."

"You have, indeed," Captain Nordstrom said, admiring Hardy's steadfast courage, but fearful for his comrade's life. He kept his own voice steady: "We do not wish to defy you, only to understand exactly what it is you need—what you demand."

"Don't try to soft-talk me, Swedish Man," she said, swinging the gun suddenly in the captain's direction.

"Norwegian," Nordstrom said. He couldn't help himself; but when he saw that he had angered her, he changed course. "And you are American, I presume."

"Presume all you like, but where I come from does not matter a damn. The world is destroyed and everything is changed. It is where I am now that counts—and who I have become. I am Ranavolana, Queen of the Malagasys and Admiral of the Oceans. You, sir, are my subject, as are all of your people. Now, let's move toward your settlement. Both of you, stay with me." To her lieutenants, she said: "Bring the men forward, at the ready. We'll establish ourselves in command of their village, and exact the tribute that is due us."

Patel and Chaudri moved to her right and left, respectively, and ordered their men to advance.

She checked her watch, a cheap old Timex that had accompanied her on her globe-trotting tours over the past decade and still worked—miraculously. The timing of the operation so far was perfect. The reinforcements from the north should be approaching the village just about now.

———

At the sound of the first shot a half hour earlier, Captain Nordstrom had put into effect the defensive plan he and General White and the Expanded Defense Committee had devised. With a prearranged signal, he dispatched Deck Officer Gustafsson to the village to carry the news and help arrange the defenses. Before the pirate queen's feet touched the sand, his trusted aide had disappeared into the darkness.

Early that morning the captain had been awakened by Gustafsson and Olav Hamsun, the *Queen of Africa*'s security officer. Run-
ners from Ulundi had arrived with news: the Madagascar invasion
force had been sighted by Inlander scouts in a cove about ten miles
to the north of Engineering Village. At dawn, one body of men—
approximately one hundred and fifty—had moved inland on foot
and headed south toward the village. The fleet, with about two hundred and fifty men aboard, had sailed out to sea and then set a
course toward the beach that served as the community's port facility. The queen's two pronged attack was launched. The captain had
transmitted this information to General White, who was prepared
to mobilize the defense forces. So, throughout the morning and
early afternoon, troops from the Engineering Village battalion had
been gathering in secret in the bamboo groves around the village.
They did not interfere with any of the wedding preparations; they
simply were not there. And in the midst of the hubbub they were
scarcely missed.

To the north, the Ulundi battalion had been deployed to intercept the land invaders; and shortly after Queen Ranavolana's fleet
sailed, they had moved into action. The one hundred and fifty pirates were on the march, slovenly and unsuspecting, when the
Ulundi force, five hundred strong—most of them young Zulus—
attacked from the hills above. The assault quickly became a slaughter. The pirates fought with desperation, but they were surprised
and outnumbered. And man for man, they were no match for the
fierce warrior descendants of the mighty Shaka. Half the invaders
were killed outright, including subcommander Yook Louie, who was
simultaneously shot through the head with a bullet and run
through the heart with a spear. Another twenty-five or so were
wounded, which left only fifty standing. These threw down their
arms and surrendered. Quickly, their hands were tied behind their
backs. The whole operation was over in less than an hour. The

surviving pirates, totally unnerved, were then forced to march south with their conquerors.

A courier on horseback brought news of the victory to General White and informed him that the Ulundi battalion, with its prisoners, was en route to the village, expecting to arrive by evening. The Defense Committee and the Coordinating Committee, meeting in a secret emergency session, were faced with a decision. It was now mid-day: Should the wedding celebration be allowed to proceed?

"Considering the alternatives," Hardy had said, "I think we should carry on as normally as possible. A sudden cancellation would throw our people into a state of confusion that would only work to the benefit of the invaders. Besides," he continued with a grim smile, "if you'll permit a personal observation, my son—who you'll note has not been informed of this meeting—is scheduled to get married in a little while, and I don't want some two-bit so-called pirates to make us change our plans."

General White agreed. "We have no way of knowing exactly where and when the invasion fleet plans to come ashore," he said. "So let's just stay alert and keep our troops at the ready but concealed. The mad queen's eventual goal is certainly the village—and that is where we will prepare to meet her. In the meanwhile, let the celebration continue." He stood up, ready for an adjournment of the meeting, but then turned toward Dr. Hardy and put a hand on his shoulder. "Just one thing, Wilson," he said in a severe tone of voice. "I'm going back to join our fighting forces. But I don't like the idea of missing a party, and I want it remembered that you owe me one!"

This lightened the mood as the secret meeting ended. Some of those in attendance filtered out to join the wedding festivities. Others, along with General White, went to rejoin the troops.

When darkness fell, the pirate fleet had made its appearance.

Ahead, Nordstrom and Hardy saw the lights of bonfires. Earlier in the day, these fires had been strategically placed to illuminate the length of the village, and orders were given for them to be ignited upon the approach of the enemy. The flickering glow now gave the scene a theatrical aspect, and the queen led her men confidently up to the small obelisk that marked the heart of the central square.

At this point, a shrill whistle was heard, and out of the shadows, on either side of the pirate force, there appeared a massed army stepping forward with practiced precision. To the invaders, this body of men appeared to be an enormous legion—a ghostly horde—arrayed row upon row and disappearing into the darkness. In reality, it was the Engineering Village battalion, somewhat less than five hundred in number, many of them armed with weapons of uncertain utility. But the most impressive-looking guns had been put into the hands of the front ranks, and the overall appearance of the force was fierce and intimidating.

Queen Ranavolana was stunned and she reflexively shivered. Chaos was the milieu in which she had risen to power. Here there appeared to be order and discipline, the nemesis of her reckless aggression. Still, she braced herself and managed to stand steady, pointing her gun ever more menacingly at Captain Nordstrom and Dr. Hardy. She was by no means vanquished by this latest turn of events. These two men had allowed themselves to become her hostages, a foolish move, she thought, which they must be very much regretting. And as soon as her land army arrived from the north— glancing at her watch she could see that they should be appearing at any moment now—they would attack this surrounding force and teach them a thing or two about battle. She knew her pirates to be ferocious fighters, each one the equal of several ordinary soldiers. Nevertheless, she was momentarily overcome by that same feeling of uneasiness she had experienced in the cove the previous evening.

As the two hostile forces stood staring at each other, fingering their weapons, General White stepped out of the ranks and walked forward to confront the queen directly. He was dressed in his precisely pressed U.S. Army uniform, golden stars ablaze in the flickering light, and several rows of battle ribbons arrayed imposingly on his broad chest.

"Madam," he said, "may I point out that you are surrounded and outnumbered. I suggest that you surrender before we have a lot of unnecessary bloodshed."

"May I suggest," Queen Ranavolana replied, "that you get out of our way before I decide to shoot you between the eyes." Confrontational talk seemed to revive the lady's spirits.

"I think this is what they call a Mexican standoff," Wilson Hardy quipped tensely; but no one was listening.

At this moment, from just outside the village, shouting could be heard. It was a crowd of warriors chanting a Zulu battle cry, at once spine-chilling and fiercely melodious. Closer and closer came the resounding chant, until suddenly Peter Mavimbela, streaked with dust and sweat, his clothing torn and bloodied, ran into view followed by a group of Ulundi militiamen. "We beat them! We beat them to a bloody pulp!" he exclaimed. "Come on in, boys!"

Queen Ranavolana and her men stood frozen, like disbelieving statues, as the Ulundi legions marched forward with the ragtag remnants of the pirate land army in tow. Mavimbela lined up the prisoners, bedraggled and defeated, heads hanging, unable to look in the direction of their queen. The Zulu warriors, some of them bedecked in animal skins and carrying large shields, struck terror into the hearts of the pirate invaders. The threatening precision of the Engineering Village battalion was now compounded by the savage menace of the Ulundi troops; it was too much to bear.

Captain Nordstrom reached toward the queen, palm upward, and said, "I will take your weapons, Your Majesty, if you please."

The tables were now turned, and Queen Ranavolana was prisoner of the very people she had presumed to conquer. Oddly, she seemed almost relieved, and her body was totally limp as two militia officers half-carried, half-dragged her to the council pavilion for questioning.

General White took charge of the interrogation of the queen and her three surviving subcommanders. He asked Pascal Ralaimongo—because of his knowledge of conditions on Madagascar—to join the proceedings. Also in attendance were Nordstrom, Hardy Senior, and members of the Expanded Defense Committee; but they observed in silence. Although it was now approaching midnight, Wil Hardy, the new bridegroom, was called to duty as recording secretary.

The session lasted for several hours, and as it concluded, the dawn of a new day was breaking. The general wanted to be absolutely certain that there were no more reinforcements waiting to land on the beach and fall upon Engineering Village. It became obvious from the dispirited answers given by the queen and her subcommanders that there were no other hostile forces to be concerned about, nor anyone remaining on their home island who had either the means or the desire to recruit a new army. Ralaimongo reassured the group that this was the case. General White then sought other information about the survivors across the Mozambique Channel; also the resources—or lack of resources—in that little corner of the world.

When the interrogation session ended and the prisoners were led away, Wil Hardy went up to his father and Captain Nordstrom and confronted them angrily. "Why did you keep us in the dark?" he said, "Herb and Tom and me? If you knew what was going to happen, we should have been called for duty with the militia." First of all, young Wil wanted to do his share like everyone else. Secondly, how could he write about important events if he had not witnessed them himself?

His father looked from Captain Nordstrom to the younger man. "Apologies, son, but we didn't want to alarm the populace and possibly give aid to the enemy. Also, to tell the truth, we didn't want to spoil your wedding day." As he noticed the sun in the East, rising out of the sea, he was almost too tired to smile.

By afternoon the Coordinating Committee was once again in session, this time trying to decide what to do with the members of the defeated army. Pascal Ralaimongo, the intrepid teacher and Malagasy elder, offered to return with them to Madagascar. He contended that without the leadership of the mad queen and her lieutenants, these brutes would not be able to function as an organized force. Besides, he was confident that with a little bit of assistance from their South African neighbors, his countrymen could organize a civil society, and that the erstwhile pirates would soon blend in with the mass of survivors. He suggested that, in a primitive tribal setting, the life of a buccaneer holds few attractions. When there is little that is worth stealing, and when survival depends mainly on group enterprise, a criminal career loses its appeal. This was a fact that the members of the Coordinating Committee had found to be true in their own community. Of course, in the long run—everyone, including Ralaimongo, agreed—as society became wealthier and more complex, human nature would be human nature, and law enforcement would once again become an important aspect of civilized society. But the long run would have to take care of itself. There were more than enough immediate problems with which to cope.

In the end, Pascal Ralaimongo's suggestion was adopted: The invaders would be allowed to return to Madagascar. With them would go vital foodstuffs and tools, and a party of volunteers from the Ulundi Circle—doctors, engineers, and agricultural specialists. While this flotilla was being readied, an effort would be made, under Ralaimongo's direction, to "rehabilitate" the scoundrel pirate army and prepare them for a useful life among the decent people of their homeland.

The queen and her three villainous aides would be kept in a makeshift jail in Engineering Village. There were those who wanted them shipped back with their army; but that was considered too risky. Others wanted them executed; but that was considered too barbaric, particularly in the absence of any legal code. Was there to be a limit to their term of imprisonment? Could they ever be paroled or pardoned? These vexing questions, by general consensus, would have to be decided "in the future."

A few days later, as the time for the fleet's planned departure was drawing near, Captain Johan Nordstrom walked on the beach studying the dozen craft that were lying at anchor. He admired especially two of them that were beautifully shaped and carefully crafted, obviously built for speedy sailing across rough seas. Suddenly, he was struck with an idea that took hold of him so forcefully that he could scarcely believe it had not occurred to him earlier. He awaited the next day's scheduled meeting of the Coordinating Committee with great anticipation.

"The outside world!" he said excitedly to the committee when they were gathered together. They were not used to seeing the captain in such a state of animation. "The outside world!" he said again, gesturing with his arms in large circles. "A couple of those yachts from Madagascar are beautiful vessels that can sail anywhere, cross any ocean. They would have to be worked on a bit, fitted out properly and adequately supplied; but it's almost as if they've been sent here to encourage us to go exploring."

There followed a spirited discussion, which inevitably spilled out beyond the confines of the Coordinating Committee into the community at large. It was amazing how quickly the populace became swept up in a passion for journeys to distant places. The presence of the sailing yachts, plus the invasion of the pirates, had reawakened an interest in other parts of the globe, a curiosity that had been lying dormant since the Event. The earliest reconnaissance, on horseback, had convinced everyone that beyond the Ulundi Circle there was nothing but a burned-out wasteland. Additional exploration, also by horse, carried out by Inlanders determined to look for loved ones in the farthest reaches of South Africa, had revealed the same: total devastation everywhere.

But what about other continents? Theoretically, they were wastelands too. Yet how could one be sure? And no matter what their fate, no matter how bleak their condition, shouldn't these survivors seek to determine it with their own eyes? Beyond concern for the present—possible fellow survivors, possible resources to be garnered—there was the future to be considered. It might be prudent to establish colonies on distant shores. Or, prudence be damned, there might be those who wanted to migrate to distant shores for whatever reason.

A few people urged that extended voyages be delayed until the boats could be fitted out with steam engines, and even more important, short-wave radios for keeping in touch with home base. But there were no prospects of having such equipment available for a long time—at least several months for the engines, and even by the most optimistic forecast, three years for radios.

Arguments for caution and delay were swept aside, and preparations for a lengthy voyage—perhaps two—were begun. The desire to explore is an endemic fever in the human spirit. The sight of those graceful yachts had set it raging.

FROM THE JOURNAL OF WILSON HARDY, JR.

When the pirate fleet finally set sail for home across the Mozambique Channel, the two most seaworthy yachts were left behind. Nobody claimed that they were the spoils of war. Rather, it seemed a fair trade—a couple of surplus boats in exchange for food, tools, and medical aid, for the necessities of life. The pirates, most of whom had given themselves up for lost, could scarcely believe their good fortune. Free, returning home, and accompanied by a foreign aid mission to boot; they were transformed magically from surly scoundrels to simple seamen, grinning from ear to ear. Nor did they seem to regret being free of their queen's command.

Millie Fox and a few of her Peace Corps people decided to join the volunteer contingent going to Madagascar; and Millie, along with Captain Nordstrom and Pascal Ralaimongo, arranged a tentative schedule for ferrying people and materials back and forth between the two communities.

"Let's keep in touch!" shouted my friend, Herb Green, as the last of the vessels hoisted anchor and turned seaward. Then muttering: "But don't call me; I'll call you."

"Oh, come off it, Herb," I said by way of reprimand. "If there are two human habitations left on the face of the earth, the least they can do is socialize."

"Okay, if you say so," he replied. "But no more invasions, please."

No sooner had the sails disappeared over the horizon than attention turned in earnest to plans for global exploration. Work began on refitting the two sloops with new canvas, and on restoring their woodwork to its original strength and beauty. When the vessels were taken out for trial runs, large crowds gathered to marvel at their speed and grace skimming the waves.

The leaders of this enterprise were the Cortez brothers: Ernesto and Jose. The two young men were put in charge when their credentials were brought to the attention of the Coordinating Committee. The brothers come from Texas, where they were sometime students at the University of Texas at Austin. Their father was a leading petroleum engineer with one of the major oil companies. Ernesto and Jose are accomplished soccer players, skillful rock climbers, and as luck would have it, experienced yachtsmen. They have often sailed with friends up and down the Gulf of Mexico, and on several occasions across the Atlantic to the west coast of Africa. Nobody here can match their experience as oceangoing sailors. Many officers and crewmen of the *Queen of Africa* have spent years on the open sea, but not in sailboats. A number of Inlanders have sailed often in coastal waters, but never across an ocean. The Cortez brothers established their fitness for command not only by past reputation, but also by their knowledge as evinced in discussions with Captain Nordstrom and his officers, and by their masterful performance at the helm.

The captain had reservations based upon the youth of the two men, and also the fact that they were known to love a party. A reputation for high spirits was not necessarily a disqualification, but it did raise doubts in Nordstrom's mind. He was reassured, however, when the young men's father vouched for their conduct. They might play hard, said Mr. Cortez, but on a serious mission they were totally trustworthy.

"You know, Captain," he added with a smile, "the family's namesake, the renowned conquistador, Hernán Cortéz, was said by his secretary to be haughty, mischievous and 'much given to women.' And just think of what he accomplished."

"We are not looking for someone to conquer a Mexican empire," Captain Nordstrom said, somewhat dourly. But he relented.

Ernesto and Jose were given their commands; but they were not given free rein in choosing routes of travel. Their first idea was to sail together around the world west to east, the two sloops lending support to each other as they checked out the continents one by one. But members of the Coordinating Committee resolved that the journeying should be limited to a year's time, and given that constraint, a circumnavigation seemed overly ambitious.

"Magellan was the first one to do it in the world that was," said Stephen Healey, "and it took him three years. Actually, I should say it took a few members of his crew three years. Magellan was killed in the Philippines, and most of the men died along the way."

"But, sir," Ernesto objected, "that was a long time ago."

Jose pointed out that back in the 1960s Sir Francis Chichester had sailed around the world alone in the 55-foot *Gipsy Moth IV*, a sailing yacht about the same size as the two now in hand. He covered 14,100 miles from Plymouth, England, to Sydney, Australia, in 107 days; and after several weeks layover, continued back to Plymouth around Cape Horn, 15,517 miles, in another 119 days, making for a total time at sea of 226 days.

"And that was nothing," Ernesto added. "There are now sailing ships that go round the world easily in seventy days. Or at least there were."

"Let's not be ridiculous," Captain Nordstrom said impatiently. "We're interested in exploration, not ocean racing. A swift trip across open water wouldn't reveal much by way of useful information."

It was finally decided that the purpose of the mission—learning about the state of the world—would best be served if the two sloops headed off in different directions. One boat would go west across the Atlantic to Brazil, then north to Florida, making as many stops in South and Central America as feasible, then back to the Atlantic coast of France, Spain, and Portugal, returning to home base along the west coast of Africa. If time and tide allowed, there could also be a visit to England and a short sortie into the Mediterranean. When someone questioned whether such an itinerary wasn't too much to tackle, Mr. Cortez Senior observed that Columbus, on his first voyage, had crossed from the Canary Islands to landfall in the Caribbean in just five weeks and had returned despite severe storms in less than seven.

Captain Nordstrom remarked, "For a petroleum engineer, Señor Cortez, you seem to know a lot about the sea."

"Only about the great Spanish explorers, Captain."

"I thought that Columbus was Italian," the captain said. But he quickly smiled and held up his hand as if to say, no, let's not go down that road.

The other boat was to sail north, partway up the east African coast, then across the Indian Ocean. After stopping at Southern India, Ceylon, and Malaysia, it would enter the South China Sea. Plans called for reaching Vietnam and China. It would be good to get as far as Korea and Japan, but that seemed out of the realm of possibility. An attempt could be made, but only if such a journey proved to be feasible within the allotted year.

The aim was to move quickly, to see as much as possible. However, if either boat were to come across a large functioning community, relatively unharmed by the Event, that boat was to return home immediately with the news.

As Captain Nordstrom told the brothers, looking at them intently: "We have been operating under the assumption that world civilization lies in ashes. If by some miracle that is not the case, we don't want to wait a year to find out."

Since the boats would be starting out almost eight months after the Event, one could hope that the burned-over fields would be regenerating, and that edible plants would be found along the way. There should be sources of fresh water at every coastal stop, and our own experience indicated that fishing would be productive. Nevertheless, the crews were to carry food rations with them and were not to sail beyond the point where such rations, plus nourishment found en route, would see them safely home.

Uncertainty about sources of food meant that the size of the crews had to be severely limited. The decision was to send six people in each boat.

Ernesto suggested that he would sail to the west and that one member of his crew would be his girlfriend, Anna Colombo, who is fluent in Italian, French, and Spanish, and also speaks passable Portuguese. Anna hails from Milan, where her father, a celebrated mechanical engineer, designed automobiles. Anna is gorgeous, and comes from a world of sleek Ferraris and chic designer gowns. As for seamanship, she has done her share of serious yachting all over the Mediterranean. I never would have guessed that her glitterati lifestyle would mesh with Ernesto's beer-drinking adventurousness. But it did, as soon as they met aboard the *Queen of Africa*, and they have been inseparable.

Jose amenably agreed to go east, but also insisted on taking his girlfriend, Peggy McManus, even though she had no special language qualifications. As it happened, Peggy was an excellent short-order cook, having shipped on the *Queen of Africa* as a sous-chef. Also, under Jose's tutelage, she had become a proficient hand with halyards, lanyards, and all that sailboat stuff.

As interpreter, Jose recruited Emily Chan, who not only spoke several Chinese dialects but was conversant with other Asian languages, her special field of study. Emily was the daughter of Gordon Chan, who was not at all happy to hear of her enlistment. In fact, he forbade her to go until he could see that she was totally determined no matter what, at which point he relented and gave her his blessing. Jose, heading east, also took a representative from the Inlanders' Indian population. And he thought it prudent to take a member of the Zulu community. However, he insisted on more than language and cultural qualifications. He wanted two young men who were congenial, athletic, and familiar with boats. Since Durban had long been the center of a lively yachting community, this was readily accomplished.

As a sixth, Jose chose one of the engineering officers from the *Queen of Africa*, a technician who served the double purpose of being handy around a boat and knowledgeable about machines, just in case any machines were found to have survived the fires and floods.

Ernesto, in filling out his crew, also enlisted two young men from the Durban sailing community, one white and one black. He then recruited a geologist and a talented machinist. Fortuitously, the geologist was female, so each of the two vessels would have two women on board.

This pleased my father and others concerned about suitable representation of women in all our activities. On the other hand, some worried that the male-female composition of the crew might make for tensions on a long journey. To this, the brothers responded as one. They had been on ocean trips with members of both sexes, and for serious sailors and mature people there should be no problems. As for their own women friends, there was a long tradition of captains' wives or consorts accompanying them on voyages. Plus, they had picked their crews carefully, confident that they were psychologically sound as well as physically fit. And, after all, a year is not forever—and this is the twenty-first century, not the nineteenth.

Work on the boats progressed rapidly, and a date was set for departure. There remained the question of giving the sloops names. Many suggestions were forthcoming, ranging from such standards as *Hope, Faith, Belief, Intrepid,* and *Dauntless* to dozens of more idiosyncratic proposals. Ridiculous as it may seem, the debates began to get acrimonious. So Ernesto and Jose were authorized to make the choice. Accordingly, the vessels were christened *Atlantic* and *Pacific*. These names, simple yet emotionally resonant, gained general approval.

One day in early August, with a festive crowd gathered at the shore and band music drowning out the sound of the surf, the two expeditions set forth.

Herb searched his memory for a poetic phrase from the past. "You know," he said to Sarah, "the one about Cortéz looking out over the ocean." Sarah obliged him with the lines by Keats:

> *Or like stout Cortez when with eagle eyes*
> *He star'd at the Pacific—and all his men*
> *Look'd at each other with a wild surmise—*

> *Silent, upon a peak in Darien.*

While the *Atlantic* and *Pacific* were being fitted out for their voyages, I was swept up in the pervasive mood of anticipation and adventure, putting behind me the bad taste left by the pirates' invasion of our peaceful community. If I had known about another expedition being planned, I would have been less high-spirited. In fact, this other journey, when I found out about it, made me sick at heart.

I learned the sad news at a meeting of the Focus Group held in October, about two months after the Cortez brothers and their crews sailed over the horizon. These get-togethers had become less frequent than they had been in the earliest days of our friendship. Marriage and busy schedules took us in different directions and we no longer felt the emotional need to check in with each other daily. Still, we never let more than three or four evenings pass without a good sitdown, often featuring the tasting of a new homemade beer. By now there were a number of different brews from which to choose, and Roxy, through her friends among the Inlanders, assured our supply.

So there we were, lazing about on a mild evening, engaged in languid end-of-the-day conversation, when Herb suddenly cleared his throat and said that he and Roxy had an announcement to make.

"We have decided to move away from Engineering Village."

For a moment there was the silence of total shock, and then everybody started to talk at once. "You can't be serious." "Why on earth?" "Hold on now." "We won't permit it." Mary started to cry. Sarah was ashen. Tom flushed. I don't know how I looked, but I felt terrible.

Tom was the first to pull himself together and ask the obvious questions: Where, when, and most important, why?

"We're moving up into the hills," Roxy said. "Right after the first of the new year. It's a question of climate." She smiled to show us that this was a joke, but there were tears in her eyes.

"No," she amended quickly, "it's not really the climate. We're moving to a kibbutz. That's always been a dream of Herb's, and it appeals to me as well."

"We're not calling it a kibbutz," Herb said. "No Israeli connotations. We're not calling it a commune, either, though that is what it will be. Commune sounds like Stalinist Russia, or American hippies, which is not what we are thinking about at all. It's just a cooperative community." Then, with a slight smile, "But I hope to organize it like a kibbutz."

"We've been thinking about this for quite awhile," Roxy said. "There are a number of people right here in Engineering Village who are anxious to give it a try. Not the engineers themselves—except for a couple—but several children of engineers, like Herb, and several *Queen of Africa* employees, like me. And there are some Inlanders, too, who will be joining us."

"We didn't want to say anything about it until the plans were set," Herb went on. "But now they are, and while Roxy was joking about the climate part of it, she wasn't kidding about the timing. Right after the first of the year. We thought of asking you—our dearest friends—to join us. We still think of it, and we do ask you. Right now. But we assumed that this wouldn't be your kind of thing."

"Well, you're right about that," Tom said. "But why, for God's sake, Herb? Why? Just when wonderful new deeds are being accomplished each day? Just as we're finally getting organized?"

"That's exactly it," Herb said. "Things are getting organized. Or, more precisely, everybody's getting ready to reorganize. Before you know it, a year will have passed since the Event and our landing here in KwaZulu Natal. That means we'll be coming to the end of the agreed period, endorsed by the Coordinating Committee, of volunteer service to this disaster-stricken community. It's been wonderful to see how everyone has pulled together, worked with a will and achieved miracles. I never would have dreamed that a community this large and this diverse could have carried on the way it has for so long. If anything, one might have expected it to go the other way. The calamity might have generated disorder and conflict, a descent into the worst kind of savagery. I give credit to the tribal tradition of the black Africans. I give credit to the good sense of the Afrikaners. I give credit to the British and their legacy of orderly government. I give credit to the spirit of Mahatma Gandhi that hovers over this place. I give credit to Captain Nordstrom and his super crew. And, finally, I give credit to you engineers, the ultimate pragmatists. You laid out a plan and got everybody to sign on. You gave the people constructive work to do and fostered hope. You generated a wholesome feeling of accomplishment that has served us well."

I had never heard Herb speak so passionately and so seriously.

"But this can't go on forever," he said. "The magical year will end, and already I sense that people are jockeying for position. The workers want to make sure they're not exploited. Entrepreneurs are making plans. Robber barons of the future. Maybe there isn't any actual money to be had, but the capitalists are already gathering at the starting gate. Also, there are politicians dreaming of power. I've heard that petty crime is starting to become a problem. Human nature is rearing its ugly head, and you technocrats are blithely going about your work, unaware of the forces that are stirring."

"Don't be ridiculous," Tom said. "We know very well that the year will end. We understand that a constitutional convention is being planned, and then elections and all that self-seeking stuff. But there's no reason to think we can't work out a political design every bit as effective as our technical projects. All the people of Engineering Village, not just the Americans, expect that our society will evolve along democratic principles. As for the South Africans, they held their first fully representative democratic election in 1994, just sixteen years ago. They've had only the smallest taste of democracy, and it has whetted their appetite for more. So, why expect the worst when everybody is ready to move in the right direction?"

"Besides," I said, "we're not starting from scratch. Just as we have the benefit of accumulated technological knowledge, so do we have the benefit of the world's experience in politics. We don't have to go through the whole damned business again—pharaohs and warrior chieftains, knights and serfs, gentry and underclass, kings and revolutionaries, Communists and Freedom Fighters. We know how to put together a decent democratic government, just like we know how to put together an electric generator."

"That's so true," Tom went on. "I'll provide the quote this time and beat Sarah to it. Santayana: 'Those who cannot remember the past are condemned to repeat it.' Well, we've learned the lessons of the past, and we are not condemned to repeat anything."

"You think you've learned the lessons," Herb said. "Pardon me,

Tom Swift, boy genius of the age, but you really shouldn't be so smug."

I thought I knew what Herb was getting at, but I wanted to make sure. "Just what is it that has you so excited?" I asked.

"You know what it is, Wil," Herb said. "You sit in on all those committee meetings, and you know what's up. The Dismal Science is about to take over."

"What in the world is the Dismal Science?" Mary asked.

"Economics," Herb said. "That's what John Kenneth Galbraith called it: The Dismal Science. And that's what this planning for the future is all about. I'm not worried about the new constitution; it will say all the right things. But our planners are getting ready to crown the actual new ruler: Property Rights, the once and future king. And do you know the precepts that will dominate his realm? Economic incentives. Competition. Lean and mean. That's what's coming, and Roxy and I don't want any part of it. We still believe in the possibilities of cooperation and brotherly love."

"You're overreacting," Sarah said. "Just look around you. It's obvious that free enterprise is already at work, and it doesn't seem to be so terrible."

Sarah was right, of course. Soon after the Event, out of the first days of chaos, there had emerged an unofficial market. I won't call it a black market, since there were no specific prohibitions. But it is a complex system of barter that testifies to the ingenuity and enterprise—and the myriad yearnings—of the human spirit. Projects authorized by the Planning Subcommittee didn't begin to address a host of the people's needs and desires.

Consider clothing. The Planning Subcommittee established a cottage industry to manufacture yarns and textiles and to provide basic clothing and blankets. "Basic" is the operative word here. Until a new crop of cotton could be grown, harvested, and processed, the only material available in quantity was wool. As can be imagined, hand-spinning and weaving yield a pretty coarse fabric. And in the absence of input by fashion-conscious designers, the seamstresses turn out dresses, shirts, and pants of the most rudimentary sort. In Engineering Village, most of the people still have the clothes that they had brought with them on the cruise. But as the need arises for additional garments, the available standard issue is drab, to say the least. For the Inlanders, who had not been afforded the protection of a ship during the Event, the average wardrobe is notably lacking in variety. In the first few weeks of crisis, the survivors were well content to receive whatever garments the Planning Subcommittee could provide. But in short order they became increasingly unhappy about what they began to call "the sack."

Pretty soon dozens—perhaps hundreds—of people were busy altering and restoring old clothes, making new garments out of any odd materials that could be found, and reshaping, dyeing, and decorating models of "the sack." Bartering began to take place, the pace of which grew increasingly brisk. It would not be an exaggeration to say that apparel became a form of currency.

Such traditional currency as people had in their possession—dollars, rands, and euros—were used hardly at all in market exchange. This was particularly so after the Coordinating Committee announced that it had no plans to ask any future government to redeem such money. The expectation was—and still is—that the future government will print new currency, backed solely by its own credit. In this regard, it is fortunate that for the the past two decades and more, most national governments moved away from using gold as a guarantee of currency. Therefore, reliance on the state's pure credit, or pledge, is a concept which knowledgeable people are ready to accept. It's ironic that we find ourselves in the land of gold and diamonds at a time when these materials have lost their value. Doubtless, they will continue to be prized for their aesthetic qualities, and it is rumored that a few Inlanders have traveled to distant mine sites with the intention of collecting private hoards. It is also rumored that the future government will nationalize, or confiscate, or otherwise proscribe such personal accumulations of mineral wealth.

In any event, the use of clothing as a medium of exchange is only one example of the free market that has emerged throughout the Ulundi Circle. Toys are another. "Leave it to engineers to forget about toys," Sarah said when she learned about the brisk trade that had arisen in handmade dolls, miniature wagons, and other such items.

There has also been a lively commerce in writing implements. The Planning Subcommittee, believing that ample quantities survived in various parts of the Ulundi Circle, and also that the *Queen of Africa* administrators were adequately supplied, felt that the matter was well in hand. They planned for future demand, but underestimated the desire that ordinary folk would have for writing materials right from the start. Consequently, there has been a great demand for hand-crafted quill pens and for inks made of carbon black and vegetable oils. A few Inlanders with access to a deposit of graphite started to make primitive pencils that were very much sought after. The wooden holders were carved, split in half, and carefully notched. Then small "lead" rods—made by mixing graphite dust with clay—were inserted and the wood reassembled.

The main supplies of paper are mostly earmarked for technical enterprises and for bureaucrats like me. As a result, late into the night, hobbyist papermakers have plied their craft, trading their prized product for other goods and favors.

There are few families that have not made an effort to improve on the rather Spartan living quarters authorized by the Planning Subcommittee. Thus, carpentry, masonry, and thatching have also been important aspects of the unofficial market.

Occasionally, when a fair barter transaction cannot be negotiated—if a child yearns for a toy and the parents have nothing to offer in return—gifts are freely given. Often, future favors are the consideration, sometimes recorded, sometimes "to be remembered." Many IOUs have been executed: "Patricia owes Joshua the equivalent of a bead necklace," or: "Harry owes Bill the equivalent of ten hours carpentry fixing up his furniture."

Obviously, when Sarah told Herb that free enterprise was already at work, she spoke truly, and Herb knew it.

Yet, in rebuttal, Herb contended that this unofficial market has a free and easy spirit that is unique to this time and place. After all, the basic necessities of life are provided without charge by "the state," and the common disaster is still fresh in everyone's consciousness. This inspires a neighborly feeling that cannot be expected to last indefinitely. Already the force of a more traditional trading impulse is manifest, and more than a few people find it difficult to suppress their acquisitive instincts. The potential for more earnest business dealings is clearly in the air. The free enterprise of tomorrow may be very different from the free enterprise of today.

———————

Whatever the prospects for the future, I thought, there must be some way to get Herb thinking in a different direction. At least I had to give it a try.

"Hey, pal," I said. "I know where you're coming from. But we can have a good society, even if we aren't altruistic angels. Captain Nordstrom has told us of the egalitarian traditions that prevail in Norway, where conspicuous consumption is considered shameful. You can help us establish such traditions here. I understand what you have against free enterprise. But it's like Winston Churchill said about democracy, it's not a very good form of government; it's just the best there is.

"Let the capitalists do their thing, to the benefit of all of us. You can join the left-wing party that keeps the robber barons in check and looks after the little guy. Also, as we rebuild, the central government will have to play a responsible role in most major industries. At the same time, we can find morally acceptable ways to put self-interest to work."

But, as Herb had a habit of saying in jest, and this time pronounced in dead earnest, "My mind is made up. Don't confuse me with facts."

Once we realized that Herb and Roxy were not to be dissuaded, we began to ask for more details. They told us that the cooperative would be based on agriculture and animal husbandry, although possibly some form of light manufacture might be added in the future.

Tom laughed. "I can't see either of you harvesting crops, much less herding cattle."

"You seem to forget that I come from Texas," Roxy protested, "the world capital of cattle ranching. And Herb is a quick study."

Sarah said, "And you'll continue your work as a champion of dance in our community, I hope."

"Oh, yes," Roxy said.

Mary added, "Herb can still practice, or rather, apply his knowledge of law. We'll need him for that."

"You can count on it," Herb said.

"Will this new commitment mean the end of your involvement in our Environmental Protection Agency?" Sarah asked.

"Certainly not," Roxy said. "We'll find time for that no matter what else we're doing." She was quiet for a moment.

Suddenly, she said in a firm voice: "You guys have to realize that when we talk about the environment, and when we plan for an idealistic community, we're dreaming about the future. We're thinking about our baby."

"Baby?" Mary asked in a tremulous voice. "Baby?" she repeated, excitedly. "You too?"

"Baby?" Now it was Sarah, also flustered. "I was going to break our news next week."

Suddenly, all six of us were laughing and crying, hugging each other in wild celebration. Everyone started to talk at the same time, all asking the same questions: "Since when?" "How many weeks?" "How do you feel?" "Which doctor have you spoken to?"

Finally, Tom put his arm around Herb, squeezed his shoulder, and said: "You can't move up into the hills now. Our kids have to go to the same nursery school."

"I'll make a deal with you," Herb replied. "They'll go to the same university. Can you get a decent university built in eighteen years?"

"I guarantee it," Tom said. "With a world-class engineering curriculum." Seeing Sarah's frown, he quickly added, "And an excellent liberal arts program, of course."

In the next few minutes we had pretty much mapped out the courses and faculty structure of this university of the future, including outstanding departments of dance, law, and the history of technology.

"It doesn't take much to put us all in a good mood," Herb said.

"Only the greatest miracle the world has to offer," Roxy said, giving her husband a big hug.

At other times, Sarah would have offered up a quotation to suit the occasion. But she realized—as did we all—that there were no words eloquent enough for this moment in our lives.

FROM THE JOURNAL OF WILSON HARDY, JR.

O come, all ye faithful,
Joyful and triumphant,
O come ye, O come ye,
To Bethlehem.

It is Christmas Eve, December 24, 2010, and the Engineering Village Carolers are wending their way along the lakeshore, singing that music which has such an eternal grip upon our hearts. Mary, Roxy, and Sarah are among the group, and I fancy that I hear their voices stand out sweetly above the others. Of course, this is my imagination; the more than twenty-five voices blend together. Indeed, all day my senses have been in overdrive. Am I living a fantasy? Here it is, the end of December, and we are entering the heart of the summer. I don't believe I will ever get used to celebrating Christmas in the summer.

Celebrating? Joyful and triumphant? Is that what we are, one year after the destruction of seven billion people and civilizations that took thousands of years to create?

If there were any desperate hopes that Jane Demming Warner's scenario of doom was overly bleak, they are now—a year later—pretty well dissipated. More than four and a half months have passed since the sailing of the *Atlantic* and the *Pacific*. That is plenty of time for one or the other to have returned with good news, if there was any good news to report. What a journey that must be, from ruin to ruin, ashes to ashes.

Yes, ashes to ashes. That is an expression we use for individual living creatures, but never expected would pertain to everything on the face of the earth. With each passing day it looks more and more as if the renewal of civilization depends solely upon what we do here in the Ulundi Circle. As Sarah said just the other night: "To the question, 'Will we survive?' must be added another, 'If we are the only survivors, will we be worthy?' "

Joy to the world . . .

The music is achingly beautiful. But joy? Mary says it's a matter of faith.

Tom says that faith is fine if it helps you; but even without it, there are things about which to be joyful. And sometimes I have to agree with him. In just one year, the industrial enterprise has made phenomenal headway. Screw-ups? Confusion? Failures? Oh, yes, plenty, as I discover almost every day at various committee meetings. But priorities are adjusted, people are reassigned, plans are redrawn, and progress resumes. They say that a steam engine is almost ready for testing. An ugly brute, by all accounts, made of low-grade materials. But it is expected to work, the first of many that will be replacing the primitive waterwheels that have been driving our sawmills, gristmills, and bellows for the smelting furnaces.

We are enjoying a second summer of ideal weather and bountiful crops. The sheep and cattle were blessedly fertile. Lucky animals: they have no philosophical qualms about how to rebuild the world.

With the weather so fine, and serviceable farm tools now in ample supply, many of the people who were working the fields are being reassigned to food-processing activities. We can look forward to a cornucopia of cheese, baked goods, salad oils, and other delicacies. At the same time, the Joint Planning Subcommittee has mandated that salting, pickling, drying, and other preservative activities be intensified. They insist upon conservative planning for the future, an approach that is greeted with universal approval.

School programs, which understandably took a while to get organized, are now running full tilt. No talk of summer vacations around the Ulundi Circle. The children are anxious to learn. Distracted on occasion, and ornery too, of course; but basically anxious to learn. The teachers are knowledgeable and anxious to teach. Given these transcendent realities, the shortage of texts and supplies becomes a minor consideration.

Higher education is handled in an apprentice arrangement, often with a mentor-disciple ratio of one to one. What university students—and faculty—would not be exhilarated by such an opportunity?

Gratifying improvements. Yet, joy to the world?

Last evening, we held a pre-Christmas meeting of the Focus Group, and inevitably the discussion turned to matters spiritual. Of course, the holiday is not totally religious, as we know from past years. The Macy's Thanksgiving Day Parade in New York City always ended with a Santa Claus float, heralding the start of the serious shopping season.

Nevertheless, after the cynics have had their say, there is still something special about Christmas. Even in the hot and humid climate of a South African summer evening, we felt familiar stirrings of anticipation—tinged, of course, with the ever-recurring regrets which are the backdrop to our days.

Mary, predictably, tried to focus our attention on the traditional holy message of Christmas: faith, hope for the future, and salvation.

I asked the obvious question: "So why wasn't the world saved?"

And she gave the obvious answer: "The nature of salvation is beyond the ken of human reason."

This proposition brought us, in short order, to a conversational dead end.

So we started to talk about Christmas music, Christmas in the movies, and Christmases of our childhood—trees, sleds, parties, and snowstorms. Sarah tried to recreate, with the rest of us chiming in, the storyline of *A Christmas Carol*. Herb favored us with a spirited recitation of "The Night Before Christmas."

Eventually, we found ourselves revisiting the theme of universal destruction, the possible ways in which we could come to grips with the catastrophe intellectually, philosophically, and emotionally.

Roxy reflected on the notion of punishment from above. "I am more convinced, as time goes by, that so-called civilized people brought the destruction upon themselves—maybe I should say *ourselves*—by becoming mean and materialistic."

"I can't agree," Sarah countered, "that society became less moral. You could argue to the contrary: what with civil rights, increased concern for the poor, and mainly the victories of democracy over despotism. That doesn't mean we didn't anger the gods. Having spent these many months among technical types"—she looked at Tom and me with affection, despite her words—"well, I have some new ideas about what might constitute the offense against heaven. I never realized before how deeply science had penetrated the physical mysteries of the universe. And I don't mean just Prometheus learning the secret of fire. We snatched metals from the earth, mastered electricity, deciphered the atom, and had begun to manipulate human genes. Doesn't this begin to threaten the supremacy of the Deity—or deities?"

"I don't think that's the problem," Roxy countered. "In my view, God doesn't resent people for being smart, only for being nasty." She picked up the Bible that Mary had brought to the meeting, and flipped through the early pages of Genesis until she came to the story of Noah.

"Here it is," she said. " 'And God saw that the wickedness of man was great in the earth, and that every imagination of the thoughts of his heart was only evil continually. And it repented the Lord that he had made man on the earth, and it grieved him at his heart. And the Lord said, I will destroy man whom I have created from the face of the earth . . .' But Noah was spared, and why? Because 'Noah was a just man . . . and Noah walked with God.' "

Roxy pursed her lips and looked intently at the book in her hands. "So Noah built the ark as he was directed to do, and then the Lord said to him, 'Come thou and all thy house into the ark; for thee have I seen righteous before me in this generation.' " She put down the book with satisfaction, and addressed us as if she were delivering a sermon: "The man was saved because he was just and righteous. It had nothing to do with intelligence or lack of it. And, of course, the animals were saved because—well, just because they deserved to be saved."

"But, sweetheart," Herb said, "how about the rainbow? How about the covenant that God made with Noah that this wouldn't happen again? Let me see that book."

Roxy showed him where she had been reading, and in a moment, Herb spoke out with a tone of challenge in his voice: "Here it is: 'And the Lord said in his heart, I will not again curse the ground any more for man's sake . . . While the earth remaineth, seedtime and harvest, and cold and heat, and summer and winter, and day and night shall not cease.' "

"It seems to me," I said, "that implicit in the covenant is the understanding that humankind will not go back to evil ways."

"Or maybe," Sarah said, "God couldn't help Himself. Maybe He doesn't control comets that come from far, far out in space, from— what's it called, the Oort cloud?"

"Or maybe," Tom said, "God never made the promise at all, and it was simply imagined by the guy who wrote the Noah story. After all, what we're talking about is a story, and the plot is probably based on some historical catastrophe."

Mary reached over, picked up her Bible, and said, "Listen you guys. In the true spirit of Christmas, I forgive you the blasphemy of playing wordgames with the Holy Book."

"Well, dearest Mary," Tom said, "if you're dispensing forgiveness, then let me tell you what I really think. I believe that the gods—with a small 'g'—or the devils, or the fates, have been playing a little game. I've thought about this a lot in the past year, and there's no other way to explain it. Just consider."

"Uh-oh," Herb exclaimed. "Mary, cover your ears."

"Maybe we ought to write this down," Sarah said, smiling. "A new version of the Apocalypse."

"No, bear with me," Tom continued. "The world is destroyed on Christmas Day, except for a small region containing a relatively small number of people. Not one righteous man like Noah, mind you, with his family and a bunch of animals; but a community just about large enough to embark on restoring an advanced civilization with a technological base. The spared population consists of proven pragmatists with many talents, and outstanding survival skills; and the land which they call home has most of the natural resources one could want. Into their midst sails a ship containing six hundred of the most proficient and knowledgeable engineers in the world, along with their textbooks, handbooks, notebooks, and up-to-the-minute plans. Also families and crew, people of many talents—mechanical, scientific, medical—plus other endowments having little or nothing to do with the sciences.

"Between the natives and the people aboard ship—the Inlanders and the Outlanders—practically all the races of the world are represented. Granted, there should be, by proportion, more Asians.

But, after all, every game has its rules, and in this one the world, as it exists, is a given. If the story took place in Asia, there would be hardly any non-Asians. That wouldn't do. At least in KwaZulu Natal, there are blacks and whites, and an astonishingly large number of people who hail from the Indian subcontinent. And, as partial compensation for the lack of Asians in the local population, remember that aboard the ship they are very well represented. This is so because Asians are prominent in the engineering profession, and also because they serve on crews in many oceangoing ships. And, who knows, perhaps Gordon Chan is right in his conjecture that there is a circle of survival somewhere on the Chinese mainland.

"Anyhow, there you have it. The game is all laid out and ready to play. Once before, human beings, extraordinary creatures, went from the Stone Age to high technology in six thousand years. Let's see if they can do it again, only faster. We'll put them back in the Stone Age—the way that General LeMay suggested the United States do to Vietnam—but leave them most of their accumulated knowledge. What will happen? Isn't it fun to speculate? Place your bets, fellow deities. Ready, set, go! Can anybody offer another theory that makes more sense?"

After a few moments of silence, Sarah spoke up. "Well," she said, "if you want to let your imagination run wild, I have a better idea. Suppose we've all been bopped on the head, like the hero of Mark Twain's *Connecticut Yankee*, or the narrator in Edward Bellamy's *Looking Backward*. In that case, everything we've lived through has been a dream, and soon we will awaken."

"A year is an awfully long time for a dream," Tom said.

"Besides," I said, "I've been dreaming a lot lately. Is it possible to have dreams within a dream?" What I didn't say was that most of my dreams have been about Queen Ranavolana. Danger, mystery, ineffable beauty, and enigmatic evil—that red-sailed ship represents everything that lies beyond my everyday world and well-ordered conscious thoughts. I have a feeling that I knew of its existence before I ever saw it and that I will dream of it forever. But all I said was, "Dreams within dreams? It hardly seems likely."

Tom ignored my musing, and returned to his hypothesis of a game conceived by the gods. "The thing I really like about my idea," he said, "is that while the gods think they've made up a game for their own amusement, the truth is they've made up a fascinating game for us. Start from ground zero and see what you can accomplish. The challenge is posed, and it is up to us to meet it. Meeting a challenge is what makes us feel most alive—at least that's true for the engineers amongst us."

"That's just dandy," Herb said. "Are you saying that the gods did the engineers a favor by destroying the world? And they did it on Christmas Day? What a lovely present. And how about the rest of us, who could do very nicely without so much challenge?"

"Well, honey," Roxy said, "it is true for everyone that your challenger, your adversary even, can be your best friend. That's like the Zen view of tennis. I read it once in a book. By making things difficult for you, your opponent brings out the best that is in you, and therefore does you the kindest possible favor."

"That reminds me of Sisyphus," I said, "condemned to roll a heavy boulder up a hill, only to see it fall back to the bottom each time he reaches the summit." Then to Sarah, "Didn't you tell me about a philosopher who said that we have to imagine Sisyphus as happy?"

"That was Albert Camus," Sarah said.

"And, by the way," I asked, "what great sin was Sisyphus supposed to have committed?"

"According to the myth," Sarah said, "he cheated Death by craftily chaining him up. So nobody died until Death was freed by Ares, the god of war. The gods were not amused."

"That's a pretty good story," Tom said. "And that's certainly one of the things that engineers try to do—cheat Death, so to speak, by helping people live in a better, safer, more comfortable world."

"At the same time that they help War do his awful work," Roxy said.

"Okay," Herb interjected, "we can weave our pretty stories, and show how clever we are. But the life we're living is neither a dream nor a game contrived in heaven. We've been tested all right—to the limit and beyond. And we can't be sure that we've seen the last of our trials. What if another comet strikes tomorrow, or earthquake, or flood, or plague? Or how about an invasion by aliens? What if it is our lot to be tormented forever?"

"Challenge is one thing, perpetual torment is another," Sarah offered. "If I thought that heaven were deliberately cruel—which I do not, by the way—I fear I would echo the words of Dostoevsky's Ivan Karamazov. After thinking about all the misery that exists, particularly the horrible anguish suffered by innocent children, Ivan says that he intends to 'most respectfully' return his ticket to God— that is, his ticket of admittance to the world."

"Hey, gang," I said, "this is the holiday season. Let's lighten up. How about a little jingle bells and mistletoe?"

"You know," Roxy said, "one of the things I've always liked best about Christmas is that it comes exactly a week before New Year's. A week to plan how you're going to party. I love New Year's Eve. It doesn't carry any of the emotional baggage of the other holidays. After Thanksgiving and Christmas, it's just what's needed. No matter where I've been in the world, and no matter whether things were looking up or down, I've always tried to celebrate the coming of January. Out with the fuddy-duddy old guy with the sickle, and in with the darling little baby. New beginning. New hope. Last year, we were in a state of shock, with nothing to be festive about. But this year I think we should live it up a little."

"There are several parties being planned, you know," Sarah said.

"Yes," Tom said, "they're ready to test one of the new steam engines at Empangeni, and the plan is to start it up at midnight of

December 31 with toasts and music. I've been meaning to tell Mary that we've been invited."

"We're not going to any party at Empangeni," Mary said. "I love steam engines. But if I have anything to say about it, we're going to celebrate with our friends right here in Engineering Village. Herb and Roxy will be gone soon enough. I think we should be together."

"I figured that's the way you'd feel," Tom said, just a touch sheepishly. "I've already told them I'd come over to see the engine the next morning."

"What I've been thinking," Roxy said, "is that this is the time for us to have another fling with our line dancing. I know we associate that with the carefree days before the Event, and we've never had the heart to go back to it. But I've been saving my cowgirl outfit, damn it, and I'm just dying to put it on again."

"But how about the music?" Mary asked. "Without electricity, there's no way we can play that boom box of yours."

"I'm way ahead of you on that," Roxy said. "A few of the guys from the band have agreed to help out. I've got them rehearsing 'Cowboy Hustle,' 'Tennessee Stroll,' 'Country Strut,' and my very best favorite, 'Dallas Shuffle.'"

She started to hum and clap her hands. "You remember 'Dallas Shuffle,' don't you? Come on, grab your partners. Just for a minute, just to see if you can still move."

We rose to our feet, awkward and uncertain. The women were several months pregnant, and it showed. But then Sarah called out, "Let's do it!" and there we were, modified sweetheart position, moving to the music. Roxy sang out the melody and continued to clap the rhythm, while at the same time she nudged Herb into position next to her. I tried to remember the old instructions: "Lift your stomach, rib cage up and in. Lift your chin so that it's parallel to the floor. Don't look down!" Pretty soon it was coming back. The body remembers. And there we were, stepping lively, feeling good, looking good, too—better still, not caring how we looked.

Thus do we answer the heavens. With dance. With steam engines. And with our babies to come.

After awhile, we sat down, out of breath, laughing—for the moment without a care. Or rather, with cares held at bay by Roxy's dauntless spirit, and by our own. Suddenly, Sarah took my hand and placed it on her belly. I felt movement, as if the little feet within were trying to mark the beat.

I began work on this book by searching for a place—a part of the world in which the survivors could, with some prospect of success, attempt to rebuild a technological society. It had to be a place endowed with temperate climate, flourishing agriculture, and large numbers of domestic animals. Other natural resources were a must—especially timber, coal, iron, and copper. Furthermore, these resources had to be close to an ocean shore and concentrated within an area that could serve as home for a functional community—say a circle with a diameter of a hundred miles or so. It was easier to describe such a spot than to find it.

A solution suggested itself one day when I pulled down from my bookshelf a copy of *The Times Atlas* and turned to Plate 1, "World Minerals." My eye fell immediately on South Africa, where the map showed several large symbols indicating an abundance of crucial materials. Other charts in the atlas, dealing with crops, livestock, and climate, seemed also to support South Africa as a promising possibility.

However, South Africa is a large country, and the information in the atlas did not enable me to zero in on an area of the requisite limited size. My problem was solved when, through the good offices of Martin Creamer, Publishing Editor of *Martin Creamer's Engineering News*, Gardenview, South Africa, I was able to retain as a researcher Dr. Kelvin Kemm, a consulting engineer from Pretoria. This professional contact blossomed into an E-mail friendship that I have come to value highly. My files now bulge with maps, charts, catalogues, technical papers, and lengthy letters dealing with South African natural resources—also such non-technical matters as Zulu names, childhood memories of Durban, stories about wild animals, etc.—much more than I could possibly use in a dozen books. Collecting the information became something of an end in itself, and as soon as the research project ended, I started to miss those lively messages from Pretoria. In addition to his valuable research, Kelvin read one draft of the manuscript and made some insightful suggestions. His cheerful enthusiasm for the enterprise was a great morale-booster.

The information I received from Kelvin Kemm convinced me that, from a geographical point of view, the province of KwaZulu Natal was the ideal setting for my story. Fortuitously, it turned out that the population of that region also met my criteria for an ideal supporting cast—multi-ethnic, technologically accomplished, and most of all, politically pragmatic.

Several other South African engineers provided support and information. In response to a letter of inquiry that Martin Creamer printed in his publication, I received friendly communiques from Bill Brunjes, Elma Holt, Wally Langsford, Philip Lloyd, and Patrick Taylor.

Once the sphere of action was established, my next task was to devise a means of destroying all the people on Earth outside of the chosen spot. With most catastrophes, such as earthquake, nuclear war, disease, and climate change, I found it exceedingly difficult to wipe out everyone in the world except for a select few in KwaZulu Natal. However, the impactor-from-space scenario showed promise, and this is the one I decided to pursue. Embarking on a journey around the Internet, I discovered a lively community of people interested in—and wary of—comets and asteroids. Eventually I found my way to the Lunar and Planetary Laboratory at the University of Arizona. More particularly, I made contact with James Head, a graduate student in the university's Department of Planetary Sciences. Calculations for the calamity scenario are his. If there are purists who are not convinced by the figures, let me just say that destruction of the world is not a field in which there has ever been much by way of agreed standards. In general, the K/T disaster theory has gained wide support, and Walter Alvarez has provided a simplified exposition of it in his book, *T. Rex and the Crater of Doom*. A more scientific treatment is "Ignition of Global Wildfires at the Cretaceous/Tertiary Boundary," by H. J. Melosh and N. M. Schneider of the Lunar and Planetary Laboratory, K. J. Zahnie of NASA, and D. Latham of the U.S. Forest Service Intermountain Fire Sciences Laboratory, *Nature*, 18 January 1990. In that paper there is reference to F. L. Whipple's hypothesis about the rain-down of fire through "molecular drag," *Proceedings of the National Academy of Sciences*, 1950.

According to my specifications, Jim Head devised a "safe zone" that sliced through the southeast shore of South Africa, providing Richards Bay as a beachhead, and KwaZulu Natal as a center of action. By happenstance, the zone also included the southern portion of Madagascar. This gave me, as a bonus setting, that incredibly exotic island. Incidentally, the quote about the population of Madagascar being "the most astonishing fact of human geography in the entire world," comes from *Guns, Germs, and Steel: The Fates of Human Societies* by Jared Diamond.

Although the geographical setting and the catastrophe scenario were my biggest research challenges, I received other assistance that needs to be mentioned.

Rich Combes provided helpful information about industrial development in Colonial North America, and details about the numbers of people required to perform specific items of work. He also read the manuscript and shared his imaginative ideas. Nora Jason, Manager of Fire Research Information Services at the National Institute of Standards and Technology, directed me to valuable material about fire storms. Other useful facts came from Captain

Enrico Ferri of Renaissance Cruises, David Pang of the American Association of Pharmaceutical Scientists, Leon Shargel of the National Association of Pharmaceutical Manufacturers, and Aristotle Tympas.

I particularly appreciate Henry Petroski taking time from his own very busy writing and teaching schedule to read portions of the manuscript and make helpful comments.

It was pleasant, as well as convenient, to be able to do some of the writing in my office at Kreisler Borg Florman Construction Company. The people there were helpful in a variety of ways, particularly Virginia Crowley, who has been our corporate secretary and my invaluable assistant for many years.

Many friends and colleagues were generous with advice and suggestions. Those whose names I have written down in connection with particular references and correspondence are Wilson Binger, Alvin Converse, Ruth Greenstein, Lois and Jerry Lowenstein, M. Granger Morgan, Greg Pearson, Allan and Craig Rubin, and Anthony Viscusi. I thank them all, as well as the many others who, in passing, volunteered helpful ideas.

There came a time when (reluctantly) I declared the research complete, and started to write. Tom Dunne, who has been my editor, publisher, and good friend for twenty-five years, gave counsel and support—and then tactfully urged me to work on a second draft, and a third. Tom's assistants, Emily Hopkins and Carin Siegfried, were cheerful and efficient coordinators of the many things that go on in a publisher's office.

However, it wasn't until Greg Tobin arrived on the scene that the "work in progress" developed into its final form. Greg resolved my difficulties with structure, and rescued me from narrative impasses. His contribution came first in the form of creative ideas, and later as words that I was happy to employ. His help was invaluable; and his consistent good cheer and unfailing faith in the project provided a sweet coating for his most radical critiques.

Finally, my wife, Judy, deserves a very big thank you. She spent many long hours working with the manuscript, from my earliest efforts on, and the prose is much crisper and cleaner than it would have been without her suggestions.

A number of people with whom I have discussed this work, and a few who read portions of the manuscript, think that, however gloomy its recipe for disaster, its view of human behavior is wildly optimistic. Worldwide catastrophe, so they say, would inevitably be followed by an era of chaos, discord, and brutality. Clearly I don't share that pessimism.

Perhaps it is my five granddaughters, to whom the book is dedicated, who have given me this faith in the future.